"Perhaps," Jason r   can satisfy you best? "

Lauren heard the rough   anguish in his eyes, but still she didn't understand. "Why are you doing this?" she whispered, unable to bear his angry contempt.

"I told you why." Very deliberately he ran a forefinger down the slender column of her throat to the bare white flesh above her gown's low neckline. Lauren quivered, feeling his touch like a brand of fire against her skin.

"Because I want you," Jason continued, his low, sensuous voice stroking her. "And I intend to have you. I'll have you again and again, 'til you can't even remember Duval's name."

"Please . . ."

"Please what?" his husky voice prodded her. "Please you? What do you like best, sweetheart? I expect I can be as inventive as Duval."

Lauren knew then. With instinctive confidence, she knew he was jealous. Fiercely jealous. The knowledge gave her a heady feeling of power. Jason desired her, Lauren thought dazedly, looking up at him. He desired *her*.

Something of her wonder must have shown in her expression, for he shut his eyes momentarily, as if he were bracing himself against pain. And when he opened them again, she could see in the brilliant blue depths of his gaze that his anger had turned to smoldering passion . . .

DESIRE AND DECEPTION

NICOLE JORDAN

ZEBRA BOOKS
KENSINGTON PUBLISHING CORP.

Other Zebra books by Nicole Jordan:

Velvet Embrace

ZEBRA BOOKS

are published by

Kensington Publishing Corp.
475 Park Avenue South
New York, NY 10016

First printing: August, 1988

Printed in the United States of America

To Ellen and Ed for always saying "you can";
To Marcy, Kate, and Bea for keeping the faith;
To my wonderful friends at OV/RWA
for their marvelous motivations;
To Betty, Renée, and John for lending an ear (and more);
And, as always, to Jay for sharing the dream.

Part I

Promise the Night

Chapter One

London, 1812

Furtive voices. Stealthy footsteps. A sharp command.

Lauren DeVries cast a fearful glance over her shoulder, glimpsing the shadowed outline of three men in the distance. The sight made her tremble. Even in the darkness, she recognized those burly forms moving slowly along Wapping High Street, carefully searching the doorways and alleys of the waterfront, like vultures hunting prey. She had seen them often enough at Carlin House. They were George Burroughs's men.

Her guardian's men.

And they were hunting *her*.

Desperate to avoid detection, Lauren slipped into the concealing shadows of a narrow alleyway. Her breath was ragged from running, her body weary from hiding out for so many days. She drew the hood of her cloak around her face and huddled against the grimy brick wall, praying they would pass her by in the darkness.

The thud of bootheels on cobblestone grew closer, and Lauren nearly jumped when a voice spoke from just around the corner.

"The girl 'as to be near. The ole tar claimed she was askin' about passage."

"Well, she gave us the slip. Let's search further upriver. Mayhap she went as far as the Tower."

Lauren held her breath, the stench from the River Thames making her stomach churn. She knew how Burroughs's men had managed to follow her. Despite her precautions of covering her bright-gold hair beneath a hood, she couldn't disguise her exceptional height, any more than she could change her husky voice. Indeed, that was probably how they had trailed her from Cornwall to Reading, where they'd overtaken her the first time. And Matthew . . . God protect him . . . had lured them away so she could escape.

Matthew. A tight ache burned in Lauren's throat as she thought of the stalwart Scot. Although he was nearly old enough to be her grandfather, Matthew MacGregor was her dearest friend—indeed, her only friend. He not only had helped her run away from Carlin House, but had given little thought to his own safety in the process. Even as Burroughs's men had battered away at the bolted door of the lodging where she and Matthew had taken shelter for the night, his first thought had been for her.

"Ye must get away," he'd said in a harsh whisper, pressing a few banknotes into her hand as he pushed her toward the casement window. "Here . . . make for the posting house on the London Road. Hire a coach to Wapping and find the inn I told ye about. I'll meet ye there if I can. And if I canna, then ye take the first ship to America, as we planned." She had protested, but his face, craggy as the Cornish cliffs, had set stubbornly. "Dinna wait for me, lass," he commanded in his soft burr. He lifted her to the windowsill then, just as the sound of a splintering door and the shouts of Burroughs's men filled the room.

Whirling, Matthew drew his pistol and fired. He hit one of the men, but a second advanced with a deadly short sword poised for a thrust, barking, "Get the girl!"

Matthew had frantically waved Lauren away. Yet she couldn't leave him there to die. With a jerk, she pushed herself from the window and fell to the floor, crying out at the sharp pain in her right knee. Her sudden movement served to distract the swordsman, though, and while Matthew rushed him, she shoved a chair at the two others, then seized her bundle of clothes from the bed and threw it at them with all her might.

The next instant she found her hand grasped by Matthew as he dragged her out the door and out of the inn.

For an endless age they raced through the dark streets, trying to shake the pounding footsteps behind them—until, finally, Matthew pushed her into a dark alley and set off again to lead their pursuers away, leaving her trembling and alone.

That had happened two days ago. Her instinct for survival had taken hold then, giving her the courage to make her way on her own. But Matthew hadn't come to the Red Lion Inn that night as Lauren desperately hoped he would. Sick with worry, she had waited another day before following his last injunction to find a ship.

Her hopes of sailing with the midnight tide were already dashed, however, for even though she had found the waterfront, she had very little money and the few sailors she had dared question had only given her leers and lewd suggestions. And in the end, it appeared that her efforts had drawn the attention of Burroughs's men once again.

Scarcely daring to breathe, Lauren waited now in an agony of apprehension for them to discover her hiding place. Finally, though, she heard the footsteps moving away.

She drew a shaky breath, then counted to twenty before cautiously peering around her hood. At the mouth of the alley, she could see stark masts silhouetted against the night sky— hundreds of them, belonging to the myriad of ships which dotted the Thames and lay anchored along the miles of wharves.

She could detect little movement. The traffic on the river had thinned to an occasional barge, while the activity on the waterfront had ceased for the night. Behind her, the shops of London's East End were closed and shuttered, although the taprooms of the numerous public houses still teemed with seamen and the bawds and cutpurses who worked the district.

Lauren caught the faint din of their drunken revelry as she stood listening to the thud of water slopping heavily against wharf timbers. She heard some soft scurryings also, which she thought might be rats, yet the idea of confronting an army of foraging rodents didn't frighten her as much as did getting

11

caught and having to face Burroughs himself. George Burroughs . . . the surviving partner and sole controller of the vast Carlin shipping empire. He was her guardian as well, and had the power to force her compliance with his slightest wish, even his personal vendettas.

Deciding that his men had truly gone, Lauren turned away from the river and sped down the filth-strewn alley. She was limping slightly, the knee that she'd twisted in her drop from the window at Reading still paining her, but she ignored the discomfort. With those bloodhounds so close on her trail, she had no choice but to continue her search for a ship. She had to leave England. George Burroughs had arranged her marriage to a man she had never met, and since she wasn't yet seventeen, she had no legal right to challenge his authority. Yet she was running from more than an enforced marriage. Her situation was far more complicated. And far more dangerous.

Her soft kid slippers made no sound on the uneven cobblestones as she made her way throught the narrow, twisting streets that were crammed with lodging houses and tenement slums. Moving parallel to the river, she headed toward the enclosed London Dock, hugging the shadows as she passed busy taverns and silent counting houses alike, pausing only once to avoid the parish night watch who was making his rounds with his latern and rattle. At length Lauren reached the great dock wall on Pennington Street that was lined with warehouses, and after some searching, found the entrance gate unguarded. She breathed more easily then, even though the odor of rotting fish and tar was nearly overpowering.

A forest of ships greeted her as she slipped inside. Slowing, she picked her way among crates and barrels which had been waterproofed with pitch and lay piled on the wharf, awaiting distribution.

A gleam of light shortly attracted her notice. It was coming from a three-masted brigantine that lay close alongside the quay, and seemed to be offering refuge. Perhaps, she thought with renewed hope, she might also find someone on board who would be sympathetic to her plight.

She descended the steps to the stone quay, and after glancing behind her to make sure she hadn't been followed, crept up the brig's gangway, the sounds of lapping water and creaking timber masking her approach. The main deck seemed to be deserted, Lauren saw as she stepped on board. The beckoning light was issuing from a lantern which hung on a peg to her left; the lantern cast a dim glow over the starboard bow, while it wreathed the stern in shadows.

Feeling like an intruder, Lauren called out hesitantly. When she received no answer, she made her way aft toward the quarterdeck, hoping to find someone with whom she could negotiate for passage.

"Stop! Who goes there?"

Lauren jumped at the unexpected challenge, then whirled in alarm. Facing her, his sturdy legs planted in a belligerent stance, was a young man dressed in the blue serge jacket and canvas trousers of a seaman, holding a lethal-looking musket at the ready. The light threw a shadow over his face, but as Lauren stood there frozen, he moved closer, giving her a better view of red-blond hair, a snub nose, and freckles.

He wasn't any older than she, Lauren realized with surprise. Indeed, he appeared a few years younger, perhaps thirteen or fourteen. She let out a sigh of relief. Even training a gun on her, he didn't seem as dangerous as the men she was running from. And oddly, she felt safer than any time since she had become separated from Matthew.

"I beg your pardon," Lauren began in her husky voice, "but could you tell me what ship this is?"

The lad eyed her warily, trying to get a better look at her face beneath the hood. He must have decided she didn't present any immediate threat, for he seemed to relax. "The *Leucothea*," he answered finally. "You lost, ma'am?"

"No, I saw your lantern light. I was hoping to speak to whoever is in charge."

"*I'm* in charge, ma'am. This here's my first night on watch."

Lauren thought she detected a note of pride in the youth's tone and hesitated, not wanting to hurt his feelings. "You command the ship then?"

A sheepish grin lit the lad's round face. "Truth tell, I'm the cabin boy . . . Tim Sutter. The cap'm let me take the watch since he's still on board."

"The captain is here? Do you suppose I could speak to him? I would like to ask him if he'll take me on as a passenger."

"A *passenger?*" Sutter seemed surprised by her suggestion. "That ain't likely, ma'am."

"I'm afraid I haven't much money," Lauren said quickly, "but I would repay him, I promise."

"It wouldn't matter how much blunt you had. The cap'm don't allow females on board ship. Besides, the *Leucothea* ain't a passenger vessel. She's a *warship*."

"Oh."

He must have sensed Lauren's fierce disappointment, for his expression became apologetic. "Truth tell," he amended, "the *Leucothea* mostly transports cargo, but sometimes she comes to blows at sea. We fought two battles with the Frogs just last month, but we gave 'em somethin' for their pains and made it through with hardly a scratch."

"Frogs? You fight *frogs?*"

"You know, *Frogs*. The Frenchies. We're at war with 'em. But we'll show ole Boney he can't defeat *us*."

"Oh . . . of course." Lauren pressed a hand to her temple, fighting a wave of exhaustion. The fear and worry of recent weeks must have taken a greater toll than she had realized, leaving her disoriented and confused; she had heard the cant term before, despite having lived in isolation for the past four years.

"Ma'am," Sutter said hesitantly. "Begging your pardon, ma'am, but the cap'm won't like you being here. You'll have to leave. I'm right sorry."

Remembering her original purpose, Lauren glanced over her shoulder to scan the dark wharf. Burroughs's men were out there somewhere, beyond the great wall. "Please . . . don't make me leave just yet."

Sutter's freckled face puckered into a frown. "You don't have a place to go, ma'am?"

"Not a safe place. There were some men following me. Please, may I stay here for a short while? They may try to return."

He studied her for a moment before finally nodding. "I'll go fetch the cap'm." He moved past Lauren, toward the stern, but

14

he had only gone a few feet when a voice spoke from the darkness.

"You seem to be doing quite well on your own, Sutter."

The boy gave a start, leveling his long carbine at the shadows. "Sir!" he exclaimed when he recognized the menace: his six-foot-four captain was standing near the door below the quarterdeck, silently observing them.

"As I'm not the enemy, lad," he said gently, "you might consider aiming that elsewhere."

Lauren, who had whirled at the sound of that velvet-textured voice, knew she must be confronting the master of the vessel, for he strode forward with the easy grace of a man used to respect and instant obedience. She wondered how long he had been eavesdropping on their conversation, but as he stepped into the lantern light, pinning her with his gaze, all thought of taking him to task fled.

Her first impression was one of overwhelming physical presence. He was a head taller than other men of her acquaintance, and his broad-shouldered frame made him appear powerful and commanding—and somewhat intimidating. He was dressed as a gentleman, though. He wore an elegant green coat, crisp white cravat, tight-fitting stockinette breeches, and gleaming topboots—all which complemented his noble features and contradicted every notion Lauren had ever held about sea captains.

In spite of herself, she couldn't help staring at his leonine magnificence. His tawny chestnut hair was thick and curling, glinting with a silver sheen in the glow of lantern light. Yet it was his brilliant blue gaze which held her attention. She had never seen eyes of such a deep, vivid blue.

He suffered her scrutiny in silence, a hint of amusement curving his lips, as if he were accustomed to such reactions from females. Finally, however, one of his heavy, slightly arching eyebrows lifted. "Do you intend to introduce me to the lady?"

He was speaking to the forgotten cabin boy, Lauren realized, at the same time perceiving how intently she had been staring. She felt a flush rise to her cheeks and was grateful for her concealing hood.

Tim Sutter stepped forward with alacrity. "Sorry, Cap'm, but she dinnet tell me her name."

The captain appraised Lauren, his calm, intelligent regard trying to pierce the shadows that concealed her face. "I'm Jason Stuart," he said mildly. "Perhaps you'd like to explain how I may be of service."

The revelation hit her with the force of a cannon shot. Lauren drew a sharp breath, her thoughts reeling. "Did . . . you say . . . Stuart," she rasped. "Jason Stuart?" But she knew the answer, even before his confirming nod. Fixing her stunned gaze on Captain Stuart, she took an involuntary step backward. "I . . . I must have made a mistake," she got out as she continued to retreat.

When the captain took a step toward her, she put out a hand as if to fend him off. That checked him for a moment. "Sutter, find her something to sit on before she faints."

"Aye, Cap'm."

"No!" Lauren said wildly as she came up against the railing. Glancing desperately over her shoulder, she spied the gangport. "I'm sorry . . . to have troubled you."

She saw Jason Stuart moving toward her again and choked back a cry of panic. Without waiting for him to reach her, she turned and fled down the gangway, praying that the shadows would swallow her up. *Dear God, how had she managed to find one of the two men in London she wished most to avoid?*

Soon she was running again through the darkened streets of the city, this time driven by more than fear. She had been truly shocked to learn the captain's identity. It didn't seem possible that the fates could be so unkind.

Three weeks ago the name of Jason Stuart had meant nothing to her; she hadn't even known of his existence. Neither had she realized how truly dangerous her situation was . . .

An argument could have been made that she herself was to blame for her present predicament. Perhaps she *should* have known better than to agree when George Burroughs offered her a home at Carlin House. But she'd only been twelve years old at the time, and alone in the world. And the six months she'd spent at the parish workhouse—where she'd been taken after her mother's death—had been horrifying. It wasn't the cold and hunger or the backbreaking work she found so hard to bear; in truth, she had been used to little better. It wasn't even the beatings. It was the way she'd been punished for breaking rules she hadn't even been aware of . . . locked in the root cellar despite her pleas and screams . . . left there in that awful blackness till her terror was so great she'd lapsed into merciful unconsciousness . . . She would have done anything to escape that. And George Burroughs had offered her a way. In return, she was to help him save the shipping line her father, Jonathan Carlin, had built.

She had never known her father, nor wanted to. She could never forgive him for what he'd done to her mother. Lauren hadn't been born on the wrong side of the blanket precisely; the blanket had slipped. Jonathan Carlin had married her beautiful, frail mother in a sham wedding ceremony—a common sport of wealthy young bucks at the time—and then abandoned Elizabeth DeVries, leaving her to face the shame of bearing an illegitimate child and the misery of constant and grinding poverty.

How terrible those final days of her mother's life had been: the pale face ravaged by hardship and illness, the thin form wracked by fever and pain. Though only a child, Lauren had continued to take in washing and mending as her mother had done, but the pittance she earned couldn't pay for the medicine Elizabeth so desperately needed to ease her suffering.

Lauren still clenched her fists whenever she remembered her helplessness; somehow that had been harder to bear than even grief and loneliness. Even as young as she'd been, she had vowed never to know such poverty again, and her time in the parish workhouse had only strengthened that vow. *That* was why she had been willing to listen to George Burroughs's strange proposition.

He'd revealed that for some years he had been a partner in her father's shipping firm, and that Jonathan Carlin had married again shortly after abandoning her mother. Jonathan had wed Burroughs's sister, Mary—legitimately this time—

and a child had been born to the couple, a daughter, scarcely six months after Lauren's birth to Elizabeth. The child had been named Andrea. But ten years later tragedy struck.

Burroughs had not gone into detail, but he'd told Lauren that Jonathan and Mary had been murdered by pirates, and Andrea tortured and left for dead. Though the child recovered physically, she was never the same mentally. Still, as Jonathan Carlin's daughter, she had inherited his tremendous wealth.

Burroughs, as her uncle, had taken over her guardianship and continued to run the Carlin Line. But the following year Andrea had succumbed to pneumonia, and so he had sought Lauren out.

She would come to live at Carlin House, which overlooked the sea atop the craggy cliffs of Cornwall, and live in the manner that Jonathan Carlin's daughter ought . . . so long as she pretended to be Andrea. There should be no problem in getting away with the impersonation. There was only one person who might know the difference—Jonathan's sister, Regina Carlin, who stood to take over the Carlin Line should it become known that Andrea was dead. Regina had never liked Andrea; indeed, she had labeled her niece a lunatic and tried to have her committed to Bedlam. But Burroughs was determined to protect his ward, just as he was determined to keep control of the shipping line out of Regina's hands. He had forbidden Regina access to Carlin House and hired men to see that she was kept out—so there should be no problem with her, he said.

And after all, Lauren and Andrea *had* been half sisters . . . only six months apart . . . both with fair curling hair, green-gold eyes, and delicate features promising great beauty. The only remarkable difference was Andrea's mental instability . . . New servants would be brought in. No one but Lauren and himself and her governess would know the truth.

Nor would the impersonation last forever, Burroughs promised. She could have her independence when she reached her majority, as well as a share in the Carlin Line. Burroughs had said that half the ships were rightfully hers, and in a way, Lauren agreed; had her parents' marriage been real, she would have legally inherited Jonathan Carlin's entire fortune.

And Lauren had only to remember her last night in the root

18

cellar to make up her mind. She agreed.

Her new life at Carlin House wasn't quite what she had expected. She rarely saw Burroughs, since he resided in London, and she wasn't allowed to associate with the servants. There was only Miss Foster, who was cold and unfeeling, like the granite of the cliffs. She did see her father for the first time . . . in the portrait that hung in the gallery. She had studied that handsome face, searching for some trace of the cruelty that had hurt her mother so, and was surprised when she couldn't find it.

But, except for the loneliness, her life wasn't a bad one. She was given an education befitting the heiress to the Carlin shipping empire, and all the material comforts even a princess could want. New gowns and shawls and slippers . . . Her half sister's jewel box was hers, the lovely lockets and pins, the ring Andrea had always worn. Miss Foster insisted that Lauren wear the ring, and also insisted on calling her "Andrea", even if they were alone, as did Burroughs.

By far the most frustrating part of having assumed her half sister's identity, though, was that she was forbidden to go beyond the house grounds. Early on, Lauren had realized that the unsmiling men who were charged with protecting her from Regina were also there to keep her in.

Yet it hadn't taken her long to devise ways to slip past her constant guards and escape to the wild, gorse-dotted cliffs with their rocky paths down to the sea. Miss Foster slept soundly, thank heaven, and whenever there was no telltale moon to reveal her presence to the patrols, Lauren would climb down the tree outside her window and set out for the cliffs and a few blessed hours of freedom.

That was how she had met Matthew MacGregor. Three months before her sixteenth birthday, on one of her nightly ventures, she had caught him in the act of stashing contraband silk and brandy in the caves below Carlin House. By all rights, he should have slit her throat when he'd found her hiding among the rocks, since her knowledge could have sent him to the gallows. But he had befriended her instead, saying she reminded him of the daughter he had lost. And after living in seclusion for so long with only a grim governess for

19

companionship, Lauren had latched on to him like a barnacle, gratefully welcoming their odd friendship, which had grown steadily over the next year.

It had only been a month ago that she had gone out to meet him and heard voices above her on the clifftop—an indistinct murmur above the rumble of the surf.

Warily, Lauren had crouched down among the shadows and pulled the hood of her woolen cloak well forward. She knew her hair would reflect the faintest light. "Bright as a beacon," Matthew always said about her golden tresses, warning her that in moonlight her hair glowed like a lantern.

The voices above grew louder, filling Lauren with unease. An argument seemed to be taking place, and although the stiff seawind whipped away the exact words, one of the voices sounded oddly as if it belonged to a woman—a frightened woman. Lauren frowned. She could think of no female but herself who would venture so near the cliffs at night.

Then her legs began to cramp from stooping for so long. She was cautiously trying to shift her tall frame into a more comfortable position when the quarrel above her suddenly erupted into a full-fledged scuffle. A muffled grunt was flung down by the wind, followed by a low curse and the rasp of dirt and pebbles falling over the cliff's edge. The next instant, a terrified scream rent the night air.

Lauren jumped, turning her head in time to glimpse a giant fluttering bat plummet past her in the darkness. She froze, her skin crawling as the scream echoed eerily off the cliff rocks.

It was a long while before she dared inch her way forward to scan the cliff above her head. Seeing nothing, she peered down. She couldn't make out anything on the rocks below, but she knew no one could have survived such a fall.

Her heart pounding as violently as the surf below, Lauren left her hiding place to scramble over the slippery granite, her breath coming harder as she negotiated the treacherous cliff path mainly by feel. When she reached the bottom, she unconsciously slowed, dreading what she would find. She climbed over the last rocky barrier, then halted abruptly, staring in horror.

Her governess Miss Foster lay there, her body twisted at an

awkward angle, her mouth open in a silent scream. A heavy woolen shawl was draped over one shoulder, while spray from the crashing waves had wet her skin, making her mannish face shine in the darkness.

Lauren swayed, feeling sick. There was something vaguely obscene about the way Miss Foster's black bombazine skirts were spread over the rocks, as if she had neatly arranged them before sitting down to the tea table.

Nausea churning in her stomach, Lauren turned away, stumbling blindly over the rocks, desperately needing to get away.

When a shadow rose up before her, she screamed—and would have screamed again, except that a broad, calloused hand clamped over her mouth, preventing her from uttering a second.

"Hush, lass," Matthew hissed in her ear. "Do ye mean to bring all yer guardian's culls down on us?"

Hearing that familiar brogue, Lauren flung herself into Matthew's arms and sobbed against his shoulder. "Matthew . . . she . . . she . . ."

"Aye, I heard the scream." After a moment, he gently disengaged himself from Lauren's deathlike grip. "Stay here, lass. I must look."

In a moment he was back, his mouth set in a grim line.

"Matthew," Lauren said hoarsely, the normal huskiness of her voice deepened by horror, "Miss Foster's fall . . . it wasn't an accident. Someone pushed her. I heard voices up on the cliff just before it happened."

"Aye," he growled, "someone pushed her. And I wouldna doubt that ye were the mark."

Lauren fixed her frightened gaze on Matthew's face. "You mean . . . someone was trying ot kill *me?*"

"Kill *Andrea.* Damme, lass, this impersonation of yers has gone far enough."

Only recently, in a vulnerable moment, Lauren had confessed to Matthew that she was really Lauren DeVries and only pretending to be her half sister Andrea, and he'd refused to let it rest until she had told him the entire story of the deception George Burroughs had staged. The revelations had not set well with him.

"Are ye a fool, lass?" he had scolded. "What made ye agree to such a thing? Dinna ye ken ye can hang?"

Not until then had she realized her impersonation was a criminal offense—punishable by imprisonment and possibly hanging. It had been the idea of prison, though, not hanging, which had frightened her most. The very thought of such confinement made her cringe.

Matthew had tried to talk her into leaving Carlin House afterward, for he'd done some cautious questioning in the village and unearthed an ugly rumor that Regina had been an accomplice in the Carlins' murders. But Lauren had no place to go. Besides, she had given George Burroughs her word.

But that was before Miss Foster had been killed. Lauren stared at Matthew now, trying to absorb the shock of his grim suspicions.

"Ye canna stay here longer, lass," Matthew said adamantly. "Regina Carlin is after yer father's blunt, and she willna jib at murder to get it. Ye must be gone from this place before 'tis too late."

Lauren shivered, despite the warmth of the June night. Matthew's accusations reminded her of a slip Miss Foster had once made—something about Regina challenging Andrea's right to the inheritance since Jonathan Carlin had lacked a will. The governess had tried to cover up what she'd said at once, and told Lauren to mind her own business. But that, as well as Burroughs's insistence on having his men protect her, seemed especially ominous now.

"I say Regina snabbled your governess," Matthew declared harshly, interrupting her thoughts. "And ye'll be next."

Lauren turned to him, her eyes pleading for reassurance he wouldn't give. Yet she knew he was right. Regina would kill her, too, if she stayed.

"Very well," she said at last, "I'll leave. But I must speak to Burroughs first. He will see that the impersonation must end."

Matthew snorted in disgust. "Are ye daft, lass? Do ye think he will let ye just walk away?"

"Matthew, he may not like me, but I can't believe he would want to see me killed."

"Aye, and he was supposed to protect your governess, too."

In the darkness, Lauren could almost see the aging smuggler's angry face. In better light, it would be as red as his hair. She laid a trembling hand on his arm. "Please, don't be angry with me, Matthew. I'll speak to Burroughs, and then I'll be free to go."

"Stubborn lass," he muttered under his breath. "Verra well, but I willna let ye stay long."

"I . . . I don't know where I can go."

"Dinna fash yerself. We'll think of a plan. Come, then," he said gruffly. "Ye must go back to the house before ye are missed."

She hesitated. "We shouldn't . . . just leave Miss Foster there."

"Yer guardian's men will find her, I've no doubt."

Choking back a sob, Lauren nodded mutely. She let Matthew guide her back up the cliff, agreeing with his advice to say nothing of what she had seen, and promising to be on her guard.

But after she had climbed the gnarled tree outside her window and was once again in her own bedroom, the horror reclaimed her and she started to tremble. She had never thought her impersonation would result in murder. And even though the Carlin ships would give her the independence she craved, she didn't want them at the price of a woman's life— or her own.

Hearing a plaintive yowl at her feet, Lauren bent to pick up the cat that was brushing against her skirts. The great, orange-furred creature had found his way into her bedroom several months ago and had adopted her. Lauren hugged him to her breast, needing the comfort of his warm body. Miss Foster had hated Ulysses and had regularly threatened to get rid of him. . . .

Reminded again of that twisted form lying so still on the rocks, Lauren desperately buried her face in the cat's fur. "Oh, Ulysses," she said in a choked whisper. "What have I done? What in God's name have I done?"

* * *

Sibyl Foster's funeral was held three days later, and the following week, George Burroughs arrived at Carlin House. Lauren paled when she was told he wished to see her in the study, but she resolutely smoothed the skirt of her black muslin gown and dried her tears. He would not be pleased, but she was determined to tell him of her decision to end the impersonation.

The study was her favorite room, even though she approached it now with reluctance. Innumerable paintings and replicas of ships crowded every wall and table, while hundreds of leather-bound volumes lined the bookshelves. Lauren had spent hours poring over tomes about the sea, learning about the brave men who challenged its power. She knew a good deal about sailing vessels as well, even though she had never set foot on one; her passion for ships was the one thing besides her height that she had inherited from her father.

Burroughs, a portly man with sagging jowls and a ruddy complexion, was standing beside the desk when she entered, looking drawn and weary after his long journey from London. His somber brown coat was wrinkled and his knee breeches were creased, indicating that he hadn't taken the time to change before summoning her. He, too, looked as if he had been crying, but Lauren knew his tears were the result of habitually watery eyes.

As she quietly shut the door behind her, Burroughs dabbed at his face with a handkerchief, fixing her with his rheumy gaze. "I have made the arrangements for your marriage," he said tersely. "The wedding is to take place shortly after your seventeenth birthday."

Stunned, Lauren stared at him. She had expected some expression of regret over Miss Foster's death. Perhaps even some effort to explain away the entire thing. But she had certainly not been prepared for this. *"Marriage?"* she stammered. "But what about Miss Foster?"

"A sad accident," he admitted.

"It was not!" Lauren replied in a hoarse voice. "I will not be a part of this deception any longer. It has gone too far."

Burroughs eyed her coldly, his lips tightening with displeasure. "I realize that you are disturbed, Andrea, so I will overlook this insubordination."

"You told me Regina wanted the Carlin Line, but you never said she would resort to murder. I won't continue—"

"That will be quite enough!" The sharpness of his tone silenced Lauren for a moment. Burroughs lowered his voice and went on as if she hadn't spoken, relating the details of her planned marriage. Nobility . . . protect . . . younger son . . . Lord Effing. . . .

A tightness in Lauren's throat nearly choked her. How she wished that she had never become involved in Burroughs's lies and deceptions. She could stand that droning voice no longer. "You promised I would be free when I was twenty-one," she challenged unwisely.

A muscle in his jaw hardened, but he ignored her comment. "I had no difficulty finding suitors for your hand—not with the Carlin Line for a dowry. Few men scruple about what sort of bride they are getting when a fortune in ships is at stake. They are even willing to overlook insanity, it seems. Yet I wanted to attract the right kind of man. I am pleased with my choice."

Lauren shook her head. How could she marry a man she didn't know? How could she draw someone else into a deception that had already resulted in murder? And in any case, she never intended to marry. She would never allow any man the power to hurt her the way her mother had been hurt.

"The Marquess of Effing is a wealthy man, my dear. The settlements he has promised are more than generous. You will never want for anything once you marry his son. The family is a noble one—"

"Do not pretend you are doing this for me," Lauren interjected.

Burroughs's expression turned coldly hostile. "I am doing it for the Carlin Line, since someone must take control when I am gone. And I am doing it to protect you from Regina. This marriage may be the only way to prevent her from locking you away in a madhouse—if she doesn't kill you first!"

Heedless of his warning tone, Lauren met his damp eyes directly. "You wouldn't care! You wouldn't care what Regina did to me, as long as you could prevent her from having the

25

Carlin ships!"

Vivid flags of anger rose on Burroughs's cheeks as he glowered at Lauren. He pointed an accusing finger at her, grinding out his words. "I have *always*, *always* met my obligation as Jonathan's partner. Even when it came to providing for his bastard daughter!"

Lauren flinched. Burroughs had never called her a bastard before. He made the word sound like an accusation, as if he would like to punish her for her birth.

Then he sighed, pressing a hand to his forehead. "In spite of how it may seem to you, you will discover I have only your best interests at heart."

Lauren laughed mirthlessly. "Oh, truly? Then perhaps you can tell me what I stand to gain? For me, it will merely be exchanging one jailer for another."

"It will not be like that."

"No? How many men do you suppose my new husband will deem adequate to guard me? Ten? Twenty? Is he rich enough to afford the army under your command?"

"I have told you before . . . my men are only there for your protection."

"Protection? Miss Foster is dead!"

"That is enough," he snapped, his face darkening ominously. "You will go to your room where you will consider what I have said."

"No! You needed me for your grand schemes, but it has gone too far. I am through, do you hear? I cannot condone murder."

"You will cease these hysterical rantings at once, Andrea!"

Lauren realized she was courting disaster but was unable to stop herself. "Hysterical!" she cried, clenching her fists. "Yes, I may be. But I am not *Andrea!*"

Burroughs covered the distance between them with a stride that belied his age, rage mottling his face as he raised his hand and slapped her hard across the cheek. Lauren's head snapped sideways, loosening the pins in her hair and sending a golden lock tumbling down her back.

Her hand going to her stinging cheek, Lauren stared at him in fear and shock. Burroughs had never struck her before— but then she had never opposed him before.

26

As if he realized what he had done, his fierce expression crumbled abruptly. "I . . . I am sorry," he stammered. And then suddenly he gasped and began to claw at the neckcloth binding his throat.

Lauren watched him warily for a moment, then instinctively reached out to help him. But he waved her away. He sank weakly into a wing chair beside the desk, taking large gulps of air.

It was a moment before he could speak again, his voice still unsteady. "I would have prevented your governess's death had it been in my power to do. Please believe me. This marriage is for your protection. The doctors say I may live only a short time longer, and I would see you settled and . . . provided for, before I quit this life."

His normally florid expression had faded to a sickly gray, but even so, Lauren couldn't shake the suspicion that he was merely using his health as a means to gain her agreement. She felt her anger rising again, giving her the courage to defy him. She shook her head. "I will not marry anyone."

"You will. The marriage will take place in September as planned. You should have ample time to adjust to the idea."

"Never." Though September was still several months away, Lauren had no intention of *adjusting* to the idea.

"You have no choice. Don't force me to do something I have no wish to do. I imagine you wouldn't care to spend a night in the wine cellars."

Terror welled up in Lauren, making her take a step backward. Burroughs *knew* about her fear of confinement. He had discovered it when he visited her at the workhouse. And later, soon after she had come to Carlin House, Miss Foster had locked her in a nursery closet as punishment for some minor infraction. She had been found hours afterward, unconscious and cold as death. The experience had brought on a rash of nightmares that still haunted her. Lauren stood there now, her back pressed against the door, staring at Burroughs in fear.

He rubbed his forehead wearily, an infinite sadness in his eyes. "Must I resort to force, my dear?"

Despising herself for her cowardice, Lauren turned and fled, yet she waited till she reached the privacy of her own bedchamber before flinging herself on the bed and giving license to her grief in a torrent of tears. She didn't doubt Burroughs would carry out his threat. He was obsessed with keeping the Carlin Line from Regina and clearly meant to have his way.

Remembering his abrupt announcement of her arranged marriage, Lauren wondered what kind of man would agree to marry a half-mad girl he had never seen. Had he been bribed with the Carlin ships? Or did Burroughs hold some other kind of threat over his head? Perhaps he didn't even know about Andrea's condition.

But whatever his reasons, he didn't deserve to be embroiled in such danger. Miss Foster had already been caught in the middle of the deadly battle between George Burroughs and Regina Carlin, and she had been killed.

Lauren was still sobbing when Ulysses leapt up on the bed, but his contented purring helped her realize the futility of tears. She wiped her cheeks and drew the huge feline into the curve of her body as she tried to consider her situation unemotionally.

Even if she went to the authorities, no one would believe her; she was supposed to be half mad. And if they did believe her story, she would go to prison for fraud, and might even hang. Prison! The very word struck terror in her heart. To be locked away, in a cold dark cell . . .

Matthew had been right. She had to leave Carlin House at once. She would put what few things she needed in a bundle and wait till everyone was asleep, then slip out to meet him.

"But I cannot take you with me, Ulysses," Lauren whispered.

The cat blinked his wide almond-shaped eyes and yawned, while Lauren stared at the canopy overhead. Matthew would help her, as he had said. Once they managed to make the nearest seaport, they could find a ship and leave England. . . .

But now, in the damp darkness of the Thames waterfront, her knee paining her fiercely, Lauren was close to panic as she recalled how disastrously their escape had gone awry. Matthew had insisted on going to London where they could more easily elude Burroughs's men, but they had made it only as far as

Reading before Matthew had nearly been killed. Then he had abandoned her, intentionally making himself a target and giving her a chance to flee. Afterward, her flight had taken her to London where she waited fruitlessly for Matthew to arrive; then to the waterfront where Burroughs's men were still searching for her; then to the London Dock where she boarded the *Leucothea* and met Captain Jason Stuart.

And that was the final blow. As incredible as it seemed, she had stumbled directly into the path of one of the men she wished most to avoid.

Jason Stuart, the man she was contracted to marry.

Chapter Two

Jason reached the gunwale in time to see his cloaked visitor flee up the stone steps from the quay. Watching her stumble through the cargo on the dimly lit wharf, he frowned, puzzled by her strange behavior.

The entire day had been rather uncommon, Jason reflected as he stared after her. When the *Leucothea* had docked that morning, he had been met with the disturbing news that the United States had declared war on England. That intelligence immediately raised the question of whether his American first mate, Kyle Ramsey, would continue to sail with the brig. Then later that day, when Jason responded to his father's injunction for a personal appearance, he had learned something else equally disturbing.

He had been too busy to consider the implications of either event until he had seen to his ship. But when Kyle finally joined him in his cabin, the two of them spent the remainder of the evening drinking Jason's best brandy and discussing the problem Kyle's citizenship posed. Years before, the Ramsey family had moved from England to a plantation on the Mississippi River, and though Kyle hadn't lived in America for long before he took to the sea, he felt a certain loyalty toward his new country.

Wanting his friend to make the choice, Jason had refrained from using his considerable talents of persuasion, but he was pleased and relieved by Kyle's decision to stay with the *Leucothea*. Only when the problem was satisfactorily resolved, did Jason mention his own quandary. "There is one more thing," he said, pausing to choose his words. "The summons from my father . . ."

"Ah, yes," his inebriated first mate interjected. "The urgent message which was waiting when we dropped anchor. Let me guess—Lord Effing ripped up at you for disgracing the family honor. Or was it merely that you didn't jump when he said jump?" Kyle snorted as he replenished his glass from the crystal decanter on Jason's desk. "You get such summons regularly, Jase. What d'you do to twig the old man's nose this time? It can't be those investments you made in the East India Company—that was last time. You should have taken me with you. I would have recommended an indulgence in spirits for my Lord Effing. Easier to stomach a rebellious son, you know." Kyle took a large swig of brandy and grinned. "On second thought, that wouldn't do. His lordship might drown in the stuff."

"He had something else in mind, however," Jason said before Kyle's loosened tongue took him off on another tangent. "My father has arranged a marriage for me."

Kyle gaped at his friend and captain, staring as if a two-tailed sea dragon had suddenly stepped into Jason's highly polished boots. "The devil, you say!" he breathed at last.

Jason wore a contemplative expression as he leaned back in his chair and drew an imaginary pattern on the desktop with a lean forefinger. "I've agreed to meet the lady."

Kyle drained his glass, then refilled it slowly. "Skulduggery must run in your family," he said, his tone remarkably sober. "The marquess is the only man I know who has more schemes up his sleeve than you do. Only he favors blackmail. Seriously, Jase, whatever possessed you to agree to such a thing? You know what he means to do, don't you? Wants you to settle down and have a passel of brats. Don't see the reason for it, myself. Your brother already has a boy of his own—succession secure and all that."

"I'm afraid my father doesn't quite see it that way—insecurity and all that," Jason returned dryly. "But what would you do if you were offered the Carlin Line for a dowry?"

Kyle's jaw dropped once more. "The *Carlin* ships?" When

he realized Jason wasn't joking, he whistled softly through his teeth. "Why, that clever, *clever* bastard. He knew that would hook you, if anything would. I take back what I said. You're a rank amateur compared to your father."

Jason chuckled and raised a hand. "Hold, man, I haven't agreed to do anything except pay a call on the heiress. You already have me leg-shackled."

"Why not? Even a bracket-faced harridan would be worth the Carlin fleet. Who's the bride, anyway?"

"Carlin's daughter. And she's supposed to be a beauty, though still somewhat young."

Kyle's brows drew together in a frown as he searched his memory. "But that's rather . . . There was a rumor some years back about a kid. Said to be touched in the head or something. Locked up in Bedlam."

Jason shook his head. "No truth to it, or so my father assures me. I am, however, to be given an opportunity to judge for myself when I pay her a visit. I thought I would set out for Cornwall in the morning. If I make haste, I could be back before repairs are completed on the *Leucothea*."

Kyle continued to frown. "I don't like it, Jase. Smells odd. My advice is to forget it. You already have a tidy pile, in spite of His Lordship's efforts to keep you a gentleman. What you ought to do is turn those brains of yours to shady dealings. That'll spike the old man's guns and make you rich at the same time. Besides, a wife won't take kindly to you fighting a war and traipsing all over the world."

Jason directed a penetrating glance at his foxed first mate. "I had thought to put the *Leucothea* under your command."

Looking down, Kyle scowled into his glass. "Damn it, Jason, I've already agreed to stay. There's no need for you to offer a bribe like that."

Jason's blue eyes filled with amusement. "You wound me, mate. I hadn't even considered bribing you. You've earned command of a ship. It was part of the deal."

"But you can't be thinking of leaving the *Leucothea* yet."

"Not immediately, but I will someday. You know I never meant to make a career of the sea. You've taught me all I wanted to know and more about sailing. Besides, if I do decide to marry Carlin's daughter, I'll have an entire merchant fleet at my disposal. It won't be the same, of course . . ."

Jason's voice trailed off as he let his gaze wander about the sparsely furnished captain's cabin. It seemed small when occupied by the two of them. Both were tall men, with powerful, well-muscled bodies and broad shoulders—although "massive" was probably a more appropriate term for Kyle. But regardless of the cabin's lack of comfort, it had been a home to Jason for nearly two years. He was as familiar with every inch of its oak-paneled bulkheads and gleaming brass fixtures as he was with the rest of the brig, and he had enjoyed every moment of being the *Leucothea*'s captain. He would miss her.

Trying to shrug off his dispirited mood, Jason picked up the nearly empty decanter. "So, then," he said, refilling both glasses. "Shall we drink to our new partnership? And to the hope that the Carlin heiress is all I've been promised?"

"Jase, are you certain about this? Just think of what you'll miss if you marry."

"The Carlin Line should provide me adequate entertainment, at least for a few years."

"Well . . . what about all the hearts you'll be breaking? There must be a dozen women on the catch for you here in London, not to mention Lisbon and Gibraltar and—"

"Not one I would consider marrying. Don't worry, my friend. I don't intend to lower my standards entirely."

Kyle hesitated, before suddenly grinning. "Hell, why not? If you're fool enough to marry Carlin's brat for her money, who am I to stop you?" He raised his glass in salute. "To the Carlin heiress. May she be comely and sweet-tempered and own a thousand ships.

"And to the *Leucothea*," he added, after drinking deeply. "The best goddamned mistress a man ever had. You know, Jase, I'm getting the better end of the deal. I'd rather have the *Leucothea* than all the heiresses in Europe. Remind me to thank you sometime. Come to think of it, you'd best be on your guard till I sober up. I may very well end up kissing you before your bride does."

Remembering their conversation now as he stood on deck, Jason wondered if he should have gotten drunk, as Kyle had.

33

Ordinarily they celebrated their victories their first night in port with a bottle and some female companionship, but for a reason Jason couldn't even name, he had postponed his departure from the ship. Yet all the liquor on board might not have been enough to dispel his heavy mood. His usual cheerful spirits had been steadily diminishing all evening—and he had no idea why. It was true that while Kyle had been mulling over loyalties, he had been giving more thought to his own future than he had in a great while. But his prospects didn't really concern him.

It wasn't even his father's autocratic arrangement of a marriage contract, since this actually wasn't the marquess's first attempt at getting him to settle down. In fact, Jason could admire his father's skillful manipulations, even when he himself was the victim.

For some years now, avoiding Lord Effing's machinations had been something of a game to Jason. Even though he had never been opposed to marriage, he preferred to choose his own bride and had no intention of rushing the business. He was willing to admit, however, that negotiating for the Carlin heiress had been a masterful stroke by the marquess.

During their discussion that morning, there had been no dissimulation between them; there had been no need, for father and son understood each other quite well. Lord Effing had known it wouldn't be the Carlin fortune itself that attracted Jason, but the appeal of controlling a vast shipping enterprise. And Jason had realized the concessions his father was making. Indeed, Jason had been rather amused to hear his sire advocating a union that had such distinct disadvantages: his future bride had not a drop of noble blood in her veins, and she was rumored to be of unsound mind at that.

Jason had accepted his father's assurances that the stories concerning the girl's insanity were without foundation. While the marquess might favor blue blood, he would draw the line at the possibility of either madness or imbecility in his descendants. But the shroud of secrecy itself intrigued Jason, just as his father had known it would. That, and lure of the Carlin ships, were strong enough inducements for him to consider the match.

He would have been a fool to do otherwise. And perhaps, Jason mused, it was possible that he and the Carlin heiress would suit. And if he would have to give up his own admittedly romantic ideal of the woman who would one day be his wife, the Carlin ships should be adequate compensation.

But that wasn't the source of the disquiet that had been disturbing him all evening. Rather, it was his odd presentiment. For the past few hours he had *known* that once he left the ship, his life would somehow change. And seeing the cloaked woman had only strengthened that feeling.

A balmy breeze ruffled Jason's gilded chestnut hair as he stood watching her vanish into the night, his strong, well-shaped hands lightly gripping the railing. Behind him, he could sense Tim Sutter's presence, could feel the boy's questioning gaze on his back.

"Maybe we shouldn't let her go, Cap'm," Tim suggested hesitantly. "She said some coves were after her."

Although normally he deplored impulsiveness, Jason had already decided to follow her. Rescuing damsels in distress wasn't his line, but he had no intention of letting her roam the streets alone at night, not in this wretched neighborhood, where thieves and procurers waited to prey on the innocent and unsuspecting. She was singularly lucky to have made it this far; even though the Thames River Police patrolled the docks and the parish constabulary boasted a large force of night watchmen, Jason himself never went unarmed. But in addition to wanting to protect her, he was more than a little curious about her startled reaction to hearing his name.

"I'll see to her, lad," Jason replied, dismissing the cabin boy. "You'd best return to your rounds."

"Aye, sir."

Making his way quickly down the gangway to the quay, Jason vaulted up the steps and crossed the wharf, passing through the wall gate in time to spy the cloaked figure some distance to his right. He had no trouble following her. Not only was she favoring her right leg, which made her easy to distinguish even in darkness, but Jason had experience tracking far more elusive game, having learned the skill from an American trapper during a year spent in the wilderness of the northern territories.

He kept her in sight, pondering her reaction as he strode briskly along the narrow, twisting streets. He found it odd that she had recoiled from him in fear. Women generally responded far differently to him. And to his knowledge, there was nothing in his reputation to make her afraid of him.

He was accustomed to being a target of speculation, of course; to his crew he was a renegade nobleman's son, a rebel and an adventurer. And some of the stories about him were even true. He was the younger son of the wealthy Marquess of Effing, and he had left home to escape his father's dictates— although he *hadn't* been disinherited when he took to the sea, as was rumored. For a short time Jason had been an officer in the Royal Navy, but his father's influence with the Admiralty had ended his hopes for a career spent in battle. He had gone to America shortly thereafter, where he'd begun building his fortune.

There were any number of rumors about how he had come by the *Leucothea*—that he had captured her, that he had won her at cards, that he had killed a man in a duel and spirited the ship away. But he had purchased the brig in America with some lucky winnings.

He was young for a captain, even now, when he was a few years shy of thirty. But he had found that command came naturally to him. His powerful physique and air of authority had gained him immediate attention—although he had had to earn the respect of his crew, all seasoned tars who accepted his leadership with wariness.

It was because of his inexperience at sea that he had formed the partnership with Kyle Ramsey and learned how to sail. Although an unusual arrangement, he and Ramsey made a good team. Kyle knew how to outrace a storm and plot a course through shallows better than any captain alive, and Jason knew men.

He had returned to England then, and for two years had fought the war in his own way: aiding British troops by transporting much-needed weapons and supplies across the channel, and harrying French vessels whenever the opportunity arose. His uncanny ability to outguess the enemy, combined with Kyle's navigational skill and their crew's courage, made the *Leucothea* a deadly adversary in battle.

There had been plenty of battles. Even though the *Leucothea* was a private vessel, she had seen as much action in the war against Napoleon as most naval ships. Only a week earlier off the coast of Spain, she had encountered two frigates that had eluded the English blockade. Unwilling to endanger his ship by facing the combined strength of longer range cannon, Jason had come about and sailed for Cadiz, leading the unsuspecting French vessels within range of a British squadron. It had been short work for three ships of the line to capture both frigates.

The next day, the *Leucothea* had exchanged broadsides with a French sloop of war, which mounted twenty-four guns to the brig's ten. In a maneuver that would have done Nelson proud, the *Leucothea* had swung alongside and inflicted enough damage to ensure the sloop's eventual capture by the Royal Navy.

Remembering the action of the past two weeks, Jason thought again of his odd reluctance to leave the ship this evening. He had no reason for it. His discussion with Kyle had been necessary, but could have been completed in a quarter of the time. He couldn't blame his procrastination on the paperwork or the necessity of finalizing plans for the ship, either. Repairing the damages the *Leucothea* had sustained would be short work for his well-trained crew, and they could see to it without his supervision.

He wouldn't even need to be present for the loading of the next cargo. The supplies they obtained were generally the best quality and rarely required inspection. There would be no maggots in the flour or spoilage in the dried meats, while the muskets and Baker rifles would be in prime working order, and the bayonets and sabers made of the finest steel. Moreover, his first mate could handle any problem.

And it wasn't as if he were reluctant to reach his destination, Jason reflected, hearing snatches of song and raucous laughter coming from a tavern he passed. It had been some weeks since he had had a woman and he was more than ready for one. Even now a lovely lady of pleasure was waiting for him at the exclusive bordello he frequented. Once the proprietor

Madame Fanchon, had received his message, she would have arranged for the exotic Lila to be free for the evening.

No, he had been waiting for something unexpected to happen. Something such as the arrival of a woman in a hooded cloak. Indeed, he felt almost as if he had been *meant* to wait for her. Which was entirely illogical, since he had never believed in premonition.

Jason banished his thoughts as the cloaked figure came to a halt. Even as he watched, she faded into the shadows of a side alley that led toward the river and the Wapping waterfront. Without hesitation, Jason lengthened his stride.

When he reached the narrow passage, he could barely make her out in the shadows. Despite her limp, she was moving so rapidly that he had to increase his speed to a jog merely to keep her in sight. She glanced back only once, but when she began to run, Jason realized he had been seen. He gave up all pretense of disguising his pursuit as she disappeared around the corner, and broke into a run himself.

The next moment, he tripped over something in his path and nearly went sprawling. Slamming a shoulder against the adjacent wall, Jason swore violently, while the unfortunate cat under his feet let out a screech that reverberated wildly in the narrow confines of the alley. But even the feline's howl failed to raise the hair on Jason's neck as successfully as the woman's scream that followed. The piercing sound resounded with rage and terror as well.

Jason felt his heart constrict as he raced the final yards of the alley. When he finally reached Wapping High Street and skidded to a halt, he could see the cloaked woman blindly fighting her three assailants.

"No!" she cried as she struggled ineffectually.

"Yer to come with us, missy."

"No! You tried to kill Matthew!"

Although her words were muffled, Jason heard them. He didn't stop to wonder if he might be intruding on a private matter, though, but gave a shout and threw himself into the fray.

It was obvious the three miscreants didn't expect him. Two of the men froze at Jason's shout—but the other one, the one holding a wicked-looking short sword, wheeled about. Jason had a pistol in his belt, but he wouldn't use it for fear of hitting the woman. He did have the advantages of surprise and sheer size, though.

Dodging a nasty thrust, he leveled a well-aimed kick at the first man, sending the hanger clanging to the cobblestones, then delivered a blow to the man's stomach that doubled him over. His grunt of pain was cut off abruptly as Jason's powerful fist contacted his jaw with a bone-crushing jar. He fell heavily to the pavement and stayed there, not moving.

Jason was flexing his aching knuckles in satisfaction when a cry from the woman alerted him to a new threat. He turned just as a second man rushed him. Reacting instinctively, Jason ducked the swinging fist and bent low to grasp the man about the thighs. Then he straightened, sending his attacker hurtling over his left shoulder to land head-first on the cobblestones. The audible crack told Jason that the fellow would be out of commission for a time, and he turned to the third.

The remaining vagrant was having a difficult time with his intended victim, Jason realized with sudden amusement. A moment ago the man had been trying to drag her away, but now it looked as if he were the defendant. The woman was struggling fiercely, scratching and kicking and clutching at his arms, successfully preventing him from either joining the fight against her rescuer or making an escape. She was taller than her attacker, Jason saw with surprise, but she hadn't enough weight behind her for her blows to do any real damage.

The next instant Jason was cursing himself for his hesitation. The man, in an attempt to protect his face from her clawing nails, had raised his arms and spun around, hitting the woman's chin with his elbow and knocking her down.

Jason waited no longer. With a fury he couldn't explain, he leapt after her assailant, tackling him and bringing him to the ground. Shifting his body, Jason drove his fists again and again into the man's face, finally stopping when his opponent was rendered completely senseless. Only then did Jason feel his anger ebb.

He was breathing hard after his exertions and his knuckles were bruised and bloody, but he felt better than he had all evening. Struggling to his feet, he staggered over to the woman. She was still lying where she had fallen, and he stood over her, swaying, trying to come to some decision about what to do with her. The street was hardly the place to go about reviving her. There was his ship, of course, but he had never before allowed a woman on board, nor would he allow his men to do so. That left only Lila, for he doubted if any of the respectable hotels would welcome an unconscious female and a sea captain who had just been in a street brawl, even should he be able to find one quickly. He wouldn't even consider his father's London townhouse in the West End.

Wondering wryly if he was making a big mistake, Jason scooped the still figure up in his arms. She was lighter than he had expected, but well curved beneath the voluminous cloak. As yet he couldn't see her clearly, but he didn't stop to look, for just then a roisterous group of seamen spilled onto the street from another tavern. Quickly Jason turned and made his way back to the alley, slipping into the darker shadows before he could be seen.

He allowed his eyes to adjust to the darkness and carefully skirted the cat who growled in protest at being disturbed again, then set out for Madame Fanchon's establishment.

As he moved away from the waterfront, the neighborhood began to take on a slightly less disreputable appearance. The cobbled streets became wider, though still dark, and the rank smell of the river gave way to other, slightly more pleasant odors.

When he reached Ratcliffe Highway with its prosperous merceries and pawnshops and public houses, the visibility was better because streetlamps had been lit at frequent intervals. He was passing under a guttering lamp when the woman in his arms moaned. Shifting his burden to make her more comfortable, Jason glanced down and saw her clearly for the first time in the flickering light. Instantly his footsteps halted, his forward progress checked as effectively as if an enemy bayonet had been plunged into his heart.

He stood there completely stunned, his attention transfixed by the vision in his arms. His first thought as he stood staring dazedly down at her was that he was holding an angel. The hood

40

of her cloak had fallen away to reveal golden hair gleaming in the lamplight, but it was her face that held Jason spellbound. Shaped in a perfect oval, it boasted a complexion so pale and smooth that the skin seemed almost translucent. Long lashes swept the cheeks like shadows, while arching brows lifted toward the temples as if in flight. It was, Jason was persuaded, one of the loveliest faces he had ever seen. The soft hollows beneath the high cheekbones added depth to the delicate features, while the pallor of the skin lent an ethereal quality.

He stared at her for several minutes before feeling suddenly flowed back into his body with devastating force, making him totally aware of his masculine urges. His gaze fastened on the angel's slightly parted lips. Her mouth was full and provocative without being too wide. Too desirable for an angel, he decided. More like a goddess. A goddess who even in sleep was capable of stimulating sensual fantasies. She was pure temptation, Jason thought with a groan.

It was only her unconscious state that enabled him to suppress the desire to capture her soft lips then and there. And only the vague remembrance that she, this golden-haired Venus he had come across in such unique circumstances, was a complete stranger made Jason resist the impulse to caress the ripe breast beneath his hand. Yet his fierce desire didn't diminish. He found himself wanting to take her somewhere so they could be alone, wanting to undress her and discover for himself if the beauty of her body matched the stunning loveliness of her face. Then he would make love to her and she would belong to him and him only. . . .

Jason shook his head to clear away his chaotic thoughts. Tearing his gaze from her, he kept it carefully averted as he forced his feet to move. His burden was still light, but his arms were aching from the strain of holding her without crushing her soft body against his chest. A thin sheen of perspiration broke out on his forehead, and he realized he was shaking. Vaguely, Jason wondered why she could remain so still and unmoving when the devil was waging a war with his soul. He wanted her to wake and experience the same torment that was gripping him. Would she feel it as well, this raging heat that burned through him like fever?

As he neared another rickety streetlamp, Jason's gaze was drawn compellingly to her face once more. And then he almost laughed, so great was the rush of released tension. He had been holding his breath, expecting to experience that great shock of flowing current again. But now he let the air out of his lungs slowly. She was but a mortal woman after all. And more girl than woman by the looks of it. Definitely younger than he had first supposed from her husky voice and shapely body.

The fever—or whatever it was that he had experienced during those agonizing moments—had died to a glowing warmth. But the madness had passed, and for that Jason was quite thankful. In that state of mind, he could easily have ravished the beautiful girl in his arms and damned the consequences.

As Jason moved through the silent, semideserted streets, he found himself wondering at the unusual violence of his reaction. There was a logical explanation, of course. It was simply that he had seen a vision of loveliness and been turned to stone. No, not stone—for he had never been so aware of the hot fires in his own body. He had been struck by a lightning bolt—that was it—and he was still feeling the aftermath. It was something that had never happened to him before.

But perhaps his response was only natural, Jason reflected. He had been in a peculiar state of bemusement all evening, and then his blood had been excited by the physical exertions of a fight. Surely under those conditions he would have lusted after any beautiful woman he had come across. Certainly he would have known the same urge to protect and defend any helpless creature he was required to rescue. But what of the extreme, intense possessiveness the girl aroused in him? That he couldn't explain. . . .

Jason swore under his breath. Hell, he didn't even know who the girl was. Or who her parents were, for that matter. Or why they should allow her to wander the streets at night alone. He couldn't bring himself to consider what might have happened to her, had he not followed and foiled the plans of those ruffians who had attacked her. The girl's father should be horsewhipped for failing in his responsibility to protect such a vulnerable beauty!

42

Feeling fury invade his soul, Jason decided that he would derive a great deal of satisfaction from just such an act of violence. But as he made his way up the back stairs of Madame Fanchon's establishment, carefully hiding the girl's face from view, Jason changed his mind. He would use chains, he decided grimly. Being beaten by chains would be a fitting punishment for a man who cared so little about his daughter that she wound up in a brothel in the arms of a stranger.

Chapter Three

Lauren moaned, caught in the grip of a frightening dream about Matthew. But then the nightmare faded and so did her fear. She suddenly felt warm, as if she were swathed in thick down quilts. Her cheek was pressed against something hard yet comforting, the texture against her skin gently abrasive, the unfamiliar scent pleasant. The strange heaviness of her eyelids puzzled her, yet she couldn't summon the strength to rouse herself—not even when a faint rapping reached her ears.

"Jason?" a softly querulous voice asked.

Jason didn't bother to knock a second time on Lila's sitting-room door, but quietly let himself in. The room lay in semidarkness, the fire burning low in the grate a testament to his tardiness.

When he kicked the door shut behind him, Lila Martel gave a start and uncurled her ample form from the chair where she had been dozing. Fully awake now, she gaped in bewilderment at the bundle in Jason's arms.

He flashed her a rueful grin as he strode across the room to the bedchamber beyond. A single sputtering candle showed that the bed had been readied for his visit, its curtains drawn back and covers turned down invitingly. He carefully lowered his precious burden to the mattress.

Behind him, Lila stared at the bed. "Mother of God!" she breathed, quickly crossing herself. "Is she dead?"

Amusement sparkled in Jason's blue eyes as he glanced over his shoulder. "Oh no, she is very much alive—and I hope to keep her that way. This may be rather an unorthodox request, Lila, but would you allow her to stay here just for the night?"

Lila eyed the prone figure uncertainly. "Who is she?"

"I don't know. I found her wandering the streets down by the docks. She was being attacked by three men who—"

"And you rescued her, the poor dear."

Jason's mobile mouth twisted in a wry grin. "I thought that might appeal to your motherly instincts."

As Lila hurried to light a lamp, Jason bent over the young woman and gently drew down the hood of her cloak. Her hair was coiled in a thick knot at her nape, and the confined tresses shone in the lamplight with the brightness of newly minted gold. Almost reverently, Jason smoothed a tumbled curl back from her face.

He wasn't the only one surprised by her stunning loveliness, though; Lila reacted with a gasp when she saw the golden hair and ivory skin. "Why she is beautiful!" Lila exclaimed, before tearing her gaze away and regarding Jason with a suspicious frown. "Jason, is this some kind of hoax? Or are you trying to tell me you need two of us to satisfy you?"

Laughing, Jason shook his head. "Believe me, Lila, this is no hoax. And you're enough to satisfy any man. But I had nowhere else to take her. Can you imagine what my crew would say once they got a glimpse of her? I'd have a mutiny on my hands within minutes. Besides, I thought it would be easier to hide her here till I could locate her parents. I'll pay for the use of the rooms, of course, plus the regular fee."

"Chivalry, Captain?" Lila replied peevishly—but then she relented. "Oh, very well, of course she may stay."

While Lila went to fetch a basin of water and a cloth, Jason removed the beauty's heavy cloak and sat beside her on the bed. Accepting the bowl he was handed, he wrung out the cloth and pressed it against her pale brow.

Lila sighed as she watched his tender ministrations. She had been looking forward to spending the evening with Captain Stuart. After the rough-and-tumble ways of her usual customers, Jason's unique combination of passion and tenderness was as pleasurable as it was exciting, and she seldom found pleasure in her life.

But the handsome, virile captain seemed totally mesmerized as he stared down at the golden beauty. That, and hungry. He looked as if he would devour the girl in one bite. A young woman like that would be helpless here. . . .

Again Lila frowned. "Jason, surely you can see she can't stay here. Look at the dress she is wearing. It must have cost a fortune."

Jason willingly obliged. The beauty was garbed in a simple empire-waist gown of gray silk that was completely devoid of ruffles and ribbons. The garment had a high collar that covered most of her slender throat, but it failed to hide the provocative swell of full breasts or the gentle curve of slender hips. Jason couldn't help speculating about the unexpectedly lush body beneath the gown. And he wanted very much to unpin that knot of richly colored hair. He wanted to plunge his fingers through bright tresses. . . .

"More than likely she comes from a good family," Lila interrupted his erotic thoughts. "Someone is probably searching for her now."

"I don't imagine anyone would think of looking here," Jason said absently as he gazed down at the girl.

"That is precisely my point. What if this young woman is an innocent? She'll be ruined if she's discovered in a place like this. And what if Madame finds out she is here? If Fanchon catches sight of her, this girl will be lucky to ever see daylight again. She'll be kept too busy—lying flat on her back servicing as many customers as Madame can fit into a schedule."

Jason reached out a finger to stroke the beauty's smooth cheek. "Nothing will happen to her, Lila."

Lila opened her mouth to speak, but then closed it again. She was wasting her time if the captain had made up his mind. Besides, if anyone was a match for Fanchon, Jason Stuart was. "I'll go and fetch some wine," she told him. "I drank most of a bottle, waiting for you."

She left by way of the hall door, and when he had completed his task with the washcloth, Jason also left the bedchamber, meaning to search the adjoining dressing room for a proper nightgown for his guest. Lauren at last found herself alone.

She waited a long moment before daring to open her eyes

and survey the unfamiliar surroundings. The throbbing ache in her head and jaw assured her it all had *not* been a dream. Her guardian's men had tried to kill Matthew—and by now they might actually have succeeded. Lauren swallowed, forcing back the tears that threatened. She couldn't allow herself to think of such things. If she did, her fears would paralyze her. Besides, she had an immediate problem to deal with. Jason Stuart. She had heard him deny knowing her identity, but once he realized who she was, he would surely force her to return to Burroughs.

Shaking her head to clear away her dizziness and rising panic, Lauren winced at the pain such movement caused. More gingerly, she raised herself up on one elbow. She recalled being caught by her guardian's men and the fight afterward, only she couldn't remember what had happened then. Obviously Jason had rescued her and brought her here to his friend Lila.

His friend? Their relationship seemed rather odd for friendship, since Jason had mentioned a fee, while Lila had spoken of servicing customers. Indeed, it reminded Lauren of one of the shocking facts of life she had been exposed to during her recent travels, one which Matthew had been extremely reluctant to explain, of how women sold themselves for money.

But she hadn't the time to speculate about Jason's association with Lila. She was grateful to him for saving her, but she couldn't risk staying here a moment longer. She had to leave at once. . . .

Her plan was forestalled, however, when Lila returned. Lauren's heart skipped a beat as she watched the curvaceous, ebony-haired woman enter the room.

"Good, you're awake," Lila said with a smile, setting the wine on the table near the fireplace and crossing to the bed. "I am Lila Martel, my dear. Goodness, your chin is already showing a nasty bruise. You were unconscious for some time."

Lauren regarded her warily, wondering if the woman could be trusted. Sultry and dark-eyed, Lila looked inquisitive but kind. "I wasn't unconscious," Lauren admitted, her voice even huskier than normal due to weariness. "Thank you for

47

taking me in."

Lila seemed surprised that Lauren had been pretending to sleep, but she didn't press the point. "What is your name?" she asked gently.

Lauren hesitated, not wanting to lie. "I think it best if you don't know," she compromised. "I can't involve you in my problems." Then she glanced uncertainly at the closed door, worrying that Jason would return any moment. "That gentleman . . . he meant what he said, didn't he? About finding my parents?"

"Jason? Why, he only means to see you safe, my dear."

"But I can't be safe. Not as long as—" Lauren broke off, realizing that she had said too much.

"But whatever were you doing at the docks?" Lila said when she was silent.

"I was trying to find passage on a ship."

Lila's expression held sympathy as she shook her head. "Jason is a merchant captain, my dear, but he couldn't oblige you by taking you on. You see, he always manages to wind up in the middle of some battle or other. He wouldn't put you in that kind of danger."

"I see that now. But I have to leave England. And I can't stay here."

When she sat up slowly and swung her feet to the floor, Lila's finely arched brows knitted with concern. "I wouldn't try to leave, my dear. Jason wouldn't like it at all if he were obliged to go chasing after you." Lauren looked up then, and Lila gave her a compassionate smile. "Of course he will help you, if only you explain what the problem is. Jason Stuart is very resourceful. Are you by chance running away from home? I'm certain he wouldn't return you to your parents without first satisfying himself that all was well."

"I must go," Lauren insisted. "Now, before he returns. Please," she pleaded when Lila remained silent. "I'm not asking for your help, only a chance to leave here."

"You are overwrought, my dear," Lila replied gently. "Surely you realize you cannot roam the London streets without protection. I'm sorry, but the best I can do is give you something to help you sleep." She reached down to rummage

48

through the top drawer of the bedside table, and after a moment, she pressed a vial of colorless liquid into Lauren's hand. "Here. Only two drops, mind you. No more, or you might be asleep for a very long time."

Lauren stared at the tiny bottle without seeing it, then absently tucked the vial up her sleeve. Gripping the bedpost then, she dragged herself up and stood there swaying, afraid that Jason would return before she could escape from the tender-hearted Lila.

"My dear, are you ill?"

Seeing deep concern in the older woman's eyes, Lauren clasped her hand to her forehead as if she were experiencing faintness. "I . . . I feel . . . it is just that I am so so hungry."

Lila's expression lightened. "Oh, but of course. You must get back in bed, my dear, and I'll bring you something from the kitchens. When did you last eat?"

"I don't remember," Lauren murmured as she obediently lay down once more. "Perhaps it was yesterday."

Lila clucked sympathetically and patted her hand, but Lauren was thinking only of escape. When she was finally alone, she lay still for a moment longer, listening to the sound of the woman's retreating footsteps. Then quickly, she rose from the bed and swung her cloak about her shoulders, covering her bright hair with the concealing hood. She limped a little as she went to the door, but she ignored the throbbing discomfort and pressed her ear against the panel. Hearing no sound, she reached for the handle.

"I see I should have thought to lock it," a steel-edged voice said from behind her. Lauren whirled, a slim white hand flying to her throat where her heart had suddenly lodged. The door to the dressing room was open, and Jason Stuart stood just inside the bedchamber.

He was just as intimidating as he had been on the ship. The aura of power he emanated was like a tangible force, reaching across the room to envelop her. Then she met the startling impact of his gaze and her breath suddenly joined her heart. His brilliant sapphire-blue eyes were regarding her intently, their expression one of silent warning. Lauren stared at him

49

wordlessly, rooted where she stood by that compelling gaze.

This was the man she might have married?

Coatless now, he was simply dressed in a loose-sleeved lawn shirt, striped waistcoat, and close-fitting breeches, yet his commanding height and magnificent leonine head lent him the formidable grace of a carved statue of Apollo. Indeed, his entire body suggested power and grace. Eyeing the breadth of his shoulders, Lauren suddenly recalled how easily he had handled those three men. Then she remembered the security of being held against that muscular chest and flushed.

His classically sculpted face was much like his frame, strong and firm, with nobility stamped in every bronzed feature. That strength, as well as a square jaw that suggested iron determination, saved his face from being too beautiful. His thick, curling hair, she could see now, was actually a light chestnut with streaks of sunlight running through it.

Lauren's gaze left Jason's hair and returned to his face, her eyes locking again with his. She stared at him for an endless moment, while the tension built between them.

"I . . . I was hungry," she stammered, finally realizing that he was waiting for her to speak.

Something flashed in those brilliant eyes at her deliberate lie, and for a moment his gaze bored into her, as if he meant to lay bare her very soul. Lauren nearly quailed under that intense blue gaze.

Then Jason moved, leaning a muscular shoulder against the doorjamb and crossing one booted foot over the other. "Indeed?" he said, his brows lifting the slightest degree. His voice was soft but unyielding, like velvet over steel, and it sent a shiver down Lauren's spine. She watched him anxiously, afraid to move.

Jason studied her in return, deciding that his shameless eavesdropping had obviously been justified. Wherever had she learned to lie like that? First pretending to be asleep, then feigning weakness, and now trying to brazen it through. But in spite of her lies—or perhaps because of them—because he still knew so little about her, Jason realized he couldn't let her go. At least not yet. He pushed himself away from the door and walked toward her slowly.

Lauren would have retreated, except that she had nowhere to run. She shrank from him in alarm, pressing her back against the door. He seemed enormous, and infinitely powerful.

Jason stopped a few scant inches away, surveying her with a frown. The husky catch in her voice suggested tears, but he was learning to recognize that as normal, and her eyes were dry. Those eyes fascinated him. They were amber green with golden flecks floating around the dark, wide pupils, and they looked strangely haunted. They held fear, he realized—fear of *him*. She needed comforting. . . .

But he clamped down on the urge to enfold her in his arms. Instead, he reached out and tugged the cloak from her shoulders, retreating a short distance.

Lauren let out her breath in relief as he moved away. She wasn't accustomed to looking up at anyone, but Jason Stuart dwarfed her. He had been so close that she could feel the heat emanating from his body, and the power that seemed to vibrate from his sinewy frame had made her feel helpless and weak and altogether too vulnerable. Even now, her heart was still pounding in response.

She watched as Jason withdrew a small package from the pocket. When he had unwrapped the cloth, he eyed the bread and cheese skeptically. Then his gaze sliced to Lauren. "This, then, does not meet the standards of your usual fare?"

Lauren swallowed hard, wondering how he had known about the food. "No," she replied lamely.

"Then perhaps you will find the truth more palatable."

Lauren lowered her gaze to the floor. She could never divulge the truth. He would likely think her mad—or worse, he would return her to her guardian.

"Would you care to be seated?" he asked, breaking the silence again.

His tone was polite, but the ring of authority indicated clearly that he wouldn't accept a refusal. Lauren decided to accede. He was obviously used to command, and despite his earlier tenderness when he had bathed her face, he would probably resort to physical violence if she challenged him openly. Yet he couldn't *force* her to speak, she reminded

51

herself. Finding the thought comforting, she crossed the room to sit in one of the chairs that flanked the fireplace.

"You're limping."

Lauren glanced at him warily, again surprised that he was so observant. "I fell and scraped my knee," she admitted cautiously.

"I'd like to see it."

"Truly, it is nothing," she protested. But he didn't seem to be listening. He fetched the basin and cloth and arranged them beside the chair before kneeling at her feet.

His familiarity startled her, and when he raised the skirt of her gown above her knees, Lauren froze. No man had ever taken such liberties with her.

Jason Stuart didn't seem to be aware of the effect he was having on her, though. Her right stocking was torn, and he was untying the garter and rolling the fabric down to expose the injured knee.

Lauren felt color flood her cheeks as his hands moved over her leg in careful exploration. His touch was firm but surprisingly gentle for so powerful a man, but the intimacy of it unnerved her. Acutely uncomfortable, she focused her gaze on Jason's tawny head, trying to ignore the warmth of his long fingers and the disturbing sensations they aroused in her as they probed around the abraded skin.

"It's bruised as well as scraped," he pronounced at last. "You should let it rest for a day or two and give it time to heal."

Lauren didn't answer, deciding it wiser not to mention that she intended to leave at the first opportunity. Instead, she bit her lip and concentrated on ignoring the sharp sting in her knee as he cleansed the wound.

Jason finished the task quickly, trying to spare her pain, but even though his movements were efficient and professional, he had more difficulty pretending indifference than he let on. The feminine limb exposed to his view was long and shapely, the skin smooth and fragrant. He wanted very much to lower his lips to that silken flesh and move upward along her thigh. . . .

But he forced his thoughts back to the problem at hand. Retying her garter below the knee, he stood up. He meant to discover why she was so afraid of him—more afraid of him, perhaps, than of those men who had attacked her.

"Now," he began, watching her reaction closely, "I'd like some answers. You are obviously in some kind of trouble, and something about the way your attackers behaved leads me to believe the incident was not as simple as an attempted robbery or—forgive me—rape. You recognized those men, did you not? And you're aware of my name, even though I haven't the slightest clue as to who you are."

Lauren determinedly avoided his gaze, alarmed that he was so perceptive.

"Where do you wish to be taken?" Jason asked, trying again. She looked up at that, but he saw the faint flicker of hope in her eyes die abruptly before she lowered her gaze once more. "The Continent isn't particularly safe at the moment for a young woman alone," he remarked.

"Neither is England," Lauren ventured at last.

Jason was pleased that he was at least getting a response, but he kept the satisfaction from his voice. "Are you aware that the United States recently declared war on England?"

He could see her hand clench involuntarily. "No, I hadn't heard," she said in a stricken whisper.

Gently Jason grasped her chin, turning her face up to his. Her eyes were deep amber-flecked pools, and their haunting loveliness tore at his heart. Unconsciously, he stroked her jawline with his thumb. "I didn't rescue you from those felons just so you could put yourself in greater danger," he said softly.

For a moment, Jason thought he had won, for her lips trembled as if she might speak. But then those incredibly long lashes lowered and hid the golden-green eyes from his view. He knew she wouldn't give in.

"Who is Matthew?" he barked so suddenly that Lauren winced.

"A . . . a f-friend," she stammered in automatic response to his commanding tone.

"Some friend," Jason said sardonically—a mistake, he realized as soon as the words left his mouth, for she stiffened and twisted from his grasp.

Pressing her lips together stubbornly, Lauren lifted her chin and met his gaze directly. "I am not one of your men, Captain. I am not subject to your orders, nor am I under any obligation to answer your questions. Even if you *did* come to my defense earlier this evening. And I will not," she added firmly, "be bullied or threatened. I assure you, I am quite immune to threats by now."

Jason couldn't help but feel admiration as he watched her. Her manner was curt and poised, as if she were speaking to a disobedient servant. Her response was a novel experience for him. He was used to men instantly obeying his orders, and he could hardly be unaware that women found him attractive. He had to smile.

The sudden change in his expression made Lauren catch her breath. Deep indentations creased his bronzed cheeks in slashing masculine dimples, making the strong planes of his face appear less forbidding, indeed, almost beautiful. He didn't seem quite so intimidating when he smiled, Lauren thought, and although her experience with men was limited, she could easily see the potential force of Jason's charm. She had little doubt women would find him irresistible—especially now, with his eyes dancing with vibrant life. Seeing the sudden sparkle in those vivid sapphire eyes, though, Lauren stared at Jason suspiciously, wondering what he was planning.

He ignored her display of defiance and rested one hip on the table beside her chair, leisurely swinging a booted foot. "So, Sleeping Beauty," he continued thoughtfully, as if working a puzzle out, "you are fleeing something or someone, and you want to go to America where you presumably have friends. But you're alone, without much money, and you need assistance. Additionally, you're determined not to trust anyone, least of all me."

Lauren shifted uncomfortably, looking down at her clasped hands. Was he a warlock, to be able to guess so accurately?

"You want to go to America," Jason mused. "It was rather foolish of you to run away from home without first providing yourself with proper funds for such a voyage."

A flush stained Lauren's cheeks, chasing away the waxen paleness of her skin. "I am willing to work my passage," she muttered defiantly.

Jason startled her by reaching for her hand. Holding it between his large calloused ones, he considered the slender appendage, his thumb swirling gently over her palm. "Soft and white," he murmured. "Unused to physical hardship. I find it hard to believe this lovely hand has ever seen a day's toil."

Angered by his presumption, Lauren freed her hand from his grasp. "There are ways women have of earning money that a man like you should be well aware of, Captain."

"Are there now?"

Lauren lost some of her composure as she met Jason's amused gaze. The glint of laughter in those teasing blue eyes unnerved her. She looked down again—although her gaze was arrested midway as she glimpsed the pistol tucked in Jason's belt. Lauren sucked in her breath. If she could distract him . . . Did she dare try?

"Of course," she forced herself to say smoothly. "Did you not come here tonight for that very purpose?" She was drawing on her recent experiences; for during the course of the past few weeks, she had witnessed more than one doxy plying her trade. Trying to remember how it was done, Lauren rose slowly, holding Jason's gaze with her own. "I could offer myself to you, for instance." Purposely she swayed toward him, then boldly pressed her hand against his chest, attempting to ignore the disturbing feel of hard muscles beneath her fingers. "Do you find me . . . attractive, Captain?"

She could tell by the sudden darkening of his eyes that he at least was interested. Encouraged, Lauren trailed her fingers slowly down his shirtfront. Jason watched her, his eyes smoldering as her hand moved still lower, till it rested at his waist. "Would you consider me worth a hundred guineas?" she asked in a husky tone that set his pulses racing.

Jason drew a deep breath at her suggestion, but he managed a chuckle. "I'm no seducer of virgins," he replied, wondering what she intended with her playacting.

"But I'm no virgin."

Her response came so swiftly, so easily, that Jason wasn't certain that it was another of her fabrications. His brows snapped together in a scowl. "You would sell yourself to me? For a hundred guineas?"

"Why, Captain Stuart," Lauren said sweetly. "Is the price too great?" Then seizing her chance, she pulled the pistol from his belt and pointed it unsteadily at his chest.

Jason gave no indication that his faculties had become instantly alert, but his muscles contracted with tension and inwardly he cursed. He had been so stirred with her beauty and the headiness of her scent that he had failed to realize her intention.

Forcing his lips into a tolerant smile as she waved his own weapon at him, he indicated the pistol with a nod of his head. "Do you even know how to use that?"

She surprised him by smiling. It was a sensuous gesture, Jason thought, watching her lips—and quite seductive. He was reminded of a cat stretching in the sun, even though she hadn't moved.

"Not at all," Lauren replied. "But it couldn't be so very difficult. You merely pull the trigger, do you not?"

Again Jason didn't know whether or not he could believe her, but he had had quite enough of being held at gunpoint. Looking beyond her, he spoke to some invisible presence, which made Lauren glance over her shoulder. In only a moment Jason had taken the pistol from her and had it safely tucked inside his belt again.

Stunned to have so quickly lost her advantage, Lauren stared at him in dismay. "That wasn't fair," she said in a voice that shook slightly and reminded him of a petulant child.

"I suppose it wasn't, from your perspective," Jason replied. But he wanted to erase the distress from her eyes and bring back that singular smile of hers. He took a step closer, and gently grasping her shoulders, drew her to him.

Caught off guard, Lauren pushed against his chest, but her resistance was no match for his great strength. Jason held her easily as he bent to brush her mouth in a kiss that was light and searching.

When he raised his head, Lauren stared up at him in shock. That brief contact had jolted her, sending a strange sensation racing through her.

He seemed to have felt it as well. Still holding her, he arched one tawny brow and regarded her thoughtfully. Then to

Lauren's complete horror, he drew her still closer. She could feel the power coiled in his hard body as she pressed full-length against him.

Slowly, he reached up to settle his palm against the side of her face. "This won't be fair, either," he warned in a velvet murmur, and lowered his lips once more.

This time he actually kissed her, his arms coming around her as he captured her mouth. Yet the effect was the same as before. A lightning bolt of sensation shot through Lauren, frightening her with its intensity.

She tried to pull away, but Jason wouldn't allow it. His fingertips caressed her cheek while his lips moved slowly over hers, as if he were tutoring her response.

And as his kiss deepened, she did respond. Had Lauren been more experienced, she would have recognized her reaction for what it was: the primitive attraction a female had for a vital, virile male. Instead, she only knew that she was trembling. His mouth was hot and urgent, and even in her innocence, she could feel the raw hunger in him. She couldn't seem to catch her breath. . . .

When he at last raised his magnificent head, Lauren simply stood there, staring up into those startlingly blue eyes and wondering at his ability to arouse such powerful sensations in her. Dazed, she raised her fingers to her burning lips.

Jason smiled tenderly down at her. "Won't you allow me to help you?" he asked gently, his voice as husky as hers.

Then suddenly his eyes narrowed, his attention arrested by the ring on her third finger. He stared at it for a long moment.

"I'll be damned," he said softly, before he began to laugh.

He released her then—abruptly—but his chuckles continued vibrating softly in his chest. Lauren watched him warily, wondering what she had done that was so humorous.

Her concern grew when his expression showed no sign of sobering. Had he suddenly lost his senses? He seemed to be trying to stifle his amusement but he was failing miserably. And when he glanced at her again, she could see the wicked sparkle in his blue eyes. Lauren began to feel annoyed by his mirth. His next words, however, set her heart slamming against her ribs.

"Sit down, Miss Carlin," Jason managed to say, his voice still full of laughter. "It appears we have a great deal to talk about after all."

Her mouth went dry. *He knew.* Somehow he had guessed. Lauren sank into the chair, burying her face in her hands.

Jason was still grinning when Lila returned with a loaded tray. He waved the food away and picked up the bottle of wine, pouring three glasses of the ruby liquid with a flourish.

Lauren didn't speak or even lift her head as she accepted the glass he offered her. But Jason smiled, his teeth flashing white against his tan. Whatever premonition he had had earlier about his life changing had been accurate, he realized.

Gazing tenderly down at the golden head bowed in defeat, Jason raised his glass high. "To Miss Andrea Carlin," he said softly. "To my runaway bride."

58

Chapter Four

Draining his glass, Jason leisurely poured himself another measure of wine. "Leave us, Lila," he said calmly, his gaze still focused on Lauren's bowed head.

"But, shouldn't I—"

"Miss Carlin will come to no harm, I assure you. We hadn't finished our discussion yet. Had we, Sleeping Beauty?"

Lauren made no answer as she twisted a pleat of her skirt between slender white fingers. Puzzled, Lila looked from her to Jason, sensing the tension that stretched between the two of them. But she knew Jason was a man of his word and decided not to interfere. As she accompanied him to the door, however, she pleaded with him in an audible whisper to remember the girl's recent harrowing experience and to be gentle with her. Lauren was left to stare at Jason's wineglass which was sitting on the table beside her.

Her heart began thudding against her rib cage as she remembered the vial of sleeping drops Lila had given her. Without giving herself time to change her mind, Lauren retrieved the tiny bottle from her sleeve and hurriedly removed the stopper. After pouring a small amount of the colorless liquid into Jason's wine, she hid the bottle beneath her chair, then clasped her trembling hands in her lap as she stole a glance at him. She hadn't been seen, she realized with elation. If only he would drink the drugged wine, she could escape—

Jason shut the door and slowly crossed the room to her side, trying to recall where his thoughts had been leading him before he had been interrupted. Lauren was watching him rather anxiously now, he realized as he picked up his wineglass and raised it to his lips. He could see a flickering light in the golden-green depths before she bowed her head again. What was it? Guilt? Fear? Uncertainty?

"How did you know who I was?" she asked quietly. "Did my guardian send you to find me?"

"I've never had the privilege of meeting your guardian," Jason answered dryly. "My ship only arrived in port today. But my father gave me a description of you when he told me of the marriage he'd arranged. And that ring you're wearing is engraved with a soaring hawk. The Carlin emblem is well known to anyone in shipping. Furthermore, you were upset to learn who I was."

When Lauren lifted her gaze, her eyes were pleading. "Please, don't return me to my guardian."

"Tell me why, sweetheart," Jason replied. "And no more lies, if you please. Burroughs, is that his name? Is it Burroughs who has you so frightened?"

"Yes . . . He would have forced me to wed you."

"I doubt that he could have done so, however—if only because I have no wish to drag a reluctant bride to the alter."

Lauren searched Jason's face, unsure whether he was telling the truth. She found herself wanting to believe him, yet the same instinctive caution that had kept her from being discovered by Burroughs's men warned her not to trust this tall, blue-eyed captain as thoroughly as she wished to.

"But let us put that aside for a moment," Jason continued. "The thought of marriage was so distasteful to you that you ran away. With . . . Matthew, was it? And then Matthew was nearly killed?"

"Yes," she replied hoarsely, thinking it wiser to answer him since he had already guessed so much of her story. "Matthew was my friend, as I said. He was helping me. When my guardian's men found us, one of them . . . tried to stab Matthew with a sword."

"And then?" Jason prompted.

Shutting her eyes, Lauren tried to ignore the tight ache in

her throat. "That's all. Matthew was determined to lead them away from me, so we separated. I spent the last of my money on coach fare to London, but those men followed me . . . and then you rescued me."

Jason pursed his lips as he contemplated her. "Well, it appears that your guardian was still within the law. You are a minor, subject to his authority. If he felt he was protecting you—"

"Protecting me!" Lauren clenched her fists in dismay. "You don't know him. He only wants to keep—" She broke off, suddenly, realizing what she had almost revealed. "I won't go back," she vowed. "I will never go back!"

Jason met her defiant gaze calmly. "Very well, you won't go back. But I will have to make some other arrangements for you. I can hardly allow you to walk the streets. And with England at war with both France and the United States, I cannot in good conscience put you on board a ship, passage money or no."

"You are not responsible for me, Captain Stuart."

Jason sighed. Getting her to listen was proving to be more difficult than rescuing a treed kitten. But he wouldn't give up. That air of vulnerability that surrounded her had aroused his chivalrous instincts—not to mention that her haunting loveliness was still playing havoc with his masculine urges. Besides, he was more than a little curious about the mystery she presented.

He supposed that had they met under more normal circumstances, he would have found her just as intriguing. But the circumstances were not normal. And it seemed that he didn't have much time to convince her that she needed his help. He couldn't keep her locked in this room indefinitely. She would likely find a way to escape, and at any rate, he had other obligations to fulfill. He had been spared the visit to Cornwall, but he still had responsibilities to his crew and country. His ship was due to sail from England within a fortnight, and it was out of the question for him to take her with him.

Moving away so he wouldn't be distracted by her nearness, Jason swirled the wine in his glass as he pondered the problem.

Lauren interrupted his musings. "It wouldn't work,

Captain," she said, causing Jason to wonder how much she had read of his thoughts. "You couldn't keep me here against my will."

Jason gave her a disarming smile, displaying the slashing masculine dimples that always won female hearts. "I'm aware of that. However, I was considering another alternative."

"Such as?"

She was immediately on her guard, he noted. He took a deep breath and gambled. "You could always honor the arrangement and marry me."

"*What?*"

"Now," he added, hearing her sharp inhalation. "At once. Without allowing your guardian a say in the matter."

He couldn't complain now that she was avoiding his gaze. She was looking at him as if he had completely lost his senses. Grinning inwardly at himself, Jason wondered if it were true. But he suspected he was in complete command of his faculties, and still he wanted her for his wife.

Had he been given the chance, of course, he would have wooed her and won her, and after a discreet interval—mainly because of her age rather than any reluctance on his part—he would have wed her. But now that she was running away, especially since she was running from *him,* he would have to take responsibility for her.

Marriage would provide the best opportunity for her protection, of course. And if he were to marry her secretly and hide her away at his small estate in Yorkshire until Burroughs could be investigated, he could then be assured of her safety. He would even exercise patience in the matter of conjugal duties, Jason thought with a mental groan, for despite her enticing figure and her regal carriage, she was still inexperienced. He had recognized her innocence the moment his lips had touched hers, even if she had denied being a virgin when she had propositioned him. And although it wasn't unusual for a young woman her age to have married or even to have borne a child, he wouldn't press her or expect her to share his bed until she was entirely ready.

"I asked you to marry me," he said more easily this time, feeling more comfortable with the idea that fate had somehow taken command of his life.

Lauren stared at him, her poise completely shattered. "You are joking, of course."

He repressed a smile at her bewildered expression. "Not at all. I've never considered a proposal of marriage to be a joking matter. And it's by far the best solution to this situation."

Lauren ran her tongue over her suddenly dry lips, trying to sort out her reeling thoughts. Marriage to him was impossible, most assuredly. He believed she was Andrea Carlin, the heiress to a shipping empire. He wanted her dowry, of course. Why else would he want to marry her, a girl with no future, no fortune, and no name, unless he wanted the Carlin ships? But even if she were willing to marry him—which she never would be—she couldn't endanger his life by making him a target of Regina Carlin's murderous ambitions.

Lauren searched Jason's handsome face, her stomach muscles suddenly tensing as she was assailed by a deeper fear. Had she misjudged him? Was he somehow in league with her guardian? Had he been sent by George Burroughs to prevent her from leaving England?

"Why?" she asked Jason abruptly, her voice breathless.

Because we were made for each other, he nearly replied. *Because fate brought us together, and now that I've found you, I won't let you go.*

But he didn't voice his thoughts, knowing such assertions wouldn't possibly be accepted. Instead, he smiled and said lightly, "I could think of any number of valid reasons. The protection my name offers, for one. Because I am better able to slay the dragons pursuing you. Because my esteemed father would be pleased were I to take a wife. The fact that you need money . . . I expect there are others."

The shock in Lauren's green eyes faded, only to be replaced by wariness and suspicion. *Cat eyes,* Jason thought, suddenly feeling uneasy.

"But you don't even know me," Lauren said slowly. And before Jason could follow up with any other reasons, she added bitterly, "Besides, you left out the one argument I would have believed. The Carlin ships. Isn't that what you were promised for marrying me? What does Burroughs mean to pay you if you succeed?"

A muscle in Jason's jaw hardened at her accusation, but he clamped down his anger. He would have to gain her trust before he could win her—and that had suddenly become the most important thing in the world to him.

"Miss Carlin," he said with strained patience. "Before this morning, when my father informed me of the agreement he had made with your guardian, I had no intention of wedding you, or anyone else, for that matter. I admit that the Carlin Line was what induced me to agree to meet you, but oddly enough, when I proposed just now I had forgotten about your dowry. And whatever else you might think, I am not involved in some heinous plot with your guardian. My main concern at the moment is seeing to your protection."

They stared at each other for a long moment. Then Jason ran a hand through his sun-streaked hair in frustration, wondering what he should try next. "Wouldn't Matthew have wanted you to be safe?" he asked quietly.

Seeing the stricken look that appeared in her eyes, Jason felt his heart turn over. In two strides he was across the room, setting his glass on the table and drawing Lauren to her feet and into his arms. When she tried to resist, he merely tightened his hold, giving her no choice but to accept the physical comfort he offered.

The tears came then. She stood quietly in his embrace, but he could feel her trembling with the effort to suppress her sobs. She was grieving for Matthew, he realized. The swift surge of jealousy that welled up in him made Jason grit his teeth, but he managed to murmur some soothing, meaningless phrases in her ear as he grazed her temple with his lips.

He didn't need to bend to do it, for her body fit his perfectly. The top of her golden head just reached his chin, and without effort he was able to rest his cheek against the silk of her hair. The soft fragrance tantalized him, filling him with the desire to twine his fingers through it. But it was a mistake to hold her like this, Jason realized. The ripe breasts pressing against his chest almost made him forget that he was supposed to be comforting her. And her thighs—he could feel the heat in his loins quickening with just this simple contact with those long, slender limbs.

She must have felt his body's reaction, or at least sensed the desire that was radiating from him, for she suddenly stiffened and pushed self-consciously against his chest. When he released her, she retreated across the room, choking back her tears and wiping her eyes.

Suddenly feeling weary, Jason lowered his tall frame into the chair. He drummed his fingers slowly on the table as he contemplated her. He had been overconfident to believe that winning her would be difficult. It was apparently impossible. Yet how many women would have jumped at the chance to become his wife? Jason's mouth twisted wryly as he thought of all the grasping females who had already attempted to trap him into marriage. He ought to find it amusing that his first proposal was being summarily dismissed—but somehow he didn't.

He watched Lauren move restlessly about the room. She had wrapped her arms around her body as if she were chilled, but her silk skirts swayed gently with the movement of her hips, displaying a gracefulness that was unmistakably alluring. She was seductive without even realizing it, Jason thought. The light from the candles caught her hair in a scintillating reflection, causing it to shine like newly minted gold, like golden guineas.

Guineas?

Jason let out his breath slowly, not even realizing he had been holding it.

"Very well," he said softly. "Take off your gown, Cat-eyes."

Her sudden stillness told him that she had heard him. After a moment, she turned slowly to face him, regarding him with eyes that were wide and questioning.

"You wanted to earn a hundred guineas, did you not? I don't carry that much gold, but I'm willing to pay a hundred pounds for your services."

"You want me . . . to *undress?*"

"I like to see what I'm getting for my money. Although my previous offer still stands."

"What . . . what do you mean to do?" she asked, a quiver adding to the fascinating huskiness of her voice.

"I intend to accept your proposition. I want the entire night, of course."

Lauren stared at Jason, certain that he must be joking. She had never meant for her suggestion to be taken seriously. She had only meant to distract him so she could take his pistol. So what was his game now? And why would he want the entire night? Was he trying to trick her? "I won't marry you," she repeated, searching the sculpted planes of his face for signs of conspiracy.

Jason flashed her a smile that radiated masculine charm. "As you wish." When she continued to stand there gaping at him, he eyed her speculatively. "Do I detect concern, sweetheart? Why, surely a woman of your vast experience would not be afraid of a man my size. You're not so fragile that you cannot support my weight. And I assure you, you will be a pleasant change from the diminutive lovelies one usually finds at Madame Fanchon's establishment."

"I . . . you . . . I didn't mean—" Lauren stammered.

"You're not as experienced as you led me to believe, is that it?"

"I . . . no."

Jason chuckled. "Well, perhaps you'll learn not to tell tales in the future. I certainly won't relish calling your bluff time after time. A relationship should be based on mutual trust, don't you agree? And I suppose I should begin by being perfectly honest—I expect quite a lot for a hundred pounds. Now take off your gown. I find myself growing impatient."

Although he felt some sympathy for her, although he knew he was taking advantage of her vulnerable state, Jason didn't regret his relentlessness. He was determined to persuade her that they belonged together, and making love to her would give him an opportunity to prove just that. It wouldn't be necessary to take her virginity, of course. The mere fact that she had spent the night in his company would compromise her enough to make his claim to her hard to refute if her guardian exhibited any objections later. He would be gentle, certainly.

Lauren obviously didn't think so. She bit her lip anxiously as she watched him. "I can't," she whispered.

"You can't or won't?" he countered. Seeing how pale she

66

had become, though, he realized how truly ner . . .
making her. He picked up her wineglass and held it ou. . . . sp
"I won't hurt you, sweetheart, I promise. Here, have s . . .
wine. It will help you relax."

Lauren hesitated, torn by indecision. She needed the money
he was offering in order to leave England—even if she did
somehow manage to get away from this captain who seemed
determined to keep her here.

She cast a worried glance at Jason's wineglass. He had drunk
barely half the contents, and he didn't seem to be falling asleep.
But perhaps the drug took some time to work—that was it.
Perhaps it would be effective enough to allow her to slip away
quietly afterward. But the money? She didn't think she could
bring herself to steal it from him while he slept. Such a step
as that would make her a common thief, and he was offering
her a way to honestly earn a hundred pounds. . . .

It was with a sense of shock that Lauren realized she
intended to accept his offer and that she was only trying to find
the courage to go through with it. What she would be required
to do she still wasn't certain, for her experience was limited to
the things she had seen in slums and alleyways during recent
weeks. She wondered if she could even bring herself to undress
for Jason, let alone allow him to touch her so intimately. But,
Lauren reminded herself, in her situation she couldn't afford
to be modest. She was on her own now, and she had to deal with
her own problems. She had to learn to support herself. Besides,
if she had to sell herself, she would prefer someone like Jason
Stuart rather than the kind of drunken, unkempt men she had
seen roaming the London streets. Captain Stuart was large and
powerful, but had said he wouldn't hurt her. . . .

Realizing that he was waiting for her answer, Lauren took a
tentative step closer, then another. When she stood before
him, she accepted his offering of wine and tilted her head back
to drink deeply, needing something to help stem a severe
attack of nerves. Finally she set down her glass. "The
fastenings are rather difficult," she said in a small voice.

"I beg your pardon?"

"The buttons on my gown are hard for me to reach."

Jason's mouth curved in a grin. "I would be delighted to

ou, my sweet, if you would but turn around. Ah, I orgot." Pulling the pistol from his belt, he placed it under the table, out of reach. Mirth danced in his eyes as he glanced back at Lauren. "The temptation might have been too great. Now you may turn around."

Certain that he was teasing her, Lauren lifted her chin and presented a stiff back to him. She tensed when his hands tightened about her waist, a tenseness that only increased when he drew her down onto his lap.

Jason smiled at her rigidness as he worked the tiny fastenings of her gown. She was as jittery as a bride on her wedding night, and not even pretending to enjoy his ministrations. After tonight, though, she wouldn't flinch from his touch. And after tonight she would be his and his alone. He would teach her to love, to experience the kind of passion he knew she was capable of.

He eased the high neckline of gray silk down a few inches, and ran a gentle finger along the satin skin of Lauren's exposed shoulder. When he heard her catch her breath, he realized how very much he wanted to turn that soft response into a gasp of pleasure. But strangely he felt no haste, no urgency to rush this particular moment. He wanted to linger in it, revel in it, draw out this precious time, their first time together. He leaned forward, pressing his lips against the curve of her neck and shoulder in a gentle caress.

Lauren shuddered as a tremor ran down her spine. His lips were warm and pliant, and aroused a disquieting fluttering in her stomach. Indeed, his very nearness was disturbing. She was suddenly conscious of his hard-muscled thighs beneath her, of the strength that radiated from him.

Until a few moments ago when she had cried in his arms, she had never noticed such things about a man before. But it was impossible not to notice when Jason held her so intimately. A A few moments before, when she had been pressed against his sinewy length and her face buried in his shoulder, she had inhaled the musky yet sea-fresh scent of him, and had glimpsed the dark golden hair on his broad chest where his shirt parted at the throat. His blatant masculinity had made her aware of her own femaleness. Acutely aware. She had never

been attracted to a man before. But then she had ne~~~~
anyone so commanding, so self-assured, so very . . .
Captain Stuart made her feel so terribly vulnerable.

"Relax, sweetheart. You're far too tense."

Relax? How could she relax? She had to remember he was
dangerous. She couldn't let down her guard as she had when he
had comforted her. Yet there was the matter of their bargain.
He was paying for her services—whatever that meant. She
supposed she ought to at least pretend to welcome his
attentions, even if she couldn't completely overcome her
trepidation. Otherwise he might change his mind and she
wouldn't be able to earn the money she needed for passage to
America.

She felt his fingers in her hair, searching for the pins,
removing them one by one. When the golden mass fell heavily
down her back, Lauren shut her eyes and tried not to think of
what was to come.

"Your hair is lovely," he murmured. "Like spun gold." He
stroked the shining tresses, glorying in the silken texture and
the elusive scent that teased his faculties. Slowly then, he drew
Lauren back against his chest, shifting her till she rested in the
crook of his arm.

Gazing down at the delicate oval of her face, Jason drank in
her beauty. He would never get his fill of looking at her, he
decided. With unsteady fingers, he traced the line of her jaw
and then the full coral lips. Her eyes were still shut tightly
when he lowered his head to capture her mouth.

Lauren shivered as his tongue rippled over her lips, teasing,
coaxing, playing upon hers. And when it parted her lips to slide
between her teeth, she fought the overwhelming urge to leap
off his lap. His kiss was having the same startling effect on her
as before—leaving her dazed and breathless.

Jason felt her resistance and lifted his head to gaze down at
her, his blue eyes caressing her, amused. "You've never even
been kissed, have you?" he asked tenderly. When Lauren
shook her head, Jason laughed softly. "Lord, you must have
been raised in a convent. No man in his right mind could resist
kissing you, given half a chance."

He regretted the words at once, for her wariness returned

69

...re she turned her head away. Although he was still holding her, Jason felt her withdrawal almost physically, and realized he had lost almost all the ground he had gained.

He settled his palm against her cheek, turning her face back to his. "You promised me the night, Cat-eyes," he chided. "So far you haven't been very accommodating."

Reminded of their agreement, Lauren gazed up at him. Did a hundred pounds give him the right to demand anything of her? "What . . . what do you want me to do?"

"Lie still and don't fight me. I'm merely going to kiss you." He bent his head then, catching the soft flesh of her earlobe between his lips. After teasing it for a moment, he abandoned her ear to blaze a trail of soft, nibbling kisses to her mouth.

"Give me your mouth, sweetheart." Lauren had no chance to comply, for he kissed her without waiting for her response. The touch of his lips was gentle but firm as he set about wooing her senses. Lauren's heartbeat quickened when his tongue delved into her mouth, but Jason's arms came around her like iron bands, stilling any protest she might have made.

She proved to be no match for his determined expertise. In only a short while, he had conquered her resistance and was purposefully attacking the defensive barrier she had erected against him. His lips moved possessively over hers, while his tongue intimately probed and caressed the recesses of her mouth.

Dazed and quivering, Lauren only vaguely realized when his passion threatened to rage out of control. He was kissing her hungrily. . . . No, he was *savoring* her. And to her dismay, she found herself enjoying the taste of him and wanting more. A delicious lassitude stole over her limbs, as desire, unfamiliar and inescapable, flooded the rest of her body.

She thought he must be feeling the same desire, for she heard Jason groan, a low gutteral moan deep in his throat. Yet she was too caught up in the spiraling heat his kiss was evoking to analyze the primitive sound.

His kiss held her entranced as he eased the bodice of her gown from her shoulders, then loosened the ribbon of her chemise. When the delicate lawn fell away and her thrusting breasts were bared to his gaze, Jason sucked in his breath.

70

Seeing where his flaming eyes were fastened, Lauren tried defensively to cover her nakedness with her arms. But one of her hands was trapped against his muscular chest, and Jason captured the other and held it at her side.

"You have beautiful breasts," he murmured, measuring the lush fullness with molten azure eyes.

Her face flushing with embarrassment, Lauren tried unsuccessfully to free herself from his imprisoning grasp. He was assessing the rose-hued areolas as if he meant to devour them. Then brazenly, he reached up to circle her right nipple with the tip of a finger. Lauren gasped as a bolt of unexpected pleasure shot through her.

"Beautiful and perfectly formed. I like full breasts on a woman."

"Why?" she said distractedly, trying to concentrate on anything but the traitorous feelings he was stirring in her body.

Jason smiled at her suspicious tone. "Because they fit my hands well when I hold them . . . like so." His hands were large and well shaped, with long fingers and a sprinkling of sun-lightened hair on the back. They bespoke his noble breeding, yet their work-roughened texture indicated that he hadn't spent a life of leisure. He cupped a thrusting breast in his calloused palm, his thumb just barely touching the quivering nipple.

Lauren clenched her teeth at the unbelievable sensation the featherlight pressure elicited. She hadn't realized her breasts were so sensitive, but the nipple had immediately hardened in response to his touch.

"And they taste good when I take them into my mouth . . . like so." Jason lowered his head as he spoke, closing his lips over the tip of one breast.

Lauren nearly bolted out of the chair as his moist tongue flicked the coral bud, but she found herself held immobile as he bent her back over his arm, leaving her breasts totally at his mercy.

A shocking warmth invaded her body as he plied and teased and coaxed the right nipple to a diamond-hard point, then lavished the same attention on the left. Lauren let out a

71

strangled gasp as he suddenly nipped the taut bud with his teeth, then soothed the throbbing ache he created with his lips. She thought she must be mad to allow him the freedom to do such things to her, but she couldn't seem to find the will or even the voice to protest.

It was only when Jason began to hike up the flowing silken folds of her gown and his hand began to slowly wander upward along her thigh that she suddenly realized what he was doing.

"No!" she gasped when his hand found the golden, downy triangle between her legs. "Please . . . you shouldn't."

"Be still, sweetheart, let me love you."

His whispered entreaty confused her. Love? What did he mean? No one had ever loved her like this. Lauren stared at Jason, searching the vivid blue of his eyes.

Seeing the confusion on her beautiful face, Jason felt his heart swell. She would be happy with him, he vowed. He would see to it that she never regretted this night, this sudden intervention of fate. For himself, he needed no ceremony to bind them together. The tenderness he felt for her was, at this moment, burgeoning in his heart, so much so that he thought it might burst.

"Ah, sweetheart, what a coil this is," he murmured. "It is no trick I am playing when I say I want you. I do, with all my heart. I want you to be my wife, my mistress, the mother of my children, my dearest love."

His words stirred turmoil in Lauren's heart. She would never love anyone. Loving meant pain and degradation and loneliness—a truth that her mother had discovered to her sorrow. Elizabeth DeVries had been trusting and innocent once, before Jonathan Carlin had used her for his own selfish purposes.

"A possession, you mean," Lauren replied bitterly, remembering the hardship and pain her mother had endured, the deprivation and shame she herself had endured. "A slave, a prisoner."

Jason's brows drew together. "Who has been filling your head with such nonsense?"

When she didn't answer, he leaned his head back against the chair and spoke quietly, the smooth timbre of his voice playing on her senses like a soft melody. "There are such marriages, no doubt, but that has never been my idea of happiness. Imagine, Cat-eyes, a union of two people. A union of souls, of minds. A husband and wife who are partners, lovers, friends. A man and woman who share a single heart. They are bound to each other, yes, but by trust and affection and passion. It could be that way between us, sweetheart."

Lauren felt herself being lulled by the velvet texture of his voice, enveloped by the warmth of his embrace. For a moment, she even allowed herself to wonder what it would be like to be married to such a powerful, persuasive man. She couldn't remember being held by anyone the way Jason was holding her now, with tenderness and reassurance. It was strange the way he made her feel cherished and protected.

He couldn't be involved with Burroughs, she decided. Not after saying such things to her. Even so, she would never have the opportunity to discover if such a marriage was possible.

As if he could read her thoughts, Jason buried his fingers in the silken mass of her hair and bent his head. His warm breath fanned her cheek as he held her gaze. "Give me the right to show you, my heart," he whispered.

Watching her, he saw the gold-flecked eyes darken with distress, saw the conflicting emotions flicker across the pale, oval face, and his chest ached with the need to comfort her. Diamond drops of tears sparkled on her lashes, and Jason bent to kiss them away before he began to rain gentle kisses over her face, her brow, her lips.

He gathered her more closely in his arms then, driven by the single purpose of making love to the beautiful girl in his embrace. His lips cajoled, demanded, pleaded, while his hands communicated wordlessly, expressing need and promising exquisite pleasure in return.

Lauren was dismayed to feel herself surrendering to him, to the vital power that was such an integral part of him, yet when Jason kissed her, she opened her mouth to him, and after a moment, threaded her arms about his neck.

Feeling her trembling response to his rising passion, he resumed his assault on her innocence, letting his hand glide along a silken thigh, stroking and caressing. Lauren stiffened

73

when his fingers claimed the golden curls that hid her womanhood, but his arousing kisses had stolen her breath away, preventing her from uttering a protest. Halfheartedly, she pushed against Jason's shoulders, trying to escape the aching warmth that was dazing her senses, yet wanting to surrender to it.

Jason's own pulse leapt wildly when Lauren squirmed in his lap. With her hips grinding against his thighs, her feminine softness was making him wildly feverish, driving him beyond the bounds of caution. He ached with wanting her, ached in every part of his body. Every muscle, every nerve throbbed with fire. But he inhaled a ragged breath, and forced himself to go slowly.

"Trust me, sweetheart. I won't hurt you." His velvet-edged voice was huskier than hers, Lauren noted vaguely, before Jason began a new agony, slowly stroking her with warm, insistent fingers, arousing a throbbing tension inside her, between her thighs.

Lauren clutched his shoulders, her tight grip betraying her fear of the wondrous sensations he was creating within her. She could feel the corded muscles rippling beneath his lawn shirt, but somehow the sinewy hardness of body only excited her more. Her head fell back in surrender.

Not only a warlock, she thought dazedly, but a magician. His skillful, knowing fingers were working magic. And his mouth. His mouth was like a hot brand, setting her on fire. It traced a flaming path down her throat to the ripe swells of her breasts, reverently kissing a rounded crest before tugging at the nipple and intensifying the burning heat in her belly and loins. And all the while his fingers were slowly exploring and tormenting her. Lauren could only writhe helplessly in his arms, her heart racing as she clung to him.

Jason felt lightheaded with triumph as she arched her hips against him, straining for a release she didn't know existed. He stroked with increased urgency, willing her to experience her first taste of passion. His own head was spinning dizzily as his fingers plied the sensitive, feminine flesh, making her breath come in ragged gasps that matched his rhythmic movements.

The heat continued to build. Lauren whimpered, feeling as if she were drowning in a hot, churning sea of sensation. Desperately, she tangled her fingers through Jason's tawny hair, gripping tightly. The fire seemed to gather in a tight central core deep within her, building and building. . . . Then suddenly it exploded in all directions, sending flames shooting throughout her body.

Jason muffled her cry of astonished pleasure with his lips, feeling but not minding at all the slender fingers that gripped his hair. He could feel the thudding of her heart as she recovered from the violence of her passion. When the shudders that wracked her body finally subsided, he cupped her chin in his hand, turning her so that he could look down into her desire-glazed eyes. Satisfied that he had at least won the first round, he pressed her head against his shoulder, smoothing her silken hair with his hand, caressing her cheek with gentle fingers.

Lauren was only vaguely aware of his warm breath brushing her temple. She felt strangely, wonderfully weak. She should not have enjoyed his scandalous attentions, though. She was doing this for money. . . .

Later, she told herself. Later she would be aghast at her wantonness, but now she couldn't speak or even think as Jason cradled her limp body in his arms. Gratefully, she closed her eyes and curled against him.

Allowing himself to relax at last, Jason shut his own eyes and leaned his head back to rest for a moment. The deep weariness that had assailed him earlier was even stronger now. He was still hard and pulsing with desire, but he felt totally drained of energy. It was an effort merely to hold her in his arms.

He didn't know how long he sat there in that dazed stupor, or how he found the strength to lift Lauren and carry her to the bed. A vague suspicion teased at his befogged brain as he lowered her to the mattress, but he was unable to focus his thoughts on anything except his throbbing need of her. He stood above her, swaying, reminding himself that he had no right to take her until he had made her his wife.

His wife. Soon she would be his.

Looking down into those incredible green-gold eyes, Jason wondered what had caused the intense sadness he saw there.

When he tried to ask, though, his tongue moved sluggishly. His speech sounded garbled, even to his own ears, so he gave it up.

It wasn't until his legs nearly buckled beneath him that Jason realized he was losing consciousness. Lauren swam dizzily in his vision, her image fading in and out of darkness.

The wine. She had drugged his wine.

Why?

God, no. Please, no.

She meant to leave him. She would disappear from his life as suddenly as she had entered it, and he would be powerless to stop her.

His one focused thought was that he couldn't let her go. Fear welled up in him, fear of losing her. He could feel her slipping from his grasp, fading away with her wavering golden image.

Jason reached out to her, fighting against the overwhelming weakness as he stumbled forward onto the bed. He landed almost on top of Lauren, startling a surprised cry from her.

He lay there a moment, sprawled halfway across her, his breathing labored. When he felt her squirm beneath him, as if attempting to free herself from his weight, the same fierce possessiveness he had known earlier surged through him. She belonged to him. He would claim her with his body and prevent her from leaving. He would make her his own, make her a part of him, bind her to him. He would make her his wife.

With a desperation he had never known before, Jason wrapped an arm about Lauren's waist, dragging her beneath him. She didn't protest, having steeled herself to submit to him, prepared to honor their agreement.

Jason raised himself up on one arm, somehow managing to loosen his breeches and free his rigid flesh. Awkwardly then, he pushed up her skirts, baring the feminine softness that only a short time ago had never known a man's touch, a softness that was still warm and moist from his caresses.

He felt her stiffen as he spread her legs with his knees. But then his arms gave out and he collapsed on top of her, pinning her beneath his large body, the impact nearly crushing the breath from her lungs.

Lauren couldn't know it, but her startled gasp served to

revive Jason for a brief while. Mingled fury and desire drove him then, and with his last vestiges of strength, he rose above her again and pressed into her, forcing himself deep within her as she twisted helplessly beneath him.

Jason heard her whimper of pain as she thrashed her head from side to side, but it was if the sound came from a great distance away. He buried his face in the mass of golden hair, pressing his cheek against hers, feeling the warm wetness of her tears.

There was no joy in the knowledge that he had made her his own, only a deep, frustrated anger at his own helplessness. But as the blackness edged aside consciousness, his fury ebbed, and so did all other sensation.

Chapter Five

Cornwall, 1812

Planting his feet firmly apart, Jason braced himself against the icy wind that blew off the sea. He could almost imagine himself on the deck of a ship as the wind, a residue of the recent winter storm, ruffled his hair and sent the capes of his greatcoat whipping about him. Looking down at the boiling waters far below the cliff's edge, it was easier still to remember the many times he had scaled the rigging and been afforded a similar view of churning waves.

He couldn't fail to be impressed by the beauty below. The frothing surf exploded continually in a violent display of nature's power, while the heavy spumes appeared startlingly white against the storm-darkened brine, presenting the only contrast to dreary gray. Jason's gaze lifted to scan the horizon. Only a thin line appeared to separate the vast ocean from the leaden sky, and he guessed that in a few hours even the sea would be obscured by dense fog rolling inward toward the Cornish coast.

Jason couldn't totally define what had prompted him to travel such a distance in order to see for himself the stage of the tragedy. He supposed it was because he wanted to learn all he could about the young woman to whom he had been so briefly promised.

Again his gaze swept the cove below. The rock which lined the coast appeared to have been ripped from the earth and thrown into the sea by some monstrous hand. Gigantic formations rose in twisting, jagged shapes from the depths, as if in agonized protest of the constant battering from the crashing breakers.

There was nothing in the savage vista to remind him of pale, delicate features and soft, feminine curves, yet the image indelibly imprinted on his memory appeared unbidden before him. By now Jason was quite familiar with the portrait of Andrea Carlin as a young girl. His mind's eye, however, persisted in adding minor details to the youthful features: a haunting luminescence to the eyes; a graceful fullness to the figure; an unconscious seductiveness to the smile. That smile had easily set his blood on fire, while the enchanting beauty of her face still tore at his heart.

Yet at the same time he wondered how faulty his memory had become in the many months since his intended bride's disappearance. He had thought her fragile and vulnerable, but she had to have been strong to have survived in this desolate corner of the world. The traumatic events in her short life had shaped her character for certain, although to what magnitude he couldn't guess.

Had she stood at this same spot on the cliffs, gazing out to sea, troubled and puzzled by her guardian's actions? But no, she wouldn't have had the opportunity. Burroughs had seen to that. The man had openly admitted to Jason his fear for his ward and the precautions he had taken for her safety.

Turning, Jason could see the great pile of gray stone that was Carlin House. The stark, forbidding structure had been built by Jonathan Carlin to resemble a castle, complete with turrets and battlements, and was set back some distance from the cliffs. Carlin House blended in well with the wild Cornish landscape, but a fanciful imagination could assign a sinister quality to the Gothic edifice. It was certainly no place to raise a young orphaned girl. Jason believed he could understand her reasons for running away.

He hadn't understood then. He had spent three frantic days searching the docks and the passenger dockets of all the ships sailing from London, before admitting that Andrea Carlin had disappeared, presumably with Lila, and had covered her trail completely. Then he had gone to the Carlin offices.

His actions that day had been those of a madman; he had nearly killed Burroughs with his angry demands to know what had become of the girl. He had finally released his tight grip of the man's throat, not because Burroughs swore ignorance, but because he pleaded a weak heart and truly appeared to be near collapse. Jason had set about reviving him, urging him to lie down upon a settee, loosening his neckcloth and collar, and forcing sips of water between his bloodless lips. It was some time before either of them were in a condition to speak calmly of the heiress.

"It is a long story," Burroughs said then. "I mean to divulge it to you, for the simple reason that I need your assistance. Your own past, Captain Stuart, has proven your capabilities, and Lord Effing tells me you may be relied upon. I would not have chosen you for my ward, otherwise."

The flexing muscles of Jason's jaw betrayed his barely leashed anger. "I am waiting," he replied dangerously.

Burroughs suddenly rose from his seat and began to pace the parquet floor, wringing his hands in agitation. "I must insist . . . I must have your word that nothing of what I will tell you will ever pass your lips without dire cause." When he paused, Jason gave a brief nod of agreement, wondering at his urgent plea for discretion.

"It began almost thirty years ago," Burroughs said in a low voice, almost to himself. "It was before I became a partner in the Carlin Line, before Jonathan Carlin wed my sister Mary. Jonathan was rather hotheaded in his youth, but even then he was imperious and stubborn. He was a law unto himself, and he would brook no defiance."

Jason's eyes narrowed as his gaze was drawn once again to the portrait of Jonathan Carlin with his wife and young daughter. Carlin stood arrogantly staring from the canvas, his long, tapered fingers resting possessively on the shoulder of the woman seated before him. Kneeling at his feet was a child, a young girl who had both arms flung around the neck of a mastiff. Her cheek was pressed against the dog's head and she was smiling slightly.

Andrea Carlin resembled neither of her solemn, bewigged

80

parents, either in expression or appearance, Jason thought. Her unpowdered hair gleamed a rich gold and contrasted brightly with her pale complexion, while her amber-green eyes glowed with a compelling light. An apt portrayal, Jason decided, except that the artist had failed to catch the smile. In the portrait, it was sweet and innocent, not beguiling and alluring.

Tearing his gaze away, he focused on Burroughs. The company's major officer was a large ruddy-faced man given to portliness in his advancing years, but he exuded none of Jonathan Carlin's aura of power and assurance. His habitually mournful expression was intensified by a watery discharge that continually streamed from his pale-blue eyes. Regardless, Jason was well aware that behind the rheumy eyes was as shrewd a brain as one could wish. Jason granted Burroughs his full attention.

"It always pleased Jonathan to be able to play God," Burroughs said with a sigh. "He liked to control people, bend them to his will. There were few who dared defy Jonathan, but his own sister Regina was one. Against her brother's express wishes, she began seeing a Spaniard by the name of Rafael. When Jonathan couldn't stop her, he had her lover apprehended. He presented Rafael with a choice—hanging or transportation. The Spaniard chose the latter, and was consigned to a slaver, with little chance for escape."

Burroughs noted Jason's raised eyebrow and replied without further prompting to the unspoken question. "The company dealt in slaves then, yes. It was how Jonathan made such huge profits in the beginning. But this was not an ordinary run. Rafael was taken to Algeria. More than a decade passed before he was heard of again."

At that juncture, Burroughs stopped his pacing and began clawing at his collar and gasping for breath. Observing the almost frantic gestures, Jason was again compelled to lend assistance by helping the man to the settee.

Once he was lying down, Burroughs waved a feeble hand in dismissal. "I am all right," he said faintly. "In addition to a weak heart, I also possess a weak stomach." He shut his eyes. "You see, I was the one who found them . . . in the caves

. . . below Carlin House."

"You found them?" Jason urged gently when Burroughs remained silent.

"Jonathan and Mary . . . and Andrea. Their . . . remains."

Jason's gaze flew to the portrait again, his mind reeling. For an instant before logic once again ruled, he focused on the possibility that Andrea Carlin was dead. Yet she couldn't have died . . . not unless her spirit had somehow returned to the flesh and she had—

Jason forcibly repressed his wild imaginings. But his grip on Burroughs's wrist was stronger than necessary and his voice had a hoarse ring when he demanded what had become of the Carlin family.

"Rafael . . . and his gang tortured them. I can't describe . . . God, there was so much blood. Vicious animals. . . ."

"But not the daughter. The girl was spared," Jason said in an unrecognizable voice.

"I suppose you could say that. Andrea was . . . She had been . . ."

Jason's heart lurched. "Rafael raped her?" he demanded, momentarily forgetting the virginal stains upon Lila's sheets.

"No, just my . . . poor sister Mary. And it was not Rafael," Burroughs replied. "He wasn't capable of such an act. Eunuchs are not . . . That was why he took such pleasure in . . . castrating Jonathan. Only he didn't stop there . . . Rafael only watched while his men, his followers, had Mary and then . . . took a knife to her. By the time they turned to Andrea, they were almost blind with drink. They slashed her thighs and arms, before she managed to escape by way of the tunnel beneath the house. She collapsed there, but Jonathan and Mary . . ."

Burroughs's words were almost whispered as he told how his sister and brother-in-law had died, but as he continued to recite, his tone became less emotional, almost dispassionate. Still, Jason thought he had never seen such horror in a man's eyes as he saw in George Burroughs's. Jason felt the horror himself. He had been exposed to the bloody ravages of war for a number of years, and thought himself inured to gruesomeness,

82

but his stomach churned as he listened.

By the end of the tale, Burroughs's breathing became more normal. He stared at the portrait, as if willing himself to remember the Carlins as they had been in life. "We had the story from the two men we caught. Rafael . . . got away."

Jason swallowed the bile that had risen in his throat. His fists clenched in apprehension, though, when Burroughs again spoke of the girl. "We thought Andrea would die, for she contracted a raging fever. I nursed her myself, I and her governess, but we couldn't stop her from screaming. She had to be tied to her bed to keep her from doing herself further physical damage.

"I will never forget the day she finally looked at me with lucidity in her eyes. It was like . . . breathing again . . . like receiving the gift of life. We were shocked to discover that she remembered none of what had happened. Nor who she was."

Burroughs slumped back on his settee, rubbing his hand wearily across his forehead. "Andrea had totally stricken the past from her mind. I engaged a doctor from London, then, who said that her reaction was normal, considering what she had endured. The trauma had been so great that her mind was unable to accept reality. He told us not to force her memory to come back, that it would when she was ready. I was only too willing to comply, so grateful was I that she didn't recall the horrors she had witnessed. Afterward she was sometimes awakened by nightmares, but there were no further consequences. Except for her loss of memory and her voice, it was as if nothing had happened."

"Her voice?" Jason repeated, remembering the huskiness he had thought so seductive at the time.

"I think her throat was damaged somehow by her screaming. Or it could have been from the ropes. There was a noose around her neck when I found her. She was just a child."

A tear followed a grooved path down Burroughs's cheek as his head lolled back against the settee. There was total silence in the room for a time. When next he opened his eyes, he met the cold fury in Jason's.

"It became my life's goal to protect her," Burroughs continued. "I always feared Rafael would return for Andrea, but he was not my only concern. There was Regina Carlin, as well. She stood to inherit Jonathan's fortune and his share in the company, were anything to happen to Andrea. At first I didn't suspect that Regina had been involved in the murders, even though one of the pirates had confessed that a woman had helped arrange their entrance into Carlin House. But when Regina learned that Andrea had survived, she came to me and proposed a scheme that would result in her legal possession of Jonathan's holdings. She—I still find it hard to believe Jonathan's sister could be so vengeful—Regina wanted to declare Andrea insane, have her committed to an institution. When I refused, she did her best to make the world believe her lies about my ward."

"Which is how the rumors of Andrea's madness got started, I presume."

Burroughs nodded. "I threatened Regina then, thinking that would convince her to give up her plans. But I also insisted that Andrea be confined to the house. She was unhappy, of course. I fear I alienated her affections, even though I had the best possible motives. I did not think it would be necessary for long, just until we managed to capture Rafael. I hired men to guard her, to see that Rafael could never succeed with any plans he might still harbor."

"These were the same men who followed your ward to London?"

"The same. I insisted there always be someone nearby to
• protect her." He didn't mention that Lauren had objected to his patrols even more than her half sister had. Sighing, Burroughs added absently, "I suppose I could have moved her somewhere else, but Carlin House is easily defended if one is prepared. Jonathan built it to last for centuries. He intended to be king of his castle, and he was, for a time. At any rate, I told Andrea I was protecting her from smugglers who roamed the area—which was partly true. For centuries the cove below the cliff had been used for illicit activities. Jonathan had even capitalized on the trade at one time. There are hidden caves that are ideal for storage. It was there that Rafael . . ."

Now, the bite of the wind made Jason recall his intention of exploring the caves below him. The receding tide was at its lowest ebb, he noted with satisfaction. Tossing his greatcoat and coat on a slab, he clamped his makeshift torch between his teeth and leapt down the first step onto the footpath.

The path's entrance was marked by two shoulder-high boulders that huddled on the clifftop like silent sentries. The exit at the bottom angled off toward a short strip of beach that would be nearly submerged at high tide. To his far left, across the cove, was an identical stretch of sand, and from there a wider path—almost a road, in fact—wound like a gliding serpent from the sea.

The recent storm had added a freshness to the tang of salt and pungent odor of marine life, but it had also rendered the hewn path that led down the face of the cliff even more treacherous. The unlevel, slanting steps were slippery with rain and strewn with rocks. The rock overhang was even more of a challenge, for Jason was required to crouch down while closely hugging the cliff. By the time he reached the short drop to the beach, his shirt and waistcoat were damp with both sweat and salt spray.

On the beach, however, he was sheltered from the wind by the large rock formations, and he could see the channel that ran parallel to the cliff. The wide expanse of water was relatively calm behind the natural barrier of rock—and deep as well, Jason guessed. It would easily harbor a small ship and still be invisible except from directly above.

He couldn't access the yawning gap in the cliff wall except by swimming, but as he moved closer, he spied an adjacent entrance in the rock. After pausing to fire his torch with a flint, Jason squeezed his way through the narrow crevice and found himself balancing precariously on a ledge. It was far quieter here. Below him was sea water, gently swelling and lapping, and he could see the high-water marks on the walls of the cave.

The ledge was the only path. About a foot wide, it led toward the back of the cave, but a rough handrail of hewn rock made walking easy.

The ledge widened gradually after some ten yards and spilled out onto an almost level floor. As before, the path seemed to end, but the light from his torch showed Jason the entrance to a passageway set at an angle in the wall. The passage burrowed

85

into the cliff rock and was scored with chisel marks, an indication that the opening had been widened by human hands.

As he entered the tunnel, his flame flickered and was reflected eerily from the damp walls. It steadied as he passed through a small cavern. The air was cool there, and still. Jason could hear only his own footsteps and a faint rumble made by the surf.

The caverns were numerous, he discovered, but none were large enough to accommodate much cargo. Except for the last. The *Leucothea* could have fit in the giant chamber four times over. Entering the vast subterranean vault, Jason instantly felt the cold—a bone-deep chill that permeated the very marrow. His small flame didn't begin to light the whole, nor did it reach the high ceiling, but the light was adequate for inspection. Jason easily discovered the entrance to another tunnel, sealed now with mortar and stone. And he found also the blackened char on the walls and dark splotches on the floor.

The largest stain was in the very center. As he moved over the spot, an icy draft fanned his face, causing his flame to sputter. For a moment, Jason saw his own huge shadow dancing spiritedly upon the wall. Then his torch steadied and the image fled. He didn't need to be told that this was where the Carlins had died in such horrible agony. Rafael and his crew had butchered Jonathan first, leaving him barely alive but reviving him time and again, forcing him to watch as they had their sport with his wife and young daughter.

There was nothing else in the cave. It was swept bare. With a grim set to his jaw, Jason left the vast cavern and made his way back through the tunnels, stopping only once when he caught the faint echo of an anguished cry. It wasn't repeated, though, and he attributed the strange sound to the distorted screech of an animal.

When he once again stood in the fading light of the winter day, he took a deep breath. The roar of the sea was almost deafening after the ghostly stillness of the underground vault. And it seemed warmer in the daylight, as well, even though he was immediately drenched with spray and buffeted by cold wind as he began the long climb to the top.

He didn't doubt Burroughs's story. The man's distress over his ward had seemed genuine, and his subsequent actions had appeared to prove his altruism: the Carlin ships had been dropped into Jason's lap as a prize to be guarded.

That first day, Jason remembered, the conversation had turned to control of the company. "You have no idea where your ward could be?" Jason had asked. "She has no friends or relatives in the States?"

Burroughs sighed. "No, none to my knowledge. I have no idea where she might have gone."

When Burroughs then suggested the possibility that she might not have survived, Jason was unable to keep the accusation from his tone. "And you have no interest in finding her alive, I gather," he said sharply.

The older man's face flushed in anger. "I resent that remark, Captain Stuart. I have always been concerned for Jonathan's daughter, just as I have always done the best I could for her, given the circumstances."

Jason clamped his mouth shut, repressing an oath. *You all but smothered her with your inept guardianship,* he wanted to rail. But instead, he listened as Burroughs outlined his plan.

"I became a partner in the company," Burroughs said, "because I was able to provide capital when it was badly needed. The Carlin Line had phenomenal success when Jonathan first founded it, but two years of unavoidable disasters at sea and some unwise investments of Jonathan's brought the company to the verge of collapse. I own half interest now, besides being responsible for the operation.

"My heart is not strong, though. I have been told that I may not have long to live. I had arranged with your father for you to marry my ward so that she would have protection after my passing. In addition, I wanted to hand the company over to someone who would be worthy of the Line. I wanted you as my successor, Captain. I did not make that decision quickly or without justification. Suffice it to say that I have been kept well informed of your exploits and that I am content in my choice." When Jason's expression remained grim, Burroughs held up a hand. "Wait, hear me out, I beg you."

He rose unsteadily from his settee and moved to sit behind a large baize-covered desk. It was his seat of power, the position from which he ran the vast shipping concern. Now it also served as a protective barrier to further physical violence on the part of his visitor.

"I hold myself greatly to blame for my ward running away. Indeed, I've made some grave mistakes in the past. Not the least was allowing my sister to marry Jonathan. But I cannot change matters now. And I am still determined to see that Regina will never profit in any manner from her actions. I would give you the company, but for the legalities involved. Yet there is a way, if you are willing to accept responsibility for my ward, as well as for the Carlin Line."

Jason regarded the portrait once more. "I am willing," he replied softly.

Burroughs nodded. "Jonathan left his share of the company to his daughter, but he left control to me. I have complete authority to act as I see fit. Even when she reaches her majority in a few years, I still retain control, unless she should marry with my approval. Then control goes to her husband. Jonathan meant for the company to stay in the family, to be passed on to his male heirs." Burroughs paused, eyeing Jason with deliberation.

Jason's eyes narrowed. "You are not," he said, his tone holding an unmistakable warning, "thinking of falsifying any documents to make it look as if a marriage took place?"

Burroughs shifted uncomfortably in his chair. "I . . . I had hoped you would understand the importance of my ward's marriage. If she is alive, I would not wager on the chances of her remaining so for long. At best, she will spend the rest of her days locked away in a cell reserved for Bedlamites. You could not prevent it. Regina is determined to gain the Carlin Line, and she will be the girl's only relation when I am gone. The only way to protect, my ward, as I see it, is to provide her with a husband who would inherit, should anything happen to her. A marriage by proxy could be arranged, one that would be recognized in any court of law."

There was an undertone of suppressed fury in Jason's voice when he replied. "You will recall, Burroughs, that your ward didn't wish a marriage of any kind. Your scheme would not only deny her the freedom of choice, but would cause me to forfeit any chance to win her regard. I want her for my wife, but I intend to manage it on my own."

"I don't have time for such scruples, Captain. I must keep the Carlin Line out of Regina's reach."

"Then do so by some other means."

"Perhaps I should find someone else whose thinking concurs with mine."

Jason's jaw clenched savagely. "You are free to do whatever you like with respect to Regina and the Carlin Line, but if you so much as consider another candidate for your false alliance to your ward, I'll send every last one of the Carlin ships to the bottom of the sea!"

His threat was absorbed in complete silence, but the ferocity in his eyes was enough to erase any possible doubt that he meant what he said. After a moment, Jason schooled his features into an impassive mask and leaned back in his chair. "I am willing to see that both Jonathan's sister and Rafael are punished for their crimes," he remarked coolly, "in addition to taking responsibility for the Carlin Line. But I will handle your ward in my own way."

Burroughs nodded in resignation, realizing they were allied in purpose, if not in method. "Very well. But the will stipulates that controlling interest in the Carlin Line must remain in the family. Under those conditions I could not even offer you a partnership, at least not one where you would be in full control."

"Then sell me the Carlin ships."

Burroughs grew quite still, an arrested expression on his face. "It would work," he said slowly. "But we must set the price at a mere pittance. Otherwise Regina Carlin would be a rich woman if . . . Andrea is unable to claim her inheritance. One pound each should satisfy the legal requirements. Twenty-four pounds total."

"No. A hundred guineas for the lot."

Burroughs raised an eyebrow in query at the sudden gleam in Jason's eyes.

"Your ward will understand the significance," Jason replied cryptically.

She might understand, but would she forgive after what had happened between them? Jason asked himself now as he reached the end of his climb. Hauling himself over the clifftop, he once again stood beside the boulders. The blood-freezing chill of the caves had left him, yet he felt achingly bereft as he turned to gaze one last time upon the horizon. It was the same sensation of total loss that he had experienced when he had woken to find the girl gone, but just now he felt the ache so deeply in his soul that he had to clench his fists to keep from striking out at something. His knuckles showed white, and he honestly believed that if Rafael or Regina Carlin or even George Burroughs had been standing there before him, he could have torn each of them apart with his bare hands.

In the time since they had made their pact, Jason had developed a better understanding of George Burroughs. And after hearing the gruesome story, he had no trouble seeing why Burroughs blamed Regina and Rafael for the death of his sister and wanted them to be punished. Yet even bonded together as they were by a common cause, Jason could find no liking for the older man. True, he had an immense respect for Burroughs's business acumen. But Jason couldn't forgive him for driving a young woman into a savage world. Nor could he forgive himself.

Bitter laughter rumbled in his chest as he thought of what little satisfaction ownership of the Carlin Line had brought him. Burroughs had sunk every shilling of the company's worth into cargo and then sold the ships worth a king's ransom to him for a hundred guineas. A hundred guineas, the same sum Carlin's daughter had named as her price.

Jason laughed again grimly as he recalled the hours before meeting her, when he had thought himself willing to sacrifice his own personal happiness for an arranged marriage and the challenge of the Carlin Line. She might never believe that he would have married her without the inducement of her fortune, or that now he would have traded it all away instantly for the simple assurance that she was safe and well.

Then perhaps he might never even find the young woman who now owned his heart. He strongly doubted that she would return to claim her rightful inheritance until she was free of her guardian. And with such a childhood behind her, she might prefer to remain in hiding forever. It was also possible, Jason knew, that by his own actions he had destroyed his dream of a quiet hearthside with children playing at his feet and his wife's golden head resting on his shoulder. He had taken her by force, raped her. It could be called nothing else.

There were any number of reasons to despair of ever achieving what he now wanted most in life. But to be denied even the attempt ... Jason swore violently, although it did nothing to lighten the burden of his conscience or ease the pain in his heart.

Part II

To Love, To Lie

Chapter Six

New Orleans, 1816

The levee along the northern bank of the great mud-laden Mississippi at New Orleans had been painstakingly erected almost a century before in order to protect lives and property from the flooding waters of the mighty river, but now the levee was vital to commerce as well. Even in winter the *batture* upstream of the Place d'Armes was lined with flatboats and keelboats and other small vessels. Frequently, sailing ships or even a steamboat, that wondrous new testament to man's ingenuity, could be seen anchored at the square. During the warmer seasons, the levee was the site of bustling activity, the hubbub attesting to the continuing expansion of a primitive riverport into a significant center of trade. Scores of sailors and stevedores swarmed over the levee, vying for space with merchandise of all kinds, and both animal and human beasts of burden crowded the wharf below.

Jason had visited the city once, years before, and as his gaze scanned the colorful scene, he absently noted the changes. New Orleans was more crowded than he remembered, as well as more prosperous, but the warm, humid air still reeked of fish, discarded produce, and unwashed humanity. Even so, the stern, unsmiling expression Jason wore wasn't caused by the stench assailing his nostrils, or by the din issuing from the teeming wharf. It was due, rather, to impatience.

Consulting his watch for the third time in as many minutes,

Jason silently cursed his own inactivity. The *Siren* had made good time crossing the Atlantic by way of the Caribbean, aided by the prevailing trade winds; just under four weeks ago Jason had been standing on British soil. But it had taken the better part of three days to navigate the silt-blocked mouth of the Mississippi and sail upriver from the blue Gulf waters to the docks of New Orleans. Another interminable delay had occurred while the port authorities haggled over fees and signatures.

By the time the sails were being unfurled, Jason was already having second thoughts about Kyle's plan to search out Jean-Paul Beauvais at once. Developing a distribution arrangement with the Creole businessman was Jason's second concern. His first was to investigate the rumor pinpointing the pirate who called himself Rafael to this part of the world.

When Kyle had proposed paying a call on the Creole immediately upon reaching port, Jason had reluctantly agreed. British-American trade, suspended during the war, had developed sporadically during the past year, while American manufacturers in the North had increasingly sought protection for their own goods. Jason clearly saw the advantages to the Carlin Line of having the backing of a prominent New Orleans citizen.

Ordinarily, Jason would have preferred to do some scouting of his own before deciding who would best suit his purpose, but he had been swayed by Kyle's staunch faith in the Creole businessman. According to Kyle, Monsieur Beauvais was a hotheaded gentleman with a reputation for considering his own interests first, but the man had done business with the Ramsey family for years and had always behaved with impeccable honor. And unlike most of his fellow Creoles, Beauvais was not above associating with Americans or Englishmen, nor above working for a living, indeed, was devoutly unconventional. He was also quite successful at any venture he undertook, and so Jason had written to him, broaching the subject of a partnership and informing him of their imminent arrival in New Orleans.

Jason's keen eyes again swept the crowded wharf in search of Kyle Ramsey's imposing figure. There was little else for him to do. He had already seen to the docking of the *Siren*, arranged for the unloading of cargo on the morrow, and given most of the crew leave to go ashore. He had also sent Tim Sutter to book rooms at a hotel, and then watched as the young man scurried off to see what could be discovered about the pirate Rafael. After that, Jason could only wait. But at least he had curbed the urge to pace the deck as the ship's orange-furred cat was doing. Instead, he stood by the railing, watching the bustle on shore and chafing at the bonds of his own idleness.

At last he spied a powerful giant of a man striding quickly along the *banquette*—a wooden sidewalk that flanked the unpaved street—headed toward the ship. Jason's grip on the railing relaxed somewhat when he noted that Kyle's mouth was split into an infectious grin. "Well?" Jason asked curtly as his friend leapt from the gangway to the deck.

"Couldn't be better," Kyle replied. "Beauvais wasn't in his offices and I had to track him down at a coffee house, but he greeted me like a long-lost son. How does an invitation to quarter upriver appeal to you?"

"His home?"

Kyle nodded. "His plantation to be precise, a few miles from here. I've been there before. Beautiful place. Calls it Bellefleur. We're invited to stay for as long as we're in port. Beauvais apologized profusely for being unable to escort us there at once, but said he had a prior engagement this evening. I told him it didn't matter, though, since I had a cargo to see to, and you had business that would keep you occupied for a few days."

When Jason didn't immediately accept, Kyle added, "It could be the perfect opportunity for you to become better acquainted and satisfy your doubts about Beauvais's potential value."

Jason's eyes narrowed. "Is he interested in dealing?"

"Oh, he's interested, all right. Beauvais is no fool. I didn't commit you, though. I only told him you were considering options. And I think he's being cautious as well. Wants some time to look you over, too. Still, it's an honor to be offered the hospitality of his home." Kyle flashed another grin. "I expect your title impressed him. At any rate, he wants to introduce you to his wife. It seems that his family has increased in size since the last time I was here. He has remarried—an Englishwoman, he said—and he now has a two-year-old son. Beauvais spent most of the time singing the boy's praises."

Jason quirked an eyebrow. "And you accepted his invitation?"

"Not for the plantation. I thought you would want to decide for yourself. But for tonight, yes. Among his many other concerns, he has connections with a high-class gaming hell on Conti. We've been invited there tonight as his guests."

For the first time in hours, Jason's mouth curved in amusement. "I can see I'll have to watch my step if he's already assuming me a pigeon."

Kyle shook his head. "You're jumping to conclusions, Jase. In the first place, the casino's a reputable establishment. And in the second, gambling isn't the only entertainment to be found there. Monsieur Beauvais thought we might be in the mood for wenching after so long at sea. I thought his suggestion rather considerate myself."

"Perhaps."

"You'd be missing quite an experience," Kyle pressed, seeing Jason's lack of enthusiasm. "I've been there before, and I assure you it's quite exclusive. The place boasts some of the most beautiful demireps to be found in New Orleans. And I for one won't mind sharing the satin sheets of a skilled courtesan. What do you say? Will you come? Someone there may have knowledge of Rafael's whereabouts, and I doubt if we'll find much pleasure at Bellefleur, since Jean-Paul is now a respectably married man instead of merely a respectable widower."

When Jason didn't reply, Kyle finally noted the faraway look that had crept into the blue eyes. Kyle knew well that blind look of Jason's, even though it appeared infrequently. And he understood the cause. What he didn't understand was how anyone, particularly a slip of a girl only once met, could have such an effect on a man, or why the intensity of Jason's feelings hadn't diminished over a period of almost four years.

Long before the fighting on the European continent had ceased, Jason had given up his command of the *Leucothea*, not in order to return to a relative life of leisure as his father had wished, but to see to his new interest—the Carlin merchant fleet—and to resume his search for a tall, golden-haired beauty. Jason had hired an American agent to look for her in the States and had sent his own people to every corner of Britain on the off chance she hadn't left the country. But she had never been found.

Kyle grunted in disapproval. "Come on, man, say you'll go. You won't be able to find better entertainment in the entire city, and if you stay here or in a hotel room, all you'll do is brood. You can at least enjoy a hand or two of cards. If the lightskirts aren't to your taste, you can leave. Hell, Jason, are you listening to me?"

Jason looked up, finally focusing his gaze. "What? Oh, yes, count me in. When did you say we would be leaving for the Beauvais plantation?"

"I didn't. I said it was up to you. We don't need to accept Jean-Paul's invitation at all, or we can go as early as tomorrow, if you like."

"Tomorrow," Jason mused. "I hope your high opinion of Beauvais is deserved."

"Then you intend to take him up on his offer?"

Jason nodded slowly. "My instincts tell me not to trust a Frenchman, even a Louisiana Frenchman, but if you're willing to vouch for him, I suppose I can go along. And as you say, he may have contacts that will lead me to Rafael."

"True. And you're better off dealing with Beauvais than a pirate like Jean Lafitte. Frankly, I never liked your idea of using Lafitte to find Rafael. Lafitte's an unsavory character, and after your last encounter with him, he may be out for blood—yours."

Jason's blue gaze hardened. "I'll use the devil if I have to."

Kyle spread his large calloused hands in exasperation. "Lafitte is a Frenchman," he pointed out. "And a notorious one, at that. Why you feel you can trust him more than Beauvais is beyond me."

"With Beauvais I'm risking the Carlin Line," Jason replied soberly.

Kyle made no comment, needing no further explanation. He

knew Jason considered the Carlin fleet almost sacred. Indeed, Jason was as protective of the Line as a first time father with a newborn babe. He would never make any decision that might jeopardize the future of the ships entrusted to him.

Jason spoke then, interrupting Kyle's thoughts. "You need a shave," he observed, "unless you mean to subject some undeserving bit of muslin to whisker burn."

Kyle rubbed the growth on his chin and screwed up his face. "Aye. And a freshwater bath, I suppose."

Jason's eyes suddenly danced with laughter. "And formal attire, if this place is as exclusive as you say. You wouldn't want the ladies to think you a savage."

Kyle groaned. "Hell, I forgot. Maybe we should go somewhere else—where I won't have to wear a damned noose around my neck!"

Grinning, Jason shook his head. "No, Kyle, lad. You have my interest piqued now. And if I could stay on board all afternoon while suffering a severe case of cabin fever, you can don a neckcloth for one evening. I doubt you'll be wearing it for long, in any case."

Kyle bent down to pick up the cat which had flopped down on the deck next to Jason's right boot. "I'd better take Ulysses below. He'll follow you all over the city otherwise."

When the cat howled in protest and swiped at him with a large paw, Kyle jerked his head back, swearing heatedly.

Jason chuckled and reached for the animal. "Allow me," he offered.

"That bloody feline will be the death of me," Kyle muttered, glaring at the cat who nestled contentedly in Jason's arms. Ulysses stared back, never once blinking his great, golden-flecked eyes. He began to purr loudly as Jason carried him away.

Watching his friend's broad shoulders disappear through the hatch, Kyle shook his head sadly. That damned cat was only one example of how Jason had changed since meeting the Carlin heiress. Jason had never cared for cats—not until he had discovered that Ulysses had once belonged to the girl. Of course the miserable animal had to be kept then, in case she ever returned.

Frankly, Kyle reflected, it would be far better if the girl never showed up. Hell, Jason was obsessed—had been since the day Andrea Carlin had disappeared.

Lauren had every intention of granting Kyle's wish, for she never planned to return to England. She was no longer pretending to be Andrea Carlin, though. To her friends, she was Lauren DeVries; to the guests at the casino, she was known merely as Marguerite.

At the moment, Lauren was sitting at her dressing table in her room at Madame Gescard's gaming house, critically eyeing the arrangement of her turban in the pier glass. Lila paced the floor behind her, reading her a lecture.

"Money!" Lila exclaimed. "That is the real reason you are going downstairs tonight, isn't it? To earn a few dollars? Goodness, but you are a stubborn creature!"

"It won't be much longer," Lauren replied. "Only a few more years and I should have enough to buy my ship. Less, if Matthew's next expedition upriver is as successful as his last. My last investment in his fur trade turned a profit of nearly two hundred dollars."

"Such foolishness," Lila declared—a familiar remark whenever the subject of Lauren's independence came up. "Heavens, Lauren, it is your pride again. Jean-Paul has said that he will make you a loan."

Lauren shook her head and began unwrapping a pair of dyed ostrich feathers from their tissue paper. "You know I cannot allow Jean-Paul to support me."

"So you live in rags!" Thinking of the simple cotton dresses Lauren usually wore, Lila threw up her hands. "Honestly, if Bellefleur weren't overrun with household servants, I believe you would ask my husband for a job as a scullery maid."

"Of course not," Lauren replied, repressing a smile. "The salary wouldn't be nearly good enough." When she caught Lila's frustrated expression in the mirror, she realized her attempt at humor had only distressed the older woman more.

Ever since that night in London four years ago, Lila had taken responsibility for her. Lila had been horrified to learn about Lauren's loss of virginity and had considered herself to blame, even though Lauren protested that Captain Stuart hadn't really hurt her. When Lauren tried to leave, Lila wouldn't hear of her roaming the London streets alone, and had insisted on accompanying her to the inn to see if Matthew had at last arrived.

Matthew was indeed waiting, but Lauren's joy at seeing him unharmed was short-lived since Burroughs's men were still on their trail. When Lila had offered to make arrangements with a captain of her acquaintance and help them board a ship without being seen, Matthew had asked her to come with them to America, arguing that Lauren needed a woman to look after her while he signed on as part of the crew. And amazingly, Lila, who had no family or future in England, had agreed.

Seeing the older woman's concern, Lauren mentally shook her head. She and Lila were a pair, with their burdens of guilt.

"I have enough for my needs," she said quietly, defending her decision once more not to take Jean-Paul's charity. "And soon I will be able to buy my own ship and hire a crew—and still have enough to support me for a few months."

"Lauren, this plan of yours to buy a ship has become an obsession. I think it's shameful the way Matthew encourages you. And Jean-Paul is no better."

Lauren bent to her task without replying. Lila would never understand her fierce determination to be self-sufficient. When they had first come to New Orleans, Lauren had obtained a job as a seamstress at the gaming house fashioning gowns for the courtesans, in spite of Lila's objections. The pay wasn't much at first—two dollars a week plus room and board, but soon her skill with a needle was in great demand and her salary increased accordingly.

She had hoarded every penny, intent on buying her own merchant ship, and with Jean-Paul's help had wisely invested her share of the profits from Matthew's fur trade. In America, where hard work was a way of life, it wasn't impossible to become financially independent or even to make a fortune. Even a woman could rise to positions of authority if she had brains and courage and determination. And although it wasn't usual for a female to own a ship, neither was it completely scandalous.

Matthew understood her need to make her own way. She had always depended on others just to survive, but now she was capable of taking care of herself. Yet she was aware that her fierce determination to be independent stemmed from her past helplessness. She had allowed herself to become George Burroughs's pawn, had allowed herself to be manipulated by his need for revenge. But she would never be controlled that way again. Never again would she give anyone such power over her. Never again would she be that vulnerable.

She planned to make Matthew captain of her vessel and in some small way pay her debt to him, for not only had he saved her life, he had risked his own defending her. But recently Matthew had been talking about settling down. He was married now, and even though the fur business he had started with Jean-Paul's backing was highly successful, he didn't like leaving his Choctaw wife for such long periods at a time, nor did he like to subject Running Deer to the hardships of his trips north.

"Matthew is leaving tomorrow, by the way," Lauren added conversationally. "Running Deer will be going with him."

Lila made a sound very much like a snort. "You shouldn't even be associating with a man like that. A smuggler! How do you know he isn't engaged in anything illegal?"

"Lila, Matthew hasn't done any smuggling since he left England. His fur trade is perfectly legitimate."

When Lila raised her eyes to the ceiling, Lauren leapt to Matthew's defense, for nothing could shake her intense loyalty to him. "I know you don't approve of Matthew, but if I hadn't had him to turn to, I would probably be dead—"

Lauren broke off abruptly, pressing her lips together. She never allowed herself to think of George Burroughs or Regina Carlin. Yet she was always aware of the danger she faced if they should somehow find her. She was always careful to preserve her anonymity when she entertained at the gaming house.

Her height couldn't be disguised, but she hid the bright gold of her hair with a liberal application of powder or an old-fashioned Georgian wig, or, like this evening, with a turban. She also wore a demimask to cover her face, and kohl around her eyes—an addition that made them appear darker and more mysterious behind the mask. Additionally she was introduced as Marquerite to the guests, and she affected a hint of a French accent in her speech.

She hated hiding, though. Hated always looking over her shoulder. Hated having to pretend she was someone else. But she didn't dare risk appearing as Lauren DeVries at the casino. It was too prominent a place to avoid detection if someone were looking for her.

Forcing her thoughts along less disturbing lines, she listened while Lila returned to her original subject.

"I really believe you ought not go downstairs, Lauren. Jean-Paul and I won't be here to protect you in case one of the customers should become overamorous."

This time, Lauren couldn't repress her smile. Lila had always been as protective as a mother tigress, but since her marriage to Jean-Paul Beauvais, she had become even more so. Indeed, after her release from a life of prostitution, Lila had become quite prudish. Her definition of "overamorous" had changed during the past few years—from blatant propositions to casual pawing, then to a mere glance or the touch of a man's hand. But it would have been cruel to point out how quickly her standards of conduct had risen.

Lauren contented herself with saying, "Yes, I heard what Jean-Paul said this morning. But I know quite well how to handle the gentlemen, Lila. Even the savage, illiterate ones from Boston."

The thrust was not directed at Lila, rather at Jean-Paul. The wealthy plantation owner considered anyone not raised in the French-Creole traditions to be ill-bred, ill-mannered, and inferior. But Lauren's veiled mockery went unrecognized. As usual, she was careful to deliver her frequently sharp remarks in a cool, even voice so as not wound the uncomplicated, kind-hearted Lila. And as usual, the older woman wasn't cognizant of the acerbity behind the barbs.

Yet Lauren's smile, that rare smile that always worried Lila with its potent seductiveness, did not go unnoticed. Seeing it, Lila said with exasperation, "I am truly concerned, Lauren. You know men cannot be contented with mere gambling."

"Kendricks will be here to take care of me," she replied calmly. Kendricks, the American majordomo of the gaming establishment, was well equipped for the job of expelling anyone who became rowdy or offensive. Not that he was often required to do so. Gambling was considered serious business; the stakes were always high and the clientele always exclusive. The regulars were either wealthy landowners like Jean-Paul, or personal friends of Renée Gescard, the proprietress.

Gambling was not the only entertainment provided, however. A patron could, if he wished, bespeak the lady of his choice and remain for the entire evening. The females Madame Gescard employed were the cream of the demimonde, and the men who frequented the casino were expected to treat them as gentlewomen. Still, there were occasions when they did not.

Lila didn't think Kendricks sufficient protection, and she said so. "Some of the out-of-town guests tonight are hardened gamblers, Lauren. Jean-Paul has told me he knows none of them well. They may not be willing to accept a simple refusal. And strangers can hardly be expected to know you are under Jean-Paul's protection."

"But I thought you said he invited them. Surely no one would abuse his hospitality."

"I wish I could be sure. But I know little about them, except that the ones from Boston are rich businessmen, and the others are men who make gambing a full-time occupation. If it were not for this ball, I would stay with you. But Jean-Paul practically ordered me to accompany him. I couldn't refuse him."

Her tone proclaimed both her reluctance to attend the ball and her wish to please her husband. Lila had never expected marriage, especially to a man of Beauvais's superiority. She had attracted Jean-Paul's attention her first night at the casino, and soon afterward agreed to be his mistress. When she had become pregnant, he had flouted convention with a vengeance and married her, not listening to her warnings that she wouldn't be accepted by his peers, because he had wanted a child. Now his son was the dearest thing in the world to him next to money.

Lauren regarded Lila's reflection fondly in the mirror. The

older woman was still quite beautiful, despite the tiny lines about her eyes and mouth that she tried to hide with layers of skillfully applied powder and kohl. The lines always deepened with worry on occasions such as now. Lauren was well aware that she was often a major cause of Lila's distress, but the older woman needed someone to worry and fuss over. Tonight, however, Lila had enough troubles trying to penetrate the closed ranks of New Orleans society. Jean-Paul's preeminence notwithstanding, the Creole elite had shunned his scandalous wife entirely, while the Americans, who had a healthier respect for wealth and power, were only slightly more forgiving.

"Very well," Lauren relented. "I shall only go down for a few hours at most, and then only to play the pianoforte. Someone must provide music for the evening, you must admit. And all the girls will be busy with the extra guests."

"Why can't Veronique take your place?"

"It wouldn't be fair to ask her."

"Veronique is a selfish little chit," Lila muttered. "She wants to be free to mingle with the gentlemen."

"But the arrangement suits me. It pays better than sewing. And you refuse to allow *me* to 'mingle.'"

"If I had an ounce of fortitude, I would insist that you remain in your room."

Lauren sighed. She would always be grateful to Lila for her kindness and generosity, but there were times, like now, when she wished the older woman weren't quite so strict. She could earn three times as much playing the pianoforte than sewing. She was also learning the intricacies of working the gaming tables—but it wasn't likely she would get to use her knowledge, especially if Lila ever found out.

She was searching for another supporting argument when Lila came up behind her. "My dear, I can't bear to see you driving yourself this way. It is but a few months till you reach your majority. Then George Burroughs will no longer be your guardian and you can lay claim to your fortune. You can repay my husband then."

Lauren stiffened, her long lashes veiling the sudden darkening of her eyes. As Andrea Carlin, she would legally be free of George Burroughs when she reached her majority, but

106

as Lauren DeVries, she had to remain in hiding. Burroughs had the power to send her to prison for her part in the deception. And Regina Carlin would still be intent on murdering her if she ever returned to England.

She had never told anyone about her impersonation, not even Lila, for she had wanted to bury the past. At times like now, though, Lauren wished she had confessed, just so Lila would forget about Andrea Carlin's inheritance. "I don't want the fortune, Lila," Lauren replied. "And I have no intention of returning to England in order to claim it."

Lila took up the large plumes and began the task of pinning them securely to the turban. "You're still afraid of Regina Carlin, aren't you?"

When Lauren was silent, Lila put a comforting arm about her shoulders. "There are laws against attempted murder, Lauren. Perhaps Jean-Paul can help. He's perfectly willing to make discreet inquiries, you know—"

"I don't want Jean-Paul to make inquiries," Lauren insisted, "discreet or otherwise. The Carlin fortune has brought grief and pain to too many people, and I want nothing to do with it."

Lila sighed. "Well, I think it unfair that an heiress should have to live in a gaming house with only a tiny room to call home. Indeed, you shouldn't be here at all. You should be living at Bellefleur where you belong."

Lauren glanced down at her hands. Jean-Paul's plantation, located some five miles upriver of New Orleans, was a beautiful place which provided far more anonymity than the gaming house, but she felt like an intruder. "I don't belong there," she replied in a low voice.

"Well," Lila observed, not letting the subject drop, "I think that your refusal to stay at Bellefleur shows a lack of gratitude for all Jean-Paul has done for us."

"You know I'm grateful, Lila. I just don't want to impose on you and Jean-Paul. You have a son to raise, and you don't need to be burdened by me as well."

"Lauren, that is nonsense—but that isn't what I intended to discuss with you," she said, returning to her original theme. "I'm dismayed because you still mean to go downstairs this evening. Jean-Paul warned you that some of the guests cannot be counted on to behave as gentlemen."

Very carefully, Lauren picked up a glittering necklace that had been a Christmas present from Jean-Paul and fastened it about her throat. A single emerald drop, the size of a small acorn, hung from a chain of small diamonds. Jean-Paul had wanted the gems to be a gift, but Lauren wore them only because they were a necessary accessory for her role as an entertainer. The large jewel nestled between her breasts, drawing attention to her deep cleavage and the low, square neckline of her gown.

Lila suddenly noticed how much of Lauren's bosom was exposed by the bodice. "Isn't that dress a trifle . . . immodest?"

"I shall wear a shawl, if you insist."

Hoping to cut short the discussion, Lauren rose from the dressing table and crossed the room to retrieve her elbow-length gloves. Lila's critical gaze followed her, noting how provocative the gown was. The green satin, comprising both the slip and parted overskirt, flattered every shapely curve of Lauren's full figure and outlined her long legs in shimmering green.

"My dear, that material positively clings to you. Don't you think you should wear a petticoat?"

Lauren had difficulty repressing a retort. The gown was one of her more beautiful creations, and not at all indecent, as Lila seemed to imply. Madame Gescard had paid for the material, of course, for Lauren would never have spent her hard-earned money on herself, even if she did have a feminine weakness for beautiful clothes.

"You know, a petticoat would ruin the lines of this gown," she replied. "Besides, another layer would be too hot." The heat was one of Lila's frequent complaints. As much as she professed to be contented within the city she had made her home, Lila never had become acclimated to the hot, humid climate. It was now only the beginning of spring and she was already vowing how glad she would be when summer was at an end.

A remark about the weather usually served to gain Lila's sympathy, but Lauren realized it wasn't to be the case this evening. As she drew on her gloves, she added consolingly, "This gown is only a costume. Anything more modest would look out of place at the gaming tables."

Lila placed her hands on her hips, prepared to do battle. "You said you would remain in the salon," she charged in her most disapproving voice. "I told you there would be strangers here tonight. Believe me, Lauren, I shall not budge one inch from this house unless you promise me to stay out of the gaming rooms. If I didn't know about your fear of confinement, I swear I would lock you in your room."

When the color drained from Lauren's face, Lila halted her tirade abruptly. On the long journey across the Atlantic on the Dutch-owned merchant ship, Lauren had accidentally become trapped in their tiny cabin. Lila had discovered her cowering in a corner, shaking with deathly cold and petrified with fright. Afterward, Lauren had refused to stay in their quarters except to sleep, and then she had insisted that the door remain unlocked and the porthole window tied open. Even then, she would sometimes wake up screaming wildly, and Lila would hold her trembling body in her arms, soothing her till her sobs quieted. Lila had had her hands full protecting the girl from both human and natural elements, for more than once both had forced their way into the cabin.

Lila viewed Lauren's pale complexion with remorse. "Forgive me, my dear! I should never have mentioned such a thing. *Of course* I would never lock you in your room—"

Lauren pressed her fingers to her temples. She had never been able to conquer her fear of enclosed places. "Please, Lila, don't speak of it. I know you didn't mean to remind me." She turned away, saying in a low voice, "You have my word. I will not go near the gaming rooms. And I will not speak to any of the guests if I can do so without appearing rude."

After a moment, Lila nodded. "Very well. But I'm still worried. I don't like to leave you to fend for yourself when strangers are present."

When she regained a semblance of composure, Lauren nodded. "I shall be very careful, Lila, I promise. I shall be so prim and proper that everyone will think me a wallflower."

"That would be impossible," Lila retorted. "But you must

remember to call Kendricks if there is the least sign of trouble."

Lauren gathered up Lila's cloak and held it out to her. "I will," she agreed again. But she was required to listen patiently to several more of Lila's warnings before the older woman would consent to leave.

When she was at last left to herself, Lauren quietly closed the door and pressed her forehead against the panel. She had suddenly lost any desire to face the company which would presently arrive. Her conversation with Lila had been too unsettling. Too many ghosts had been disturbed. That long-ago nightmare seemed so unreal now, but there were times, like this evening, when the memory of it would catch her by the throat.

Her reaction had not shown, except for her sudden paling; she had watched herself in the pier glass earlier. Her face had remained serene, her expression remote. But inside she was shaking. She needed time to compose herself.

Lauren went to the small window under the eaves and drew back the curtains. Her room was located on the third floor at the far end of a wing, as far away as possible from the activities that went on nightly in the establishment.

She stood gazing down at the enclosed courtyard. It was deserted because the evening was still too young, but the scene was carefully staged for lovers. The sweet scent of jasmine wafted gently on the soft spring breeze, while the light from a single Chinese lantern cast a gentle glow over the tiny garden and trickling fountain at its center. The rest of the flagged courtyard with its crape myrtle bushes and climbing vines was cloaked in darkness, purposely providing concealing shadows for the male guests and their chosen companions of the evening.

Lauren could hear little now except for the fountain, but more than once she had lain awake at night, listening to the whispers and soft laughter which drifted through her window.

Perhaps it wasn't surprising, Lauren thought, that the sound of lovers should remind her of Jason Stuart. After all, he had been the one to show her what pleasure could be found in a man's embrace—or at least in his embrace. She had never

110

again experienced anything like being held in Captain Stuart's arms. Indeed, she had never felt the slightest attraction for any of the men she had met since Jason Stuart.

Although she had known him but a few brief hours—almost a lifetime ago, it seemed—Lauren still remembered him quite well. His sapphire eyes had been so intensely alive, his arms so strong and comforting. His gentleness had seemed reassuring at the time, and for a moment he had swept away her pain and sorrow and fear. She had come so very close to laying her head on his shoulder and sobbing out her story. There were even times in the four years since, in her loneliest moments, that she wished she hadn't put the sleeping potion in his wine. Had he been furious when he woke to find his intended bride gone?

She had taken his money, only the hundred pounds she thought he owed her, but it had been three years before she realized she hadn't truly earned it. She had also learned that such an enormous sum was an outrageous price to pay for one night with any courtesan, let alone an inexperienced, green girl who didn't even know how to kiss properly. How very ignorant she had been then!

Veronique had explained that to her, and much more. According to Veronique, her experience with Jason had been unusual. The pain of losing a maidenhead was normal, but most men weren't so considerate as to satisfy the woman first. Generally, the man derived all the enjoyment, while the woman merely pretended to feel pleasure.

Lauren hadn't been required to pretend. She had truly felt those glorious sensations. But now, whenever she recalled Jason Stuart's boldness, she blushed with shame. How easily he had made her body respond! She could still feel the warmth of those strong, well-shaped hands on her breasts, the intimacy of those long, arousing fingers between her thighs.

She must have been truly desperate to allow a total stranger the license to make love to her like that.

But she had been desperate. Recalling how very alone and frightened she had been, Lauren shuddered. She was far different now from that naive young girl who had fled England. That frightened girl no longer existed. She was a good deal older and wiser, and she could take care of herself.

Yet loneliness was still her worst foe. Lila had Jean-Paul, Matthew had Running Deer, but she had no one. Not unless Felix Duval counted. A regular gamester at the casino, Felix had been pursuing her for some time. She didn't care for him, though, not the way a woman should care for a man. The truth was that she was *afraid* to care for him, afraid to expose herself to hurt and pain, afraid to become vulnerable the way her mother had been. And if ever she found herself longing for a warm hearthside and someone to love, she never allowed herself to dwell on it. All her energies were concentrated on establishing financial independence.

She found solace in work. She drove herself till she wanted to drop, till she was too tired to feel, suppressing her feelings of loneliness and desire with a slavish determination, never allowing herself the luxury of tears. And she was close to achieving her dream.

So why lately had she been feeling more restless and dissatisfied than usual? Occasionally she would experience a sudden sharp longing for laughter and gaily chattering people, and sometimes her heart would give a sudden leap when she heard a masculine voice lower in a gentle caress. Lately, too, Jason Stuart had been a frequent visitor in her dreams. Those particular dreams always left her with an uncertain yearning, an unfulfilled ache.

He had wanted the Carlin fortune, of course. But it was pleasant to imagine that he might have wanted her for herself. What would it have been like, she wondered, to be married to such a man as Jason Stuart? To feel his arms around her each time she went to sleep? To receive his caresses, his kisses, each night? To lie beneath him as he made love to her, stroking and fondling and belonging. . . .

Lauren was unaware of the clock ticking away, but a light rap on the door made her lift her head sharply. What was wrong with her? Letting herself dream about something she could never have was the height of foolishness. There was nothing she could do to change the past. Nothing. She could only see to her future, barren though it might be.

Bidding entrance, Lauren wasn't surprised when a buxom redhead swept into the room. There was a definite pout on

Veronique's painted mouth as she complained in lilting French, "Really, Lauren, six flights are far too much for me to climb. You might have been more considerate. I waited for hours and hours for you to come. One more song and I would have swooned. It is the truth."

"Oh?" Lauren replied, repressing a smile. "Have the guests arrived then?"

"But yes! And they are ever so handsome. Or at least two of them are. One is old and fat, and the rest merely passable. I suppose I shall end up with the fat one, and it will be all your fault, *mon chou*. This is how you repay me for taking you under my wing."

Veronique, for the past few months, had been helping Lauren perfect her French, as well as providing instruction on a number of other enlightening subjects. Lila thought Veronique a bad example and would have preferred to keep the two of them apart. But Lauren had learned one could say what one pleased to Veronique without fear of censure. And with Veronique, one could laugh—even Lauren, who rarely showed any sort of emotion.

Lauren went to the pier glass to secure her demi-mask. "But I thought you said it did not matter what the clients looked like," she reminded Veronique in a wry tone.

The redhead threw up her hands. "Of course I said that, imbecile!" she exclaimed, exasperated. "But it is better to sleep with a handsome rich man than an ugly rich man."

"Or any man who is not poor."

"With my luck, the fat one will be poor. Here is your fan, Mademoiselle Impudence. Now will you please hurry? The fish will be snapped up before I even have a chance to dangle the bait."

Taking a last look in the mirror, Lauren tucked a loose curl beneath her turban. "Such excitement over a few fish."

Veronique held the door wide. "Hah, even you would be excited over the size of these, they are so very big."

Gathering up a light shawl, Lauren draped it about her shoulders. "Perhaps they would look well stuffed and served on a platter," she remarked as she was firmly ushered from the room. "But I don't suppose I shall even see them, unless one swims by. Lila has forbidden me to leave the parlor."

"Lila is wise," Veronique said with a knowing glance at Lauren's revealing gown. "That dress is all the lure you would need to attract a man's attention. Me, I think it is good for the rest of us that you have never developed a taste for fish!"

The gaming house was typical of New Orleans architecture. Delicate ironwork in lacy weblike patterns distinguished the plain stucco facade of the exterior, while a high, arched passageway tunneled back from the wide front entrance to an open courtyard, rimmed above by railed galleries.

The ground floor was occupied primarily by cardrooms, but there was also a parlor and a smoking room, as well as a dining room where a late buffet supper was served. The elegant suites on the second floor were reached by a graceful curving staircase in the foyer or wrought-iron stairways in the courtyard. In the cardrooms, the guests had their choice of pique, chemin de fer, maccao, faro, E.O., and even roulette.

Jason could find no fault with the arrangements. The sport was competitive yet congenial, while laughter and conversation blended to provide an agreeably intimate atmosphere. Too, the redhead who hovered determinedly at his side while he played faro promised a delightful conclusion to the evening. Her gay smile and light touch proclaimed her availability as she waved her fan languorously, calling attention to the curve of her full breasts and sending a hint of some exotic perfume his way.

When the first tinkling notes of a pianoforte drifted through the open French windows, Jason was too pleasantly occupied to take notice. But when a husky voice lifted in song a short while later, his entire body tensed.

He told himself that Carlin's daughter had been too much on his mind of late, that the fascinating huskiness of the singer's voice could belong to a hundred other women, yet he couldn't prevent himself from being drawn by that siren's call. Excusing himself to the other players and the vivacious redhead at his side, he folded his hand and rose from the table.

The night enveloped Jason as he stepped into the shadowy

114

courtyard and moved silently across the flagstone. He could feel his heart driving against his ribs as he neared the source of the music, and his breathing was shallow. Yet he stopped breathing entirely as he stood staring beyond the doors of the well-lit parlor.

The room was furnished in gilt and rosewood and decorated in creams and pale golds. Mirrors lined the far wall, and at one end, a waiter served various wines and liquors from a sideboard. Jason, however, saw nothing but the woman seated at the pianoforte.

She sat half facing the long French windows, remote and elegant and regal, as she sang in the throaty contralto that caressed his senses with pain and pleasure. She appeared lost in the music. The plumes of her headdress swayed gently with the movement of her body, while her head was slightly bent.

He would have known her anywhere. Even though the golden hair he remembered was completely covered by a turban and the delicate features he had memorized that long ago night were half hidden behind a mask, the haunting loveliness that had tormented his dreams was the same.

There were differences, though. The pale complexion was tinged with rouge at the cheekbones, the full lips were so red they had to have been painted.

Then she raised her head and seemed to stare straight at him. Behind the mask, her eyes appeared the same hue as the vivid material draping her body: a deep emerald. But he could imagine the luminous gold flecks floating in the irises, the sensuous amber glow of a cat's eyes.

For a moment Jason was held by the spell of those eyes. Then his gaze dropped, following the curve of the slender swanlike neck to the smooth sloping shoulders and the soft white skin bared by the revealing gown. He stiffened in anger and arousal, staring at the darkly tempting shadows between her full breasts as they pushed provocatively against the satin bodice. The décolletage barely seemed to cover the peaks.

His fingers curled into fists as a myriad of questions assailed him. Had she been here all along? Had she needed to earn her way by selling herself to the rich patrons who frequented the casino? And where was Lila? Yet there was one question that

115

he dreaded above all else: *Had he driven her to this?*

Anguish as great as he had ever known invaded Jason's soul. That he had purchased her innocence for a hundred guineas and an unwanted proposal was bad enough, but that she should have been reduced to this . . .

Even as he stared, an elegantly attired dark-haired man came up behind the beauty and laid a possessive hand on her bare shoulder. Jason drew a sharp breath. The man was Felix Duval, a local cardsharp and gambler. Jason had met him just moments ago, and had sensed a cunning slyness beneath the suave polish that did little to merit admiration or respect.

When Duval bent to kiss the smooth shoulder where his hand rested, Jason clenched his fists convulsively, feeling a strong desire to kill the bastard for simply touching her. Yet it was her reaction that made Jason's anguish turn to fury. She didn't flinch or shy away, but looked up at the gambler and tilted her head to one side.

"Felix," Jason heard her husky voice saying in a lilting accent, "are you leaving for the ball?"

"Yes, my beautiful Marquerite. But I shall count the moments till I return."

She gave Duval a cool smile that was seductive because of its very remoteness, and Jason's fierce oath escaped in a guttural growl. *Lovers.* He hadn't been mistaken. The proof was there before his eyes. Jonathan Carlin's daughter, the heiress to a great shipping line, was employed as a common prostitute. God help him, he had wanted her as his wife.

Jason took an involuntary step closer, but he stopped abruptly as he realized Duval was leaving. His gaze shifted again to the beauty, and he caught sight of the huge gem between her breasts. That necklace must have cost a fortune. Had Duval given her that? It would be preferable, of course, if she had found one man who would give her protection and support. But somehow that was no easier to swallow than the thought of her spreading her legs for any man rich enough to afford her price.

Jason didn't know how long he stood in the courtyard with black thoughts swirling in his head. His shoulder brushed a spray of starry yellow blossoms, but the fragrant scent went unnoticed. If he had seen his dream crumbling before, it now

116

lay shattered at his feet. The innocent young woman he had held once in his arms and thought to cherish and protect was a common harlot.

After a time, Jason forced himself to relax his clenched fists. He couldn't fault Duval for desiring her. What man in his right mind wouldn't want her in his bed? Nor could he blame her. She might have had to resort to this type of work just to survive. But he had to know how it had come about.

Wearily, he passed a hand over his eyes. He had no answers to the questions that tormented him, but nothing would reduce his determination to discover the truth or shake his resolve to take her away from this flesh market and the smooth-tongued gamester who had claimed her smile.

When Jason at last left the dimly lit courtyard to return to the gaming room, his face might have been carved from the glacial ice of the North Sea. Seeing him, Kyle immediately gave over his place at the table to one of the interested spectators and followed Jason wordlessly.

They found the smoking room deserted. Settling into a comfortable chair, Kyle lit a cheroot and watched his friend and one-time captain. Jason was restlessly pacing the floor as if the room were the upper deck of a ship. No, not quite, Kyle amended, for on a ship Jason never lost his air of calm assurance.

"I've found her," Jason said in a voice taut with emotion, and then proceeded to relate his discovery.

Kyle frowned as he listened. He wasn't surprised that the girl was the cause of that arctic expression, of course. Jason had been so certain he would find her someday. But discovering the heiress here, in this house, wasn't exactly what either of them had expected.

When Kyle voiced his doubts as to her identity, Jason retorted that he had spent half an hour in the courtyard, watching her, and he needed no further proof that the young woman was indeed Andrea Carlin.

Yet it was obvious that Jason hadn't yet recovered from the shock of seeing her, for he merely nodded absently when Kyle suggested that some reconnaissance was needed.

*   *   *

When Kyle sauntered into the parlor a short while later and claimed a chair close to the piano, Lauren was no longer singing but was playing a Scottish folk song.

Seeing the stranger studying her so intently, Lauren nodded politely, a slight smile curving her lips. Veronique had not lied. The gentleman was tall with massive shoulders, and his size reduced the smaller Frenchmen in the room to the status of minnows. Yet he was extremely attractive, she decided as her gaze was drawn to him again. He had dark chestnut hair worn rather long and hazel eyes that glinted with hues of amber.

Stealing another glance, Lauren found him still watching her. He was no rich businessman, she concluded. The lines on his bronzed, rugged face proclaimed he had often been exposed to weather, and although his evening clothes were of a somber color and well cut, the way he tugged at his neckcloth suggested that he found his clothing uncomfortable. He did look somewhat out of place surrounded by the delicate furnishings, Lauren thought: a medieval warrior in a doll's house. In fact, the gilt chair on which he was seated looked in danger of snapping under his weight.

When she finished the song, Lauren saw him rise. She was a bit startled when he made a direct line to her side, for it seemed as if he meant to run her down.

But the Viking merely stopped before her, giving her a deep bow and a smile that warmed her. "You play superbly, miss," he said in a pleasantly deep tone. "Is yours the voice that so enchanted me a few moments ago? I vow I heard angels singing. Dare I hope that you might favor us with another song?"

"But of course, monsieur, what would you wish to hear?"

One craggy eyebrow rose in surprise. "You are French? Pardon me, for I was just then comparing you to the most beautiful of native English roses."

"But that must surely be a compliment, monsieur," Lauren responded as she wondered if she truly did look English. "Please do not take it back."

After a moment he shrugged his muscular shoulders. "Oh, no, I wouldn't take it back, for you would adorn a garden of any nationality. I suppose it's just that you reminded me of someone I once knew. Have you never been to England?"

Lauren forced herself to remain relaxed, but she was glad for the disguise which hid her most revealing features. "I think you must be, how do you say? Sick in the heart for your home."

When she clasped a hand to her breast, his gaze dropped to the pale swells covered by green satin. "Homesick," the gentleman supplied. Then he seemed to recollect himself and cleared his throat. "Well, I suppose I might be, except that I'm an American now. I was born in England, but my family moved to Natchez nearly twenty years ago." Reaching out a giant paw to shake hands, he grinned. "I'm Kyle Ramsey."

That explained why his speech was slightly more clipped than the soft, drawling accents of the Americans she knew, Lauren reflected. Relieved, though, that he had given up trying to determine her origins, she smiled. She ignored his outstretched hand, which was strong and calloused, and presented her slender fingers to be kissed. "And I am Marquerite, Monsieur Ramsey."

The large man hesitated before carrying her hand to his lips, his grin fading to a puzzled frown. "Marquerite?" he repeated quizzically. "Merely . . . Marquerite?"

Lowering her eyes to the keyboard, Lauren said gently but with implied rebuke, "Monsieur, here we use only the first names. There is need for no other, *n'est ce pas?*"

He studied her a moment longer, before drawing a chair forward and seating himself beside her. "You must think my manners atrocious," he said mildly. "Perhaps it is because I have spent so much of my life at sea and am unused to being in polite company."

The candor of his admission made Lauren smile. "*Mais non,* monsieur. I think you refreshing."

When he remained silent, Lauren realized with a sense of chagrin that Kyle Ramsey was staring at her—or more precisely, at her lips—in fascination. She didn't need Lila to point out that her smile was what caused that arrested expression in his eyes. Veronique called that curve of her lips her *sourirer seduisant.* But as Lauren had no intention of seducing the gentleman, she allowed her smile to fade.

Adopting a noncommittal tone, she asked, "But what is your pleasure, monsieur?" Her choice of words was inappropriate. Though she had only meant to inquire as to his musical preference, she could tell by the sudden gleam in his eyes that he had given the question an entirely different interpretation. "The song, Monsieur Ramsey," Lauren said hurriedly. "What is it you wished to hear?"

"Song?" Kyle asked slowly, his jaw suddenly hardening. "Oh, the song, of course. I fear I don't know many, except—perhaps you should choose . . . mademoiselle."

His voice trailed away, but his cool tone unaccountably made Lauren feel like she owed the handsome giant an apology for some unknown offense. "I think I would much enjoy hearing of your sea travels, monsieur," she said uneasily, "for you look to be a man who has seen much of the world. But Madame Gescard will be angry with me if I do not play for the guests." Lauren gave an apologetic shrug of her beautiful shoulders. "So you see . . . ?"

"And later?" he queried in response, his boldness taking her by surprise.

Lauren shook her head. "Later, I shall be otherwise occupied," she said firmly, running her hands lightly over the keys to put an end to further conversation.

He did not, however, leave her side immediately in search of a more willing partner, and Lauren was given ample opportunity to wonder at Kyle Ramsey's odd behavior. He seemed still to be puzzled by her, for he was studying her with an intent frown. She could read perplexity and disappointment and—could it be pity?—in his hazel eyes.

Lauren was rather relieved when after a quarter hour or so, the gentleman at last rose. He brought her fingers to his lips easily this time, without any trace of his earlier awkwardness, as he politely thanked her for the entertainment and expressed his regret that he must leave her. "For my friend will be wondering what has become of me," he said with a grin that did not quite reach his eyes. Lauren thought the excuse rather feeble and wondered what she had done to earn his displeasure.

She watched, somewhat wistfully, perhaps, as Kyle Ramsey strode from the room. Oddly, she couldn't dismiss the notion that she had somehow failed him. Not failed in the usual sense, because he had offered for her and she had refused. But because he had discovered something in her that he could not quite like.

Lauren returned to her music, trying to recover her composure. Earlier, her spirits had been dealt a severe blow by Lila; now her enjoyment of the evening fled completely under this new assault from a disapproving stranger. It seemed that she was forever fighting to prop up her hard-won self-confidence, to keep her self-imposed seclusion from overwhelming her.

She closed her eyes as the crushing loneliness assailed her. At the moment, even Felix Duval would have been welcome, but he had left for the same ball that Lila and Jean-Paul were attending.

Felix was the one man who continued to pursue her, in spite of her unattainability. Intrigued by her very aloofness, he had propositioned her frequently during the past year. Recently, he had even offered to set Lauren up in her own establishment as his mistress.

But though his offer would provide her security and wealth, at least temporarily, and though she would be getting a home and affection of a sort, Lauren had refused him. Gently, of course, for Felix was fond of her, even if his primary reason was that she challenged his ego. Moreover, she didn't want to alienate him entirely, for she was benefiting from his attention. The rumor had somehow started that she was Felix Duval's special property—strictly off limits to the gamesters. Few were willing to force the issue and face the threat of pistols at dawn with the volatile Duval.

It had never come to this last, Lauren was thankful, but Felix was becoming too possessive for comfort. His frustration at not being able to have her was growing out of hand.

He thought she was holding out for marriage, she knew, yet her answer would have been the same had Felix offered for her hand. She wouldn't marry him—couldn't marry him. Not under false pretenses. She could never tell him about her past. Not unless she trusted him, and trusting any man would be difficult after her mother's experiences with Jonathan Carlin and her own with George Burroughs.

Giving a sigh, Lauren transferred her gaze to the clock on the mantel. Only a few more hours. Then she would be free of her duties and would climb the stairs to her room. Quite alone.

When Kyle returned to the smoking room, having learned little of what he set out to discover about Andrea Carlin, he found Jason pacing the floor again. Kyle shook his head, acknowledging his lack of success. "I'm damned if I can tell, Jason. At first I thought it was Miss Carlin, for her voice and eyes were just as you described. But she seemed so . . . at home here. If she was faking that French accent, I couldn't tell. She said her name was Marquerite."

His report seemed to fall on deaf ears, for Jason merely said grimly, "She's Andrea Carlin."

"But what the devil is she doing in a place like this?"

Jason's jaw hardened as he shot a glance at his friend. "She must have come here with Lila."

"Then perhaps we should try to find Lila."

"I'll find her, all right—if she's still in New Orleans. But at the moment I'm more concerned about how to get Miss Carlin out of here without raising an alarm."

Kyle frowned and ran a hand through his hair. "I only have one question. Have you bloody well lost your mind?"

"Perhaps," Jason said, smiling humorlessly. "But I have some unfinished business with the lady. And if I know you, my friend, you have more than just one question. So out with them now, if you please."

"Very well. Where do you plan to take her? And if you have that figured out, how do you plan to deal with the bruiser who was at the door when we came in? What about the Gescard woman? Do you suppose she will thank you for stealing one of her . . . er, ladies away? And Duval. What if his interest in Miss Carlin isn't mercenary? What if he isn't aware that she's an heiress? And," Kyle finished lamely as he saw his objections were having little impact, "Marquerite said she was occupied later this evening. What if she would prefer—"

"My money should be as good as the next man's," Jason

returned, his voice low and harsh.

"Jase, you can't just abduct the woman," Kyle began, before Jason eyed him warningly. Kyle sighed, realizing that in this instance at least arguments were fruitless. He would have more luck trying to stop a hurricane in full force than Jason Stuart when he was roused. "What do you want me to do?" he offered.

"I have a hackney waiting in the rear alley," Jason replied. "I can leave with Miss Carlin by way of the courtyard if you will keep the majordomo occupied."

Kyle was reminded of the countless times in the past when he had heard Jason issuing orders in that same uncompromising tone. But at least he seemed to be approaching the problem logically now, without allowing the strong emotion that had gripped him earlier to interfere with his thinking. Kyle nodded slowly. "And then I should disappear for a time?"

Jason grinned, although his blue eyes remained cold. "You can have Veronique. The way she was eyeing that great hulk of yours leads me to believe she won't be disappointed by the exchange. I'll take Miss Carlin to the ship. I imagine I'll be staying there for a few days, at least long enough to determine what to do with her inheritance. I can send you word at the hotel, or here, if I need you."

"You relieve my mind," Kyle said dryly. "I thought for a moment that you had forgotten your original purpose for coming here."

"Not at all," Jason replied ominously.

Seeing his friend's grim expression, Kyle felt a sudden sympathy for the young woman he had just met. He reached out to grasp Jason's arm. "You might also remember that you wanted to marry her, not cause her any more trouble."

Jason's only response was a flexing muscle in his jaw.

Kyle released his grip and ran a calloused hand through his hair once more. "Hell, I still can't figure out what the heiress to a tremendous fortune is doing in a whorehouse."

Jason gave a derisive snort. "That, my friend, should be perfectly obvious."

*   *   *

When the last mellow chord of her song faded, Lauren left her place at the pianoforte and made her way to the refreshment table. She wasn't surprised to have been forgotten by the harried waiter; the parlor was more crowded than usual and the waiter was fully occupied with ensuring a steady flow of cognac and champagne for the guests. But she needed something to drink. Her throat was parched from so much singing, and the husky rasp of her voice had deepened.

As she gratefully accepted a glass of champagne, she caught sight of Desirée Chaudier clinging to two florid-faced gentlemen. Desirée was one of the dealers at the casino, and the only woman with whom Lauren didn't get along. When their glances met, Desirée flashed her a look of veiled savagery, but since Lauren had learned to deal with the spiteful, jealous Desirée by simply ignoring her, she turned away.

She was just taking her first sip of wine when she suddenly froze, the crystal rim held to her lips. In the mirror, she could see an image of a man. A tall man with sun-streaked chestnut hair. And . . . heaven help her . . . intensely brilliant blue eyes. Those eyes were watching her, gauging her. She shut her own, but the image was still there a moment later: intimidating, powerful, vital.

She wasn't imagining him. The other guests had noticed him, too, for she could sense heads turning as he moved slowly across the room. Yet how could anyone not notice, when he dominated the room with his masculine beauty and magnetic, compelling presence? He looked impossibly handsome in his elegant evening dress: a form-fitting coat of blue superfine, gleaming white cravat, and buff stockinette trousers.

He was moving toward her, walking with the leonine grace of leashed power, stopping only a yard away.

Slowly, Lauren turned to meet those startlingly blue eyes, and the impact almost took her breath away. A dim roar of rushing blood sounded in her ears.

She was unaware when the glass slipped from her nerveless fingers to fall with a dull thud on the carpet. But she was quite conscious of the blue gaze which slowly raked her figure from her satin slippers to her fashionable headdress, then down again to her breasts.

Lauren stared back at him, her own gaze dropping against her will to his lips. She flushed in remembrance. Those chiseled lips had once pressed against her bare breasts, and she didn't need to look down to know that her nipples had suddenly hardened to aching points.

He seemed to have noticed as well, for his mouth twisted in an ironic quirk before he raised his gaze to meet hers.

For the life of her, she couldn't look away. Not even when she felt him searching her face, as if trying to see behind the mask.

Thankfully, that devouring gaze left her as he bent down to retrieve her fallen goblet. But it returned again in full force as he held the glass out to her. "Yours, I believe," he said gallantly.

She still remembered that velvet-textured voice, although she could hardly hear it above the thudding of her heart. Wordlessly, Lauren nodded, although she couldn't force her fingers to accept his offering.

Jason stepped past her to exchange the empty glass for a full one. But when she wouldn't take that, either, he lifted it in a salute. "When Kyle told me he had discovered a goddess, I had to come see for myself. To your beauty, Mademoiselle Marquerite."

Lauren stared at him, trying to assimilate what was happening. He had made a similar toast once before, yet this time he had called her Marquerite. Was it possible that he didn't recognize her after all?

Unexpectedly, she felt a sharp stab of disappointment. How could he have forgotten so easily something that had affected her so deeply? Yet if Captain Stuart didn't remember her, she might yet escape retribution for drugging him four years ago.

With an effort, Lauren inclined her head graciously and forced a slight French accent into her speech. "I do not think, monsieur, that we have been introduced."

His eyes flashed briefly, glittering sapphires in his tanned face. "No," he replied, his chiseled features once again hardening, "we have never been properly introduced."

She could not have known that her fate had hung in the balance as he waited for her response. He had hoped—with his very soul, he had hoped—for a different answer. She knew who he was, he was certain. She hadn't been able to hide her initial trepidation beneath the mask she was now wearing.

He threw back his head and tossed off the champagne. Then with determination strengthening the already powerful line of his jaw, he forced himself to smile, to play her game. "Jason Stuart, mademoiselle, of the *Siren*, at your service. My ship could have been named for you, I think. I could easily believe you to be a siren, luring hapless sailors to their doom."

Lauren eyed him uncertainly. "Perhaps you mean to be flattering, Monsieur Stuart, but—"

"Jason, please," he said smoothly. "Then, a goddess, if you care not for the other. Your beauty is quite devastating. Do I dare hope that I might have the pleasurable company of one so lovely this evening?"

Her lashes lowered, veiling the gold-green eyes behind the mask. "I fear that will not be possible, monsieur." She almost jumped in shock when Jason gently grasped her fingers and raised them to his lips.

"Ah, mademoiselle, do not deny me, I beg of you," he murmured, his voice thick as honey. "I am but a mere mortal worshiping at your feet, a humble supplicant for your favors."

In spite of herself, Lauren sucked in her breath when he pressed his warm lips against the sensitive pulse of her wrist. His mouth was sending hot sparks shooting up her arm. She tried to withdraw her hand, but he held it firmly in his own large one, capturing her gaze just as inexorably.

Lauren shuddered, realizing now what it was about Jason that as a sixteen-year-old she had been too naive to recognize: raw, male virility. That was what held her gaze riveted to his as her knees quivered with feminine weakness. And that was what made her gasp as Jason's tongue flicked out to swirl slowly over her palm.

It was more than time to put an end to her breathless attraction.

"Monsieur," Lauren exclaimed, less forcefully than she would have liked. "I think you do not understand. I have a previous engagement for the rest of the evening."

"No, I will not allow it." He shook his head, a slow grin

spreading across his firm mouth, causing slashing masculine dimples to crease his cheeks. "I will speak to the hostess and have her release you from your other duties."

"Madame will not agree," Lauren protested while her eyes flickered around the room in search of help. He obviously thought she was one of the ladies of the house. But better that than for him to realize she was his runaway bride, the one who had stolen his money. She was thankful that Lila had chosen this particular evening to be away, for Captain Stuart would surely have recognized his ex-mistress and connected the two of them. If she could manage to get away now, she might be able to avoid him while he was in New Orleans. She needed someone to distract his attention. . . .

Looking around, Lauren saw no sign of Kendricks or Madame Gescard, or even the waiter. The gay crowd was thinning somewhat, as some of the couples disappeared through the open French doors. Those guests who remained were occupied with their own amusements. She would get no assistance from them, most assuredly, unless she physically struggled. And if she caused a scene now, Lila would never let her return.

Adopting her coolest manner, Lauren turned back to Jason. "Please, Monsieur Jason. I am aware of the honor that you pay me. But I must insist that you release me. I truly must go."

He bent his head, bringing his lips so close that his warm breath fanned her cheek. "You will give me no hope?" he said softly, intimately, gazing into her eyes with an intentness that seemed to seach her very soul.

Lauren stared up at him, breathing in the warm scent of him, clean yet hinting of masculine spice. His overpowering presence made her dizzy, unable to think. At last she shook her head, wishing she didn't have to say no.

He released her hand, only to take her arm in a gentle grasp. "Very well, mademoiselle. I release you on one condition—that you stroll with me in the courtyard for a brief moment. The moonlight is so very inviting. I would wish for a thousand such nights with you."

As he spoke, he propelled Lauren gently toward the darkness. But he didn't force her when she hesitated on the threshold. Instead he offered his arm, waiting for her to choose.

Glancing up at him, Lauren was confused by the look he bestowed on her and by the hard smile playing about his lips. She was confused, too, by her own foolish longings and the tension building inside her. The attraction she felt for him was so forceful as to be almost tangible.

She should refuse his request, she knew. There was danger in this commanding, powerful man. He would kiss her, and . . .

Or would he? She couldn't fathom the glitter in his eyes, but somehow it didn't bring to mind desire. And his tone was not impassioned or ardent, in spite of his flowery phrases and smooth flattery; it was cold and as hard as granite. He didn't appear to be in a mood for romance. Indeed, he seemed more prepared for battle.

There was no moonlight, either; the courtyard was enveloped in shadows. Lauren could see nothing of the other couples as they sprawled on various benches or stood in close embraces, though she could hear low whispers and an occasional sigh.

Still, the soft night breeze seemed to beckon, and the heady scent of jasmine was a strong lure. More than that, a strong, attractive man was at her side. The man who might have been her husband. The one who had wakened her to passion. The same man who had been so much a part of her dreams.

Lauren was shaken from her thoughts as Jason brought a finger up to her cheek to stroke her skin with a featherlight touch. She stared up into the blue eyes, unable to decide.

Mesmerized as well, Jason outlined her lips with a gentle finger. The tenderness of the gesture convinced Lauren that she need not fear him. She was only committing herself to a brief stroll in the garden, after all. Indeed, there was no reason for the sudden trembling of her hand as she obediently placed it on Jason Stuart's sleeve.

Chapter Seven

Lauren didn't scream as she was propelled through the courtyard gate and lifted into the waiting hackney coach; the suddenness of Jason's attack had scattered her wits, while his hand covering her mouth effectively prevented her from making a sound. She was released as the shabby coach began to move, but she didn't scream then, either; she was incapacitated by pure, simple terror. The interior was wrapped in almost total darkness, an airless void that rose up to choke her. Her first sound was a low whimper.

Hearing it, Jason flashed a suspicious glance at the woman beside him. He had been prepared for a struggle, and the ease of spiriting her away from the gaming house merely put him on his guard. But when she didn't protect or demand to be told where she was being taken, he searched the side pocket for a light.

In the golden gleam of lamplight, he saw her huddled in the corner, cringing as if she expected a blow from his fist, her bare white arms inadequately covering her head as she pressed tightly against the side panel. Jason felt the first pangs of doubt. The green satin of her gown shimmered with the swaying of the coach, while the gems at her throat flashed with a magnificent brilliance, but, at the moment, the regal beauty looked more like a frightened child than a hardened prostitute.

Again Jason heard the terrified whimper, and his eyes narrowed as he tried to determine if her fear was real or merely a ruse. The crushed ostrich plumes in her headdress only added to her appearance of helpless femininity. Jason found himself fighting an absurd desire to gather her in his arms and console her.

"I don't intend to beat you," he said in a tone laced with irony.

The sound of his voice penetrated Lauren's panic. Her one conscious thought was that she was not alone, that she had not been left alone in the dark, cramped space. And when she forced her eyes open, she realized that it was no longer dark. Gasping for breath, Lauren stretched out a trembling hand and stammered in a hoarse, unrecognizable whisper, "P-please . . . please . . . can you . . . open the . . . window?"

Jason's mouth tightened. "So you can call for help and bring every male above the age of ten rushing to aid a lady in distress? I think not, sweetheart."

Lauren reached up and managed to clutch the curtain with trembling fingers before an iron grip closed around her wrist. But she was too weak to pull away—or to do anything more than sink back against the cushions when Jason began to untie the strings of her mask. "P-please . . . I will do anything you say, if you will just . . . let down the . . . window."

He wanted to remind her that she was hardly in a position to bargain, but he refrained as he stripped the mask away. His hands stilled abruptly as he saw the result of his handiwork. Fear, stark and vivid, shone in her eyes, while the color had drained from her face, leaving only artificial vermilion staining her pale cheeks and lips. She was truly suffering, he realized, cursing himself silently for his skepticism.

Immediately he leaned across her and let down the window. A swift rush of humid air invaded the coach, chasing away the musty smell of rotting leather and horsehair. Lauren's soft gasps began to subside, and Jason himself breathed more easily when the color began to flow back into her face.

Yet her continued stillness concerned him. When he touched her cheek, his fingers brushed skin that felt like ice. Wordlessly, he shrugged out of his coat and draped it over her bare shoulders, tucking the edges around her before pulling her against him.

He received an earful of ostrich plumes in the process and

130

bit back an oath. "Does this thing come off?" Jason muttered impatiently, fumbling for the pins holding her turban in place. When he succeeded in loosing the headdress, he tossed it in the opposite seat, then settled Lauren in the crook of his arm.

She felt him pushing a soft curl from her forehead. His gentleness was reassuring, but when she glanced up at him, all she saw was the hard line of his jaw.

She should make an attempt to get away, she told herself. She should, in all reason, put up at least a token struggle, since whatever he intended for her could not be pleasant. But she was reluctant to rouse his anger further.

Not that he would allow her to escape him, she realized as Jason glanced down at her and their eyes locked. She read determination in his blue gaze. And promise—though of what she couldn't guess. That formless thought crystallized as she stared up at him. She had been mistaken, she realized now. He *had* remembered her. He knew who she was . . . or at least he *thought* he knew. Her heart began to beat erratically.

"What . . . what do you want of me?" Her huskily voiced question brought no response except for the reflexive tightening of his jaw. And then the coach slowed.

Jason brushed the curtains aside to peer into the night. "We've arrived. I trust you won't make a scene?"

Lauren swallowed, wishing she had taken Lila's advice and stayed upstairs in her room. Again she thought of running, but she knew it would be impossible to elude him. Besides, she told herself nervously, she owed him a much-needed apology for that time in London when she had drugged him and taken his money.

She accepted Jason's assistance from the carriage and allowed him to readjust his coat over her shoulders, just now remembering that she had left her shawl lying on the pianoforte bench at the casino. As he turned to pay the driver, Lauren glanced uneasily about her, realizing they were near the river. A murky, drifting mist obscured her vision, and the sounds of drunken revelry swelled from the darkness. She was quite glad when Jason returned and offered her his arm.

The music and raucous laughter faded as they neared the deserted levee. Lauren glimpsed a faint light glowing from somewhere in the distance, much as it had that night four years ago, and she guessed that Jason was taking her to his ship. An overwhelming sense of powerlessness came over her, a feeling of being swept along by a force too strong to resist. She hesitated when the skeletal mast of a schooner loomed above them, disappearing into the fog. But then Jason's arm slipped about her waist and she took a deep breath, realizing that this meeting was inevitable.

The fog curled thickly about them as they boarded the *Siren*. Part of the main deck was illuminated by a steadily burning lantern, yet when Tim Sutter suddenly materialized in the gloom, Lauren couldn't stifle a gasp.

Feeling Jason's arm tighten about her waist, she peered up at him and could barely make out his features in the lantern's glow. The strands of flaxen in his chestnut hair glinted silver, while his heavy, slightly arched brows were drawn together in a frown. His silence unnerved her. She dragged her gaze away, feeling an odd, fluttering excitement in the pit of her stomach.

Jason sent Tim back to his duties, then pressed his hand firmly in the small of Lauren's back, directing her up the steep steps of the quarterdeck to the companionway hatch.

Lauren stiffened at the sight of the opening that gaped blackly at her feet. Not even if she risked incurring Jason's wrath could she force herself to descend into that dark hole. "I . . . cannot . . ." she said in a choked voice. "It is too dark."

Jason shot her a speculative look, but made no comment as he left her to retrieve the lantern. When he returned, she surprised him by tightly clutching his hand. "There's nothing to fear," he said, managing a soothing tone. "This leads to the officers' quarters and passenger cabins."

He went first to light the way, and Lauren followed, still holding on to his hand. But she walked as if she might be swallowed up by the shadows.

He halted before a door and fit the key in the lock, pausing when he felt her gaze touch him. Turning, he looked directly down into emerald pools sprinkled with gold. Her lovely oval face was tilted up to him, framed by golden tendrils that had escaped the tight chignon at her nape. A golden goddess, he thought, feeling himself bending closer, the better to inhale

132

her fragrant scent.

But then his gaze settled on her full lips with their shading of red, and the brazen image of another man claiming that luscious mouth rose up to smote him. Jason drew back, clenching his teeth. He pushed the door open, and taking Lauren's arm in a grip more forceful than he intended, ushered her into the spacious cabin.

Lauren had a momentary impression of gleaming mahogany and brass fixtures, and also noted a massive desk on one side of the cabin and an even larger bunk on the other, but her attention remained on Jason as he shut the door and hung the lantern on a peg, then strode to the porthole and flung open the casement.

"Thank you," she murmured, grateful for his consideration. He appeared not to have heard. Lauren watched uneasily as he went to the liquor cabinet near the desk and lifted down a decanter. She was puzzled by the smoldering tension she sensed in him. Of course, she had expected him to be angry for drugging him and taking his money, but not *this* angry. She could feel his rage coiled within him, tangible and explosive.

He paused in the act of reaching for the glasses, then turned, his blue eyes searing her, compelling her to return his gaze. "But perhaps you don't care for brandy. Would you prefer a glass of sherry? It isn't drugged."

Lauren took a deep breath, steeling herself for a battle. So he had recognized her. But of course he thought she was Andrea Carlin. George Burroughs would never have revealed her true identity, not as long as Regina could inherit the Carlin ships. "No, thank you, Captain," she replied in a small voice.

"I no longer captain a ship. Kyle Ramsey commands the *Siren,* while I'm merely the owner. But what of you? Marguerite is not the name you use regularly, is it?"

"No." Lauren watched him place the crystal snifter on the desk and pour out a measure of liquor. He seemed calm enough, in complete control of his emotions, and there was none of the harshness in his voice she had heard before. But he still looked powerful and commanding, even in his shirtsleeves and silk-flowered waistcoat. His leonine head had the sculptured look of marble, while in contrast to the gleaming

133

white cravat, his features appeared molded from bronze.

When he glanced up at her, one brow raised quizzically, she recognized a hardness in his eyes that dared her to lie. He was waiting, obviously expecting more from her answer. "Lauren," she said quietly, "Lauren DeVries."

Jason exhaled his breath softly. "I wondered for a very long time if you had made it to safety."

She was the first to drop her eyes. "Why did you bring me here?"

"Why else but to avail myself of the wares you are displaying so . . . charmingly? You didn't seem inclined to break your other engagement."

Lauren didn't quite know how to respond. "I . . . I expect you would like your money back. It was wrong of me to take it. I should be able to bring it to you first thing—"

"Keep it. I would rather have what I bargained for that night in London."

The reminder brought a flush to Lauren's cheeks, and she pulled his coat more closely about her. "I'm sorry if I inconvenienced you—"

"*Inconvenienced?*" Jason's lips twisted as he remembered the anguish he had suffered, imagining her dead or worse, at the mercy of the scum that roamed the London streets. Then he thought of the gaming house, of the men who must have enjoyed her charms, Duval in particular, and jealousy ran rampant through him. He raised his glass to his lips, tossing off the contents with complete disregard for the quality of the wine. "Is that what you think? I beg to differ, Cat-eyes. Inconvenienced is far too mild a term for the torment you put me through."

Lifting her chin, Lauren gave him her coolest frown. "I said I was sorry."

"So you did."

"I came here to apologize."

His eyebrows shot up. "How remarkable. And I was under the impression I had to use force in order to bring you here."

Lauren felt her own temper flaring, realizing that he was deliberately trying to provoke her. "I truly am sorry for what I did to you, but I . . . I didn't have a choice."

She could see Jason's eyes blaze, could feel his anger leap across the distance between them. Nearly flinching at the impact of that molten gaze, she continued hesitantly. "I tell you I didn't have a choice. I had to leave England, and at once. My guardian . . . his men had already tried to kill Matthew. If you had become involved, they might have killed you as well."

His blue eyes narrowed dangerously. "Try again, sweetheart. I was your betrothed, remember? I had nothing to fear from Burroughs."

"You . . . you don't understand."

Jason swept her a regal, mocking bow. "Then perhaps you should explain it to me. In truth, I've been waiting an age for an explanation."

Lauren stood staring at him, quelling the urge to run. She had told the truth about not having a choice; she had almost gotten Matthew killed by dragging him into her affairs, and even if Jason Stuart had been willing to help her, she could not have involved him in such danger, nor let him risk his life for her as Matthew had done. She could never have repaid such a debt. But neither could she tell Jason the truth about her impersonation. Only some version of it.

"Perhaps Burroughs would not have harmed you," she murmured, "but that wasn't true of my aunt. Regina Carlin wanted me dead, and she would not have let anyone stand in her way."

"Why?"

The harshly voiced question nearly made her jump. "What . . . do you mean?"

"Why did she want you dead?"

"Because . . . she would inherit the Carlin ships if anything happened to me."

Jason's blue gaze bored into her for such a long moment that Lauren wondered if he could read her thoughts just by staring at her. But then he forcefully set down his glass and stepped behind the desk. "How much do you earn in an evening, Miss Carlin?" he asked, jerking open a drawer. "Or should I say *Mademoiselle Marguerite?*"

"Please. . . . I would prefer that you call me Lauren."

"Very well—Lauren." He rummaged till he found what he

was searching for, then lifted a leather pouch and tossed it at her feet. The clink of the coins seemed to echo about the cabin. "I'll add that to sweeten the pot, Lauren. Is it not enough? It should keep you in satins and jewels for some time."

She stood dumbly gazing down at the bag, realizing he was offering to buy her services. That he should think such a thing of her . . .

Without lifting her head, she said in a breathless voice, "You . . . you think me a whore."

"Do you deny it? I'll admit," he said with mock gallantry when she was silent, "that you're far above the common class."

Slowly, Lauren raised her gaze to meet his. "Should I be flattered? I would think any woman could service your needs just as well."

"Perhaps, but I've already paid for you. You'll recall that you left before fulfilling the terms of our bargain—one night in my bed."

Lauren winced at his words, at the pain that twisted inside her. Jason Stuart didn't want *her.* He wanted what any woman could give. "I said I would return your money."

"And I said I didn't want it. I won't even charge you interest for the period. What has it been, nearly four years?"

"I'm not for sale!" Lauren snapped.

His hand swung out in an impatient arc. "Come now. Someone must pay for the sort of gown you're wearing. Or do you earn enough to pick and choose your lovers?"

"I shall not"—her chin lifted—"dignify that remark with an answer. I think it is time for me to leave." She turned and took a step toward the door and then halted. Jason had moved swiftly across the cabin and was blocking her way.

Lauren regarded him warily. Not knowing what else to do, she shrugged off his coat and held it out to him. "Thank you for the loan." When Jason made no move to take it, she laid the coat over one of the barrel-backed chairs in front of the desk.

Jason watched her nervously smoothing out the folds of the garment, and knew a gathering sense of frustration. He was already hard with wanting her, and if that weren't torment enough, she tantalized him by stripping off his coat. Those

136

ripe, voluptuous breasts begged to be bared to his touch. . . .
"So now you intend to walk the streets?" he asked thickly, his
eyes dropping to the brazenly displayed curves.

Somehow Lauren managed to maintain her composure, even
though the heat of his gaze singed her. "I do not. I will hail a
hackney."

"And how do you expect to pay? I doubt you have the fare
hidden in your bodice. That gown couldn't conceal a penny."

"I will manage."

"How—by services rendered?" Seeing anger flash in her
eyes, Jason gave her a tight smile. "How far do you think you'll
get in that gown? There isn't a man alive who could see you and
not have ravishment on his mind."

"Not all men are as base as you are, Mr. Stuart."

"Oh, no? Show me one who isn't."

Lauren made no reply, feeling tension vibrating like a live
thing between them as he fixed her with his unwavering stare.
But she was determined not to show her trepidation. She stared
coolly back at him, with her head held high, her shoulders held
proudly erect.

Jason's anger flamed higher. She looked as regal as a queen,
standing there in that superbly, indecently tailored gown, with
those expensive gems sparkling at her throat. She was every
inch Jonathan Carlin's daughter and heiress to a fortune.
Surely she couldn't have thrown away her future to become a
high-class strumpet.

Assuming a casualness he didn't feel, Jason leaned back
against the door and crossed his arms across his wide chest. "I
take it Lila was willing to brave this danger with you," he said
levelly.

Lauren realized he wouldn't let her go until she explained.
"Not . . . not at first," she replied. "But then I told her about
Burroughs . . . and about Matthew. Lila felt rseponsible for
me, whether I wanted her to or not, and she wouldn't let me
search for Matthew alone. When we found him, she helped us
book passage on a ship, then decided to come with us. She had
no family in England, no reason to stay. And I think Matthew
told her I was too young to be going to America with only him
to care for me."

"She's here in New Orleans, I presume?"

"Yes, but she's married now, to a very kind man, Jean-Paul Beauvais. It . . . would be better if you didn't see her, I expect. She doesn't need to be reminded of her past, and Jean-Paul has a jealous temperament."

"I'll consider your advice," Jason returned sarcastically. He stood considering her across the small distance that separated them, an ominous glint in his eye. "I'll wager you never told Lila about our arranged marriage."

"Not . . . until later."

"I can just imagine her reaction. She would have been horrified to think that she had allowed your seduction in her own bedroom. I suppose," he ground out slowly as Lauren bowed her head, "that you wept copious tears, pleading with Lila to save you from the debauched villain who had stolen your virginity."

When she didn't answer but stood twisting her fingers together, Jason clenched his fists, almost choking on the rage that boiled inside him. Abruptly, he strode over to the desk and poured more brandy in his glass, eyeing his own unsteady hand with something akin to disgust. "That is, if I were the first," he said after a time.

"Of course you were the first," Lauren whispered.

His eyes burned darkly with suppressed fury as he shot her an impaling glance. "Then why did you agree to give yourself to me, if you don't mind my asking? You could have waited a while longer for your drug to take effect."

"I . . . didn't know if it would," she said honestly. When Jason's mouth twisted in contempt, Lauren added, "I needed the money, so when you suggested the bargain, I felt obliged to fulfill my part."

"Such a sense of honor," he mocked. "And now I bear the burden of guilt for having set your dainty little feet on the sinful path."

"That isn't true!" she cried. "I tell you I didn't have a choice."

With her answer, Jason's fury erupted. He slammed his glass down, shattering the crystal, and reached Lauren in three

138

strides, making her head snap back as he seized her shoulders in a crushing grip. His eyes blazed with blue fire, his nostrils flaring as he snarled, "You had a choice, damn you! I would have taken you as my *wife*. I would have cherished you, protected you, given you everything I owned."

Lauren gasped with pain as his fingers bit into the soft flesh of her arms. His face was just inches from hers, his eyes alive and blazing with emotion, and for the first time she was afraid of him. She struggled, pushing against his alarmingly broad chest. "You wanted the Carlin ships!" she cried, trying to twist from his grasp. "You didn't want me!"

Her efforts left her panting for breath and no less a captive as Jason hauled her full against him, against his powerful, sinewy body. "Wrong, sweetheart!" he rasped, his eyes crystal slits of fury. "I wanted you. I *still* want you. And I mean to have you."

His lips came down on hers fiercely then, claiming with brutal possessiveness. The taste of brandy filled Lauren's senses as his tongue savagely assaulted her mouth, punishing her, robbing her of breath.

Lauren's attempts to free herself failed pitifully. Clamped as she was against the hard length of him, all she did was arouse Jason further. Arouse him in a different way. She realized his new intent almost at once, even before she felt his hard body tighten.

When he raised his head, she stared up at him, shaken, breathless, furious, into eyes that were hot and glittering, and she became truly frightened. What did she know about Jason Stuart, after all? She had dreamed of making love to him, of being in his arms again, but not like this. Not with anger and fear raging between them.

Desperately Lauren tried to avert her face, but his powerful hand cupped the back of her head, holding her still while he lowered his mouth again. He kissed her with a bruising, controlled passion that left her gasping. Her hands flailed helplessly around his shoulders as he filled her with the taste of him, the hot searching stab of his tongue.

His kiss was brutally lustful . . . yet somehow sensual. Lauren couldn't control the wild pulse of excitement that quivered through her at his rough handling. Even so, she fought him, pounding her fists ineffectively at his broad shoulders.

Jason easily subdued her, forcing her hands behind her back as he bent her back over his arm. Lauren whimpered, wildly aware of his muscular chest crushing her breasts, of the explicit pressure of his arousal pressing against her thighs. But her resistance only seemed to increase his determination.

He held her wrists in one hand while the other slid up her satin bodice to the yielding swell of her breasts, roaming freely, caressing boldly. Then, bending, Jason pressed his lips against her hair, nuzzling her ear. "Play the whore for me, Lauren. Show me how well you do it."

She was shocked by his husky command, and shocked further by the brutal rush of feeling that flooded her. The primitive leap of hunger assaulted her so sharply that she moaned.

"Is Duval a good lover?" Jason continued in that hoarse, relentless voice. "Does he make you moan like this? Can he make you cry out with passion?"

His hard fingers closed over her breast, relentlessly pressing and releasing the nipple beneath the satin. Lauren gritted her teeth as her flesh involuntarily contracted into a tight, aching bud. She was hardly aware of what Jason was saying. Duval? Felix had never done anything like this to her. And how did Jason even know about him anyway?"

"No . . . you're mistaken. . . ." she gasped, fighting her body's traitorous response.

Suddenly Jason was turning her and urging her backward. Caught off balance, Lauren clutched at his shoulders, having no choice but to move with him as he pushed her up against the desk.

There was nowhere to run. The edge of the desk bit into her buttocks while Jason's granite-hard thighs held her prisoner, molding against her softness. Feeling herself falling, Lauren threw her hands out behind her and found herself half sitting, half lying on the desktop, with Jason's arms staked on either side of her shoulders, his hard body pressing her down, holding her immobile.

140

"Perhaps," he rasped, "we should hold a contest. Who can satisfy you best? Who can make you moan the loudest?"

She heard the rough catch in his voice, saw the hooded anguish in his eyes, but still she didn't understand. "Why are you doing this?" she whispered, unable to bear his angry contempt.

"I told you why." His gaze dropped to her straining breasts. Very deliberately he ran a forefinger down the slender column of her throat to the bare white swells above her gown's low neckline. Lauren quivered, his touch feeling like a brand of fire against her skin. "Because I want you," Jason said, his low, sensuous tone stroking her. "Because I've wanted you every night for four years, every waking moment. And I intend to have you. I'll have you again and again, till you're so filled with me you can't even remember Duval's name."

"Please . . ."

"Please what?" his husky voice prodded her. "Please *you*? What do you like best, sweetheart? I expect I can be as inventive as Duval."

Lauren knew then. With the instinctive confidence of a woman, she knew he was jealous. Fiercely jealous. The knowledge gave her a heady feeling of power that she had no time to analyze. Jason desired her, Lauren thought dazedly, looking up at that hard, virile face with its noble, sculpted planes. He desired *her*.

Something of her wonder must have shown on her face, for his eyes shut momentarily and his jaw went rigid, as if he were bracing himself against pain. "Oh, God." It was as if the groan was dragged out of him.

And when he opened his eyes, she could see in the brilliant blue depths of his gaze that his anger had turned to smoldering passion.

Her lips parted in breathless anticipation as she waited helplessly for his next assault. She was startled when, with incredible gentleness, he tugged on the bodice of her gown, freeing her full breasts from their confining satin.

His gaze fixed hungrily on the silken crests as he drew in a sharp breath. "Those magnificent breasts, just as beautiful as I remember them. I remembered doing this . . ." He cupped her

141

breast in his palm, his tenderness infinitely arousing after the violence that had preceded it. "And this . . ." His hard thumb circled the sensitive tip, sending a stab of quivering, almost painful delight through her body. "And this . . ." He lowered his mouth to claim the lush flesh, his tongue flicking out to taste, to tantalize, to torment.

Startled by the raw hunger that curled inside her, Lauren moaned, and with one hand clutched blindly at Jason's shoulder. Impossibly, his caresses became more gentle. His warm mouth pulled at the aching nipple, then pressed featherlight kisses on the tight bud, alternating with slow, sensuous licks of his rough, wet tongue, while his hand reached up to attend her other breast with a plucking motion of his fingers.

Lauren shuddered at the fierce pleasure he was arousing in her, a sensation like liquid heat gathering between her thighs. Jason's response was a low, hungry growl deep in his throat.

After a moment he lifted his head, letting his gaze rake Lauren's flushed face. "I want you, sweetheart," he whispered hoarsely. "I ache with wanting you."

He bent again, his mouth trailing hot, nibbling kisses along her throat as he reached down to slowly raise Lauren's gown to her hips, baring the secrets of her femininity. His warm fingers spread over her silken thigh, skimming upward, caressing the shivering flesh. "Yes, I want you. I want you hot and lusting . . . for me . . . only for me."

When he found his mark, the moist, yielding cleft, his sharp inhalation was audible. "I haven't even begun and already you're burning for me."

Lauren closed her eyes as his fingers began to move, desire running like fire in her veins. "Please . . ." she whimpered, not even knowing what she was pleading for.

"That's it," he urged, his slow, sensuous stroking driving her into a mindless frenzy. "Moan for me, sweetheart. Go wild for me."

She arched wantonly, straining against his hand as she tried to ease the throbbing, pulsing ache between her thighs. Her flesh was burning. Her skin was on fire. Her nostrils were filled with Jason's heat, with the musky, sensual scent of him.

She let her head fall back in surrender, her breath coming in soft pants as she gave herself over to the wild, heated dimness. Through a haze of desire, she could sense Jason watching her, could sense his hot gaze fixed on her face as he sent her flaring passion nearly out of control. Yet he seemed to know just when she could no longer stand his tender torment. His burning gaze remained on her face as he unbuttoned his breeches and freed his swollen, rigid hardness. He let his weight fall forward, pressing Lauren back, his aroused flesh burning her thigh, probing, seeking entrance.

She could have stopped him. In that brief moment when their eyes clashed, she read a question in the blazing azure of his gaze. But she didn't want to stop him. That was what terrified her; this feeling of being swept out of control. It was as if she had been craving this for years, as if desire had been building inside her for four years, stoked by her dreams and her memories. Every dream, every fantasy, every feeling of suppressed desire had been leading up to this moment.

She closed her eyes, reaching up to twine her fingers in his thick, sun-gilded hair. Jason instantly recognized her surrender. His hands slid under her hips as he lifted her, then pressed into her slowly, powerfully, entering her in continuing thrusts that filled her completely.

He held himself still then, poised above her, sheathed within her, as he gazed down at her beautiful, flushed face. Lauren's eyes were closed, her lips slightly parted as her breath came in ragged gasps. Jason's doubts about her innocence, his concerns for her vulnerability, were forgotten. "Look at me, Lauren," he ordered raggedly. "Damn it, look at me and know who is loving you."

She heard his voice through the flame-shot darkness, and her amber-flecked eyes flew open. She stared up at him, mesmerized by the intense, burning desire in his blue gaze. Slowly Jason began to move inside her, arousing her, making her body quiver in response. Her hips arched instinctively, her body welcoming his thrusts, his hard, pulsating fullness.

"God, four years . . ." she heard him rasp, and she wound her long legs about his waist. Abruptly, his movements became more urgent. His arms closed fiercely around her waist, his

143

taut body quivering with the effort of maintaining control as he groaned and buried his face and mouth in her shoulder.

Lauren clung to him, her fingers digging into the corded muscles of his arms as he took her with savage intensity. She was filled with his incredible hardness, sobbing with the sweet, sweet pain of it. Waves of pleasure washed over her again and again, lifting her up with their ever-increasing swells as Jason possessed her. The waves grew to gigantic proportions. She was drowning, drowning in a stormy sea, pitched and tossed by churning waves.

She sobbed, clutching him as his powerful body went rigid. He contracted, straining with hungry violence, and she plunged down, deep, deep, deep. . . . The sea erupted, sending violent surges crashing through her body as he poured himself into her.

The devastating shocks pummeled Jason as well. Shaken by one last, brutal shudder, he collapsed upon Lauren, his face buried in the damp hollows of her throat, his breathing harsh and ragged as the last vestiges of passion drained from his body.

Lauren lay beneath him, unmoving, vaguely aware that it was over. Jason's hard, muscular length was sprawled heavily on her, his weight only partially supported by his arms. Her breasts rose and fell slowly as she inhaled the sensual, sweat-dampened scent of him. The ragged sound of his breathing was loud in her ear.

Then in a low growl, so low that Lauren thought she might have imagined it, Jason swore.

Chapter Eight

"Bloody, *bloody* hell," Jason mumbled again under his breath.

The insane jealousy that had kindled a blind rage in him was fading, leaving behind guilt and self-contempt. *Again*, he thought disgustedly. Again he had attacked the woman he had planned to make his wife. He couldn't remember when he'd last lost control with a woman, but in his desire to have Lauren, he hadn't even waited to shed his clothes. He had taken her like a trollop from the streets, pounding into her with a relentlessness brought on by four years of frustrated longing.

And yet she had reached the pinnacle with him. She hadn't feigned that writhing response or those cries of passion. Had she learned in her trade that such ardor made a man feel his own power? How many men had she given herself to with such abandon?

Not that those questions mattered now. His dream was a mere obsession, an aberration of the mind. He couldn't take a high-class Cyprian to wife, regardless of his personal feelings. He owed more than that to his name, to his breeding, and he had an obligation to the illustrious title he had inherited but never wanted.

He would fulfill his promise to Burroughs, of course. She wouldn't be required to sell her body again for gold, for she would be rich enough to afford whatever she desired. And when he completed his business with her, after he handed over her fortune, he would sail for home and not look back—if

145

he could.

Jason lifted his head to search her face, his brows knitting with concern. "Are you all right?"

Hearing the grimness in his husky voice, Lauren regarded him in confusion. All right? She was still dazed by the shattering experience of the last few moments, her body limp and exhausted. Her position was awkward and uncomfortable, to say the least, and she found it hard to breathe. Yet she felt warm and sated and more completely alive than ever before. She wanted to savor Jason's closeness, the heat and heaviness of his powerful body.

When she nodded, Jason eased his weight from her and stood, adjusting his clothes. Shakily, Lauren raised herself up on her elbows, and was shocked when she looked down at herself. Her breasts were bared lewdly, her nipples glistening and swollen from Jason's attentions, while her skirts were bunched up around her waist and her pale thighs still parted in an erotic invitation. This couldn't be her. Not this wanton creature with the flushed skin and disheveled clothes. Feeling a sudden wave of embarrassment in the silence, Lauren pushed her gown down to cover her bare limbs and slid from the desk to her feet.

She was straightening her bodice when Jason held out a linen handkerchief. "You look like a Haymarket doxy with that paint on your face," he said quietly. "Wipe it off. You need no artifices to enhance your beauty, and I need no reminder of your occupation."

Lauren flinched before giving him a wary glance, and for a moment Jason thought he would have to force her compliance. But then she silently began to scrub away the traces of the cosmetics. Jason raked his fingers through his hair, wondering how he was going to repair the shambles he had made of this evening. Catching sight of the broken crystal on the desk, he retrieved another glass and poured himself a large measure of brandy, then sank heavily into one of the chairs.

Lauren watched him, trying not to think of what had just happened between them, of how effortlessly Jason had brought her to that shattering, gasping release. It had shaken her that he should have such control over her. And his silence now made her feel like she had committed some dire offense, or more painfully, that he had made love to her and had found her wanting. As the dull ache between her thighs began to throb, she made a shaky attempt to gather her shredded pride about her. "Was I so very bad?"

His blue eyes found hers, and she was surprised to find his gaze held uncertainty. "You know very well you weren't. But I didn't mean to take you so roughly. My only excuse is that it has been some time since I've been with a woman. Forgive me, please."

Lauren smoothed the green satin of her skirt. "Well," she replied after a time, "if you are quite finished with me, perhaps now I may go. You can have no further need of me."

Jason's mouth curved with self-mockery as his desire suddenly rekindled. "I wouldn't say that precisely, Miss Carlin."

"I . . . I wish you wouldn't call me by that name."

"Why not? You prefer to remain incognito? Don't you intend to claim the fortune you left behind in England?" When he saw the flicker of alarm in her eyes, Jason cocked his head to one side, contemplating her. "Have I stumbled onto a secret? You don't wish anyone to know you're an heiress?"

Lauren only stared at him, wondering what he was driving at.

"It seems I've discovered a point of leverage," he added when she remained silent. "But never fear, I'm prepared to bargain. Are you not curious to hear my . . . proposal?"

Lauren found her voice. "I don't care for your bargains and conditions and proposals. They don't interest me."

Jason leaned back in his chair, crossing his long legs at the ankles. "You were willing enough to bargain four years ago. And I was going to promise my silence in exchange for—" He shrugged his broad shoulders. "Ah, but you said you weren't interested."

"In exchange for what?" she demanded with a frown.

"I still want the night you promised me."

His reply was low and soft, a velvet murmur that stroked her, but Lauren's eyes widened at his audacity. He was blackmailing her!

Yet she couldn't dismiss his offer without careful consideration. In the first place, she still owed him money, and she didn't like being indebted to a man who could wield such power over her with merely the force of his personality. Moreover, he could expose her to Burroughs if he chose.

"And then you will let me go and not say a word about knowing who I am?" she asked, realizing she couldn't risk refusing him.

"If you truly wish it," Jason said softly.

Lauren searched his face, trying to determine whether or not she could trust him. At last, she said in a voice that trembled slightly, "It seems again, you leave me no choice."

The gentle look in his eyes faded. "No, sweetheart. You will always have a choice. But whether you're wise enough to make the right one remains to be seen."

"You are very sure of yourself."

"Sure of myself, yes," he said solemnly, "but not sure of you. The last time you drugged me and ran away. I can't help wondering what tricks you will try next. Even now, when I seem to hold all the trump cards, I'm not at all certain of winning."

Lauren regarded him with puzzlement. "You speak in riddles. What trumps? What game are you playing?"

Jason waved his hand in dismissal. "Nothing. Come, Lauren, I'm waiting for your answer. You are free to go. The choice is yours."

Lauren's glance went to the door and then back to Jason. He was wrong, she thought as she took one hesitant step toward him. She had no choice, or at least no will to resist the force that seemed to draw her to him.

He seemed to sense her capitulation, for his expression softened. "Come here," he ordered, the quiet timbre of his voice playing on her senses.

Slowly she closed the distance between them, until she was near enough to touch him. Her pulse skittered wildly as Jason rose to his feet and stood towering above her.

"Now, kiss me."

It was his fascinating aura of power, Lauren decided as she obediently closed her eyes and tilted her head back to receive his kiss. That was why she felt so helpless and overwhelmed whenever she was so near him.

"No, sweetheart, I expect you to do the honors. I don't want to be guilty again of forcing you."

Lauren's lashes flew up as she looked at Jason questioningly. He was watching her intently, a glimmer of amusement in his eyes. Oh, those blue, blue eyes. Fathoms deep. A woman could drown in those blue depths. Taking a deep breath, Lauren moved closer and stood on tiptoe. Pursing her lips, she planted a brief kiss on his chiseled mouth, being careful not to touch any part of his large body.

Jason gave her a wry smile, shaking his head. "Nor do I want the kind of salute reserved for cousins. You can kiss better than that. Put your arms around me and do it properly this time. And have pity on me, I beg. Make it last a while. I might not be the recipient of your favors again."

Pity was not what Lauren was experiencing as she warily placed her hands on his shoulders. Confusion, breathlessness, desire, and a great deal of mistrust, yes. But she couldn't imagine anyone feeling pity for this man who seemed to be the very ideal of masculine beauty. Taking a deep breath, she braced herself against the startling physical attraction she felt for him and slowly encircled his neck with her arms.

He refused to make it easier for her by lowering his head, so she was forced to move closer, pressing almost full against him. She felt herself suddenly quivering, but Jason stood very still, his hands at his sides, waiting. If it weren't for the gleam in his blue eyes and the rapid heartbeat that seemed to mingle with hers, Lauren might have imagined herself attempting to embrace a statue.

Except that the lips that waited for her were infinitely warm and tender. She wasn't at all prepared for the melting rush of feeling she experienced with that kiss. It was gentle enough to draw the very soul from her body. And it had every nerve ending in her body clamoring for more.

Her lips parted beneath his, hungering for the taste of him, and when he wouldn't give enough of himself, she slid her tongue into his mouth. Her boldness gained her the response she was seeking: Jason's breath quickened as his arms came around her.

Lauren pressed even closer, tangling her fingers in his sun-kissed hair. It was hard to convince herself she was doing this for a debt owed. She *wanted* to kiss him. The vital current that flowed between them was warm and vibrant and infinitely arousing, and she wanted it.

She could feel her pulse beating wildly as Jason's hands slowly stroked her back, gliding effortlessly down the smooth satin to caress her buttocks, and up again, to fondle the silken skin at her nape. And by the time his fingers gently cradled the back of her head, she was trembling. His arousal pressed against her thigh, hard and demanding and urgent. . . .

She was startled when Jason lifted his mouth, breaking off the heated embrace.

He was breathing heavily as he cupped her face in his hands. "Lauren," he said hoarsely, urging her to look at him, "before this goes any further . . ." He wanted her to understand why he had been so angry. And he needed to explain his reasons for bringing her on board the *Siren* before he lost control of himself again. He had known where a kiss would lead.

His searching gaze caressed the perfect oval of her face, the golden-green cat-eyes, the lips that had tasted like wine. "I have a confession to make. I never intend for you to return to the gaming house tonight. And when I demanded a night with you in exchange for my silence, I wasn't being completely honest. I want more than a night with you. . . . I want all of you."

Lauren gazed up at him with passion-glazed eyes. "I know," she replied, her voice a husky murmur. "You are very obvious about what you want, Jason Stuart."

The same passion flared hotly in his eyes. "And you want me as well," he said softly, his thumbs brushing her delicate cheekbones. "Say it, Lauren. You want me, too."

Her soft smile made Jason's heart stand still. "I . . . I want you, too."

He never completed his explanation. His intentions of telling her about Burroughs and the Carlin Line fled as he began to press small kisses randomly over her forehead, eye-lids, cheeks, chin, before at last he captured her mouth again.

This time when he made love to her, however, he was infinitely gentle and patient. He took the time to remove her gown, to loose her flowing hair from its pins, to divest her throat of the glittering gems, before lifting her up and carrying her to the wide bunk. And this time, as he stood over her, drinking in the sight of her naked beauty, his senses were drugged, not with an opiate, but with the headiness of passion.

He stepped back to shed his clothes, and Lauren lay silently watching him, a mixture of desire and wonder in her eyes. His waistcoat went first, then his shirt, exposing powerful shoulders and corded arms. His broad chest was lightly furred beneath a golden tan, and tapered to a flat, hard stomach and lean hips. Then he removed his boots and trousers.

The sheer magnificence of his body took Lauren's breath away. In the golden glow of lamplight, he looked vital, bronzed, beautiful. Yet beautiful in a supremely masculine way. His powerful, sun-gilded body was sleekly muscled and superbly sculpted. And he was undeniably aroused. Lauren couldn't stop her gaze from dropping to the place where his tan ended, where his virile hardness leapt proudly from a dark nest of curling hair, overwhelming in its size and power.

The Sun-god Apollo, Lauren thought, startled by the sharp stab of desire that filled her. She wanted to touch him, to move her hands freely down the length of his magnificent form that was so different from hers.

Flushing, Lauren lifted her gaze to Jason's face and caught her breath. The sapphire eyes seemed to hold great tenderness even while they regarded her so intently. No, his eyes were smoldering, and she felt the heat of his gaze where it touched her. There were flames in his eyes. She was drowning in a deep blue sea of fire.

He came to her then, moving with fluid masculine grace as he stretched out beside her. Lauren gasped when he drew her against the full length of his hard body. The fine hair covering his chest rasped sensuously against her breasts, while his long steel-muscled legs molded against hers, sending heated stabs of awareness throbbing through her.

He didn't speak as his warm hands stroked her silken back, nor as they slowly began winding tortuous paths over the rest

151

of her skin. Lauren quivered as she submitted to his sensuous caresses, yet she wanted to explore Jason, too. Breathlessly, boldly, she began to reciprocate, letting her touch roam at will.

His body seemed to have been hammered from pure steel. His skin was rough and smooth at the same time, the texture of raw silk, with rippling sinew beneath that suggested superb physical conditioning. He closed his eyes and shuddered when her slender fingers discovered unknown territory.

Her hand froze when she felt his response. She had only wanted to satisfy her natural curiosity about the swollen hardness that had given her so much pleasure, and was surprised to find it felt like heated satin. But when she saw Jason's face contort in sensual pain, she slowly began to stroke his arousal, needing to give in return.

The next instant Jason groaned and grasped her ministering hand. Lauren glanced at him questioningly when he shifted from her reach. "This time is for both of us," he rasped, his voice unnaturally husky.

Gently he pressed her down upon the pillows while he supported himself on one elbow. Gazing down in eyes of golden emerald, he traced the outline of her parted lips with his fingers. "My beautiful Lauren, why did you run from me?" His murmur was nothing more than a whisper, and sent shivers of longing racing through her. "Ah, but it doesn't matter. Nothing matters but this night."

Lauren returned his gaze, her hand moving of its own volition from his cheek to his strong jaw. "No, nothing else matters," she breathed as she drew Jason's head down, seeking his mouth.

Their breaths mingled, then lips, then tongues. And as Jason kissed her with slow, savoring possession, the embers started to smolder again. Lauren moaned against his demanding mouth when his muscled thigh began moving between her legs. He was touching her everywhere with expert caresses, his hands warm and knowing.

She moaned again when his mouth traced a heated path down her body to her lush breasts, and when he paused to fondle tight, rosy nipples with his tongue, she felt as if flames were licking her skin, scorching her.

152

And then he was shifting his weight, settling himself between her thighs, sliding into her welcoming heat, filling up every inch of her. Lauren arched against him, wanting him with a fierceness that shocked her.

But Jason refused to hurry. "Not yet, my love," he said, pressing a light kiss on the corner of her mouth.

"Please, Jason. . . ."

"Patience, sweetheart."

He moved with exquisite slowness, letting the heat of passion build. Lauren had to be content with moving her hands feverishly over the flexing muscles of his back, urging him on.

Only when shimmering heat waves danced around her did his rhythm slowly escalate, and that by that time, Lauren was whimpering with need. At last his thrusts increased in power and urgency, and he arched into her with unrestrained possessiveness, his forceful tenderness making her gasp.

A white-hot explosion racked Lauren's body. She rose up against him, crying out his name, while Jason shuddered, groaned, and twisted his fingers in her hair.

They both floated down with the warm ashes of the aftermath.

"Lauren, my beautiful . . . precious Lauren," he murmured, pressing soft, tender kisses against her mouth. "You are fire . . . and ice."

She heard his husky words through a haze of contentment. Not wanting reality to intrude, she wrapped her arms around Jason's neck and buried her face in the sweat-dampened hollow of his throat.

Jason didn't even try to pry himself away. Instead, he rested his cheek against the golden silk of her hair, savoring the joy of meeting some unspoken need of hers.

Only when her fervent grip relaxed somewhat did he ease his weight from her and roll on his back, gathering Lauren in his arms. His fingers threaded through the tangled veil of her hair as his free hand stroked her bare shoulder.

After a time he sighed. "My love, we must talk," he said, knowing his revelations would shatter the peacefulness of the moment. Yet when Lauren raised her head from the comfortable curve of his shoulder and returned his gaze so trustingly, Jason hesitated. He was reluctant to sever the tenuous bond that had sprung up between them. He found himself, instead, asking about her fear of the dark.

Lauren regarded him uncertainly before resting her head again on his shoulder. She was surprised that his question engendered no frightful memories; the specters seemed to be held at bay when she was lying safe and warm in Jason's arms. She found that the words came easily. "It isn't darkness I fear, but close, confined places," she said quietly. "I see these hideous images . . . like evil shadows . . . and I hear screams. It's like a nightmare, only worse. I'm so terrified that I can't move. And then I go cold all over and my throat closes up, like someone is choking me."

"Have you always reacted this way?" Jason asked quietly.

"Yes, as long as I remember. I've tried to conquer my fear, I truly have, but I can't seem to control it. I can't even ride in a closed carriage or lock the door to a room without seeing those phantoms and hearing those ghastly screams. They petrify me. I even dream about them. Sometimes I think—"

When Lauren broke off, her voice shaking, Jason pressed his lips to her brow. "Tell me," he urged.

"Sometimes I wonder if I truly am going mad."

Jason's arms tightened about her. "You seem very sane to me, Lauren. From your description, it sounds rather like you suffer from a phobia, perhaps brought on by some unpleasant experience. Your situation isn't so unusual."

Lauren shuddered at the memory. Not wanting to discuss the disturbing topic further, she abruptly changed the subject. "Jason, why are you here? In New Orleans?"

"I could ask the same of you," he countered. "Is this where you've been hiding out all these years?"

She nodded, then sat up, her eyes searching his face. "Did you mean it when you said you wouldn't give me away?"

Jason was distracted momentarily by the sight of her disheveled hair tumbling around her shoulders and a tress that curled around her bare breast. He wanted to reach out and fondle the ripe flesh, but he had noted the gravity in her tone. "What must I do, Lauren, to convince you that I care what happens to you?" Jason said slowly. "Do you realize that it

154

sickened me to discover you working as a doxy in a gaming house? Selling yourself like used goods at a market? Don't you know I feel guilty as hell for having been your first customer?"

The throbbing anguish in his voice touched a sensitive chord within her. She hadn't intended to divulge anything about her past life, for with his perceptiveness, Jason might guess the secret that she had hidden for so long. But, inexplicably, she didn't like having him think her that kind of woman. She had to tell him about her reasons for working in the gaming house. She had to explain—as much as she could.

"It isn't what you think," she said in a low voice. "I have an arrangement with Madame Gescard."

"I can just imagine."

His sardonic tone made Lauren stiffen. Her lashes fluttered down to veil her thoughts as she responded with her own brand of sarcasm. "But of course you can," she returned sweetly. "You know all about such things, don't you, Jason Stuart? Tell me, how do you find the 'goods', now that you have had a sample? How do I compare to Lila, or to the girls who work for Madame Gescard? Or to any of your other women, for that matter?"

Jason's mouth tightened. "There is no comparison." He reached out to place a warm, possessive hand on her breast. "I don't want you returning to the gaming house, Lauren." He felt the sudden leap of her heart against his palm before she quickly drew back.

"Are you asking me or telling me?" Lauren said in a calm tone that carried no trace of her underlying bitterness.

"I'm asking. I'll kneel at your feet and beg, if I must."

"Why?"

The question was casual and indifferent, yet Jason was aware that he must tread cautiously. He searched her beautiful face, looking for some trace of emotion behind the cool, expressionless mask she wore. He could find none, nor any sign to betray her sudden wariness; she returned his gaze steadily. Even so, he sensed the tenseness in her body. And he knew that even after the passion they had shared, even after she had confided her deepest fears to him, she still didn't trust him. She had

155

retreated from him—not physically, for she was trapped in the narrow space between himself and the bulkhead—but emotionally. She stood remote and untouchable on the far side of a gaping chasm.

Determined to bridge it, Jason reached up and curled his fingers behind Lauren's neck, drawing her face down to his. When she strained away, averting her mouth, he began planting delicate kisses on her throat and nibbling his way to her ear. "Why? Because I'm jealous of any man who touches you," he murmured huskily. "Every time I picture you with Duval, I want to do something highly uncivilized, like bash his face in." Gently then, Jason grasped Lauren's chin, forcing her to look at him. "When you give yourself, I want it to be my gold that matches the gleam of your hair, the glitter in your tempting eyes."

The sensuousness in his voice made Lauren shudder. She sighed heavily as she laid her head on his shoulder. "There have been no other men, Jason," she said quietly, feeling the strong beat of his heart beneath her cheek. "Not since that night in London with you has any man—"

She wasn't even given time to complete the sentence before Jason reacted with startling swiftness. Lauren found herself on her back once again, this time looking up into eyes that blazed with anger, not desire.

"You can save your lies," Jason said between clenched teeth. "I've already agreed to pay. I'll meet your price willingly, without any strings attached. But hear me well, Lauren. The one thing I'll always demand from you is honesty. Total and complete *honesty.*"

Taken aback by his sudden fierceness, Lauren stared at him. "You have no right to demand anything of me," she returned. "But I'm telling the truth. Felix isn't keeping me. I'm a seamstress at the casino, and occasionally I play the piano— nothing else. And I've known no man but you."

Jason's blue eyes narrowed to mere slits as he seized her shoulders. "You allow me to take you like a common trollop and then expect me to believe you?"

"You said I wasn't common."

She gasped as Jason's fingers bit into her skin. She thought he might shake her, for his powerful body had gone rigid and his handsome face was dark as thunder. "I'm telling . . . the truth!" she managed to say between breaths. "Madame Gescard . . . pays me to entertain . . . the guests by singing and playing. You're . . . hurting me," she protested when the pressure of his grip increased painfully.

He released her shoulders, but his teeth remained clenched. "Think yourself fortunate, sweetheart. I'm trying very hard not to wring your neck."

Before she could reply, Jason had flung himself from the bunk. Lauren shivered, immediately missing the warmth of his large body. Covering herself with the quilt, she lay curled on her side, watching him warily as he sifted through the garments strewn on the floor.

"Why . . . don't you believe me?" There was no answer. "Tell me," she challenged as his silence stung her, "do you treat all your women so violently? Lila never mentioned it."

Jason's gaze sliced to her as he pulled on his breeches, making Lauren aware that his anger hadn't abated one degree. He didn't reply, though, and his grim silence disturbed her. She couldn't understand what she had done to provoke him, but oddly enough, she preferred facing his wrath to being ignored.

She knew she was playing with fire when she smiled tauntingly, yet she did it to cover her own hurt. "Are the wages for a night's work always so generous, monsieur?" she asked, adopting Marguerite's French accent. "If so, I might consider a full-time position as your *chère amie*. Unless you mean to cover me with bruises, of course. Please tell me. I should like to know what your paramour can expect."

Her inclusion of the accent had been calculated to wound, but she dropped it when she got no response. When Jason jerked open the lid to a large chest and selected a fresh shirt, Lauren offered hesitantly, "You said you wanted honesty. Very well, I thought your lovemaking . . . quite enjoyable." Nothing. Not even a glance.

"Perhaps I will accept the money you offered me tonight, after all. I could buy the satins and jewels you suggested. In spite of what you think, I'm not wealthy."

157

Still there was no answer. "Won't it help assuage your guilt if I take your money?" Lauren said in her most sarcastic tone. "I no longer feel such things as guilt, you see. I lost my heart long ago. George Burroughs saw to that."

That succeeded in getting Jason's attention for a moment. But then he stooped to pick up the bag of coins. He eyed the leather pouch intently before locking it away in the bureau. Then he proceeded to lock every cabinet and drawer in sight.

Lauren watched his actions, first with wariness, then with increasing alarm. "What are you doing?" she exclaimed, already regretting having taunted him.

"I'm securing the cabin."

"You can't mean to keep me here!" Lauren cried, her voice holding a definite trace of panic. He couldn't mean to make her a prisoner. He couldn't!

"I do," Jason admitted with tight-lipped control. "But please feel free to make yourself at home. I'll leave the lantern if you give me your promise not to set fire to the ship."

"Yes, but—"

"Have no fear that I'll lock you in to prevent you from running away. I can't trust you not to attempt an escape, but I expect that not even you would try to leave with only a quilt to hide your nakedness." He scooped up her gown and necklace and slippers, then strode to the door and jerked it open.

"But where are you going?" she nearly shouted.

Jason spared her one brief scowl. "I presume Lila can confirm your story? Well then, you have nothing at all to be worried about, do you?"

The reverberation seemed to echo loudly about the cabin as the door slammed shut behind him.

Chapter Nine

Lauren stared at the closed portal in disbelief. She had pushed Jason too far, she knew, but that didn't explain why he had been so angry to learn she wasn't a harlot. Nor did it excuse him for storming out like that, leaving her without any clothes, a virtual prisoner on his ship. And he had reneged on his last promise, as well. She had been willing to give him the night he demanded, but he hadn't allowed her to fulfill her part of the bargain and end his claim to her. But Jason Stuart had underestimated her if he thought he could keep her captive for long.

Gathering the quilt around her shoulders, Lauren went to the door and found that the handle turned easily under her hand. She peered out into the companionway. The darkness made her shudder—but at least no one was guarding the door. Shutting it once more, she turned to survey the cabin, noticing things she hadn't noticed before.

In addition to the bunk, desk, and chairs, the cabin was furnished with a large sea chest, an unlit brazier, and a shaving stand, while the mahogany-paneled bulkheads were lined with latticed cabinets. Through the leaded panes, she could see leather-bound books and various navigational instruments, including a sextant and spyglass, but she had no luck in opening the doors. She didn't see any usable weapons, either, for the pair of mounted pistols which hung behind the desk proved to be unloaded.

She decided to try the sea chest next, but as she passed the shaving stand, she caught sight of herself in the mirror. Halting abruptly, she stared at her reflection in astonishment, hardly recognizing herself. She looked just like Veronique did after a night with an arduous lover. Her cheeks were flushed, her lips red and swollen from Jason's kisses, and her hair spilled over her shoulders in wild disarray. But her eyes seemed to have undergone the most change. They were bright and animated, not remote and shadowed. She felt different as well. Her skin was glowing with warmth, while her stomach fluttered with anticipation and excitement.

"My God!" Lauren murmured as a new thought struck her. Even if she could have done so, she wouldn't have changed what had happend that evening. She was actually *glad* Jason Stuart had found her, despite the fact that he had virtually kidnapped her and imprisoned her on his ship. She couldn't guess what he intended to do with her. But even if she couldn't find a way to escape, she wouldn't worry yet. He would let her go after he saw Lila.

Lila! God, what would Lila think? Distractedly, Lauren pushed a lock of golden hair back from her face. She had had an excuse for letting Jason make love to her that long-ago night in London, but not by any stretch of the imagination could she be pardoned for this evening's revels. How could she explain the wanton way she had responded when he kissed her? She had wanted him to make love to her, had wanted his strength and warmth and passion.

And what of Lila herself? What would Lila feel when her past lover suddenly appeared to disrupt their lives? And Jean-Paul? He was volatile enough to call out any man who threatened his honor.

Oh, why did Jason Stuart have to come to New Orleans just now, when she had managed to bury her past? And why was she so elated by his presence? There could never, never be anything between them, not as long as George Burroughs and Regina Carlin continued their deadly battle over the Carlin Line. She couldn't put Jason's life in danger by dragging him into her affairs.

Besides, he still thought she was someone else, and she couldn't risk telling him the truth, at least not yet. She didn't

160

trust him enough yet to give him such a powerful weapon to hold over her head.

So why was she standing here like a fool waiting for him to return?

Tearing her gaze from the mirror, Lauren bent over the basin and quickly splashed water on her face, trying to remove the lingering traces of passion. She had no brush or comb, so she did the best she could with her tangled hair by using her fingers. Then she turned her attention once more to her escape.

First she had to find some clothes, she decided as she knelt before the chest that had contained Jason's shirt. With one of her hairpins, which she found on the floor, she set about trying to pry open the lock.

After a quarter of an hour and a broken fingernail, she gave up in frustration. The heavy lock proved impossible to budge, and she was shivering because the quilt kept slipping off her shoulders. Rubbing her arms, Lauren looked around the cabin again. The desk! Of course. She should have first searched the desk for the keys.

She managed to open the top drawer with the hairpin, but there were no keys among the various papers and rolled parchments. She was about to close the drawer and try another when she noticed a familiar handwriting on one of the letters. She froze, her gaze drawn to the scrawling signature. *George Burroughs*. The name leapt up at her like a rabid dog, snapping and snarling and dripping its poisonous venom.

For a long moment, she couldn't move, couldn't think. She simply knelt there, staring with cold fear, her pounding heartbeat echoing loudly in her ears. Finally she reached a trembling hand for the letter.

It was dated a few years earlier and concerned the sale of a ship—an East Indiaman in the Carlin Line—and it was addressed to Jason.

Lauren wasn't aware of the angushed denial that escaped her lips, or that her cry could be heard outside the cabin. She didn't want to believe that Jason was connected with her hated guardian. Yet here was irrefutable proof that he was taking orders from Burroughs.

161

Pain knifed through her as she realized the full impact of Jason's betrayal. He had lied to her! He had tricked her, just like Jonathan Carlin had tricked her mother, proposing to her, making love to her, when all he had wanted was the Carlin ships. What a stupid fool she had been! She had been so concerned with protecting him, yet he must have known about the deception all along. It was even possible that he had ordered those men to kill Matthew.

Lauren shuddered, realizing suddenly the danger she faced. If they needed "Andrea Carlin" alive in order to maintain control of the Carlin Line, then Jason probably meant to return her to England where she would again be in George Burroughs's power. And if they had found some way to do without her, they might consider it wiser to be rid of her altogether. Then no one would be able to expose the deception. Either way, her life was in danger.

The rapid pounding on the cabin door made Lauren jump. She looked around wildly for a place to hide or a weapon to arm herself, but Tim Sutter burst into the cabin before she could move.

"Crimes!" he breathed, drawing up short. He looked shocked to find her kneeling on the floor, the quilt slipping from her bare shoulders. And the deathly pallor of her face must have alarmed him, for he immediately grabbed the brandy decanter from the desk. "Lord, please don't swoon, ma'am," Tim pleaded, kneeling beside Lauren and holding a glass to her lips. "Here, drink this. You'll feel better."

"No, I don't want it. . . ."

In spite of her protests, he managed to force some of the liquor down her throat, which made Lauren choke and gasp for breath. The burning spirits revived her color, however, as well as her wits, and she realized she would have to overpower Tim Sutter if she hoped to escape the ship.

When her gaze fell on the decanter beside her, she knew she had the weapon she needed. Not giving herself time to change her mind, Lauren grasped the decanter with both hands, closed her eyes, and swung.

The blow struck Sutter on the temple, knocking him out at once. Lauren stared with remorse at his unconscious body. She hadn't wanted to hurt him. But she had to get away—as fast and as far as possible.

She took a deep breath to steady herself, then went to the door to close it before returning to Tim's side. Although she tried to ignore the thin trickle of blood at his temple as she divested him of his trousers and shirt, her hands were shaking so badly that the task took twice as long as it should have. Finally, however, she was dressed in Tim's clothes—*sans* boots, since she decided stockinged feet would be quieter. She lifted the lantern down from its peg, intending to use it to guide her way, and slipped out of the cabin.

As she moved along the companionway, she felt as if she were reenacting one of her terrifying nightmares. She even heard voices as she mounted the steps to the main deck. But they were human voices, Lauren realized with new alarm. She and Tim Sutter weren't the only ones on board.

She doused the light automatically and dropped to her knees, her heart pounding in her throat, just as it had when she was sixteen years old and running from her guardian. When her eyes adjusted to the darkness, she could just make out two men standing near the gangplank. Neither resembled Jason Stuart, and Lauren suspected they were men who had been ordered to stand guard.

She crept silently away, edging toward the far side of the ship. She crawled over coils of rope and folds of canvas sail, and twice she collided with cables that were invisible in the curling fog.

When she reached the gunwale, she inched herself up to peer over the side. Oh God, she thought, staring at the glistening black water of the Mississippi. Why had she never recognized such a vast deficiency in her education before now?

She had always been proud of her accomplishments. She could design gowns fit for courtesans or queens, she could sing and play a skillful accompaniment, and she could make investment decisions with a shrewdness that startled even Jean-Paul. She also had learned a great deal from her friends at the casino: the art of Creole cuisine from the Negro cook, the use of firearms from Kendricks, and the complexities of the French language from Veronique.

Yet with all her efforts to make something of herself, she had never learned to swim.

Even drowning, though, was preferable to facing the terror she had left behind in England, just as it was preferable to waiting for Jason to put an end to her existence.

She threw one leg over, then the other. Then taking a deep breath, she jumped.

When the river closed over her head, she was almost surprised by her own calm. *I'm going to die,* she thought as her lungs began to feel the strain of being unable to breathe. The thought wrapped around her, embracing her, chilling her mind like the cold black water was doing to her body. The sensation was so different, yet so similar to her nightmares. . . .

Then denial welled up in her. She didn't want to die! She began struggling against the sucking forces that dragged her down, lashing out in a blind panic. Her hand struck something, a piece of driftwood, and she clung to it instinctively as her head broke the surface. Gasping, choking, she drew great gulps of life-giving air into her lungs.

Her body was racked with spasms as she coughed up water time and again, but she kept a desperate grip on her precious piece of wood, knowing it was her only salvation.

When she had recovered enough to get her bearings, she glanced over her shoulder. Through a veil of wet hair and fog, she could see the faint outline of the *Siren,* for the decks were ablaze with lanternlight. They were already searching for her, she realized when she heard the shouting. Now, more than ever, speed was imperative.

The night closed around Lauren. She floated for some time, unable to tell how far downriver the current was taking her, before nature or a kindly providence swept her close to the north bank. When she had clawed her way up the muddy incline and lay panting and exhausted upon the levee, she realized that she hadn't drifted far. And she knew where she had to go in order to find safety—Matthew.

It was only as she was making her way furtively through the dark streets of the Vieux Carré that she realized the flaw in her plan. Lila would tell Jason about Matthew, and his cabin would be the first place Jason looked when he discovered her missing.

For the same reason, she couldn't go with Matthew and Running Deer on their trading expedition. Lila knew they would be leaving before first light and she would have no trouble figuring out that Lauren had gone with them.

But perhaps she could make that work in her favor. It would entail lying, but she had to take advantage of every opportunity, for one thing was certain: Jason Stuart would come after her.

Another thing was certain, as well. She needed money, clothes, transportation, and food if she intended to leave New Orleans. The first two, Lauren knew, would be the easiest.

A short while later, she found herself knocking quietly on the door to Veronique's bedroom.

It eventually opened, and Veronique let out a startled gasp when she saw Lauren standing there in the light of a flickering oil lamp, her figure hidden by shapeless, overlarge masculine garments that dripped muddy water upon the polished floor. "I need your help," Lauren said in a hoarse whisper.

Without hesitation, Veronique stepped out into the corridor and shut the door carefully behind her. Then enfolding Lauren in her arms, she listened while Lauren explained about Jason being in league with Burroughs and her own need to leave New Orleans.

"Wait here, *mon chou*. I have some money in my room." Disappearing into her room again, Veronique returned with a purse which she pressed into Lauren's hands. "This is all I have with me, I regret—not quite a hundred dollars."

"It will be enough. Thank you, Veronique." As Lauren accepted the money, she tried to swallow the ache in her throat. "Tell Jean-Paul to repay you from my savings," she said shakily. "And tell Lila—" Her voice broke, but she took a deep breath to steady herself. "I doubt if I will see Lila again. Please tell her why I have to leave New Orleans. She will understand."

"But where will you go?"

Lauren hesitated, regretting that she had to lie. "North, the River Road. I'll be going with Matthew and Running Deer, so tell Lila not to worry. Matthew will take good care of me. And Veronique, thank you for your friendship. It has meant so

165

much to me. I will—"

The words died on her lips as the door suddenly swung open behind Veronique. Kyle Ramsey stood there, his huge, muscular body half naked, a sheet clutched around his hips for modesty. It took Lauren a moment to remember that he was now the captain of Jason's ship.

Her gaze locked with Kyle's, yet somehow she managed not to betray the trepidation she felt. *"Pardonez-moi, mon capitaine,"* she said with only a slight tremor. "I am sorry to have disturbed you. Veronique is *très merveilleuse* with the fishing." Lauren pointed to her very wet garments. "As you see, I am not such an expert. *Je m'excuse, s'il vous plaît?"*

Lauren turned then, holding her shoulders back and her head proudly erect, and walked away, while Kyle watched with mingled astonishment and admiration.

He didn't say a word until after she had disappeared around the corner of the corridor, and Veronique tried to distract him with her voluptuous body. "Not now, my dear," he murmured, gently disengaging himself. "Something tells me I had better return to my ship." Then he favored Veronique with a long, assessing look. "Now why could that be, do you suppose?"

Chapter Ten

"Keep your head down, ma'am," a disgruntled voice warned Lauren in a harsh whisper. "That hair of yours is as bright as a new-minted gold piece."

"Perhaps I should have worn a bonnet," Lauren retorted, although she did as she was told. Sinking down behind the protective outcrop of rock, she shielded her eyes from the harsh glare of the noonday sun. "What do we do now?" she asked Ben Howard, the guide she had hired to lead her through the Mississippi Territory.

He indicated the rifle he was holding. "We wait. We conserve ammunition and water. We pray like hell that they decide we're not worth the trouble to come after us."

"Is that likely?"

"No," Howard answered grimly. Then he gave Lauren a long, assessing look. "That scalp of yours will make a pretty trophy. You should have run when you had the chance."

Lauren shook her head, recalling the opportunity she had missed. She and Howard had traveled for nearly a week, avoiding white settlements and Indian villages at her request. They had encountered no one but a French trapper until a few hours ago when they had been attacked by a small band of Creek warriors. Howard had meant to try and hold them off, giving Lauren a chance to go back the way they had come, but she had refused to leave him. Instead, they had abandoned their packhorse and ridden north at a mad gallop. Their mounts had been nearly dead of exhaustion when Howard had spotted the rocky summit. Grabbing their weapons and a canteen, he had pulled Lauren up the bare-faced slope of the hill to the shelter of the rocks. She had loaded the rifles while Howard fired methodically and carefully at the charging band. The Indians had scattered then, and only occasionally would one leave the cover of the trees below and ride into the open—testing his range, Howard said.

For the past three quarters of an hour total silence had reigned, while the merciless sun baked the rocks around them. In the sweltering heat, Lauren could feel rivulets of perspiration running down her back and the hollow between her breasts. Her homespun cotton dress was soaked in places, and she continuously had to wipe her brow with her sleeve to prevent sweat from getting in her eyes. She thought Howard looked relatively comfortable in contrast. He sat with his back against the rock, a rifle slung across his knees. He didn't seem disturbed by the quiet as she was. In fact, he had only broken his silence when Lauren had raised her head above the rock to peer down the slope.

"Why don't you try to get some sleep?" Howard said now. "They won't try another attack until nightfall. But I don't hold much chance . . ." His voice trailed away. After a moment, he added in his slow drawl, "Have you ever seen what the Creek do to their captives, ma'am? I have. And I saw what was left of Fort Mims, after a thousand of the savage devils broke through the stockade."

He had Lauren's full attention; she looked at him questioningly. "Fort Mims," Howard repeated. "The fort north of Mobile. Only a handful of settlers escaped. The government sent Andy Jackson to put a stop to the killings. 'Sharp Knife', that's what the Creek called Jackson. I fought with him at Horseshoe Bend. We won and the Injuns had to give up most of their lands in '14, but they're still fighting the white man. Like that band down the hill. Those braves probably came from a hundred miles east of here."

Pulling a pistol from his belt, he held it in his palm. "Double barrels," he said grimly. "One for you, one for me. I never thought I would have to use it." He looked up to find Lauren watching him steadily. "Do you understand what I'm

168

saying, ma'am?"

"Yes." Her voice was low and hoarse.

"Well, it's your choice."

You will always have a choice. The words echoed in her head, but it was Jason Stuart's voice she heard. Was this what he had meant? That a quick death was preferable to suffering? She would never know. "Very well," she said slowly. "One for you, one for me."

Amazed by her calm acceptance, Howard shook his dark head. "You're the damndest woman. You're not a bit scared, are you?"

She raised her chin at his tone. "Of course I am."

"You don't look it. You're like a . . . I don't know what. Cool as an icicle, though."

At his choice of words, Lauren's lips curved in a faint smile. "Perhaps I truly am melting. I thought it was just my imagination."

It was the first time Ben Howard had seen her smile. He stared at her for a moment, mesmerized. Then recovering with a start, he busied himself untying the kerchief about his throat and wetting it with a few drops of water from the canteen. "Here." He handed the cloth to her. "We can spare it. It only has to last till tonight. How come you didn't take off when I told you to?"

Grateful for the cooling moisture, Lauren wiped her brow. "I couldn't leave you to fight them by yourself." She sent him a worried glance as a disturbing thought struck her. "Would you have stood a better chance without me?"

Howard grinned. "Nope. If you hadn't been here to reload, they would have swamped me. I s'pose I have you to thank for saving my hide."

"I . . . I am sorry for having gotten you into this."

He shrugged. "It goes with the job. But as long as we're apologizin', I'm sorry, too, for letting it come to this. It was my responsibility to keep you safe." When she did not answer, Howard said, "You mind if I ask you a personal question, Miss Demarais?"

"How personal?" Lauren replied guardedly. She had told Ben Howard almost nothing about herself, saying only that her name was Margaret Demarais.

Hearing the defensive note in her voice, Howard stretched his lanky frame out on the rough ground and propped his head up with his elbow as he considered the young woman who sat but a yard away.

Even though the sun had burned her pale complexion and there were shadows of circles under her eyes, she was still a beauty. She was curved in all the right places—the faded blue cotton dress couldn't disguise the fact that she was an armful of woman. But she held herself so stiff and proud that he had never seriously considered overstepping the boundaries she had drawn. There was an elusiveness about her, even a slight chill, that told him she wasn't for the likes of him. And her eyes were the same—beautiful, but cool and remote, like a cat's. Still, there was a kind of vulnerability about her that made a man want to protect her. Ever since she had hired him, Howard had wondered about her.

"You said you didn't want questions, I know, but I was just wonderin' why you wanted to leave Louisiana so bad. And why you picked this way, through the wilderness."

Looking away, Lauren twisted the kerchief between her fingers. "I can't answer that, Mr. Howard."

He watched her for a while. "I'm usually the kind that minds my own business, but when a man's gonna die, he wants to know what he's dying for. Someone chasing you or something?"

"No. I just had to leave."

"Well," Howard shrugged, "whatever he did, he must have been a pretty rough character."

His assumption surprised a startled glance from Lauren. "Why do you say that? How do you know I didn't steal some money or kill someone?"

"You're not the type. And you chose a murderin' band of Creek Indians over going back to New Orleans. And something had to cause those nightmares of yours. Still, looking at you, I wouldn't have guessed you to be the kind to run away. Wouldn't have thought anyone could ruffle those feathers of yours."

"Mr. Howard," Lauren said carefully as she returned his

170

gaze, "I have no wish to discuss this topic further. But I promise that if we should happen to meet in another world, I will explain it to your entire satisfaction."

His dark eyes widened perceptively as he stared at her. Then suddenly he chuckled. "I think I better go first and warn the devil you're comin'. Get some sleep, ma'am," he said when she smiled again. "It may be a long day."

It was a long day. The grueling miles of unaccustomed riding, the lack of rest during the nights when she tossed feverishly upon her bedroll, the suffocating heat and humidity, all had served to drain Lauren of strength. But although she was nearly drooping with fatigue, she couldn't sleep in the broiling sun. And even though her weary body cried out for release, her thoughts kept her awake. The afternoon stretched endlessly before her as she listened almost resentfully to Ben Howard's slow, monotonous breathing. At last she closed her eyes and drifted into a fitful doze, only to wake at dusk, stiff and sore and parched.

Ben Howard was already preparing for the attack, fortifying the cracks in the rock with stones. There was no food, but they shared a ration of water. Then he made her practice loading a long-barreled Kentucky rifle with her eyes shut to simulate darkness: priming the pan with powder from a paper cartridge, dumping the rest down the muzzle, and ramming home the greased wad of cloth that contained the bullet. When a quarter moon rose, however, she could see fairly well in the pale light. Howard blessed the lack of cloud cover, saying that at least they wouldn't be surprised by one of the savages sneaking up the hill.

She could hear them below. The strange chanting to the beat of drums made her shudder, while the intermittent war cries caused her to clench her hands and dig her nails viciously into her palms to keep fear from overwhelming her.

Suddenly everything grew quiet. The moon trailed a silver path across the sky while they waited. After a time, the silence became even more unnerving than the sounds had been. Lauren's nerves were strung so tightly that she felt sick to her stomach.

When she heard the thud of pounding hooves, she knew the

171

Creek braves were preparing to make their move. Howard shifted beside her, sighting carefully along the long barrel of his rifle.

But the explosion never came.

Nor did the expected attack.

"What the hell?" Howard finally muttered in silence. Swiftly, he moved across the narrow chasm to climb the rocks behind Lauren. He stayed there for some time without speaking, his eyes searching the darkness below. Lauren decided that if he didn't say something soon, her nerves would shatter in a million fragments.

Howard slipped coming down and cursed quietly as a small avalanche of pebbles bounced off the rocks and sprayed Lauren with a cloud of dust. Then he dropped beside her. "No one there," he whispered. "The bluff's almost sheer and impossible to climb, but I thought they might be trying to get at us from behind. Stay quiet. It's some kind of trick."

And so they waited once more. Lauren clamped a hand over her mouth to prevent herself from releasing the unbearable tension in a scream. *It isn't the idea of dying that is so frightening* was the thought that flitted through her mind. *It's the waiting.* The eternity of waiting, the uncertainty of not knowing.

Then someone called her name.

"Did you hear that?" Ben Howard whispered as the voice echoed off the rocks behind them.

"Lauren!" They heard it again. Howard raised his rifle as a shadow moved below.

"No, wait!" Lauren gasped, and gripped Howard's sleeve.

Again the familiar velvet-edged voice called out. "Jason," she breathed.

"Who's he callin' to?" Howard asked in puzzlement.

Lauren didn't reply, for the world was spinning behind her eyes. She swayed, seeing black-and-silver wheels in her vision. They shrunk to tiny pinpoints, then disappeared altogether as she fainted.

She dreamed she was floating in a warm dark sea. Contentment washed over her in silken waves as she drifted languorously in the darkness. When the familiar nightmare-specters intruded on the peace she had found, Lauren whimpered in protest. "Hush, love," a velvet voice soothed. "Sleep." A hand softly stroked her hair. The visions went away, and so did her dream.

The yellow glow behind her eyes grew stronger, widening in a circle, till Lauren felt surrounded by warmth. Her eyelids fluttered open. The pearl-gray light in the sky heralded dawn, but the glow came from a crackling fire. She recognized Howard as he bent to pour himself a cup of coffee from a pot.

Lauren closed her eyes again, savoring the warmth of the blanket covering her body. It had all been just a nightmare. She was alive. Howard was alive. The Creek warriors didn't exist. Nothing had happened. When morning came, they would break camp and continue on their journey.

She was about to drift to sleep again when a horse whickered, calling her attention to the quiet murmur of voices. Lauren sat up suddenly, raising a hand to her brow. The conversation broke off as her gaze flew rapidly around the clearing.

They were camped in a sparse forest of red gum and hickory, she saw, looking around. Their horses—several of them—were tethered to a rope stretched between two hickory trees, the saddles lined up neatly on the ground. Two unoccupied bedrolls were spread near the fire, while sitting a short distance away were two men. They were both watching her. One of them was Howard, the other, Jason Stuart.

Lauren stared at Jason in horror, her heart pounding against her rib cage. He wore a buckskin outfit similar to Howard's, and several days' growth of beard covered the well-remembered features of his face. His jaw was set in an uncompromising line.

When he rolled slowly to his feet, Lauren gave a choked gasp and shrank back. But Jason didn't approach her. He turned his back to the circle of firelight and stood silently gazing into the shadows. Ben Howard rose then, to bring her a cup of hot coffee and a plate of food.

Lauren ignored his offer, feeling stunned and betrayed. When he set the plate on the ground, she drew her knees up to

173

her chest and wrapped her arms about them, burying her face in the scratchy wool blanket. A burning sensation welled in her throat, making it ache. She wanted to cry but her eyes were dry; the pain cut too deeply for tears.

For a time no one spoke. Then Howard went down on one knee beside her. "You have to eat somethin', Miss DeVries," he said gently. "We have a long way to go. We stopped here only so you could rest, but it isn't safe for us to stick around."

Slowly Lauren raised her head, giving him a look of such anguish that he was startled. "Go to hell," she whispered. "Go straight to hell and leave me alone."

He reached out to touch her shoulder. "You've suffered a shock, ma'am, so it's understandable—"

"Yes." Lauren gave a low laugh that was tinged with hysteria. "A great shock. But I think I would have preferred to take my chances with the Indians."

"You don't know what you're sayin'. Stuart risked his hide to rescue us—"

She brushed away his hand. "And did he tell you what he stood to gain? Did he tell you about the Carlin fortune? Or did he lie to you, too? Oh, God, how could you have listened to him?"

Ben Howard shook his head. "Ma'am, I think you should hear the whole story before you judge."

"Do you, Mr. Howard? How much gold did Jason Stuart pay you? Or was it silver? Thirty pieces?"

Tossing aside her blanket, Lauren climbed unsteadily to her feet. "Perhaps *you* should hear the whole story. Four years ago I had to leave England. Did Jason Stuart tell you why? Did he tell you I was being forced to marry him? Did he admit that he was part of a conspiracy with my guardian? Damn it, because of them I've had to live like a hunted animal these past four years! Because of them—how could you have believed him?"

The voice that rang out in the small clearing was grim and edged with steel. "No one forced you to leave England, Lauren," Jason interjected. "You made that decision on your own."

Lauren whirled to face him, her hand going to her throat in a defensive gesture. Jason was watching her, but she couldn't

174

read his expression. His blue eyes were hooded and his face hidden in shadows.

What did he intend? she wondered. Would he, like her guardian, threaten to lock her up if she refused to go along with his plans? Or would he kill her now and be done with it? She was beyond caring. She only wanted to strike out at him, to hurt him the way he had hurt her with his betrayal.

"How you must have laughed," she observed bitterly. "Captain Jason Stuart *protecting* me from my guardian's men. So conveniently at hand to rescue me. I should have known you were part of it all along, especially after your sudden overwhelming desire to marry me—offered under the guise of wanting to protect me. You knew if I left, you would lose a fortune, didn't you? What did you intend by coming to New Orleans now? Were you planning on taking me back to England so I would be in Burroughs's control again? Or did you think your original plan the best—to marry me for the Carlin ships? Perhaps you want it all. How soon will I disappear after the wedding?"

Ben Howard was watching her with concerned dismay, but Lauren never noticed; her attention was focused entirely on Jason. Her voice dropped to a pained whisper. "You *lied* to me. After all that talk of honesty. Did you tell him about Matthew, Jason? How Matthew risked his life trying to defend me? God . . . they nearly killed him." She faltered, her throat aching with unshed tears. Jason must have known about Matthew, perhaps even ordered his death. And she had given herself to Jason like an unsuspecting, innocent, *stupid* fool.

She couldn't bear to face him or herself any longer. Turning abruptly, she went to where the horses were tied. For a moment she struggled with a heavy saddle before she managed to lift it to the back of the nearest animal, a chestnut with white markings. Neither man moved. Neither man spoke. The tension in the small clearing crackled like the flames of the campfire.

The silence ate at Lauren, arousing in her a perverse need to wring a response from Jason. "How did you intend to explain Matthew's death, Jason?" she asked with a vicious jerk on the saddle chinch. "How do you excuse murder?"

Jason took a step toward her, then stopped, his hands clenched at his sides. "I had intended to tell you the truth," he said slowly, "but I can see you aren't prepared to handle it. I doubt if you ever will be. When you can't face up to your problems, you run. Go ahead then. Run, Lauren. No one will stop you. But neither will anyone aid you. If you go, you go alone."

She shrugged defiantly, but then her shoulders slumped in despair. Wearily she leaned her forehead against the chestnut's neck. "Far better than going back to New Orleans where you can carry out whatever schemes you and George Burroughs have planned."

"That's another of your erroneous conclusions about the past. I couldn't return you to Burroughs, even if I wanted to, for the simple reason that he's dead."

"I don't believe you!"

"Believe what you choose. But he died of a diseased heart less than six months after you disappeared. He's buried in Cornwall, in the cemetery behind Carlin House."

Lauren whirled to face Jason again, her gold-flecked eyes full of pain. He was lying. He was telling her this so she would accompany him without protest. But she wouldn't allow him to dupe her again. She wouldn't allow him to hurt her this way again. Her fist came down hard on the saddle, even though her whispered words were almost a plea. "Damn you, I trusted you."

Jason shook his head slowly, holding her gaze with unyielding intensity. "No, you never trusted me. You don't know the meaning of trust. You *use* people, Lauren. You use whoever is available, whenever it is expedient. You used Matthew, Lila, me, Howard—you nearly got Howard killed yesterday. And if you hadn't run away in the first place, Matthew never would have risked his life. You're responsible for that, and you know it."

"No." Her denial, barely audible, was uttered without conviction. Jason had managed to strike at the heart of her guilt. She did feel responsible for endangering Matthew's life. But she wasn't at fault for trying to extricate herself from the nightmare of murder and greed Jason had conspired to create.

176

Again the pain of his betrayal raked her. "Bastard." The word was expelled on an anguished sob. "Filthy, bloody, lying bastard."

When Jason advanced another step, panic gripped Lauren. Desperately, she picked up a rifle that was leaning against the base of a tree and leveled it directly at his chest. "Stay away from me, do you hear? Don't come near me! I know how to use a gun now, Jason, and I swear, if you take one more step, I'll kill you!"

Chapter Eleven

She thought she imagined the look of pain that crossed Jason's face, for it was gone in an instant.

"Then shoot, Lauren. Aim for the heart. Unlike you, I still have mine." Jason's tone was caustic, but he stood quite still as her finger trembled on the trigger. "Or are you too afraid? You've let fear rule your life until now. Why should this be different?"

When Lauren raised the muzzle another inch, Ben Howard let out his breath in a rush. "Damn, are you crazy, ma'am? He saved our lives!"

"Why? So he could have the Carlin fortune?" Lauren was surprised to hear how calm her voice sounded, for it seemed that her whole body was shaking. She should fire the gun, she told herself. She should pull the trigger. One slight movement of her finger would end her misery. *One for you, one for me.*

Her aim wavered as she gazed at Jason. It seemed that nothing would come into focus but his eyes. They held hers, communicating silently, offering comfort that she couldn't accept from him.

But she couldn't do it. She couldn't take Jason's life, not even to save her own. She lowered the weapon and let it slip unheeded to the ground, then turned and stumbled blindly from the clearing, her breath coming in shuddering gasps. Shortly she began to run, yet when she fell to the forest floor some time later, she lay there, without the will to go on, dry sobs racking her body.

Then someone was kneeling beside her, strong arms were lifting her up, enfolding her.

"That's enough, Lauren." Jason's voice was hoarse, anguished, but she didn't care. She didn't want him to touch her. Her body gave a reflexive jerk, but his arms tightened around her, holding her against him.

"I hate you!" she sobbed, wanting it to be true.

His lips covered hers then, demanding and desperate, as if he could drive away her despair with the sheer force of his will.

She struggled, pushing against his hard chest and imprisoning arms, yet through the haze of her pain, Lauren felt heat flare between them. His mouth was hard and searing, compelling a response from her. Even the rasp of his unshaven jaw against her skin excited and aroused her. How could she hate him so much, yet feel such wild longing for him? His kiss was subduing her, draining her of the will to fight. In a moment she would surrender to him completely. . . .

When her struggles eventually ceased, Jason loosened his hold, but his lips continued moving tenderly over hers, then over her cheeks, her closed eyes.

Lauren tried one last time to pull away, pushing weakly against Jason's chest, but he pressed his cheek against her hair, murmuring, "Don't, Lauren. Don't shut me out."

For a long time, he held her, stroking her hair, soothing her trembling body, his touch gentle and patient.

Lauren at last lay quietly in his arms, and her exhausted senses gradually focused. After the rough bristle of his beard, Jason's buckskin shirt felt soft against her cheek. It was saturated with his warmth and the musky, male scent of his body, and beneath thrummed the steady beat of his heart. Lauren gave a ragged, quivering sigh. "You . . . you were right. It was my fault that Matthew risked his life."

His lips moved briefly against her hair. "You weren't entirely to blame. Burroughs's hirelings simply became over-zealous in obeying orders."

Reminded again of Jason's treachery, Lauren stiffened and started to pull away, but his fingers closed over her chin, forcing her to look at him. "I want you to believe me, Lauren. I never lied to you about knowing Burroughs. No, don't speak."

179

He pressed a finger against her lips. "Just listen for a moment. That night in London when I first met you, I had only just returned to England. You can check the *Leucothea*'s log if you wish. I remained on board later than usual that night, or I would have missed seeing you entirely. I followed you simply because I didn't like the idea of a lone woman roaming the docks after dark. I didn't realize who you were then, and everything I knew about the Carlin ships was hearsay. I had only just learned about our betrothal. Earlier that day my father had told me of the arrangement he had made with your guardian for me to marry the Carlin heiress."

Jason searched her face in the dawning light, trying to interpret her silence. "I intended to leave for Cornwall the next day to pay you a visit. To meet you and see if we could reach an understanding. I had never been enamored of arranged marriages, but the Carlin ships had always intrigued me. I couldn't turn down such an opportunity without investigating first. But when I met you, all thought of the Carlin fortune left my head. All I knew was that when you looked at me with those beautiful eyes of yours, I wanted you. For yourself, Lauren. I didn't know who you were, or what your background was, but I could see that you were in trouble. Damn it, you wouldn't even tell me your name! You were so very determined not to trust me. And when I guessed that you were really my intended bride, I started to believe in fate. I decided then that I couldn't let you leave, that you would have my protection whether you wanted it or not. I thought I was being clever, for I meant to compromise you and then present the evidence to your guardian as a *fait accompli*. You would have to marry me then, to save your reputation. Or so I thought."

She was watching him. And she was listening. He took a deep breath and plunged on. "My ineptitude put me in such a rage that my men avoided me for weeks. And when I couldn't find you, I went to the Carlin offices. I nearly killed Burroughs, for I blamed him for your disappearance."

"What did he tell you?" Lauren asked quietly.

Jason let out his breath in relief, knowing he had at least penetrated the defensive barrier she had erected between them. "Burroughs told me he wouldn't live much longer. He knew when he tried to arrange our marriage that his heart was weak. But he thought he was providing for your future. He cared for you, Lauren, in his own way. If I hadn't known that for certain, I would never have agreed to help him find you. Do you believe me?"

Her gaze was fixed on his face. There was still doubt in her eyes, but the terrible despair was gone from the green depths. "I don't know," she said gravely. "You still haven't told me why Burroughs would write you about the Carlin ships."

"Here, Cat-eyes, sit beside me and I'll explain. Kneeling like this is getting rather painful." When Jason had settled himself into a more comfortable position, he drew Lauren against him, nestling her in the crook of his arm. "I shouldn't have left you to find that letter," he observed softly. "What you saw was Burroughs's agreement to the disposal of an East Indiaman. She was one of the first Carlin ships, long past her prime. I convinced Burroughs that she was no longer making a profit on overseas routes and later sold her to a merchant who planned to transport goods from Liverpool to London."

Lauren shook her head. "That doesn't explain how you became involved with Burroughs."

"Well, before he died, Burroughs took me on as a partner. I've been in charge of the Carlin Line almost since your disappearance. The other night, on board the *Siren*, I intended to tell you about it. But somehow I was distracted."

"I thought . . . you had lied to me."

"I could have guessed by your response. Who taught you to swear like that? Not Lila, I'll wager."

When he received no answer, Jason tilted Lauren's face up to study her expression. He watched carefully as he told the story of how he had bought the Carlin ships for a hundred guineas. Lauren stared at him speechlessly during his entire explanation. "Now will you believe me," Jason said at the conclusion, "when I say I don't want you for your dowry? I already have it." His blue eyes were laughing gently, inviting her to share in his amusement. After a moment, his humor spread to the corners of his mouth and he grinned. "Regina nearly had an apoplectic fit when she realized the company was worthless."

"Regina?" Lauren said with sudden breathlessness.

"Your aunt, Regina Carlin. When you disappeared, she tried to take over the Carlin Line. She wanted to have you declared legally dead, but without proof of a body, the courts wouldn't act until an interval of seven years had passed."

Lauren shuddered as she thought of her aunt's determination. Regina would still be intent on murdering her or locking her away in an insane asylum—unless she found out the Carlin heiress was an imposter. Then it would be prison and possibly the gallows. . . .

Then Lauren realized what Jason hadn't said. Never once had he mentioned the deception or referred to her as anything other than the Carlin heiress. A shock rippled through her. *He doesn't know,* she thought. *George Burroughs never told him I'm not Andrea Carlin.*

Lauren lowered her eyes, unsure whether to be relieved. Now the charade had to continue . . . unless she were to confess to Jason. . . .

But she couldn't tell him. Even if she could forget the pain of his betrayal with Burroughs, there was always the possibility Jason was still lying to her because he wanted the Carlin ships. What kind of weapon would she be giving him to hold over her head? She would be giving him the power to send her to prison. No, there was no reason to tell Jason. Not yet. She would wait till she was certain.

Jason bent his gaze to search her face. "What are you thinking?" he murmured as he traced her lower lip with a finger.

"I . . . I was wondering about Burroughs," she equivocated. "He's really gone?"

"Yes, he's gone."

Lauren looked away, avoiding Jason's scrutiny. She had feared Burroughs, perhaps even hated him, and knowing he couldn't threaten her again raised an oppressive weight from her spirit.

"Burroughs left you his share of the Carlin Line, incidentally. Added to Jonathan Carlin's half, it makes you a very rich young woman." That comment brought Lauren's gaze flying back to Jason's. She stared at him as he continued. "As your trustee, however, I intend to abide by the original terms of your father's will. You'll inherit the entire estate when you reach the age of twenty-one, or whenever you marry, whichever comes first."

Lauren was too astonished to even protest that she didn't want the Carlin fortune, for she realized what Jason's revelation implied. "Do you mean to tell me," she asked incredulously, "that *you* are now my legal guardian?"

"I'm afraid so, Cat-eyes. But I know your opinion of guardians, and I confess I've never particularly cherished the idea of having you for my ward." He gave her a grin, his blue eyes dancing. "As far as I'm concerned, you're old enough to be in charge of yourself. I do plan to retain control of your fortune for the time being, of course, but you needn't fear that I'll adopt any of Burroughs's methods of forcing your submission."

When Lauren finally found her tongue, her own eyes were flashing with anger. "No, you have your own means, don't you? Like leaving me without any clothes."

"Well"—Jason's grin broadened—"I was trying to be clever again. You can see how far it got me. And poor Tim Sutter is abed with a broken head."

His reminder immediately deflated Lauren's ire. "Was . . . was he badly hurt?"

"Not from the crack you gave him. But I imagine he's still smarting from my tongue-lashing. I would have discharged him if I hadn't had known from personal experience how slippery you are. Do you realize this is the first time I've even seen you in daylight?"

"I . . . it doesn't seem possible."

"No, it doesn't, does it?" Jason raised a gentle hand to brush a tendril back from her forehead, but dropped it when Lauren closed her eyes. "I think you need some time to take this all in," he observed. "Howard was right—you've sustained a shock, and you're physically exhausted. But it's unwise for us to linger here any longer. I wouldn't put it past that band who held you hostage to decide to follow us. You can rest tonight. There will be time later for us to talk on the trail . . . if you

183

return to New Orleans. Will you come?"

There, he was doing it again, Lauren thought. He was giving her a choice. But there really was no choice. She hadn't the stamina or skill to survive in the wilderness, and at the moment she was too tired to offer further resistance. Later, when she had regained her strength, she would decide what needed to be done.

She nodded, knowing nothing had been settled.

Jason got to his feet. "Come," he urged, reaching out a hand to her. "Howard will be waiting for us."

Lauren hesitated, still not quite trusting Jason or his motives. But then he smiled and the tenderness in his blue eyes reassured her.

She took his hand, for the moment giving herself into his care.

Lauren spoke little the rest of the day, for keeping her weary body upright in the saddle required her full concentration. Jason had offered to take her up with him on his horse, but she declined. She didn't want to be that close to him while she sorted out her confused thoughts.

That Jason was obviously a wizard at persuasion, she couldn't deny. One moment she had been screaming at him and throwing curses at his head, nearly determined to shoot him, and the next she was in his arms, allowing him to convince her that her suspicions were unfounded. She couldn't even say why she was inclined to believe him when she had so many reasons to doubt.

Their party generally rode single file with Jason in the lead, though when the sparse forests gave way to level coastal meadows, Howard urged his horse up to ride abreast of Jason. The men's quiet laughter sometimes drifted back to Lauren, but in the sultry heat she didn't have the energy to wonder what the two of them were discussing.

In a vague way she realized Jason was waiting for her to come to grips with the situation. Frequently he would glance over his shoulder and give her an encouraging smile that bolstered her flagging strength, but he was obviously determined to leave her alone. He made no move to approach her, even when they stopped to rest the horses.

Lauren was grateful for his restraint. She was far too exhausted to keep her wits about her.

That night when they made camp, she didn't even wait for supper before crawling gratefully beneath her blanket. She fell asleep at once, not waking until Howard shook her the next morning.

She felt greatly refreshed by her long sleep and ate hungrily at breakfast, even managing a smile when Jason teased her about her appetite. It was a congenial group that broke camp, and Lauren occasionally made an effort to join in the men's conversation.

That day, they stopped before dusk because Jason wanted fresh meat for their supper. He went hunting at once, which satisfied Lauren, for she wanted a private word with Ben Howard.

They set up camp beside a stream flanked by cypress and cottonwood trees, and while Howard tended the horses, Lauren mechanically began to make preparations for the evening meal: placing dried beans in a pot to soak, putting coffee on to boil, arranging a spit for whatever game Jason brought back, and pressing moistened cornmeal into flat little cakes before wrapping them in leaves and laying them in coals to bake, the way Running Deer had taught her.

When Lauren broached the subject of her previous outburst, however, Howard casually shrugged off her apologies. "I've been told to go to the devil more times than I can recall, Miss DeVries. Though maybe not by someone as . . . as ladylike as you." He flushed slightly when Lauren raised an eyebrow. "Maybe I shouldn't say this, ma'am, but I'm mighty glad things worked out the way they did. If it hadn't been for Stuart . . ."

"I know," Lauren said softly. "'One for you, one for me.' What happened that night?"

"Not much. Stuart sent those Creek devils packing, and after you fainted, he came up. For a minute there, I think I wanted the savages back. He wasn't very happy about finding you unconscious with me holdin' you. But we got that cleared up. He thought it best we get the hell . . . not stick around. You rode double with him for a few hours. Then he decided to make a temporary camp 'cause you were whimpering in your sleep. You know the rest. But it's a good thing the Shawnee and Creek are friendly to each other."

Lauren gave him a puzzled look.

"The Shawnee live up north in the Ohio valley, but their tribes move around a lot. Some of 'em even get down this way to the Mississippi Territory. They have dealin's with the Creek, even share the same villages sometimes."

"That still doesn't explain how Jason managed to send them away."

"He used to trap near a tribe of Shawnee. Said his partner had a Shawnee wife and he learned some of their customs from her. I don't know quite what he said to those Creek warriors, but it was enough to rescue us—and our horses and packs, too."

At the mention of their rescue, Lauren remembered the accusations Jason had made. He had said that she let fear rule her life and that she used people. Perhaps it was true. Certainly she had put Ben Howard in danger along with herself. He might have lost his life trying to help her, just as Matthew had nearly done.

Lauren considered Howard thoughtfully. She hadn't even paid him the entire salary he had earned, having spent most of Veronique's money on horses and supplies for the trip.

"Mr. Howard?" Lauren said quietly. "I'll pay you the rest of what I owe when I get back. I don't have quite the full amount with me at the moment."

Howard shook his head. "That won't be necessary, ma'am."

"But I insist."

He ran his fingers through his hair as if he were suddenly uncomfortable. "Stuart's already taken care of that. More than generous, he was. Why don't you talk it over with him?"

Lauren decided not to press further. "Perhaps I will," she replied before retreating into thoughtful silence once more.

When Jason returned, she found her gaze continually straying to the stream where he was cleaning the rabbits he

186

had brought back. Even though his features were shadowed by a golden-brown stubble, he looked nowhere near as unkempt as she felt. He wore the buckskin clothing of the native Americans with a natural grace, and appeared as much at ease in the wilderness as any warrior. Try as she might, though, she couldn't picture Jason—with his aristocratic blood, his vivid blue eyes, and almost fair hair—associating with Indians. The slashing dimples in his cheeks were prominent at the moment, for he was chuckling softly as he listened to something Howard was saying.

Jason looked up then, meeting Lauren's gaze, and as she stared into azure eyes that were dancing with laughter, she suddenly decided she was wrong. Jason Stuart would be at home no matter where he was, enjoying whatever life he chose. And he would choose, she was certain. No buffeting by circumstances for him. He would be master of his own fate, whatever his situation. He had more than just physical power; one could almost feel his inner strength. He radiated confidence and control.

Lauren felt inadequate and insecure in contrast. And yet, when Jason quirked a brow at her serious expression, his look one of teasing concern, an unexpected warmth filled her, and she suddenly felt almost capable of conquering mountains, past and future.

"What are you contemplating, Cat-eyes?"

His question caught her off guard. Unwilling to admit she had been pondering the strange effect Jason had on her, Lauren prevaricated. "I was wondering how you managed to follow me from New Orleans."

An amused grin curved Jason's mouth. "It wasn't easy. After finding you gone, I headed north toward Natchez and managed to catch up to Matthew and Running Deer on the River Road, only to discover they hadn't seen you. By the time I returned to New Orleans, though, Kyle Ramsey had picked up your trail. Your height is difficult to disguise, and the stableboy where you hired your horses remembered you."

"Thank the Lord," Howard interjected.

"Yes," Lauren added quietly. "Thank you for coming."

187

"My pleasure. But I'd be grateful if in the future you would avoid situations that require me to rescue you. This last time scared ten years off my life, and I've only so many to waste."

The teasing smile on Jason's lips invited her to share his laughter, but the challenging light in his blue eyes made Lauren aware that he was quite serious. Recalling the debt she owed him, she felt rather small. She was glad when Howard entered the conversation again and changed the subject.

That night Howard's snoring woke Lauren from a restless sleep. A sliver of moon bathed the campsite with light, and as she sat up, she saw that Jason's bedroll was empty. Throwing off her blanket, she went in search of him.

She found him a hundred yards upstream. He was sitting with his back against a cottonwood tree, one arm resting across his upraised knee, a rifle beside him. He watched her approach in silence.

When she received no invitation to join him, Lauren seated herself beside Jason and nervously smoothed the skirt of her gown. She had planned what she wanted to say; she intended to end his claim to her once and for all. Yet she was reluctant to disturb the peaceful silence. Silvery darkness surrounded them, while stars shone with brilliant intensity, lacing the sky like interwoven strings of diamonds. The night was warm and still, with only the hum of crickets and the deep, resonant croak of a bullfrog to provide a backdrop to the beating of her heart.

Wondering why he remained so silent, Lauren glanced up at Jason. His strong profile was etched in moonlight, his expression schooled into impassivity. She placed a hand on his sleeve and was surprised by the tension she felt flowing beneath her fingers.

"I promised you a night," she said quietly. She could hear the momentary cessation of Jason's breathing, but he didn't respond. Slowly she reached up to unfasten the buttons on the front of her gown.

"That's far enough, Lauren." His voice was low and taut, as if he didn't trust himself to speak.

Her hand stilled as she searched his face. His jaw was

188

clamped, while a muscle flexed beneath the surface.

"But I intend to repay you for saving my life."

"I was afraid you would reach that conclusion. I'll have to decline, I'm afraid."

Faintly bewildered, Lauren stared up at him. "You saved my life. I don't want that hanging on my conscience."

Jason muttered a soft oath as he rose to his feet and stalked off a few paces, flexing his fists. Lauren's gaze followed him. She could sense the tight control he exercised over himself, could hear the tension in his voice when he said, "You don't owe me, Lauren. And certainly not for preventing you from being taken captive. I would have done the same for a stranger."

Lauren rose slowly, keeping her attention fixed on Jason. "Those Indians would not have taken us captive. Ben Howard was going to shoot me first and then himself." She heard Jason's sharp intake of breath before he turned to face her. "So you did save my life, Jason. Just as you once provided me with the means to escape my guardian. And I'm indebted to you, whether you admit it or not. I should like to cancel that debt once and for all."

She reached up and loosened her hair from its pins, then shook her head, sending the gleaming tresses flowing down her back. Jason thought she looked like some pagan goddess offering herself to the moon. Her pale skin reflected the luminous rays, while her shimmering hair shone more silver than gold. It required a great effort for him to relax the rigid muscles of his fists.

"Well?" she challenged. "What are you waiting for? Are the terms not to your liking?"

He raked a hand through his hair, as if he were fighting for control. "No, the terms aren't to my liking. But I would refuse them under any conditions. I have no intention of bargaining for your body again."

Lauren raised her chin stiffly. "You were willing enough before."

"When I thought I was one among many who sought your favors, yes."

189

"Very well, so you won't accept payment for saving my life. But I still owe you one night."

"I don't intend to hold you to our bargain."

Lauren felt a flush of humiliation creep into her cheeks. It had never occurred to her that Jason would refuse her or that she would have to beg him to make love to her. "Don't you want me?" she said in a small voice. "You refused to take any money in payment—"

"Of course I want you," he returned thickly. "More than I've ever wanted any woman." He moved closer, as if he couldn't help himself. Placing a finger under her chin, he tilted her face up. "Understand me, Lauren," he said softly, hoarsely. "It isn't you I'm rejecting. You threaten my very sanity with your beauty. I ache with wanting you, with wanting to stir that singular fire in you. But I won't take you in order to settle some imagined debt."

Lauren stared up at him, into eyes that glinted like molten silver, and a familiar shiver of awareness ran through her. His warmth was overwhelming her senses again, stirring an urgent hunger within her. She knew then that she had been deceiving herself. She *wanted* Jason to touch her, to caress her as he had before. She wanted his hard body pressing against hers, his heat enveloping her. She wanted him, with a fierceness that shocked her.

"But what if," she asked breathlessly, "I said that I wanted you as well?" That much was true. Her blood was racing at his nearness, her body throbbing with need.

His hesitation was perceptible. "I would be honored . . . and pleased by your honesty. But it wouldn't make any difference. I won't make love to you."

He stepped back a pace then, putting a safer distance between them, and the finality in his action moved Lauren to anger. "I swear I don't understand you!" she exclaimed. "I've been offered a fortune for what you just refused."

The corners of Jason's mouth twitched. "I don't doubt it. I offered you one myself, you will recall."

Lauren's temper soared when she heard the laughter in his voice. "Was I too immodest, is that it?" she said sarcastically.

"Do you prefer your women more reluctant?"

"No, Cat-eyes, but I have a responsibility toward you now."

"That's precisely what I'm trying to end."

"Sweetheart, what kind of guardian seduces his own ward?"

That gave her pause. Staring at him, Lauren realized Jason intended to take his self-imposed role seriously. But then she mentally dismissed his claim of guardianship. Perhaps he was the trustee for the Carlin Line, but he had no right to control her. No man had that right. "You aren't my guardian," she replied tightly. "I don't acknowledge your authority."

"Even so, a gentleman doesn't make love to young females of good breeding—especially not one under his protection—without benefit of marriage."

"I didn't expect you of all people to give me a lecture on morality."

Jason slanted her an odd look before he returned to his station under the cottonwood. Lowering himself to the ground, he stretched his long frame upon the grass and propped his head up with his hand. "I said nothing of morals, Lauren," he finally replied. "But I rather fancy passing my name on to my children."

"What are you talking about?"

"Illegitimacy has always had a certain . . . stigma, wouldn't you say?"

Startled, Lauren glanced down at him. Did his question mean that he knew about her past after all? He was watching her intently, his gaze seeming to bare her soul.

"If I recall," Jason said slowly, "you weren't exactly overjoyed by the prospect of marriage to me. You drugged me the first time I proposed. I presume you haven't changed your mind?" When she didn't reply, he smiled faintly. "And I have no wish to sire any bye-blows, no matter how much I desire you. We therefore find ourselves at an impasse, wouldn't you say?"

Lauren let out her breath, realizing that he wasn't talking about her own illegitimacy. Trying to seem nonchalant, she shrugged her shoulders. "I know how to prevent pregnancy."

Jason raised an eyebrow. "And you came prepared?" His

191

teeth flashed in a maddening grin. "I didn't think so. Therefore, it will have to be abstinence. But my frustration will be far easier to bear, now that I know you're suffering as well."

"I'm not suffering! Except perhaps because I must endure the dubious pleasure of your company."

"No one is forcing you, sweetheart. You can always find your way back to camp."

Lauren fell silent. Was he sending her away, or was he merely reminding her she had a choice? She couldn't tell by his expression. Well, she would choose. With a stubborn twitch of her skirts, she sank down upon the grass.

She refused to acknowledge Jason's chuckle. But even though his amusement annoyed her, she was unaccountably relieved that he had refused her as payment for saving her life. Somehow it would have cheapened the value of her offer had she given herself to him under those terms. And more obscurely, she realized that such intimate physical contact would only have served to strengthen the bond that seemed to be developing between them, and it wouldn't do to become too dependent on him.

Yet she didn't want to be alone just now. Pillowing her head on her arm, Lauren settled herself beneath the star-filled sky. The quiet of the night swept over her, filling her with a strange peace. Her contentment, though, had less to do with the beauty of the night, she knew, than because Jason was near. She could feel his warmth, his strength, even across the space that divided them.

After a time, Lauren turned her head so that she could see Jason. He was pulling idly at a blade of grass, but he was still watching her. Lauren's pulse quickened when she saw his gaze fixed on the curve of her bosom. She knew instinctively that he was remembering what was hidden beneath her cotton bodice.

She stirred as a responsive tightening of her nipples caught her by surprise. The memory of Jason's hands cupping her breasts, his mouth working magic, returned to her with stunning clarity.

Her slight movement elicited a similar reaction in Jason, for he shifted slightly, his eyes dropping the length of her body. The hot sweep of his gaze sent a sharp thrill through Lauren.

192

She could sense if not see the sudden flare of undisguised lust in his eyes, and realized that Jason wasn't as indifferent as he pretended. For a brief moment, she even wondered if he would change his mind about making love to her. But she knew he wouldn't touch her again unless . . . unless what? What was it he expected of her?

She would have to consider it.

Chapter Twelve

Lauren buried more deeply under the blanket to ward off the early morning chill. Remembering vaguely that Jason had carried her back to camp sometime before dawn, she recalled that he had kissed her then—no more than a soft brush of his lips, but his warm mouth had stirred memories of that night in his cabin when he had made love to her. The resultant dream she had experienced had left her body flushed and aching.

It didn't help her equilibrium either when she opened her eyes to find Jason standing half-naked only a few yards away. He was engaged in the very masculine, very personal, and very intimate act of shaving. He must already have washed in the stream, she decided, for he wore no shirt, and drops of water on his bare back and shoulders sparkled in the morning sunlight.

The blatant sensual appeal of his magnificent physique held her spellbound. She watched the play of hard muscles beneath smooth bronzed flesh, and in spite of the chill, felt herself growing warm.

As if he sensed her absorption, Jason glanced over his shoulder. When he met her gaze, Lauren was unable to look away. She was caught by the magnetic attraction of those startingly blue eyes.

"Good morning." His tone was soft, amused, and it brought Lauren to her senses, making her realize how intently she had been staring.

She blushed hotly as she threw off her blanket and rose abruptly. She avoided looking at Jason as she went to kneel

194

beside the stream, and after twisting her hair on top of her head, splashed water on her face, trying to cool her flushed skin.

She heard Jason's chuckle before she realized that he had come to stand beside her. Lauren lifted her head slowly, her gaze rising from his soft leather moccasins to the deerskin trousers that encased his long, steel-muscled legs and lean hips. Her eyes widened to see the strong bulge below the waistband of his pants, for it left no doubt of his virility. They widened further when she looked up to see Jason grinning down at her. His face was clean-shaven, his hair damp and curling. The sparkle in his eyes was half humorous, half mocking.

"It doesn't help, does it?" he taunted softly.

Embarrassed color stained Lauren's cheeks as she realized he had read her thoughts. "I am sure I don't know what you mean," she managed to respond with dignity.

"Oh, I think you do, my sweet." Jason's voice lowered to a husky murmur as his eyes held hers. "And there's only one way to cool your blood—and mine. Let me know if the strain proves too great." He turned away before Lauren could find her tongue.

She clenched her teeth as she returned to her ablutions. Cool her blood, indeed! Did he think she had no control over her own body's responses?

Lauren stayed by the stream until all trace of warmth was gone. By the time she rose, her teeth were chattering and her lips were tinged a faint blue.

When she returned to camp, Jason was occupied with making breakfast. He surveyed her appearance and shook his head knowingly. "Come over here by the fire, sweetheart, before you turn to ice." His tone was so innocently considerate that Lauren felt a strong urge to slap him.

She shot Jason a resentful look as she retrieved a comb and some hairpins from her saddlebag, then settled herself on a log before the fire. "You and Howard should collaborate," she suggested with exaggerated sweetness. "Perhaps together the two of you might achieve a more original description of me."

Jason poured out a cup of coffee and offered it to her. "Howard thought you a cold fish, did he?"

"He did not—" she began. Then looking around her, Lauren realized they were alone. "Where is Mr. Howard?" she asked, sipping gratefully on the steaming brew.

"Do you miss him already, or are you merely afraid to be alone with me?"

There were blue devils dancing in Jason's eyes, and his levity annoyed her. "Neither," Lauren returned, giving him a frown that was intended to quell his marvelously high spirits. "I merely wondered where he had gone."

Jason went down on one knee to feed the fire with broken branches. "He's on his way back to New Orleans. A man who earns his living can't afford to sleep away the morning like a certain heiress we both know." Jason glanced up from his task and laughed softly at Lauren's rigid expression. "Don't be concerned that you might be indebted to me for his salary. I plan to take his fee from your inheritance."

"Why didn't we go with him?" she asked as Jason returned to his task.

"I thought we would make a more leisurely journey. Snatching a few hours' sleep each night with no time even for a proper shave isn't my idea of comfort."

He seemed determined to provoke her this morning, Lauren decided as she studied the top of Jason's tawny head. Well, she wouldn't allow him the satisfaction. She would remain calm and serene . . . and get some of her own back.

Her lips curved in a smile as she set down her cup and began to use the comb on her hair. "Did you think to ask Mr. Howard what payment I had promised him for his services?" she asked provocatively.

"Oh, no, my girl. I'll not fall into that trap again."

"Just so you understand that I'm not a . . . a strumpet. You didn't believe me when I said you were the only one who had made love to me."

"Oh, I believed you, all right. Unfortunately, that was after you had told me about your job at the casino. By that time the damage had been done."

Her comb came to a halt. "But why did you get so angry?"

she asked, puzzled. "That didn't make sense, particularly when you had just declared you were jealous of anyone who touched me. Why would you be angry to learn that I was *innocent?*"

"You're clever enough to figure that out."

"I suppose," Lauren said slowly as she began to comb her hair again, "that you felt guilty for taking advantage of me."

Jason raised an eyebrow, his eyes brimming with teasing laughter. "Take advantage of you, sweetheart, when you beat me at my own game? Not once but twice now? I will say one thing, I've learned not to underestimate you."

Lauren frowned. "Then you didn't feel guilty?"

"I felt guilty as hell for treating you so savagely. But that isn't why I was angry."

"Well then, was it because you thought Lila might find out?"

"No. In fact, she gave me her blessing."

"She did *what?*" Lauren regarded him with horror. "You didn't tell her!"

The grin Jason flashed her was positively wicked. "Tell her that you threw yourself into my arms and into my bed? That you couldn't resist me, charming devil that I am? That you lured me with your seductive wiles till I was mad with desire for you?"

In spite of her resolve, Lauren lost her careful poise. "That isn't what happened! You kidnapped me and forced me on board your ship. You pressured me into feeling guilty because I had reneged on our original bargain. You insulted me by throwing a bag of gold at me, saying I looked and behaved like a . . . a . . . trollop!" Her voice rose. "You duped me into believing you cared what happened to me. Then you pretended to know nothing of my guardian and left me a prisoner on your ship, without a stitch of—"

"You deserved it all you know," Jason interjected casually. "And it's your ship."

Lauren gave him a startled look. "Mine?"

"The *Siren,* named after you, by the way. One of the Carlin Line, along with some thirty-odd others."

"And you made me lose my temper," she added lamely, her thoughts spinning.

Jason smiled. "And that, I suppose, is the greatest of all my sins? But at least now you don't at all resemble a cold fish, mayhap a fishwife. . . ."

Lauren hardly heard the jibe. She hadn't yet wanted to face the problem of what to do with the Carlin inheritance. She would refuse to accept it, of course; the Line had caused too much bloodshed and heartache already. Besides, she was capable of supporting herself now. But her more serious problem was Jason himself. It seemed that he truly meant to set himself up as her guardian, yet she had no intention of letting him dictate to her.

She caught her lower lip between her teeth. "You realize, of course, that the idea of you being my guardian is perfectly ridiculous."

"I quite agree. I would far rather be your husband."

There was a long, shocked silence.

Looking up, Jason blandly met Lauren's startled gaze. "And not," he said with emphasis, "because I'm after your inheritance. I do have some wealth of my own—certainly enough to deny the charge of being a fortune hunter."

Hoping that he was jesting, Lauren made a desperate attempt at recovery. "*Are* you pursuing me, Mr. Stuart?"

"Are you running, Miss DeVries?"

Lauren raised a hand to her brow, wondering why all her encounters with Jason left her breathless and shaken. "You are deliberately trying to confuse me."

"Not at all." Then he added casually, "We could be married as soon as we return to New Orleans."

Lauren stared at him, her mouth half open. If he intended to keep her off balance, he was certainly succeeding. "I don't wish to marry you," Lauren at last said slowly. "But even if I did, I don't understand why you should want to marry me."

"You really don't know?"

"No." She shook her head. "No, truly."

Jason rose then, and dusted off his hands before he came to stand before her. He stood looking down at her for a long moment, his expression suddenly quite serious. Lauren held her breath.

"Then I'll show you," he said softly. Reaching for her

hands, he drew Lauren to her feet. Then he bent his head, slowly, almost as if he were afraid of what would happen.

Lauren watched, spellbound, as Jason's sensuous mouth moved closer. The clean scent of his shaving soap assailed her senses, making her lightheaded. When his lips touched hers, she realized exactly what he had meant. The warm, arousing current that flowed between them was almost tangible. And it was growing. It was powerful enough to sweep away rational thought, to melt any resistance. . . .

Lauren was trembling when Jason pulled away. She opened her eyes and stared at him dazedly. His eyes had darkened to a midnight shade, and his voice, when he spoke, was as husky as hers.

"Don't tell me you didn't feel that, Lauren."

Lauren found it difficult to breathe, let alone speak. "That . . . was just physical attraction . . . merely . . ."

"Lust?" Jason supplied with a grin. "I beg to differ, Cateyes. No other woman ever succeeded in turning my vitals inside out with just a kiss. Whatever there is between us is far more than lust. I don't have a name for it, but I wouldn't mind spending a lifetime trying to discover what it is."

She couldn't name it, either, but it was there—a magnetic, vibrant force that drew them together. That same force had been working between them since the first moment they met.

When Lauren made no reply, Jason said softly, "Perhaps now you can see why it was a mistake for me to make love to you. It's doubly hard for me now, being so close and yet so far, having been given a taste of the wine but denied the pleasure of the full cup."

Lauren remained staring up at him. After a moment, Jason's hands dropped from her shoulders. "I think I'll take a turn at the stream," he announced. "You did say the water was cold, did you not? Maybe I'll get lucky and discover it has turned frigid."

Jason didn't seem disturbed by her refusal of his marriage proposal. Nonetheless, Lauren felt unaccountably depressed as she rode beside him that day. The sultry weather continued, as well, making the journey even more miserable. There seemed to be no way to avoid the heat, even when they paused in the shade to rest the horses.

Lauren was rewarded for her uncomplaining fortitude, though, when Jason pulled up well before dusk, declaring they would spend the night there. Her spirits lightened considerably when she spotted the deep, blue-green pool fed by an underground spring. The idea of a bath after the miles of hard riding in the scorching sun was infinitely appealing. Just that morning she had exchanged her faded cotton gown for a fresher one, but it would be a joy to remove all the layers of grime and sweat that had accumulated since then.

After they set up camp, Jason affably volunteered to stand guard for her while she bathed. He settled himself in the shade of a willow tree where he could be close to Lauren, yet still keep his back turned. When he didn't hear any telling splashes, though, he glanced over his shoulder and found her searching the water. "What are you doing, Cat-eyes?"

"I'm looking for the shallowest spot. I don't know how to swim."

There was an ominous silence. "Do you mean to tell me," Jason said, his tone soft and threatening, "that you jumped ship in the Mississippi and *you can't swim?*"

Lauren cast him a startled glance. He had risen to his feet and was moving toward her, his expression thunderous. Involuntarily she took a step backward as an iron hand closed around her wrist.

"Damn it, Lauren, you're lucky to be alive. Don't you know how treacherous the currents of the Mississippi are? That river has an undertow that could drown an ox!"

She stared up at Jason, bewildered by the blazing fury in his eyes. "I'm sorry," she stammered.

"Sorry! Sorry that you could have killed yourself? You have to be the greatest idiot alive. Anyone in his right mind would have stayed the hell away from that river."

Realizing suddenly that his anger was due to concern for her, Lauren felt an odd pleasure at his reaction; she was conscious of a deeply feminine sense of satisfaction that a strong male should want to protect her. "I won't do it again, I promise," she said in a small voice, wanting now to placate him.

"Devil take it, what do you think you're doing right now? That pool is deep enough to be over your head. And you can't swim!"

"I'll be careful, Jason."

"What good will that do? I'll still be forced to watch you to ensure you don't drown!"

"Is that why you're angry? Because you'll have to *watch* me?"

She knew, even before she heard his growled oath, that she was right. Lauren returned Jason's gaze unflinchingly as he glowered at her. He still looked like he might explode, but she wasn't intimidated any longer. Indeed, she could hardly refrain from laughing, he was so obviously reluctant to see her without her clothes.

The opportunity to repay him for his provoking remarks of that morning was too great to resist. Her lips curved in a roguish smile as she reached up and slowly began to unbutton her gown.

Jason clenched his teeth, his eyes narrowing at her in suspicion. "Is this my punishment for last night?"

"No," Lauren replied sweetly. "For this morning. But I find it surprising that you should ask, since you always seem to be able to read my mind."

"I can only guess," he grumbled. But his tone had lost its fierce edge, and knowing that she was safe made Lauren more daring. She leaned closer to Jason, almost brushing the hard wall of his chest with her breasts.

"Then tell me what I'm thinking now," she murmured, deliberately using her huskiest voice.

When she ran a fingernail languorously along the line of his clean-shaven jaw, Jason jerked his head as if he had been burned. Lauren's eyes widened with demure innocence. "I only wanted the soap, Jason. May I have it, please?"

He blinked, then slowly shook his head. "I ought to turn you over my knee," he muttered, rueful exasperation lacing his voice.

She smiled up at him provocatively. "But you won't."

201

As Jason fetched the soap from his saddlebag, Lauren found great satisfaction in teasing him further about his modesty. Fortunately, though, her remarks served to deflate his anger rather than increase it. She could tell by his twitching lips that he was struggling to maintain his grim expression.

He handed her the bar and spun her around, giving her a gentle push in the direction of the pool. "Make haste, wench," he commanded with mock gruffness. "Stay close to the edge and yell if you start to drown, for I don't mean to watch you bathe. I find it hard enough to keep my resolve without seeing you flaunt your beautiful body."

Returning to his spot beside the willow, Jason made himself comfortable, then addressed Lauren over his shoulder. "Incidentally, that puritanical gown of yours is hardly better than nothing at all. Makes a man want to discover what you're hiding. Have you nothing else decent to wear?"

Lauren's answer was slightly muffled since she was pulling her gown over her head. "Only my green satin . . . and two others like it—"

"I said decent, not brazen. Don't you have anything in between? Something with a modicum of style and taste?"

"I'm afraid not." Her subsequent gasp told Jason that she had entered the water and found it amazingly cold.

"Poor girl. At least now you're rich enough to buy all the beautiful gowns your heart desires. By now Kyle should have opened an account for you in a New Orleans bank. A thousand to start with." Hearing her catch her breath a second time, Jason added, "That's dollars, not pounds."

When Lauren made no reply, he turned to eye her quizzically. He was relieved to note that although she had turned to face him, she was submerged up to her slender neck in water. Still, the pool was quite clear—so clear, in fact, that he could easily see the pale outline of her nude body. She had begun to lather her hair and her hands were poised above her head in way that made her full breasts thrust out temptingly. Jason shifted uncomfortably, trying very hard to ignore the stiffening in his loins.

Lauren didn't notice his discomfort, even though she was staring at him again. She was frankly astonished by the sum he had mentioned. But it wasn't the amount of money or even the subject of her supposed inheritance that had startled her. It was that Jason had planned for her return. She searched his face intently, not even realizing when the bar of soap slipped from her chilled fingers. "You were certain I would come back, weren't you?" she said slowly.

Jason's blue eyes locked with her wary gold-green ones. "I was only certain I would try my damndest to find you," he replied solemnly.

The silence stretched between them until Jason spoke again. "By the way, I didn't disclose your identity to anyone. Kyle already knows the story of your disappearance, but he was to make the deposit in the name of Lauren DeVries. I left it for you to explain to him why you aren't going by Andrea Carlin." There was another pause before he added, "I do hope you realize there's no longer any reason for you to remain in hiding. Burroughs is gone and Regina has no cause to harm you."

At the mention of her past, Lauren felt the familiar panic well up inside her. Perhaps she no longer had to remain in hiding, but she couldn't return to England; Regina Carlin would still be intent on locking her niece Andrea away in a madhouse. Lauren shuddered. At the very least she would face criminal charges if her impersonation were ever discovered. The threat of prison was still very real. No, her past lay buried and she would have to keep it that way. If Jason would let her.

Seeing his discerning gaze fixed on her face, Lauren stirred uneasily. Why did she always get the feeling he knew more than he let on?

When she remained silent, Jason grinned. "Isn't a thousand dollars enough?"

She was grateful that he didn't press her. Turning her back to him again, she made a show of looking for her soap. "Why is it that you always seem to be trying to give me money?" she asked lightly, trying to recover her poise.

"Probably because it's yours."

"Mine? Next you'll say the gold you offered me that night on board the *Siren* was mine as well."

Jason chuckled. "Wouldn't that have been intriguing?

Using your own money to buy your services. I should have thought of it."

Lauren ducked under the water to retrieve her soap. When she came up breathless and sputtering, Jason returned to the subject of money. "A thousand dollars should be sufficient to purchase an adequate wardrobe. Of course, you can have more if you need it. But I should warn you that as your trustee, I expect to be kept generally informed of how you mean to spend your fortune. I'd like to be certain you won't just give it away to the first man who turns your head. Like that loose fish Duval, for instance."

"I haven't allowed Felix to turn my head."

"You've certainly turned his. Lila says he offered you an extremely attractive proposition."

Lauren cast a glance over her shoulder to gauge Jason's reaction, but his head was turned. "I suppose Lila told you my life story," she muttered as she began to soap her body.

"Some of it. She also says that you're determined to be independent and that you plan to buy your own ship."

"Is there anything Lila didn't tell you?"

"I'm persistent. What do you intend to do with it?"

"My ship? I mean to go into trade. In a year or two, I'll have enough capital to start my own business."

"I would have thought Beauvais could afford to finance a loan."

"He offered, but I didn't want to become indebted to him."

"I think I'm beginning to see how your mind works, Cat-eyes. To you life is a tally sheet of debits and credits."

She could hear the faint amusement in his voice. "It wasn't Jean-Paul's responsibility to support me," Lauren said defensively, not wanting to explain her fierce need to maintain her independence.

"I suppose not, but I would have preferred you had chosen a different way to earn money. What was Lila thinking of, letting you work in a gaming hell?"

"Lila isn't to blame."

"I didn't think she was," he said dryly. "She warned me you were rather stubborn. I can see we'll have to find you some other means of employment if we think to keep you away from

204

such improper places."

Lauren tossed her head. "Improper! You, I'll warrant, didn't find anything 'improper' about a gaming house. And I'll not believe that gambling was the only pleasure you were seeking."

Jason raised an eyebrow. "I could almost imagine I detect a note of jealousy in your tone."

"Not jealousy. Envy." Lauren threw him a smile, even though he wasn't looking. "I'm envious of your freedom. You're free to do as you like, move about the world whenever you wish, chase as many skirts as you have the money and inclination to chase."

Jason tried ineffectually to smother a chuckle. "A gentleman does not 'chase skirts,' my dear Lauren. And for an heiress—an unmarried young lady, at that—your language is deplorable, even scandalous."

"Hypocrite," Lauren accused, enjoying their banter. "You've said far worse things to me. Indeed, you should accept some of the blame for corrupting me. Before you, I never knew such things as bordellos existed."

"You're determined to heap coals on my head, aren't you?" He shook his head in exasperation. "I suppose it's fortunate that you haven't moved about much in polite company. You'd set society on its ear with your talk of bordellos—and the gossips would have torn your reputation to shreds by now. But don't think I mean to abandon you. In truth, I intend to do my utmost to redeem you."

"*You* redeem *me?*" Lauren asked skeptically.

"I feel obligated to rectify the damage wrought on your character, since I was the one to lead you astray."

"Because you seduced me, you mean. You're beginning to sound as stuffy as Lila, Jason. And you can't imagine how proper she has become."

"And you're beginning to sound as if you crave vice and corruption."

"I do not!" Lauren laughed, feeling truly lighthearted.

The throaty sound made Jason lift his head. He could see Lauren's face in profile, and the soft smile that curved her lips sent a fresh surge of desire flooding through him. "Lord," he said on an exhaled breath, "it's no wonder I thought you a

205

strumpet. That siren's smile turns a man's blood to fire."

She sent him another provocative glance, tilting her head slightly, her gold-flecked eyes alight with mischief. Jason watched, mesmerized, as having finished her bath, she moved toward the bank. She was shivering and her hair was dripping wet.

"Honestly," Lauren declared impishly when she reached the water's edge, "I don't see how you can be a proper guardian. You didn't scruple to introduce me to the woman who was your mistress. Who replaced Lila, if I may ask?"

Determinedly averting his gaze from the sight of her lovely body rising from the water, Jason disciplined the arms that begged to surround her and held up a dry blanket. "You may ask. But unless you claim to be jealous, I don't intend to satisfy your vulgar curiosity. *You* weren't available, you will remember."

"And if I had been?" she asked as he wrapped the blanket around her.

Jason looked down at her then, and his lips curved in a slow grin. "I would have married you for your fortune, of course."

When Lauren's expression instantly sobered, Jason's grin deepened. "Well," he murmured, "we're making progress. Two days ago a remark like that might have gotten me shot."

"I don't see how you can jest about it," Lauren chided, frowning up at him.

"But I claim the privilege of teasing you, after all the torment you put me through." When she shivered, he gently reached up to brush a wet tendril of golden hair back from her face. "Sit in the sun, Cat-eyes. It should warm you quickly."

Lauren obeyed, settling herself on a patch of spring grass with her back to the pool. She had no intention of watching Jason while he took his turn, although to be honest, her decision wasn't motivated by modesty. Rather, she feared a return of the weakness she had experienced that morning.

For a time, she successfully managed to keep her thoughts focused on something other than Jason. But as she combed the tangles from her hair, the late-afternoon sun began to lull her with its warmth. Lauren then discovered another reason to curse being plagued with a vivid imagination.

She could see the tableau without looking: Willows trailing long tendrils of green. Fronds of palmetto and patches of coral-red jewelweed by the water's edge. A shimmering plane of aqua reflecting a cloudless sky. A muscular, perfectly formed body, magnificently virile, beautifully masculine. And her imagination carried her further: The flash of sunlight glistening on naked skin. The rippling muscles of a powerful torso. Strong, lean hands working up a soapy lather, rubbing it over a lightly furred chest. Lauren shut her eyes, trying to will away the vision.

She was relieved when a new medley of splashes indicated that Jason had finished bathing. She turned to watch him swim the length of the pool and back.

That was a mistake, Lauren quickly discovered. Even his strokes reminded her of the last time he had made love to her. Strong, sure, deep, unhurried, slowly increasing in speed and power.

He swam for a long time before making a final dive beneath the surface and coming up with a burst of spray. Then, as the waves lapped over him, he floated lazily, his head thrown back, his eyes closed. Finally he turned and struck out for the bank.

In spite of her resolve, Lauren couldn't help watching as Jason rose from the water—a magnificent male, bronzed and powerful. Again the comparison to Apollo came to mind. Sunlight glinted off his hard golden body, reflecting warming rays that buried deep in her own body, evoking a sudden aching yearning that shocked her with its intensity.

It took every ounce of determination Lauren possessed for her to look away.

When he joined her, he was wearing his deerskin breeches again, but no shirt. Her heart gave a queer leap at the sight of Jason's broad-shouldered torso. She caught herself staring at the damp sprinkling of golden-brown hair on his chest, almost able to feel the silken rasp of it against her bare breasts.

When he spread another blanket upon the grass and threw himself down, Lauren started talking in order to cover her nervousness. "You never did tell me how you rescued us from those Creek warriors. How ever did you manage it? Did you offer them a dozen scalps for our freedom, or did they recognize you for a fellow savage?"

Jason reclined on his side, supporting himself on one elbow. "My, my, Howard has been filling your ears."

"Actually he was quite impressed by your knowledge of the Shawnee, although he thinks they're almost as bad as the Creek. And he admired your courage for facing those warriors alone."

"It wasn't courage, it was desperation. I wasn't about to leave you to their tender mercies."

"What ever did you tell them to make them let us go?"

Jason grinned at her. "You won't like it."

"Please, you have piqued my 'vulgar curiosity'."

"I told them you were my woman."

Lauren felt warm color flood her cheeks at the possessive term. "And that was that? They gave you no argument?"

"The Creek have always been allies of the Shawnee," he replied, plucking a blade of grass to chew on. When Lauren continued to regard him with that mixture of archness and expectation, though, Jason raised an eyebrow. "Are you really interested in hearing the details?"

Lauren studied him for a moment, realizing that an affirmative answer would mean some sort of commitment on her part; she would be admitting that she wanted to know Jason better. But she did. "Yes," she said at last. "Yes, I am. I don't know any Indians but Running Deer." Lauren wondered if the gleam in Jason's eyes was one of satisfaction, but she soon forgot about it as he told her of the year he had spent trapping in what was now the Indiana Territory.

"My partner's wife was Shawnee, and came from the tribe led by Chief Tecumseh. Tecumseh was one of the Shawnee's greatest leaders—but more to the point, I once brought down a bear who was attempting to maul one of his cousins. In gratitude, he gave me a rather valuable knife inscribed with the tribe's symbols. It was his name I invoked when I treated with the Creek braves."

"You mean they let us go because you saved someone from another tribe?"

"It isn't as farfetched as it sounds. Tecumseh was killed in the fighting a few years ago, but his name is still highly respected. For most of his life, he tried to organize a confederacy of tribes—including the Creek—against the white man."

"You sound as if you approved of him."

Jason shrugged. "He was only protecting his people. For years American treaties had been depriving the Shawnee of their homes and hunting grounds. And the British weren't much better. They provided political advisers to the Shawnee who actually encouraged hostilities, using Indian tribes as a buffer between America and Canada. The Shawnee are fighting for survival, just like the Creek who accosted you."

"But you weren't involved in the fighting—you were a trapper. So what brought you to America in the first place?"

"I expect for the same reason you want your own ship—I needed to control my own destiny. My father had certain ideas about what was expected of a marquess's son, which I disputed frequently. The life of a pampered aristocrat never appealed to me."

Lauren regarded Jason curiously. She couldn't imagine him being under anyone's thumb, even a father as high-ranking as a marquess.

"I suppose," Jason added, "that I also wanted to prove myself. The wilderness fascinated me, and so did the simplicity of the life-style. But it was challenging, both mentally and physically."

"You sound as if you enjoyed it," Lauren observed quietly.

Jason's gaze focused on some distant point beyond her shoulder. "It was one of the happiest times of my life."

"Then why did you leave?"

He didn't reply at once. A mockingbird trilled in the nearby willow, sounding loud in the silence. "Several reasons," he said at last. "Responsibilities. It wasn't my world. England is my home and always will be. And I had no wish to cut the ties with my own family." He didn't add that he hadn't found what he had been searching for—a feeling of completeness, of purpose—and so had moved on.

His gaze settled on Lauren then, and Jason again resolved to be patient. Even wrapped as she was in shapeless dark wool, she was totally desirable. She had tucked her blanket under her

209

arms, leaving her shoulders bare. Her slender white feet and ankles showed as well, since she had drawn her knees up to provide a rest for her chin. Her drying hair spilled down her back in a golden cascade. Jason could barely resist the urge to run his hands through the silken mass.

Lauren felt the impact of his gaze like a caress. Determined to combat the effect it was having on her pulse, she changed the subject. "Those buckskin clothes of yours, is that what Shawnee braves wear?"

Amusement glimmered in his eyes. "A slightly more civilized version. Normally men wear only breechclouts in warm weather, with leggings to ward off the cold in winter. I had to give Little Eagle an extra horse to make breeches for me in place of the traditional clothing."

"She made your clothes?" Lauren's eyes widened as she wondered what else the Indian woman had done for the handsome man lounging at her feet.

"It certainly wasn't work for a man," he replied, his tone warm and teasing. "The Shawnee woman handles tasks like curing hides and making clothes. She's also responsible for the harvest and for raising the children—at least until the boys reach a certain age and are ready to test their manhood."

"The women are treated as mere slaves, then," Lauren remarked derisively.

Jason lay back on the blanket, lacing his hands behind his head. "You might be surprised to realize how much power they wield. The wife has complete control of the home—it is her word that is law. The husband's main responsibility is to provide protection for his family, but if he wants something as simple as an ear of corn for his own purposes, he must offer his wife a gift in exchange. And the Shawnee don't consider females mindless idiots as so many of our countrymen do. She can have a considerable influence on the decisions of the tribal council, and can even rule as chief of her village if she gains the respect of her people as a leader."

Lauren looked pensive. "And what must she do to gain this respect? Must she fight her enemies?"

"Certainly she must prove her abilities, but it's rarely in battle. There are any number of other ways to show bravery, courage, wisdom. But enough about the Shawnee." Jason turned his head to glance at Lauren. "We should be discussing your future. Tell me, besides having the freedom to chase skirts, what do you want to do with your life?"

"Must we talk about it now?" she protested, not wanting to spoil the magic of the afternoon. Stretching lazily, she lay back with her arms over her head and looked up at the sky. The blue had changed to soft hues of crimson and gold, heralding the setting sun and the day's end.

"You haven't considered what you will do when we get back to New Orleans?"

Lauren closed her eyes and sighed, feeling languor creep into her limbs. "It's so peaceful here," she murmured drowsily. "Maybe I won't go back."

Jason rolled on his side again, raising himself up on one elbow. His breath caught in his lungs as he took in the sight Lauren presented. Her hair was splayed over the grass in glorious profusion, while her ivory skin was bathed in a warm, golden glow. Jason's eyes moved from her face, down her smooth throat, to the beginning swells of her breasts as they rose and fell softly. How he wanted to free those lush white mounds from their imprisoning cocoon. . . . "Well, then"— he couldn't rid his voice of its sudden huskiness—"where would you like to live?"

Lauren's eyes flew open. She was startled by his question, and by the intensity of Jason's blue gaze when she saw the long, searching look he was giving her. "I plan to stay in New Orleans. Why do you ask?"

"Because the legalities of transferring the bulk of your inheritance will have to be taken care of in England. Of course, if you mean to stay in New Orleans for any length of time, I can handle the whole. But it will only be a few more months before you have charge of the Carlin Line."

"But I don't want it. I have everything I want right now."

"Everything? What about the ship you intend to buy?"

Lauren absently pressed a hand to her temple, thinking how ironic it was that she was refusing a fortune in ships. Once she had been willing to give ten years of her life to have what he was holding out to her. "That's different. That will be my

211

own business."

"Yet even if you can afford a vessel, you'll need to know how to choose a worthy one. And you'll need to know about buying and selling the goods she'll carry."

"I plan to employ an able captain."

"And you have the experience to hire one?"

"No, but I'll manage. And I won't take the Carlin Line."

Jason's brows drew together. "Would you like to tell me why?"

"I didn't earn it," she said lamely, feeling a prick of guilt at all the half-truths she would be forced to tell in order to maintain the charade.

There was a long silence while Jason stared down at her. Lauren endured his contemplation in silence, wondering uncomfortably if he could somehow read her mind. At last he said softly, "You don't *earn* an inheritance, Lauren. It is left to you. Your father meant for you to have his fortune. He stated so in his will. And Burroughs left you his share of the Carlin Line."

"I don't want it," she returned just as softly. "If you insist, I'll give it all to some worthy charity."

He paused, then shook his head. "As your trustee I would have to object. No charity would be set up to run the Carlin Line, nor would they have the expertise. Lauren . . ."

As if unable to prevent himself, he leaned closer. His face was only inches from hers, and she could feel his warm breath softly caressing her face. "Lauren," he breathed in barely a whisper, his intimate tone arousing a flickering heat in her. "I want your trust, Lauren. Your love." His hand came up, his fingertips gently brushing her cheek. "I want to share mine with you. Marry me, sweetheart."

Lauren's lashes fluttered down to cover her eyes, hiding her tormented thoughts. What he was suggesting was impossible. Even if she could forget her mother's bitter experience, even if she could convince herself that Jason wanted her rather than the Carlin ships, she couldn't accept his proposal without confessing who she really was. And she wasn't ready to trust him that much.

Besides, there was the factor of her illegitimacy. What

212

would Jason say if he knew she was a bastard? He might be a renegade, but he was still a nobleman's son. Her origins would prevent her from making a respectable marriage with a man of his station.

Carefully, she forced all emotion from her reply. "I can't marry you, Jason."

"Why not?"

"Please . . . I just can't."

His thumb moved slowly over her lips, tracing the soft outline. "You don't trust me, do you?"

Trapped by his tender gaze, Lauren gazed back at him in anguish. She didn't want to trust him. How often had she heard her mother warning her about men who would use her, then leave her? "I don't know," she admitted hoarsely.

"Lauren"—his velvet-edged voice caressed and soothed—"you are both more and less than the woman I thought you would be. But unless you've given your heart to someone else, you still have it. You're just not prepared to give it to me."

Lauren shut her eyes tightly. She wanted . . . But it didn't matter what she wanted. "No, I . . . I can't," she murmured.

Jason's sigh was audible, but then he shrugged and drew away. As if he had never deviated from the subject, he went on. "I'd like to feel confident you can handle the responsibility when I turn over the Carlin Line to you. Therefore, I'm going to take advantage of your penchant for bargaining and suggest another one. I mean to set up an office in New Orleans for the Line, but I'll need the support of your friend Beauvais in particular to establish a successful distributorship. That's where you can be of help to me. If you'll apply yourself to learning about the shipping industry so you can aid me, I'll find a merchantman for you to buy at a reasonable price and teach you how to ensure a profitable trade. Is that agreeable to you?"

Lauren searched his face, his inscrutable expression, and wondered what he intended to gain by this new proposal.

Jason gave her a brief smile. "Come now, you're not frightened by such a prospect, are you? The woman who traveled across the Atlantic at sixteen with only a hundred guineas in her pocket? The same one who helped hold off an

213

attacking band of Creek braves? The one who can look a man straight in the eye and tell him to go to hell?"

"No," Lauren lied. "I'm not afraid."

"If it will help you make up your mind, I'll agree to stop pressuring you about marriage."

That would be a relief, Lauren reflected wryly. And there were other advantages if she agreed to his bargain. She could learn a great deal from Jason, since he had experience sailing his own ships as well as running the Carlin Line. And at least his proposition offered her reprieve for a time, until she could find a better solution for what to do with the Carlin inheritance. *If* she could manage to control her attraction for Jason. . . . "Yes," she replied, determined to start at once with this last resolve.

But it seemed Jason had other ideas. He took her hand and raised it with slow gallantry to his lips, making her heart beat faster. "Partners, then?"

Feeling a surge of warmth, Lauren nervously pulled her fingers from his grasp. "Yes, partners."

"Good." Jason smiled as he reached out to trace the delicate line of her jaw with one long forefinger. When Lauren shivered, his touch became even lighter, his fingertips skimming the outer rim of her ear. Then, giving in to the urge, he let his hand trail downward to brush the vulnerable hollow at her throat with a featherlight stroke.

Lauren's gold-flecked eyes widened perceptively when Jason's caress slowly dropped lower. He meant to pay her back for taunting him earlier, she concluded. She tensed, preparing to withstand the sensuous assault that would be her punishment, determined not to give him the satisfaction of knowing how easily he could make her respond, even if her pulse was racing like she had run a great distance. But when Jason's fingers moved still lower to curve around the top edge of her blanket, Lauren couldn't pretend to be unaffected any longer. She clutched at Jason's hand. "No, enough, please!" she begged, wanting to end the game.

Jason, however, had just started. "Relax," he warned, sounding amused. "This isn't a proposal." He gave a gentle tug, and when the folds of the blanket fell apart, his sharp intake of breath was audible. "God, you still have the most beautiful breasts I've ever seen." His voice was suddenly husky, his blue eyes as warm as the rays of golden sun that kissed her naked skin.

Quivering, Lauren closed her eyes. Again that exquisite, melting weakness was assailing her, draining her of will. He drew a lazy finger along the silken valley between her breasts, a long, arousing passage that detoured to stroke the full, creamy undersides. Then he began a new pattern, rubbing light circles on her curving flesh, slow swirls that deliberately avoided the swollen, rose-hued nipples. When Lauren whimpered, Jason smiled, watching her start and shiver at his maddening caresses.

"Please, Jason . . ." She faltered, not sure she had the strength to end his torment. Her nipples were aching with the desperate need to be touched.

"Please what, Lauren?" His voice was a throaty, savoring rasp as he bent his head. "Don't arouse you? It's too late. You're as taut as a bowstring."

His lips joined the sensual attack then, nuzzling her ear, the soft skin beneath her jaw, pressing beguiling kisses along her throat, while he filled his palms with her straining breasts. When his mouth at last claimed an engorged nipple, the moist heat shocked the breath from her.

Dazed, her blood singing, she looked down and vaguely noted that one of her long tresses had brazenly draped itself over his shoulder; the gold of it glinted in the fading sunlight, mingling with the silver strands in his gilded chestnut hair.

He attended the erect and aching nipples thoroughly, his lips pulling at their ripeness, tongue plying the pebble-hard buds to rigid arousal. Mindlessly, Lauren clenched her hands, her fingers digging into the soft wool blanket, her breath coming in ragged spurts.

When Jason pressed a knee between her thighs, she realized that it wasn't a game, that it never had been. He didn't mean to stop. His hand was stroking her stomach and moving lower, stirring her passion. "But . . . you . . . said . . ." she began a feeble protest.

Shifting his position slightly, Jason let his lips follow the

215

path of his hand. "What I have in mind doesn't result in children," he murmured, his breath whispering against her belly.

Lauren gasped when he nuzzled at the cluster of blond curls between her thighs. "No, Jason. . . ." Frantically, she clutched at his hair, trying to make him lift his head. "No. What are you . . . doing?"

"I'm giving you what you wanted last night."

"I didn't . . ."

"You did." His lips danced across the portal to her womanhood, showing her exactly what he had in mind. Then he looked up into her hot, pleading eyes. "Tell me you want me to stop, Lauren, and I will."

"Oh, God." She closed her eyes, knowing she was already lost. "I can't."

Jason laughed tenderly as he gently seized her hands. Pinning them at her side, he proceeded to claim her with soft quick strokes of his tongue.

Lauren thought she would die from the piercing sweetness. She drew a long, sobbing breath, her hips arching upward uncontrollably as his tongue flicked like fire over the most intimate part of her body. She writhed, trying to escape, but Jason's hands slid under her hips, cupping her hot flesh, refusing to allow her to move. A guttural sound of satisfaction rippled from him as Lauren moaned.

He went on savoring her, alternately, lapping at her with his tongue and then drawing at her with his lips, plundering, devouring. Lauren wanted to scream when the tip of his tongue penetrated her delicate warmth. Lances of pleasure shot upward through her, destroying the last of her sanity. Her head tossed wildly back and forth as she clung to Jason, her nails scoring his sleek, muscular shoulders. It wasn't long before a sharp spasm of ecstasy ripped through her, followed by another, then another.

The echoes of her throaty cries were the only sounds to disturb the quiet of the golden afternoon.

Chapter Thirteen

During the remaining three days of their journey, Lauren discovered that Jason was entirely serious about involving her with the Carlin Line. He started by telling her of the China and West Indian trade, the foundation upon which Jonathan Carlin's fortune had been built, then described the organization of the current company which he now controlled.

Lauren was impressed by the magnitude and complexity, for she hadn't realized the firm was so large. "And you make all the decisions?" she asked as she rode beside him that first day.

Jason flashed her a grin. "Hardly any, if the truth be known. I have a reliable man to oversee most of the details, and the London office has an efficient staff. Normally I'm only required to give my approval, though sometimes I come up with an idea or two of my own."

But when Jason related some of the problems and challenges the fleet constantly faced, Lauren realized Jason was drastically understating the impact he had had on the continuing success of the Carlin Line.

"Still," she observed, "you must have found it difficult at times, managing such a vast enterprise."

"Actually it's been a great deal of fun. Burroughs taught me a great deal before he died." Noting Lauren's sudden silence, Jason gave her a speculative glance. "Burroughs was actually quite brilliant when it came to making business decisions. It's a shame that he should have been such a complete addlebrain when dealing with you. I suspect he was afraid of you."

Lauren eyed Jason skeptically. "Of *me?*"

"He was scared to death of the responsibility. I must admit he didn't handle it at all well."

"You make him sound almost human."

"And so he was, with human failings like the rest of us, Lauren. I don't expect you can ever find it in your heart—mind what I said—to forgive him. But perhaps some day you'll understand why he did what he did."

Lauren pressed her lips together, unwilling to consider the possibility or to discuss Burroughs further.

"Have you ever considered becoming a governess?" Jason asked suddenly, causing her to regard him with puzzlement. "That tight-lipped frown of yours would strike terror in the breast of the most stalwart child."

Lauren made an effort to relax, and even favored Jason with a faint smile.

"Better," he laughed. "I shouldn't like to think my new partner was planning to desert me when I need her help."

"Help?"

Reining in his horse, Jason brought their small cavalcade to a halt so he could study the trail. Lauren watched him, fascinated that he could make anything of the jumbled tracks crisscrossing the ground. He was apparently satisfied with the signs, for he urged his horse on and continued the conversation where they had left off.

"You'll understand, once you speak to Beauvais. He wanted to call me out for my behavior the night I barged into his house. I refused his challenge, of course, for I was in something of a hurry, and fortunately Lila managed to calm us both down. Even so, I'll be lucky if Beauvais considers accepting my apology for the things I said to him—the least insulting of which was to disparage his intelligence for letting you work in a gaming hell."

"But Jean-Paul had nothing to do with it," Lauren defended.

"I know, it was all *my* fault," Jason said good-humoredly. "But I'm counting on you to smooth things over with him. Actually, I liked Beauvais when I met him. He would find that quite a compliment if he knew me better. I have a strong aversion to all things French. Comes from having to keep my

218

homeland from being overrun by a pint-sized Corsican with a corpulent ego, I don't doubt."

"Does he know about your past relationship with his wife?"

At her innocent tone, Jason shot Lauren a wry glance. "Not to my knowledge—and I don't plan on telling him, either. Lila wasn't concerned about it, and that particular intelligence might have a definite effect on our profits, if not my life. Kyle thinks we need Beauvais's assistance to start a reliable distributorship." Jason then went on to explain his plan to open an office in New Orleans.

"It sounds exciting," Lauren observed wistfully, not hiding the envy in her voice.

"Rather dull stuff, actually. But I'm glad you don't see it that way, for you're to be in charge." Jason grinned when she looked surprised. "You didn't think that I would let you fail to hold up your end of our partnership, did you? You'll be quite busy, sweetheart. Worn off your feet, even. Too tired, I hope, to even think about playing the pianoforte for a melee of lecherous gamblers."

One delicate brow lifted. "And what will you be doing while I am working my fingers to the bone?"

"Keeping you out of trouble, I trust." The humorous gleam in Jason's blue eyes deepened at the arch look Lauren bestowed on him. "I get to be your adviser. And I'll also have to supervise the warehouse construction."

"Would there be any jobs for Matthew MacGregor, do you suppose? I had planned for him to captain my ship, but he says he's getting too old."

"Tell me what you know about him."

"He was once a smuggler," Lauren announced, curious to hear Jason's reaction.

His mobile mouth twisted wryly. "I don't find that difficult to believe, knowing the colorful pasts of some of your other friends. But Lila already told me that much about him. I confess I wasn't shocked. I prefer to stay on the right side of the law myself, but still, I can admire an enterprising fellow. I'm more interested in MacGregor's trading skills. His prior occupation doesn't concern me, so long as he's trustworthy now."

"Matthew has always been trustworthy," Lauren declared,

not hiding her intense loyalty. She then told Jason about Matthew's fur trade and how he had managed to develop it into a successful business.

Jason nodded thoughtfully. "You may be right. We might be wise to involve him in this venture somehow. I'll talk to him when he returns."

After that, their topics of conversation ranged widely, from the shipping industry in general, to their personal histories, to plans for the immediate future. When Jason asked Lauren about her life during the past four years, she found herself talking to him as if she had known him always. It was only later that she realized the ease with which Jason drew her story from her.

Later, when she spoke of Lila's marriage, Jason asked how she had weathered the war between America and England. Lauren told him of the impending attack by British troops two years before that had had the entire city of New Orleans in a state of panic. Even though the American government had sent Andrew Jackson to defend the city, his forces were ill-equipped and mostly comprised of civilians.

"Lila was frantic," Lauren admitted, "primarily because Jean-Paul was involved in the fighting. We were prepared to leave Bellefleur at a moment's notice if New Orleans fell, but as it turned out, there were very few American casualties, and Jean-Paul received hardly a scratch."

"While the British lost two thousand troops," Jason put in grimly.

"I know. It was horrible. They said it was the bloodiest battle of the entire war. And the terrible irony was that it took place two weeks *after* the Ghent peace treaty was signed."

When Lauren wondered out loud if the fighting in Napoleonic wars had been as fierce, Jason told her something of his own past experiences and his battles at sea. He actually said very little about the dangers he had faced, but the realization that the virile, handsome man riding beside her could have lost his life many times over left Lauren strangely disturbed.

One other thought also disturbed her: the memory of what had happened that day beside the pool. Although she tried not to dwell on it, she couldn't forget how easily Jason had aroused her and brought her to a shattering, gasping release, or the way she had surrendered without a single protest.

She had thought she was safe from his advances since he had vowed not to make love to her until she agreed to marry him. And, strictly speaking, Jason had kept his word. He hadn't taken her, nor had he had any physical gratification himself. He had merely succeeded in heightening her already intense awareness of him. Every time he came near her, she remembered the scent of his skin and the heat of his mouth, and a shaft of unwelcome desire would quiver through her—which only served to increase the tension in her body and make her even more aware of the current radiating between them.

He had been right about that, Lauren reflected uneasily as she glanced at Jason. There *was* a compelling, ever-present physical attraction between them. It existed, smoldering like banked embers, ready to flame into life at the merest touch.

Her biggest problem now would be ensuring that it never had the opportunity to do so again.

The unusual dry spell ended the next day, and twice Lauren and Jason were caught in a torrential downpour. Even so, the last miles of their journey passed pleasantly and with remarkable swiftness. When they finally arrived in New Orleans after ferrying across the Rigolets Channel, it was still raining and dusk was setting in.

That was when Lauren realized she might have made a dreadful mistake by agreeing to Jason's proposal. He took full advantage of any license implied by a partnership by refusing to let her return to the gaming house, even to fetch her clothes. Nor would he hear of her living alone in Matthew's cabin.

"I won't live at Bellefleur," Lauren declared. "I've taken advantage of Lila's hospitality far too often as it is."

"She doesn't think so," Jason returned. "Besides, I intend to stay there if Beauvais can be brought to renew his invitation."

"Maybe Jean-Paul will refuse to accept your apology."

"Lauren, I can only uphold our bargain if we spend some

221

time together."

"Then perhaps we should forget the whole thing."

"I'm sorry you feel that way," Jason replied blandly. "April is a pleasant month for weddings, don't you agree?" When Lauren scowled, he laughed. "You know, sweetheart, you're the first woman of my acquaintance who could be *threatened* with marriage."

Lauren was quite out of charity with Jason by the time they reached Bellefleur. When they halted in front of the magnificent, galleried plantation house, she didn't even wait for Jason's assistance to dismount. Giving him only a curt farewell, she ran swiftly up the wide front steps into the house. Jason stared after her for a long moment before gathering the reins of the two spare horses and starting back down the wide oak-lined drive toward New Orleans and his hotel.

Lauren had another reason, she discovered after he had gone, to be angry with Jason. Lila greeted her with the inevitable tears and remonstrations, while Jean-Paul demanded a complete accounting of what had happened.

The slender, dark-eyed Creole frowned the entire time Lauren was making her apologies and explanations, but when she had concluded her abbreviated tale, Jean-Paul directed a challenging stare at her, much in the manner of an irate father. "Where is this . . . this Lord Effing now?" he demanded.

Puzzled, Lauren glanced at Lila for an explanation. The older woman shifted uncomfortably. "Jason Stuart is a marquess now, Lauren. The Marquess of Effing."

"He promised," her husband interjected, "to do the honorable thing and wed you."

Lauren was so taken aback that she simply stared at Jean-Paul.

"He took you to his ship, compromised you—"

"Jason *told* you that?" Lauren asked in amazement, finally finding her tongue.

"*Oui!* Do you deny it?"

Lauren clamped her lips together, realizing now what Jason had meant about having Lila's blessing. Of course Lila would take his part. He had agreed to a marriage! And now Jean-Paul was adding his weight to the argument. How *dare* Jason not

222

warn her what to expect? And how *dare* he divulge anything of what had happened between them?

Trying to school her expression into a semblance of calm, Lauren nodded. "I do deny it," she replied. "Jason—his lordship—exaggerated greatly. Just because I accompanied him to his ship doesn't mean he compromised me."

"But Lauren, you were with him for several days, alone," Lila pointed out, before Jean-Paul added firmly, "He must be made to marry you at once."

Lauren stood her ground. "Jean-Paul, that is ridiculous. I have no intention of marrying him."

"He made no advances toward you, then?"

Lauren glanced at Lila and hesitated.

"I shall call him out!" Jean-Paul declared in ringing tones, gesticulating with his hands to emphasize his determination.

A similar thought had occurred to Lauren, but when Jean-Paul spoke with such conviction, she wondered if he really meant it. "Jean-Paul," she said sharply, not pausing to consider the incongruity of suddenly finding herself Jason's champion. "This talk of dueling is absurd."

"Then there must be a marriage. If Lord Effing has dishonored you, he must be made to—"

"May I remind you that you are *not* responsible for me? I appreciate your concern, but it is my future you are arranging without my consent. I shall not marry Jason Stuart, *ever*. He is merely the trustee of the Carlin Line, and he means to teach me about the shipping industry. He and I are partners for a time, that is all. I had hoped to gain your support for the new distribution system he has in mind, since Jason says you would be a great asset, but I see you aren't prepared to listen. I shall continue this conversation in the morning, when you have had ample time to adjust to the idea. Good night, Lila." With a regal inclination of her head, Lauren turned and swept from the room, shutting the door firmly behind her.

The silence she left behind was pronounced. Lila twisted her fingers together in agitation, her eyes trained blindly on the carpet. Then Jean-Paul gave a soft laugh and drew his wife into his arms. "Something troubles you, *ma chérie?*"

Sighing, Lila rested her dark head on his shoulder. "You

223

would not truly call him out . . . ?"

"Of course it will not come to that," Jean-Paul reassured her. "If his intentions were not honorable . . . Well then, that would be another matter entirely. I predict that by summer our beautiful Laurie will be safely wed."

"They would be so good for each other. But Lauren won't marry him, I know it."

"Do not worry so. Monsieur Stuart strikes me as being able to handle the matter. He has already progressed farther than I would have thought possible."

Had she heard Jean-Paul's prediction, Lauren would have hotly refuted it. At the moment she was upstiars in the elegant bedroom that was hers whenever she stayed at Bellefleur, making a vow to keep as far away from Jason Stuart as possible. It made her furious to realize how easily she had been manipulated.

She had been a fool to agree to Jason's proposition, she could see now. She had given him a decided point of leverage at no cost to himself. And now she would have to endure Lila's compulsory lectures, as well. Jason might have agreed to drop the subject of marriage, but Lila never would.

Lauren's guess was correct; at breakfast the next morning, Lila immediately launched into the arguments she had prepared.

What truly incensed Lauren, however, was the discovery that Jean-Paul had turned over her entire savings to the bank where the Carlin Line funds were deposited, effectively giving Jason control of all her hard-earned capital. Lauren lost her normally cool temper then, roundly informing Jean-Paul that she had no intention of acknowledging Jason's claim of guardianship, despite whatever papers he had to the contrary, adding that she had had enough of dictatorial guardians to last her a lifetime!

Lila broke into their disagreement then, trying to smooth over the troubled moment by pointing out the advantages of marriage to Lauren. But by ten o'clock, Lauren had listened to all she could bear of Lila's gentle attempts at persuasion and had taken refuge in the garden.

When Jason was announced by a house servant a half hour

FREE

BOOK CERTIFICATE

ZEBRA HOME SUBSCRIPTION SERVICE, INC.

YES! Please start my subscription to Zebra Historical Romances and send me my free Zebra Novel along with my first month's Romances. I understand that I may preview these four new Zebra Historical Romances Free for 10 days. If I'm not satisfied with them I may return the four books within 10 days and owe nothing. Otherwise I will pay just $3.50 each; a total of $14.00 (a $15.80 value—I save $1.80). Then each month I will receive the 4 newest titles as soon as they come off the press for the same 10 day Free preview and low price. I may return any shipment and I may cancel this arrangement at any time. There is no minimum number of books to buy and there are no shipping, handling or postage charges. Regardless of what I do, the FREE book is mine to keep.

Name _____

(Please Print)

Address _____

Apt. # _____

City _____ State _____ Zip _____

Telephone (_____) _____

Signature _____

(if under 18, parent or guardian must sign)

Terms and offer subject to change without notice.

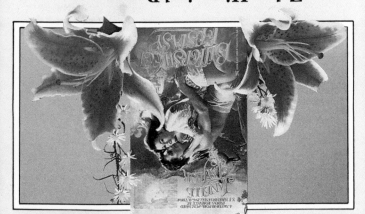

later, Lauren was still seething with indignation. The rain had stopped, but the bench where she had settled was damp, and she made a great show of meticulously brushing moisture from her skirts when she saw him approaching. He looked impossibly handsome and elegant in a dove gray coat and trousers, but she dragged her gaze away, silently deploring the way her heart leapt at the mere sight of him.

"Well, does Beauvais mean to forgive me?" Jason asked when he received a terse "good-morning" in return to his greeting.

Lauren studiously avoided his eyes, keeping hers trained on the ground. "Yes, but I shall not, my lord."

"My lord? What ever happened to Jason?" When Lauren said nothing, Jason eyed her warily. "Poor Lauren, was it so very bad? Did I err in leaving you to face the wolves alone?"

Her head remained bowed, her hands folded primly in her lap.

"Lauren, look at me, please." When she didn't respond, Jason gently grasped her chin, compelling her to meet his gaze. His heart sank at what he saw in her eyes. The glitter in the gold-green depths was cold, hard, brittle.

Those gold-flecked eyes widened innocently. "Why, whatever is the matter, Jason?"

"You tell me," he countered.

"Why, nothing, nothing at all. I enjoy being scolded and harassed and chided and coerced all morning!" Lauren twisted her head, making him release his grasp. Her voice suddenly became accusing. "How *could* you have told Lila you made love to me?"

Jason casually propped a booted foot up on the bench beside her. "I don't recall being nearly so graphic."

The hint of laughter in his tone made Lauren want to slap him. "It amounts to the same thing! And you *knew* what she would say, what Jean-Paul would say."

"Which was?" Jason prompted.

"Which was that I should marry you. Don't deny it!"

"Oh, are we engaged now? Is it acceptable for me to kiss my fiancée then?" Before she realized his intent, Jason had taken her hand and raised it to his lips.

Lauren snatched her hand away and glared. "Don't be absurd! Of course we aren't engaged. I will not marry you, now or ever. And as far as I'm concerned, any bargain we made is no longer valid."

"I never imagined you could be so easily flustered."

The teasing look Jason bestowed on her was tender and intimate, and it made Lauren clench her fists. "Damn you, Jason! I am not—" she began before she realized that her normally calm voice had risen. With an effort, she spoke more evenly. "I am *not* flustered. I just don't care to be tricked. You could have at least warned me what to expect."

"Did you stop to consider that I might have done exactly that, had you stayed to finish our conversation last evening instead of running away to sulk like a child?"

"Oh, you are insufferable!"

Lauren leapt to her feet, intending to return to the house at once, but Jason forestalled her by grasping her arm. He turned her to face him, his jaw hardening in determination. He didn't intend to apologize for simply wanting to marry her. No, not simply, Jason amended. Nothing was ever simple where Lauren was concerned. At least now he understood something of how Burroughs had felt—walking a tight line between truth and obligation, the ground beneath his feet as fragile as crystal. He made an effort, though, to keep a rein on his temper. He had driven her away with anger before. He wouldn't do so again.

"I will speak to Lila," he promised softly. "I think I can persuade her to stop troubling you. Now go and put on a bonnet. I have a carriage waiting."

Lauren lifted her chin stonily. "I don't intend to go anywhere with you."

The corner of Jason's mouth curved in a half smile. "You haven't even asked where I mean to take you. I thought we would go shopping. The dressmaker's first, to buy you a new wardrobe."

"I won't be manipulated, Jason. And I don't want any new clothes."

The amusement in his blue eyes deepened. "You shall have them regardless. I don't intend to have my partner shaming me by looking like the veriest ragamuffin."

Lauren wrenched her arm from his grasp. "We don't have a partnership! What are you doing?" she demanded when Jason slipped his hands around her waist. "Let me go! You can't force me, Jason."

She struggled, but Jason only drew her closer, then bent his head, seeking her lips. When Lauren averted her face, Jason merely nuzzled at her ear, tugging on the soft lobe with his teeth.

"Of course I can't force you," he agreed in a velvet whisper. "But neither do I mean to argue about this one, sweetheart. I shall simply kiss you until you either give in gracefully or we wind up in the grass. Your choice."

Lauren pushed against his chest to no avail; he wouldn't release her. And when his tongue traced the outer swirl of her ear and then suggestively teased the inner shell, her traitorous body sprang into response, flooding with unwelcome heat. To her dismay, she discovered she was no longer fighting Jason. Rather she was struggling against the delicious sensations that his tongue was arousing. "You wouldn't dare," she exclaimed breathlessly.

"Oh, I would, Cat-eyes," he asserted, letting his hand brush boldly over her breast. "I would." Feeling the nipple instantly harden, he stroked it with his thumb, then pressed it seductively, making her gasp. "What do you suppose Lila would say if she found us locked in a compromising position?"

"Jason, please . . ." It was impossible to understand this wild longing. Impossible to stop herself from responding, melting, wanting. . . . His hips were pressed against hers, his shaft hard and throbbing against her, leaving no doubt as to what *he* wanted. "All right, yes!" Lauren gasped.

"Yes?"

"Yes, I'll go with you."

His breath was warm and rapid against her cheek. "And our partnership still stands?"

"Yes," she conceded, pressing her palms against his hard chest until he at last released her. She held a hand to her heart, as if to slow her own breathing. "But it is strictly a business arrangement. Do you understand?"

Jason bowed with exaggerated gallantry. "Of course. What

else, Miss Carlin?" Then he stepped aside so she could precede him to the house.

Lauren found out quickly how Jason interpreted her condition. During the drive into town, he didn't even speak except to answer a question of hers, replying that, yes, he had purchased the phaeton and pair of high-stepping bays that morning. He didn't seem angry, merely bored.

Yet he's acting as if I am the one at fault, Lauren thought with resentment as she watched his hands dexterously handling the reins. Then she flushed, realizing she had been remembering the feel of long, sensitive fingers caressing her skin.

To her annoyance, the contrast between Jason's previous attentions toward her and his attitude now was even more pronounced when they arrived at their destination. His indifference immediately dropped away when he addressed the modiste—a pretty woman in her thirties, who eyed his tall form and leonine good looks with appreciation and interest. In response, Jason subjected her to the full force of his magnetic charm and smiling blue eyes—even flirting, Lauren silently fumed—and had no trouble getting the service he required.

He didn't consult Lauren in the requirements for her wardrobe. Even when she did express an opinion, the modiste always looked to Jason for confirmation. His assumption of authority nettled Lauren, yet she could hardly object to his choices; his taste was faultless. He unerringly recommended styles and shades that would subtly flatter her full figure and coloring without exposing half her charms for all the world to see.

Still, his behavior was maddening, for he subjected her to a critical perusal each time a new material was draped across her bosom. When she at last tried on a ready-made carriage dress, a dark rose in shade with a cream-colored spencer, his suggestions concerning the necessary alterations across the bosom brought a flush to her cheeks.

"I trust you are satisfied," she told him irritably when she had once more donned her own faded cotton gown.

Jason leaned back in the chair that had been provided for his comfort. "Quite satisfied," he admitted, subtle humor dancing in his eyes.

"Then may we leave? Or do you intend to provide assistance to the modiste for all her other customers?"

He smiled at her tolerantly. "You're being ungracious, Miss Carlin."

"The name is Miss *DeVries*. Honestly, Jason, I don't mean to be unappreciative, but I'm a seamstress. I could have made my own gowns."

"You won't have the time."

"Even so, I didn't need your advice."

"Based on your past choices," he returned wryly, "I wasn't certain."

"Do you *always* get your way?" Lauren asked, giving him a look of exasperation.

He grinned back at her, his eyes sparkling. "Nearly always."

His good humor was infectious, and as he rose to his feet, Lauren shook her head. Why did she suddenly feel like laughing? A moment before she had been ready to dump a dozen bolts of cloth on his head and fill him full of pins like a pincushion.

While the carriage dress was being altered, Jason escorted her to a cobbler's and milliner's shop, and upon their return, Lauren changed into the new gown. She found herself sighing with pleasure. It was marvelous, she had to admit, to look neither like a servant nor a Cyprian.

When she modeled for Jason, he gave her a slow smile that stroked her senses with heat. Realizing suddenly that she was beginning to crave his approval, Lauren made a determined effort to calm her racing pulse as Jason stepped aside to speak to the modiste.

He directed her to send the completed gowns to the Beauvais plantation and the bills to his bank. At the mention of banks, Lauren was reminded of her chief grievance with Jason—his appropriation of her savings. When he offered her his arm, she stood looking up at him with uncertainty. "I'd like to see for myself the account you had opened in my name," she announced, waiting for his reaction.

If he was discomfited, he veiled it with a wry smile. "What is this? You don't trust me, your partner?"

She searched his face, her brows drawing together. "I don't

think so," she replied quite seriously.

"At least that's honest," Jason said, tucking her hand beneath his arm with easy masculine grace. "Very well, Cat-eyes, you shall see for yourself. But first we eat. Dressing a lady always serves to increase my appetite."

Lauren was uncomfortably aware of the muscular arm beneath her fingers. "Surely you mean undressing," she said in an undertone.

"That, too," Jason chuckled as he held the door for her.

They bypassed several crowded coffee shops that catered primarily to men, and chose a café that was small but offered a delicious cuisine. Lauren found it hard to concentrate on her menu, for the activities of the busy establishment intrigued her.

And as she eyed the other diners with undisguised interest, she noted the admiring glances Jason was receiving; his commanding presence attracted the attention of men and women alike. Lauren could identify quite well with their fascination. Power emanated from Jason like a vital life force. That, combined with his unmistakable virility and refined elegance, made for a devastating combination.

She also noticed what the other women were wearing, and found herself mentally comparing their fashionable ap-pearance to her own. Intent on watching them, she wasn't aware that she herself attracted a number of appreciative masculine glances.

As soon as they had been served, Jason leaned closer to her and ordered Lauren to open her mouth. When she turned her attention back to him, he fed her a prawn. "Now, chew." He grinned and held up a hand. "I know, sweetheart. You're capable of feeding yourself. But I was growing worried that you would starve. One would think that you have never eaten out."

Lauren flushed. "I haven't," she replied simply. "Or at least not in a place like this."

He regarded her thoughtfully. "You needn't be concerned about your appearance, Lauren. You look exquisite."

She had needed to hear that. In the company of all these genteel, well-dressed people, she had begun to feel insecure and unsure of her ability to fit in. She smiled at him, a fragile

230

smile with an unconscious seductiveness that could bring a man to his knees.

Jason's heart soared, then settled back to hammer against his rib cage. Gazing into her luminous eyes, he realized suddenly how he could so easily have mistaken her for a courtesan. She had the smile of a siren, the body of a goddess, and the bearing of a queen. What man wouldn't want her in his bed?

Cool and remote, she was breathtakingly beautiful, Jason thought as he surveyed her. The color of her gown brought out the rose in her smooth complexion and her provocative lips, while the narrow-brimmed bonnet framed her lovely face, not quite covering the sweep of golden hair. Jason found himself aching for the sight of those tresses spilling around her naked breasts. Growing silent, he let himself remember every exquisite moment of making love to Lauren on board the *Siren*.

The memory would have to suffice, Jason told himself. At least for a time, until he could break down the barriers of cold reserve she was constantly surrounding herself with. Meanwhile, he would just have to hold his desire firmly in check.

But there were other compensations he could find in her company. Just watching her today had been a joy. The evident delight Lauren had shown in being well dressed, the almost childlike interest she had taken in her new surroundings, had touched his heart. He had known then that he would always find pleasure in gratifying her slightest wish. He had no fear that her sudden wealth would give birth to greed or an insatiable yearning for material objects, for the years of deprivation had taught her the value of a coin. Lila had told him how hard Lauren had worked to save for her ship, how she had refused to take Beauvais's charity. Her fierce determination to remain independent was understandable. And while he would have preferred a different occupation for her, the job at the gaming house had been honest work.

How hard the years must have been for her. Measured in terms of wealth or any other standard, Lauren's life had been far more difficult than his had ever been, Jason reflected. And it couldn't have been easy, living with the constant fear that at any moment her whereabouts might be discovered by

Burroughs. He could understand why she felt driven to control her own destiny, and why, after what she had endured, she would consider her freedom more important than gold or jewels. But he could also see how starved her soul was for new experiences, and his new determination to see that Lauren began to enjoy life overrode even his own wish to make her his own.

But he would teach her, Jason vowed. One step at a time, he would show her each aspect of a close, loving relationship, until she saw the value of the whole.

His gaze lingered tenderly on the stunningly lovely oval face. He would be the luckiest man on earth, Jason thought, if Lauren could return but one-tenth of the love he desperately wished to lavish on her.

Chapter Fourteen

Lauren made her way along the gallery of the Beauvais plantation house slowly, reluctantly, as if she were being drawn by an invisible, magnetic source. It was odd the way she could sense Jason's presence. She had heard a horseman arriving at Bellefleur, and although she hadn't seen the visitor, she had known it would be Jason there in the study with Jean-Paul.

She should keep away from him, she knew. He was far too dangerous, for he seemed to be able to bend her to his will. But actually, she very much wanted to see him. Tucking a stray curl behind her ear, she nervously smoothed the skirts of her apple-green muslin, one of the new dresses that had arrived during the time Jason had been away from New Orleans.

His trip had taken her by surprise. He hadn't told her where he was going or the reason for his absence, merely that he was leaving town for a few days. She still remembered his parting words, when he had teasingly asked if she would miss him. Her tart denial had made him laugh.

But to be truthful, Lauren had missed him. That brief interlude in the Vieux Carré, when Jason had squired her about the shops and then taken her to dine at the fashionable café, stood out in her mind as one of the most enjoyable days in her memory. After finishing the delicious meal, they had gone to the bank where Monsieur Sauvinet, the bank's owner, had treated Lauren like visiting royalty. Curiously, Sauvinet had taken Jason aside for a few minutes to hand him a note. Jason had read the missive, glanced once at Lauren, and then nodded. They had left shortly thereafter, with Lauren's reticule heavier by a hundred dollars.

"And what do you intend to do with such a sum?" Jason asked casually as he took her arm and directed her toward the square.

"I have to repay Veronique's loan."

"Ah, yes. The loan which financed your escape."

Lauren gave him her coolest frown. Returning a bland smile, Jason steered her in the direction of the levee, saying he needed to visit the *Siren*.

On the way, they detoured through the French Market, an arcaded structure of stucco brick. As usual, it was extremely noisy and crowded with every conceivable kind of person: tradesmen, greengrocers, fishermen, ragged children, well-dressed customers, Negresses dressed in bright colors wearing turbans wrapped around their heads, and Choctaw and Chitimacha Indian women draped in handwoven blankets who sold reed baskets and other handmade goods.

At a stall where jewelry was sold, a string of blue beads caught Lauren's attention. Fingering the smooth bits of glass, she found herself comparing their brilliant color to the fathomless depths of Jason's eyes. When she looked up to discover Jason watching her, she saw he was regarding her with that same odd expression that so often disturbed her. "Is something amiss?" she asked self-consciously.

"No," Jason said softly. "I was just picturing you with a necklace of sapphires about your throat. But if these have caught your fancy—"

"It isn't that!" Lauren exclaimed quickly, unwilling to admit just what had attracted her to the beads, unwilling also to acknowledge the implication of Jason's remark. She didn't want him to spend any more money on her, either. "I only wanted to see how the beads were strung," she prevaricated, handing the necklace back to the vendor.

A short while later, they boarded the *Siren*. Kyle Ramsey seemed reserved when he greeted her, but he offered to show her around the ship. Since Jason excused himself, saying he had a few matters to take care of, Lauren politely agreed to a tour.

The *Siren* was a two-masted schooner, smaller and far more elegant than the kind of vessel Lauren had dreamed of owning. The crew was hard at work scrubbing decks, checking blocks and rigging, and inspecting endless yards of shrouds, sheets, and staysails for damage.

Following Kyle as he pointed out various details, Lauren discovered to her dismay that her thoughts kept straying to the last time she had visited the *Siren*. She was grateful Kyle didn't take her below decks, since Jason had disappeared in that direction and she had no wish to encounter him in his cabin. She still grew warm whenever she recalled her experiences there at his skillful hands.

Tim Sutter's presence also reminded her of that night. She knew a moment of embarrassment when the young man saluted her smartly, but recovered when she saw the undisguised admiration on his face. Pausing to speak to him, Lauren made him a gracious apology for hitting him on the head and inquired about his injury. Tim turned a fiery red and mumbled a disclaimer, and after hastily begging the captain's permission to return to his chores, he scurried off, leaving Kyle laughing and even Lauren smiling a little.

Kyle didn't introduce her to any of the other men on board, even though she was the object of more than one interested glance. "I hope you can forgive being subjected to an inspection," he remarked, noting the attention she was attracting. "You're the first female I've allowed on board the *Siren*. I haven't told my crew yet that you're the real owner of this vessel. Sailors are a suspicious lot when it comes to women and ships, and I thought it better for my men to get a good look at you before I let them know they were really working for you."

Lauren was uncomfortable with the direction their discussion was headed. "Actually," she admitted, "I would prefer that nothing be said about it."

"You still don't want anyone to know you're Miss Carlin?"

She was avoiding his gaze, so she only heard the surprise in his question. "I . . . it's just that I have gone by Lauren DeVries for so long that it would feel strange to change."

235

Kyle shrugged his broad shoulders. "I understand, but you might want to reconsider. If you plan to spend any time on board the *Siren*, your ownership will provide you a measure of protection."

"Protection?" Lauren shot him a startled glance. "But your men don't seem disrespectful."

Kyle's grin was wry. "They wouldn't dare. Not when Jason brought you on board and while I remain by your side. This lot was handpicked, so they're a cut above the normal lot of seamen, but I've seen more than one man lose his head over a beautiful woman, risking position, name, everything in a moment of madness." He paused to study Lauren, his hazel eyes becoming quite serious. "Indeed, for a number of years, I was convinced that was what Jason had done. I must say, you aren't at all what I had imagined. I thought Jase was caught in the coils of some scheming hussy, even if you *were* worth a fortune."

"You thought that of *me?*" Lauren said weakly.

There was another long pause, before Kyle added, "Jason tried for a long time to find you. He even sent me here to the States a few years ago to look for you. But I never expected . . . I've been to New Orleans once or twice since then, but I suppose you were too well hidden." His serious expression relaxed then, and he regarded her with a rueful smile. "This ship is even named after you. I'm afraid it was my idea to call her the *Siren*. And it wasn't meant to be flattering. It didn't help to find you in that gaming house, either. But . . . well, I should have known you wouldn't be mixed up in that kind of business. I'm just sorry I, er, propositioned you."

"It was understandable, Captain," Lauren murmured, discomfited by his apology. She was relieved when Kyle changed the subject.

Her tour was interrupted a short time later by Jason's reappearance. He was carrying a bundle under one arm and a basket under the other. "Some books for you to read on the shipping industry," he said, indicating the leather-bound volumes. "And Ulysses." With that cryptic remark, he presented the basket to Lauren.

Hearing a muffled but decidedly mournful howl, Lauren

236

gave Jason a quizzical look, then carefully peeked under the lid. When an angry orange ball of fur tried to leap out, she hastily shut it again. Stunned, Lauren glanced from Jason to the basket and then back again. "My cat," she breathed.

She looked adorably bewildered, Jason thought, glad that the occupation of his hands kept him from sweeping Lauren into his arms. He cleared his throat, directing his thoughts back to the cat. "I wouldn't let him out till you get home," he advised. "I had the devil of a time coaxing him in there. And as fond as Ulysses is of Kyle, he might not want to leave the ship."

Lauren knew she should say something, do something, but she was too astonished to speak. She was also unable to tear her gaze away from the tender light in Jason's eyes. She hardly heard Kyle's remark that she was welcome to the damned beast and a reward, too, for taking Ulysses away.

She hadn't recovered from the first shock when Jason announced that he had sent for the carriage but that he would be unable to drive her home. He apologized to Lauren, explaining that a matter had come up that required his attention and that he would probably be away from the city for a few days.

Lauren stared at Jason, puzzled, wondering what mysterious mission could possibly take him away from New Orleans, and even though she intercepted the look that passed between him and Kyle, she could read nothing in their silent communication. When Kyle gallantly offered his services as driver, Lauren accepted absently.

It was after she had been handed into the carriage and the parcels had been stowed away, that Lauren asked Jason what his business was. His answer as he stood looking down at her was evasive. "It doesn't concern you or the Carlin Line directly."

"Forgive me for prying, then," she said curtly.

Seeing the stubborn set of her chin, Jason flashed her a grin. "You were the one who wanted to keep our relationship impersonal," he reminded her. "Business partners only, if I recei your warning correctly." When her lips tightened, he cocked his head at her in amusement. "Do I dare hope you will miss me, Cat-eyes?"

"Dare whatever you wish," she replied haughtily.

He raised a quizical brow. "*Whatever* I wish?"

At his intimate tone, Lauren felt vivid color stain her cheeks. She managed to return his gaze steadily, though. "I doubt your absence will cause anyone any particular distress, my lord," she said sweetly. "Certainly not me. I am sure to discover *something* to occupy my time."

"You have the reading material I gave you. You should find it informative, if a bit dry."

The sparkling devils in Jason's eyes suddenly made Lauren suspicious of his motives. Her own eyes narrowed. "You've thought of everything, haven't you?"

"Probably not," Jason laughed. "But Kyle will be here to watch over you. I trust you won't lead him on any wild chases." Taking her hand, Jason brought it to his lips. Even this simple gesture sent a flood of warmth surging through Lauren, and she nervously withdrew her hand from his grasp.

Jason released her reluctantly. He didn't want to leave; he felt far more than she the loss of parting. But he didn't intend to jeopardize his goal with a premature action.

When he spoke, however, he failed to maintain his light tone. "Take care of yourself, Lauren," he murmured, gazing at her intently. "I'll see you as soon as I return."

Held by the spell of that vivid blue gaze, Lauren was almost glad when Kyle gave the horses the office to start and Jason was left behind.

For much of the return drive to Bellefleur, Lauren remained silent. Then she bestirred herself to question Kyle about the suddenness of Jason's trip.

"You know as much about it as I, Miss DeVries," Kyle replied guardedly.

Lauren's raised eyebrow declared her disbelief. "But you do know where he's going?"

Kyle arched his neck, as if his collar had suddenly become rather uncomfortable. "You wouldn't expect me to betray a confidence, would you?"

"I suppose not," Lauren conceded. "Is Jason going to Barataria?" When Kyle gave her a startled glance, she realized she had hit upon the truth. "Don't be alarmed. You didn't

238

actually divulge any secrets."

Kyle looked at her in amazement. "Was that merely a wild guess, or do you have the same outstanding powers of deduction that Jason has?"

She smiled. "It was only a guess. A trip to the swamps might take several days, and I couldn't think of anyplace else he might go that he wouldn't want to divulge. Besides, at the bank I saw Monsieur Sauvinet give Jason a note. Everyone knows that Sauvinet has connections with the smugglers. He's said to have handled Jean Lafitte's affairs for years."

Kyle pulled the horses down to a jog. "Are you acquainted with the pirate?" he asked curiously.

"Not personally. Jean-Paul is, of course, but I only saw Monsieur Lafitte once when he was walking along the street. And I understand he prefers to be called a privateer, not a pirate."

"Same thing, to my mind, considering the fate of British merchant ships at his hands. I understand that all his property was confiscated after the war."

Lauren nodded. "*After* he earned his pardon by fighting for the Americans. Jean-Paul was outraged at the way he was treated. Now Lafitte has challenged the government in court in order to regain what was taken from him. But does that have anything to do with Jason? He wants something from Lafitte, doesn't he? Else he wouldn't be going to see him."

Kyle kept his gaze trained on the horses. "I can't tell you, Miss Car— Miss DeVries."

"You mean you won't tell me. I don't see why it's such a secret. I've been exposed to smugglers all my life. Very well, then," she said when Kyle remained silent. "Will you tell me if what Jason is doing might be dangerous?"

Kyle sighed. "I don't think it is. Unless Lafitte has nursed a grudge all these years." He glanced at Lauren and noted the question in her eyes. "That was how Jason acquired his first ship. He won a British frigate from the pirate on a throw of the dice."

"Jason told me he didn't care to associate with Frenchmen. Was he telling the truth?"

"Most certainly. It's his greatest prejudice. And I doubt if

239

Jason would ever willingly lie to you," Kyle said carefully.

"You have great faith him," she returned, her tone dry.

"I should. You might say that Jason changed my life. With the reward money he received for returning the frigate to her owner, plus a little that he had saved, Jason bought the *Leucothea*, his first vessel. He signed me on to teach him what I knew about seamanship, in exchange for half interest in the ship."

Remembering her own agreement with Jason, Lauren glanced down her hands. "Was it . . . did you find you had made a good bargain?" she asked after a moment.

"The best."

Each of them became lost in their own thoughts then, and they were more than halfway to Bellefleur when something else occurred to Lauren. "Has anyone ever succeeded in outwitting Jason?" she asked suddenly.

Kyle grinned at her question. "Only you, to my knowledge."

Lauren shook her head. "Oh, no. If I had, I wouldn't be here with you." Seeing Kyle grimace, she smiled ruefully. "I didn't mean quite mean it that way. It's just that again Jason managed to get me to do precisely what he wished. I meant to pay a visit to Veronique, but I was so surprised when Jason said he was leaving that I forgot. I suppose you wouldn't consider taking me back to town?"

Kyle hesitated. "Jason wouldn't thank me. The casino isn't exactly a proper place for a lady."

"So I've been told," Lauren said wryly. But she accepted his answer as a refusal and withdrew a roll of bills from her reticule, holding it out to him. "Then will you give Veronique this when you next see her? It's the money she loaned me the other day."

Kyle whistled. "She must be rich. Do you suppose I've found myself an heiress?" he asked with a laugh as he pocketed the wad.

"Veronique understands the necessity for being frugal," Lauren replied stiffly. "She is saving for what she calls her lean years."

"I'll wager they'll be a long time in coming."

"Would you?"

Subjected to Lauren's cool stare, Kyle looked as if he might like to squirm. "Have I said something I to offend you, Miss DeVries?"

Hearing his contrite tone, Lauren lowered her gaze. "No, I'm sorry. I just don't care for jests about heiresses."

"Poor taste, was it? How about honor among thieves, virtue among— No, that's worse. Perhaps I'd better keep my mouth shut. You and Veronique are close, are you not?"

"Very close. She's one of the few people I know who doesn't try to wrap me in swaddling as if I were a child."

"Is that a hint, ma'am? All right, then. I can't share Jason's reasons for leaving town, but I don't see why I can't tell you how it first started."

As Kyle proceeded to relate what he knew of Jason's past, Lauren listened attentively.

"Jason's the younger son of the sixth Marquess of Effing— an interfering old autocrat if there ever was one. Jason attended Oxford because his father wanted him to, but found it easier to keep his independence by refusing the income Lord Effing offered. Which means that while other young gents frequented gaming hells for sport, Jason did it from necessity.

"Lord Effing got on his high ropes when Jason used his gambling winnings to purchase a commission in the Royal Navy. The marquess considered a naval career an unfit occupation for someone of Stuart lineage, you see, and he used his connections in the government to make Jason's position extremely uncomfortable. So Jason gave in gracefully and resigned, then removed himself from Lord Effing's sphere of power by going to America."

"That's when he became a trapper?" Lauren asked.

Kyle nodded. "And that was the same year he acquired the *Leucothea* as the result of a wager. I met him shortly afterward, and we made the bargain that proved profitable to us both. In all, Jason was here for nearly two years. After he returned to England, his father tried again to bring him in line, insisting that he marry and settle down. Jason refused—until the marquess made that arrangement with your guardian.

"I probably shouldn't be telling you this," Kyle admitted with a frown. "Whatever is—or will be—between you and

241

Jason is for you two to work out. I promised not to get involved. But Jase is dearer to me than a brother, and I care what happens to him. I've never seen a man change so . . . Well, he was just different after you left England." Kyle paused, noting Lauren's bent head. "But the Carlin Line has been good for him. Gave him something to think about. He's treated those ships as if they were his own children, Miss DeVries. And made you a lot of money in the process. Of course, he set London on its ear. A marquess in trade is next to sedition in England. But Jase has never been one to sit back and let others work. He nigh gave his father an apoplexy every time he started some new venture."

Disturbed by the turn their conversation had taken, Lauren nevertheless tried to keep her tone casual. "I presume Jason inherited the title from his father? He neglected to mention anything about it."

"Well, I suppose he considers it unimportant here. Americans don't put much stock in titles. But Jason is Lord Effing now. He never expected to inherit, but two years ago his older brother and nephews were killed in a fire, a tragic accident. Jase never thought much of his brother, but I think he would give quite a lot to have him back. Of course, now he has to marry, carry on the line. The old lord would have wanted it. Jason rarely was what you could call a dutiful son, but I think he feels obligated to respect his father's wishes."

Lauren kept her gaze carefully averted. "But surely he could have found a wife before now."

"Oh, I don't doubt that at all," Kyle said mildly. "In England, the ladies were standing in line."

"Then why did he not?"

Kyle gave her a long, penetrating look. "That's not hard to explain, Miss DeVries. He was waiting for you to return."

Lauren felt her cheeks grow warm, knowing there was no reply she could make. She was beginning to understand the depth of Jason's determination to marry her, but now more than ever she could see what a misalliance that would be. A marquess was such an exalted position, close to royalty. Lauren mentally shook her head. Renegade nobleman or no,

242

Jason could never marry a bastard. He would face social ostracisim.

And then there was her involvement with Burroughs's deception. Jason would be swept into a horrendous scandal if she went to prison.

Deploring this recent tendency of hers to blush, Lauren lapsed into silence once more. Neither she nor Kyle said another word until the plantation was reached.

Lauren found herself counting the days till Jason's return. It wasn't that she had too little to occupy her time. Kyle called daily and took her for long drives around the countryside, and he even brought Veronique along once. When Veronique told her Felix Duval had been asking about her, Lauren wrote the gambler a long missive, saying that Marguerite regretfully declined his offer of protection and adding that she would no longer be entertaining at the casino since she was leaving the city. She hoped he would accept her explanations at face value.

The books Jason had given her on the shipping industry also kept her busy. She discovered, to her chagrin, that complete concentration was required if she were to understand one-tenth of what she read, yet she doggedly plowed through the heavy material since it gave her enough background to ask intelligent questions during her discussions with both Kyle and Jean-Paul.

And of course there was her wardrobe. Lila was ecstatic that Lauren was at last dressing like a lady of quality, and Lauren frequently had to bite her tongue while Lila supervised the final fittings and offered detailed and mostly unneeded advice.

In all, Lauren was quite, quite busy. During all this activity, though, she was aware of a budding sense of anticipation and excitement. She refused to admit that it was because she was looking forward to Jason's return, and instead attributed it to her plan to rid herself of the Carlin fortune for good, along with Jason's unwelcome attentions. The idea had occurred to her one day when she was talking to Jean-Paul about the new office.

243

She had already discovered, much to her surprise, that while Jean-Paul was willing for her to marry the "English lord", he was unwilling to commit himself to the distribution venture. He wanted to hear more about such things as assets and debits and insurance underwriters and profit margins before throwing his weight behind the project. He had not become rich, he said, by investing in firms that had no strong guiding hand.

Since she was unable to respond knowledgeably about the stability of the Carlin Line, Lauren deferred that discussion till Jason returned. But she did argue that Jean-Paul would not be required to make any investment.

"Ah, but there you are wrong, *m'amie,*" Beauvais countered. "You ask me to stake my reputation, my honor. I have heard of the Carlin ships and their success, but what of their future? Perhaps it is true that your Englishman, as the trustee, has been responsible for this success. But what will happen when he is no longer there to offer you advice? Could you run the company yourself? Would you even wish to do such a thing? For many men it would be difficult. For a woman with no experience, nearly impossible. Let us say, for hypothetical purposes, that I agree to this distribution scheme. I obtain the customers you seek. For a time everyone is satisfied. Then one day your ships fail to deliver what has been promised. Ppff! My reputation is diminished, my integrity is questioned. Non, Laurie, *ma belle.* It is better for me to avoid such risks altogether. Without some guarantee that my investment is protected, I should have to decline."

"And I suppose," she said warily, suspecting that she was again being manipulated, "that such a guarantee might come in the form of my marriage to a man who could run the company?"

"That would be the most convincing argument I could think of, yes. But I understand your feelings. You do not wish to marry. So that is that."

Lauren focused her cool stare on the Creole. "No, that is *blackmail.*"

Jean-Paul shook his dark head. "*Mais, non!* It is smart business." He did, however, have the grace to look the tiniest bit ashamed. "But I do not pressure you to accept this marriage you do not want. It is your choice. To me, your happiness is more important than the fee I might earn. My Lila thinks you would be happy with this Anglais, but it is you who must live with the decision. If you cannot, then you cannot."

"I cannot," Lauren declared with determination. "But there must be an alternative. What if Jason agreed to remain as the trustee, or perhaps a permanent officer of the company?"

"Then I would reconsider. But I do not believe he will agree to such a thing. Think, *m'amie!* Would you if you were in his place? He could marry you and gain all the Carlin ships, since the law says all property belongs to the husband."

"Do you think that is why Jason offered to marry me? Because of the Carlin ships?"

"I expect he has thought of that, yes. But do not underestimate yourself, Laurie. You are a beautiful young woman. And he is a man. If he could have both you and the ships, why should he wish for less than the whole?"

"He will have to be satisfied with less. Jason understands that I won't marry him. Actually," she added thoughtfully, "he already owns the ships. I suppose I should just refuse to take them back, for then he would have control."

"You would be giving up a fortune," Jean-Paul reminded her.

Lauren looked up at that. "Yes," she said slowly. "I would be giving up a fortune. But," she added, "if I accept the Carlin inheritance, I would probably have to live in England, which I don't want. And to be fair, Jason deserves to be rewarded for his efforts. According to Kyle, were it not for Jason, the Carlin Line might not even have survived. So, what would your position be if Jason just kept the ships?"

Jean-Paul nodded. "There would be no problem for me. Of course I would have to speak with him first. I will do so when he returns, if you are sure that is what you want."

"I am sure," Lauren replied. "At least one person died because of my father's fortune, and I want no part of it."

Nor could Jason convince her to change her mind, Lauren added to herself. She wouldn't allow him the opportunity. For that reason, she was glad Jean-Paul had volunteered to talk to him. Of course, Jason couldn't *force* her to take the Carlin inheritance. But still, she didn't trust her ability to withstand Jason Stuart if he decided to truly exert himself at persuasion.

It was two days after this conversation that Lauren heard Jason's arrival at Bellefleur.

The Beauvais plantation wasn't exceedingly large by current standards, but it was quite profitable, boasting a small refinery for its prime crop of sugarcane. The house itself was spacious and elegant, and sat well back from the river, surrounded by moss-covered live oaks. Typical of Creole residences, it was built upon brick pillars to minimize the danger of flooding, with turned-wood colonnettes and wide, graceful galleries. The lower floor of the house was used only for storage and laundry and as service quarters. On the second floor were the main rooms and sleeping apartments for the family, all of which had direct access to the outdoors via tall French windows.

As Lauren moved slowly along the gallery, her heart gave a queer leap, for she could hear the soft resonance of Jason's voice through the open doorway of the study. Jean-Paul started to reply to Jason's comment, but when he saw Lauren, he broke off the conversation and gestured to her, bidding her enter.

Lauren was surprised to find Jean-Paul's young son Charles with the two men. She was also surprised when Charles didn't run to her the way he usually did, for Jason was holding the boy on his lap. As Lauren entered, he set the child on sofa and politely rose to his feet.

Lauren took two steps into the room, then halted suddenly, nearly gasping at the warm shock that raced through her. She had forgotten the effect Jason's brilliant blue gaze had on her. For a moment, as their eyes met, she even had difficulty controlling her breathing. And by the time she was able to, Jean-Paul was speaking. It was all she could do to listen to him.

"Lauren, Lord Effing has refused your offer of the Carlin ships. I have explained how matters stand with me, however, and he has agreed to remain your adviser, so long as you need him. It is this assurance that permits me to commit my services. I have proposed to put him in contact with men who can be of help in this distribution venture. I have also suggested that he and his friend, Captain Ramsey, remove from their hotel. His lordship has accepted my offer to stay here while they are visitors to New Orleans."

"I . . . I see," Lauren said slowly, not quite knowing how to greet this news. If Jason had refused the Carlin Line, then he must still believe she could be coerced into marriage. It was impossible to tell from his expression what he was thinking, though. He hadn't said a word. He only stood there, silently watching her.

Yet she was entirely aware of his overwhelming physical presence. Feeling herself succumbing to the fascinating aura of power that radiated from him, Lauren clasped her hands tightly together. "Thank you, Jean-Paul. But cannot his lordship speak for himself?"

A humorous gleam crept into the blue eyes, before Jason made a slight bow. "Certainly, Miss DeVries. Was there some point in particular that was beyond your understanding? I myself thought Monsieur Beauvais expressed himself with adequate eloquence. There remains only for me to thank him again for the gracious offer of his hospitality."

Lauren's eyes flashed warningly, but she managed to maintain a calm tone. "Then it is all or nothing?" she asked.

Jason did not pretend to misunderstand her. "It has always been so," he replied quietly. In his voice, there was an underlying ring of determination, and his intent look compelled her gaze to remain locked with his. "But realize, Lauren, it is not a declaration of war. There can be two victors."

She shook her head slowly. "No," she whispered. "I don't believe that." Then collecting herself, Lauren said firmly, "But neither do I wish to speak of it. Why don't you tell us about your trip? Was it a success?"

"It is too soon to tell," he replied, refusing to be baited.

Jean-Paul made some comment to young Charles then, but Lauren hardly heard. Again, as always when she was with Jason, she had the strange sensation of being alone with him. It was as if only the two of them existed in the world. To break the spell, she made herself turn and retrace her steps. With her

247

back to him, she said in low voice, "You will not be happy with 'nothing', I think."

There was a long pause where even the child was quiet. In the silence, Lauren could hear the beating of her heart.

"Nor will you," Jason said at last.

Lifting her skirts, Lauren almost ran from the room.

Chapter Fifteen

By unspoken agreement, the contention between them wasn't referred to again, even though it was there, simmering beneath the surface. Jason had openly declared his intention of winning her hand as well as the Carlin ships; Lauren was determined he wouldn't succeed.

She would have preferred to shun Jason's company altogether. His uncanny ability to read her mind alarmed her, and she was afraid that she would succumb to the sheer force of his compelling personality. But because they were guests in the same house, and because their bargain required they spend their days together, she found it impossible to avoid him.

Her days began to assume a pattern. Normally she would rise early and breakfast with Jason and Kyle. Then one of them would drive her into town while the other rode beside the phaeton.

That first morning, they met with a solicitor who showed them various buildings and lots near the waterfront. Their primary order of business was to find a building with a central location which could be converted to an office for the Carlin Line, the secondary one, to choose a site for their soon-to-be-built warehouses, with proximity to both the River Road and the city.

It took nearly a week for the decision to be made and the sale to be finalized. Much of that time Lauren spent on board the *Siren*, their temporary headquarters, learning about ledgers and bookkeeping and accounting, and she found herself becoming more involved with the Carlin Line than she ever intended.

In the end, they purchased a small brick building on Levee Street, whose refurbishing proved a big challenge. Filth and cobwebs littered the interior, while rats infested the woodwork, if the frequency of odd scufflings was any indication. Disgusted by the unsanitary conditions, Lauren volunteered to set the building to rights, and the next morning when she came down to breakfast, she was wearing one of her old cotton gowns. Jason raised an eyebrow at her appearance, but beyond warning her that she had a difficult task before her, he made no comment.

Lauren was determined to uphold her end of the bargain, though. She borrowed nearly every indoor servant at Bellefleur from Lila, along with an arsenal of mops and brooms and buckets. For the rats, she brought Ulysses.

Both Jason and Kyle were banished from the premises, and when they were allowed in three days later, they were given a tour of a spotlessly clean building. Lauren basked under their praise, even going so far as to laugh when Jason wiped a smudge of dirt from her cheek.

"I suppose I could provide references if you should ever decide to become a scullery drudge," Jason offered.

"I'm far more ambitious," Lauren said with a smile. "An upstairs maid is much more my style."

After that, she saw little of Jason during the day. He was busy hiring a crew to build the new warehouses, while she supervised the painters and carpenters and drapers at the offices.

She was never alone. Because the neighborhood was not the best, Jason had insisted that two men from the *Siren* be with her at all times. Usually this included Tim Sutter, whom Lauren grew to like. An elderly black woman from the Beauvais plantation was also present to lend respectability. Veronique was a frequent visitor to the new offices, and Lila stopped by to check on the progress whenever she came to town to shop.

Surprisingly, though, Lauren found herself missing Jason's company. And without realizing it, she began to change her routine at home so she could see more of him.

Upon Jason's arrival at Bellefleur, she had begun retiring early to her room, pleading fatigue as an excuse to avoid him. But now, she lingered in the drawing room until well after the tea tray was brought in. Occasionally she would join the others in a game of whist or piquet, and sometimes she would play the pianoforte, but usually she would settle into a corner with a book or a piece of embroidery and watch Jason from under lowered lashes.

That he puzzled her, she couldn't deny. He treated her with the friendly warmth that he might have shown a favorite hound, and gave her little cause to think she was being wooed. Even so, she wasn't convinced Jason had given up on the idea of marrying her to gain the Carlin ships. She was wary and distrustful and determined to keep her distance.

More and more, though, Lauren found herself letting down her guard. Jason Stuart was the kind of man who *compelled* trust, and she often forgot to be wary of him. Unconsciously, she even began seeking his approval, accepting his guidance without protest, even when she suspected she was complying too easily.

Had she guessed that Jason was following a careful strategy to win her trust and affection, Lauren might have admired his determination, even while resisting his every attempt to breech her defenses. But his methods were a masterpiece of subtlety, appealing to her logic and pride.

After the offices were completed, Lauren saw less of Jason during the day than before, since he spent most of his time down at the waterfront where the new warehouses were being constructed. But he kept his end of the bargain also, and saw to it that she learned the inside operation of the shipping line. In fact, Lauren was fully occupied, developing the bookkeeping system and organizing the ledgers.

Kyle showed her how to make an inventory of easily accessible goods, and under his direction, she learned to match routes of the Carlin ships to current points of trade. Their plan was to develop a network of commerce instead of having goods sold by captains of individual ships. It wasn't that the method of trade was new, but the scale on which Jason meant to operate was almost staggering to contemplate.

They hired two clerks for the office, and when Matthew MacGregor returned from his latest trip upriver, he also accepted a job working for Jason. Although Matthew protested that he wasn't qualified to handle the bookwork, he shortly dispelled any doubts about his abilities as a salesman. Armed with the list of potential customers suggested by Jean-Paul, Matthew set out to establish a market for the furniture, fine fabrics, and manufactured goods from England's factories that the Carlin ships would import, and to find adequate sources for the cotton, sugar, leather, furs, and tobacco to be exported to Europe.

Lauren was surprised to discover how smoothly the venture proceeded from there. Shortly they had orders to be filled both in England and the West Indies. Jason approved the initial schedule Lauren developed, deeming it adequate for the fledgling branch, then promptly wrote to his overseas agents, setting the plan in motion.

She also was surprised by Jason's familiarity with a number of America's prominent statesmen and entrepreneurs. The volume of his correspondence was quite large, but he refused Lauren's offer of help, saying that when he returned to England, he would turn the lot of it over to his secretary and make the fellow earn his salary.

Lauren found that comment unaccountably depressing. She realized, of course, that the situation between them couldn't go on indefinitely, but she didn't like contemplating the thought that Jason would leave some day.

She knew him better now, and she could see his faults and weaknesses. Besides possessing a temper that could rage with white-hot fury, he could be persistent and tenacious to the point of stubbornness, and occasionally he was self-indulgent, often taking comfort and luxury for granted. His fondness for young Charles rivaled that of the boy's father, and he tended to spoil the child, if the frequent complaints of the boy's nurse were to be believed. On the credit side, however, he had a number of qualities Lauren admired, including a depth of intelligence that was startling to watch in action. And in spite of all her efforts to keep her distance, she was drawn to him.

It was curious, the effect he had on her. He made her feel

alive, sharpening her senses and wits, and when she was in his company, the restless loneliness she had known for so many years disappeared. Even the terrible dreams that had plagued her for so many years rarely tormented her since Jason had come to Bellefleur. Ulysses's presence in her room had a soothing effect, of course, but after the first time she had awakened from a nightmare to find Jason holding her trembling body and murmuring comforting words in her ear, she knew that if she needed him, he would be near.

Still, the cloud of her past was always there. And when sometimes Lauren caught herself wondering what her answer to Jason's proposal would have been had she been free to make the choice, she firmly admonished herself for daydreaming.

Yet her physical attraction for him was especially difficult to ignore. Often, as she lay alone in her bed, she would recall the feel of his body moving against hers, and the arousing warmth of his hands on her breasts, and desire would spring up in her, hot and wild, making her ache with longing.

She missed him most during the evenings when he remained in town, either alone or with Kyle, and she couldn't stop herself from wondering what Jason was doing each moment. When eventually she learned, though, the discovery hurt unbelievably.

Veronique had come to visit the new office and was lamenting the fact that her handsome Kyle had left to visit his family in Natchez. While complaining how boring New Orleans was without him, Veronique let slip that she sometimes saw Jason at the gaming house.

Seeing Lauren's stricken expression, the redhead beauty added hastily that it was only to be expected. "He does not go upstairs with any of the girls," Veronique explained. "Or at least, I have only seen him do so once."

Lauren tried to swallow the ache in her throat. She had no right to demand fidelity of Jason, she knew, but the thought of him with another woman filled her with anguish. "Who . . . who was he with?" she said hoarsely.

Veronique wrinkled her nose in distaste. "Desirée Chaudier." When Lauren stiffened at the mention of the malicious dark-haired beauty, Veronique leaned forward to pat her hands consolingly. "It means nothing, *mon chou*. Men do not look on these things as serious. You should put it from your mind. You know how that slut Desirée always boasts of her clients. Half of what she says is not to be believed." A mask had descended over Lauren's face, though, and Veronique had no trouble recognizing it for what it was: a guard against further pain. "What do you intend to do?" she queried, frowning.

Lauren's chin came up. "I find suddenly that I have grown tired of patiently sitting at home while Jason enjoys himself. Look for me tonight at the casino, for I shall be there."

Veronique eyed her skeptically. "But what of M'sieur Jason? He will not be happy with this. Will he give his permission?"

"It isn't Jason's place to say what I may or may not do. Besides," she added with a bitter smile, "you've always told me that a woman who could not get what she wanted from a man was a disgrace to her sex."

"I said also that a man who could not stand up to a woman was no real man. I think this is a mistake you are making, *miette*."

Lauren pressed her lips together. "Perhaps. We shall just have to see, won't we?"

That afternoon Lauren disregarded Jason's wishes for the first time, and instead for waiting for him to collect her at the office, she set off on foot for the waterfront, accompanied by her protesting bodyguards. When she arrived at the *Siren*, where Jason often worked, she didn't bother to knock on the door to his cabin, but went directly in, with Tim Sutter hard on her heels.

Jason was writing at his large desk. He hardly gave them a glance, but when Tim began to speak, Jason waved him away. The lad retreated obediently, leaving Lauren to pace the cabin while she waited for Jason to conclude whatever he had been doing.

"Sit down, Lauren. I shall be finished in a moment" was his only comment.

Hearing the hard note in his tone, however, Lauren realized that he was angry. Perhaps, she admitted with sudden apprehension, her impulsive action had been ill-considered.

254

With unaccustomed meekness, Lauren obeyed. Sitting in one of the chairs that had been pulled up before the desk, she placed her hands in her lap and willed them to be still.

The silence grew more ominous with each passing minute; only the scratch of Jason's pen could be heard. Lauren eyed Jason warily. He was casually dressed, having doffed his coat, and she could see the muscles of his arms rippling under his shirt of finest lawn. She would be completely defenseless, she knew, if Jason ever unleashed his powerful physical strength on her. She tensed when he put down his pen.

The look he directed at her was lengthy and penetrating, and she fought the urge to squirm under his brilliant blue gaze. When at last he rose and came to her, she found it difficult not to shrink from him.

But surprisingly, he didn't chastise her. Bending slightly, Jason cupped her face in his hands, tilting it upward, his eyes flicking over her features. "You are tired," he observed quietly. "And angry. I've come to know that little furrow that appears between your brows." As he spoke, his thumbs smoothed the tiny crease, then traced gentle semicircles beneath her eyes.

Lauren found she had forgotten completely what she had meant to say. Jason's nearness was having a shattering effect on her senses. Her lips parted in breathless anticipation as she returned his gaze.

He didn't kiss her as she expected. Instead his hands moved gently downward, sweeping the column of her throat before coming to rest on her shoulders. His fingers began to work, then, kneading gently the taut muscles in her neck, massaging her stiff shoulders and arms. Lauren closed her eyes. A delicious languor was spreading throughout her body, draining away her tension and anger. She sank back in her chair, relaxing under his skilled ministrations.

Sometime later, his hands stopped working their magic, and she heard Jason speak as if from a great distance. "Now what is all this about?" he asked softly.

Her gold-tipped lashes lifted slowly. Jason was half sitting, half leaning against the desk, his arms crossed in front of his broad chest. His jaw was set in a stern line, but there was a faintly humorous gleam in his blue eyes.

The suspicion that she had been neatly outmaneuvered occurred to Lauren, but she couldn't summon the will to fight. "I . . ." she began, only to pause, trying to remember what she had meant to say. "Are you going to the casino this evening?" she finally murmured. Now why had she said that? She hadn't intended to ask, but merely to inform Jason that she herself was going out.

Jason tilted his head to one side as he considered her question. "I hadn't planned on it, no. Actually, I had thought to spend a quiet evening at home."

"Well, I mean to go. It isn't fair that I should have to languish at Bellefleur while you amuse yourself in town. That wasn't part of our bargain."

Lauren returned Jason's gaze defiantly, daring him to forbid her. She didn't truly want to go to the gaming house, but neither did she intend to let Jason carouse with a woman like Desirée Chaudier. It had nothing to do with jealousy, of course. She merely wanted to protect Jason from the clutches of a scheming, greedy witch.

Jason didn't seem troubled with her announcement, though. "I regret your decision, Cat-eyes," he replied lightly. "Especially since I had arranged an alternate entertainment for you. . . . But perhaps you aren't interested?"

"Interested?"

Repressing a smile, Jason shrugged his broad shoulders. "In accompanying me to the theater one evening next week. I found someone willing to loan us their box. The play will be in French, but I thought you might enjoy it. Besides, you deserve to be rewarded for all the work you've done. I had planned a late supper afterward, but if you don't care to come . . ." Jason let the words trail off as he pushed himself away from the desk and retrieved his coat from a hook on the wall.

As he silently donned it, Lauren struggled against the urge to tell Jason just what she thought of his underhanded methods. Damn him! Again he was giving her a choice—in the form of a bribe! She could go to the gaming house this evening, in which case he would withdraw his invitation for the play. Or she could do as he wished and enjoy an *acceptable* form of entertainment. But she truly wanted to go to the theater, for she had never been before. Not very graciously, Lauren nodded her acquiescence.

When Jason didn't even acknowledge her acceptance, she realized he had known all along what her decision would be. With rising anger, she watched as he cleared the desk and put away the papers. One day, Lauren promised herself, she wouldn't allow herself to be so easily managed.

"Incidentally," Jason said, "I've found a ship for sale that should meet your needs. If you don't have anything pressing this afternoon, I'd like you to take a look at it."

Wondering if this were another part of his plan to secure her obedience, Lauren eyed him warily. "What is the cost? You've convinced me it's smart business to accept Jean-Paul's loan, but I don't want to be indebted to him for life."

"You can afford it. The owner came down a bit on his original asking price after I talked to him."

"Is there no one you cannot manipulate?" Lauren remarked bitterly.

At first it seemed that Jason would ignore her waspish comment. "Unless you direct otherwise," he continued easily, going to the cabin door and holding it open for Lauren, "I intend to complete the deal." As Lauren rose, however, Jason gave her a mocking little bow. "Of course I do not wish to be thanked for performing so insignificant a service for such a charming lady. It is, after all, in my best interest to convince the world that my partner is not the selfish child she so often resembles."

Lifting her chin militantly, Lauren glared up at him. "You think me a selfish child?"

Jason's lips curved in a wry smile. "Quite frequently. But I have hopes that you will grow up one day. I expect you'll make quite a woman when you do. Shall we go?" he added with a laconic lift of his brows.

Since Lauren could think of no appropriate retort, she swept past him with an angry rustle of skirts.

Her anger dissipated, however, the moment she saw the ship Jason had chosen for her. It was the kind of vessel she had always dreamed of possessing: a three-masted, schooner-rigged merchantman, tall and graceful, yet sturdy enough to carry tons of cargo across three or four thousand vast miles of ocean.

The *Kite* rose high in the water, her holds empty, her raking masts bare of sail. Lauren watched silently as they rowed out to board her, not saying a word as Jason lifted her from the skiff to the *Kite*'s boarding ladder.

When she had somewhat awkwardly negotiated the climb and stood on deck, surveying the gleaming stretch of scrubbed-wood planking, a warm rush of feeling surged through Lauren. And as she gazed skyward at the endless intricate web of rigging, the thought crossed her mind that her obsession with ships was interwoven just as intricately with her past.

How many times in Cornwall had she and Matthew talked about buying their own ship? How many times had she dreamed of sailing away with him and leaving her past behind? For that was what ships stood for: freedom, independence, control. And this, the purchase of the merchant ship *Kite,* was the fulfillment of a lifelong ambition. She felt a burden lifting from her heart. Slowly she mounted the quarterdeck and went to stand at the helm.

From his position by the gunwale, Jason watched her, wondering at her thoughts. She reached out to touch the wheel, caressing the smooth wood, then turned to smile at him, her eyes bright as topaz and emeralds, making him catch his breath. If he hadn't given his heart to her long ago, it would have been stolen by that smile. When she looked away, he went to join her.

"I want to call her the *Matthew MacGregor,*" Lauren murmured when she felt Jason's presence, the huskiness of her voice betraying emotion that her cool features never would.

Jason gazed down at her, his eyes caressing her face, taking in its haunting loveliness. "Matthew would be honored . . . any man would be. But Matthew is a man's name. Are you sure you want to flout convention so drastically?"

Lauren looked up to find Jason watching her. His blue eyes were filled with tender amusement and a deeper smoldering light that made her heart skip a beat. "What's convention?" she replied, trying to ignore his burning look.

Jason laughed and flicked her nose. "Something I've been doing my damndest to get you to acknowledge, Cat-eyes—although I don't seem to be having much success, what with your woefully neglected upbringing. Very well, call her the *Matthew MacGregror* if you like. But don't apply to me if you wind up with a mutiny on your hands."

And so the *Kite* was to be rechristened the *Matthew MacGregor*. Lauren went to see the ship's namesake the very next day, intending to offer Matthew a position as captain.

Since he didn't work for the Carlin Line on Saturday, she expected to find him at home, but when she drove up in the gig she had borrowed from Bellefleur, only Running Deer came out of the cypress-log cabin to greet her.

Not attractive by any standards, the Choctaw woman had squat, olive-toned features and coarse ebony hair that hung to her waist. She was wearing a beaded doeskin tunic and moccasins, and her expression registered surprise. "Lauren, I not expect you," she said in her soft musical voice.

"Probably because I've been frightfully negligent," Lauren replied with a smile. "I should have come to see you before now. But I have good news. Where is Matthew? I have to tell him about the ship we're going to buy."

Oddly, a wary look crept into the luminous dark eyes. "He see to traps."

"Does he mean to return soon? If not, I can go look for him."

"No."

Lauren's smile faded. Running Deer was standing at the foot of the cabin steps, twisting a fringe of her tunic and looking very much ill at ease. Lauren couldn't understand her lack of warmth, for generally she was as gentle as the forest animal whose name she carried. "Running Deer, are you angry with me for some reason? Have I done something wrong?"

The Indian woman hesitated. "No."

"Well then, what is it? You usually invite me to to tea."

"Come in, Lauren. You welcome always." She turned to mount the stairs then, leaving a puzzled Lauren to stare after her.

Lauren tied the reins of the gig to the porch rail and

followed, entering the two-room cabin in time to see Running Deer hanging a rifle above the fireplace. "Something *is* wrong," she challenged. "You never greet visitors with a gun."

Running Deer shot her a nervous glance. "I make tea now."

"Please, Running Deer, I don't want tea. I want to know why you have to keep a rifle loaded."

Her dark eyes lowered. "Mat angry if I speak," she said softly.

"Is he in trouble? For God's sake, he's my friend. You can tell me."

"Matthew say you not to worry. You marry soon and be happy."

"Marry—" Lauren realized then that Running Deer and Matthew must be expecting her to marry Jason, but she let that mistaken assumption pass in her concern for Matthew. "Running Deer, you might as well tell me. I won't let it rest until you do."

She sighed softly. "He . . . he lose money. He play cards and lose."

"How much money?"

"Five thousand dollar."

"Five thousand! I don't believe it! Matthew would never be so foolish as to gamble his life savings away."

"He drink too much. And the man cheat."

"What man?"

"Duvo."

"You mean Duval? Matthew was playing cards with Felix Duval?"

Running Deer nodded, worry apparent on her dark features. "The man give one week to find money. He come soon. Mat not have, go to jail."

Lauren stared at her, hardly believing. She had only seen Matthew briefly during the past week, and hadn't noticed any particular difference in his behavior. But then he wouldn't have wanted her to know he had gotten into debt. She couldn't understand, though, how he could have become mixed up with a man like Felix Duval. Felix usually patronized the higher-class gaming hells, where Matthew would never be invited. "Don't worry, Running Deer," Lauren said briskly. "Matthew isn't going to jail."

The Indian woman gave her a grateful smile. "The man have vows. . . ."

"Vowels? That's an I.O.U.—a promissory note showing the amount of the debt, but it doesn't matter. Vowels can be bought back. Where is Matthew now? I want to talk to him."

When Running Deer said that he was trapping near the stream that ran through his small property, Lauren went in search of him. Before she was a hundred yards from the cabin, though, she saw the brawny flame-haired Scotsman coming out of the woods. He was dressed in fringed buckskin, and had half a dozen carcasses of small animals slung over his shoulder.

His stride slowed as soon as he saw her, and his grim expression suggested he knew why she was there. "Go home, lass," he said quietly. "This isna yer battle."

Meeting the gaze of the man who had been like a father to her, Lauren returned a look of affectionate exasperation. "That has to be the most absurd comment you've ever made. You saved my life four years ago. Do you think I wouldn't give my help if you needed it?"

Matthew shook his head without replying, then strode past her, headed toward the curing shed in back of the cabin. Lauren followed, carefully picking up the skirts of her muslin walking dress as she entered the shed to avoid the clutter of stretching frames and dried furs. She had often visited Matthew there while he worked, and was familiar with the pungent odor, but even so, she tried not to breathe too deeply as she settled on a rough-hewn wooden bench.

Matthew had dropped his load and set to work on a beaver carcass, peeling back the fur with deft strokes of a knife. Lauren watched him in silence for a moment, before saying, "Running Deer told me Felix cheated."

"Aye, the cards were marked. And he had more inside his coat."

"Can you prove it?"

Matthew grunted in reply.

"Then you'll have to pay back the debt."

"I dunna have such a sum."

"But together we have enough."

261

"I canna let ye do it. Ye're to buy yer ship."

Lauren didn't tell him that she had already found her ship, knowing it would make his refusal more adamant. "It doesn't matter. I'm not letting you go to jail. How much longer do you have?"

"Till day after next. But I willna take yer money. 'Twas I who acted the fool. Ye'll no' pay for that."

"Well, at least borrow the money from Jean-Paul if you won't take mine."

"Nay, the mon cheated! I'll no' give him one penny."

She could see she was wasting her breath. "Then what will you do?"

"I dunna ken."

Lauren rose then, brushing out her skirts. "Very well, Matthew. If that is how you feel, I won't argue." She had no intention of leaving it at that, certainly, but she knew better than to tell Matthew what she was planning.

He was too familiar with her ways, though, not to wonder at her meek capitulation. "Ye'll no' do something daft, lass?" he asked, giving her a suspicious glance.

"Certainly not," she replied wryly, returning an innocent look. "I'm merely going to take tea with your wife. We have to plan what items to bring you when we visit you in jail!"

Eight hours later, wearing her green satin gown, powdered wig, and mask, Lauren descended the sweeping staircase of the gaming house. The reticule hanging from her wrist contained five thousand dollars.

She had had some difficulty persuading Monsieur Sauvinet to release so large a sum on such short notice, but it had been relatively easy for her to carry out the next part of her plan. First she sent a note to Felix Duval, requesting that he meet "Marguerite" that evening at the casino and allow her to redeem Matthew's vowels. Then after supper, she pleaded a headache and retired early to her room, avoiding Jason's penetrating glance and Lila's concerned one. When it grew dark enough, Lauren wrapped herself in a cloak, took a horse from the stables, and rode into town.

Veronique was delighted to see her, but gave Lauren's plan only a lukewarm reception, saying that gambling debts were male matters and should be left for men to settle. Veronique did agree, however reluctantly, to lend her support by keeping any guests away from the smoking room when Felix arrived.

He was already waiting when Lauren entered and carefully closed the door behind her. His dark face lit with a charming smile. "Chérie," he murmured as he moved toward her and took her hands. "How I have missed you."

Lauren was relieved by his greeting, for she hadn't known if her message would reach him, or if he would agree to her request. As always, he looked quite handsome; his elegant, slender build adapted well to formal evening clothes, and his black hair contrasted with his starched white neckcloth. "Felix," she said in her French-accented voice, "I am glad to see you as well. Thank you for coming."

When he carried her fingers to his lips, she had to control her impatience at his gallantry. "Did you bring Matthew's vowels? I have with me the amount he owes you."

Duval hesitated, gazing at her with a faint smile. "It pains me to refuse you, *ma belle*, but I cannot take money from so lovely a woman."

His answer startled her. She hadn't considered that he would refuse to accept the money. "But I am prepared to give you five thousand dollars. Are you saying you won't allow me to redeem Matthew's debt?"

He chuckled. "The debt has served its purpose. I had hoped it would bring you out of hiding."

"You had hoped—?" Lauren searched his face, wondering what he meant. Then quite suddenly she remembered an incident several months before, when Matthew had come to see her at the casino and she had introduced the two men. Afterward Felix had asked if Matthew was her lover, and she had laughed, claiming that his jealousy was unbecoming. She had shortly forgotten about it, but Felix obviously hadn't. That must be the reason he had sought out Matthew and cozened him into losing such an enormous sum. To get to her.

She stared at Felix, realizing that the faint signs of dissipation etched on his features had deepened since she had last seen him. Realizing also that she had dropped out of her role of Marguerite, Lauren smiled the cool, seductive smile that never failed to set male hearts aflutter. "But how clever you are, Felix. And now that you have found me, what do you intend to do with me?"

His dark eyes flashed with a gleam that she had no trouble recognizing as lust. "What do you think I intend, *ma belle?*" he asked huskily as he moved closer.

When he slipped his arms around her waist and bent to kiss her, Lauren hastily averted her face. "You are very bold, m'sieur," she said somewhat desperately—which fortunately made her voice merely sound breathless. "And not very gallant, I fear. You have set the stakes and the rules, and not given me a fair opportunity to play."

One eyebrow rose skeptically. "What are you suggesting?"

"You are a gambler. You should not be opposed to engaging with me in a game of chance. Chemin de fer, perhaps?"

He gave her a patronizing smile. "And for what stakes shall we play, chérie?"

"Matthew's vowels, of course. And if you win, you shall have a night with me."

"Merely one night?"

Lauren reached up to run a slender finger along his lower lip. "A week, then. I am worth it, I think."

"Agreed, mademoiselle, if I will at last be allowed to view the lovely face behind the mask."

Jason would kill her, Lauren thought as she returned a provocative smile. But it seemed the only way to save Matthew from jail. She didn't have great faith in her ability to defeat Felix at cards, but she thought she could manage to make the play challenging enough to give him a scare. And that might lead him to make a very big mistake.

Easing herself from Felix's embrace, Lauren turned and led the way to the crowded gaming rooms. She wanted to be very certain there were other people nearby when she exposed Felix Duval as a cheat.

As luck would have it, Desirée Chaudier was working the chemin de fer table. The beautiful brunette scowled the moment she saw Lauren. "I see the Amazon has returned,"

264

Desirée said nastily, calling attention to Lauren's height.

Lauren ignored the slur and flashed a cool smile at the five men already seated at the table. "M'sieurs, you will kindly allow us to join you, *non?*"

At once, all five gentlemen rose and made a great show of inviting the husky-voiced Marguerite to participate. Desirée took immediate exception. "You cannot! Madame Gescard will forbid it."

"Tonight I am a guest," Lauren replied as she allowed a balding overweight gamester named Smithson to seat her. "And my great friend M'sieur Duval wishes to play with me."

Other than cause a scene, Desirée had no choice but to back down. She acceded with poor grace, while the players made room, less enthusiastically, for Felix Duval.

He wound up sitting two seats to Lauren's left, which pleased her. She had chosen chemin de fer because it offered numerous opportunities for a cardsharp to execute a sleight of hand. The dealer changed frequently, and the initial two cards each player received were turned facedown, making them easy targets for marking or substitution. In order to catch Felix at cheating, however, she had to be close enough to see him.

The decks were shuffled and cut, then placed in the dealing box called a shoe. Lauren bid low when the deal was auctioned, for she wanted to see what Felix would do. The Creole seemed to be waiting also, since he allowed the deal to go to the bald gentleman.

"The bank is three hundred dollars," Smithson announced, before beginning the first hand.

The bets were conservative at the start, with Smithson winning the first three coups, then losing on a natural eight. When the deal passed to the left, Lauren increased the betting in order to drive up the stakes. Her first two cards totaled five, but when she drew another, it was a queen, which put her over the required count of nine.

"A pity, chérie," Felix remarked with mild sarcasm.

Accepting her loss with a shrug, Lauren flashed him a challenging smile. "But can you do better, m'sieur?"

"Watch and you shall see."

Lauren did watch, carefully, as Felix bancoed by matching

the entire bank with his wager. She could see no indication, though, that his play was anything but aboveboard, for he made no extraordinary moves, and he hadn't had time to mark any of the cards. His impassive face revealed no emotion as he added the value of his cards and elected to stand.

An eight to the dealer's seven, Lauren saw with disappointment when the card was revealed. As long as Felix won so handily, he would never be desperate enough to try anything underhanded.

To Lauren's dismay, he continued to win—at least until the deal had gone once around the table and again belonged to her. Then Duval's luck took a downturn, while Lauren's improved. Twice she had a natural—a count of nine—in the first two cards, and since she was holding the bank, she won all bets. Felix's confidence remained strong, however, even when he began losing steadily.

The deal went around the table once more, with Lauren again winning several hands. When it was Felix's to deal, she watched him carefully out of the corner of her eye. If he were to make a move, she thought, it would probably be while he controlled the cards.

She was right, although she almost missed his deft sleight of hand; Duval slipped a card from the shoe and let it fall to the floor so smoothly and quickly that Lauren knew he must have practiced the motion regularly. She resisted the urge to cry foul, though, knowing a charge of cheating would only stick if he were caught redhanded.

Her impatience was growing thin by the time Duval won several more coups, for he still hadn't reached for the fallen card. Lauren took a deep breath and gambled. "Banco," she declared, hoping that the bank of five hundred dollars would be too large for Felix to risk losing.

All smaller bets had to be withdrawn, and Smithson, who had also been losing, decided to fold. As he left the table, Lauren counted her points. The total came to four, so she had no choice but to draw. She could feel her palms sweating as she asked for another card.

A four. She was still in. She glanced at Felix, realizing as she met his penetrating dark gaze that her own calm expression was no more revealing than his own. Smiling slightly then, she tried to look as if she were repressing excitement over a winning hand.

Elation coursed through her when she saw Felix draw a lace-edged handkerchief from his pocket. When he dropped it as if by accident, then bent to pick it up, Lauren knew the fallen card would be concealed in its folds. She opened her mouth to denounce him, just as a tall, tawny-haired man dressed in a blue coat and buff breeches moved into her range of vision.

"M'sieur Stuart!" Desirée crooned, while Lauren nearly jumped.

"How careless of someone," Jason drawled as he bent casually to pick up the card he had purposely stepped on. "The two of spades was lying beside your chair, Duval." He flicked the card on the table, then smiled dismissively at the other gamesters, managing to defuse the potentially explosive incident with his unconcern.

Felix kept his face carefully blank as he added the spade to the discards. Lauren would have seen a muscle in his jaw tighten had she been watching, but she was staring at Jason in dismay. She had been startled by his sudden appearance, then angry when he had foiled her carefully prepared trap, yet she could only bemoan her ill luck in silence.

When he greeted Desirée with a liberal dose of masculine charm, Lauren nearly ground her teeth in frustration. He turned to her then with a polite bow, his gaze locking with hers. "Mademoiselle Marguerite, is it not? I had the great pleasure of hearing you sing some weeks ago."

She was taken aback by the smoldering anger in his blue eyes. Realizing she would be lucky to get home with her skin intact, Lauren managed to murmur a reply. She was too disquieted, though, to protest when Jason asked to join the game and seated himself at the table. She didn't even smile when she discovered she had won the bank of five hundred dollars with her hand of eight. With the two of spades, Felix's total would have been nine.

The play turned deadly serious after that, probably, Lauren decided, because Felix seemed determined to win at any cost. He didn't have much luck against Jason's phenomenal skill, however, nor did anyone else. One by one the other gamesters dropped out, making it a contest between the two men. By the time three hours had passed, Felix had lost more than five thousand dollars, and Jason's winnings were nearly double that.

"You are very lucky, m'sieur," Felix said at last, barely keeping his tone civil.

Jason raked in the proceeds from the last coup, then looked up to fix his gaze steadily on the Creole. "Some hold the belief that a man makes his own luck. I would have thought you agreed. Or did the two of spades just happen to fall off the table by itself earlier this evening?"

Felix's face darkened in anger. "Is that an accusation?" he demanded in a dangerous voice.

Lauren stirred uneasily in her chair. The other players had drifted away, so only she and Desirée were left to observe the brewing confrontation.

"I see no need to make any accusations," Jason replied evenly. "Madame Gescard will hear of the incident, I don't doubt, and take the proper precautions. But perhaps you ought see that no stray cards end up in your vicinity in the future. It could be rather embarrassing for you."

"This issue should be settled on the field of honor!" Felix exclaimed, his voice taut with fury.

"Please, Felix," Lauren said quickly as the Creole leapt to his feet. "There is no need to get upset."

Unconcerned by Duval's outburst, Jason leaned back in his seat, a ghost of a smile wreathing his mouth. "I would be happy to oblige, of course—"

"*Non!*" Desirée interjected. "One of you could be killed."

"—but a duel," Jason continued, "would not be particularly good for a gambler's reputation. You would find it hard to avoid the stigma of cheating afterward, even if you were to win. Which, I must warn you, is unlikely." When Felix remained standing there, clenching his fists and glaring, Jason raised an eyebrow. "Come now, Duval, you're not a stupid man, sit down. You're making a scene, in addition to disturbing these lovely ladies. Besides, I have a proposition for you that will allow you to cut your losses."

268

Felix continued to glare, but he resumed his seat. "What proposition?" he demanded. Lauren let out her breath, not realizing that she had been holding it.

"I believe you're holding a note of hand belonging to a friend of mine," Jason said, pushing a stack of bills across the table to Duval. "Here's five thousand for the note, plus another thousand for your trouble."

Felix's brows drew together in a frown. His suspicious gaze sliced to Lauren, before returning to Jason. "This MacGregor seems to have a great number of friends."

"I wouldn't know," Jason lied. "MacGregor happens to be in my employ, so I have a vested interest in keeping him out of jail."

The Creole hesitated a long moment, before he smiled philosophically and reached into his coat pocket for the note. "Forgive me, chérie," he said to Lauren, "for backing out of our wager. But you see how it is. You will be achieving your goal, at any rate." Picking up the money, Felix stuffed it into his pocket as he rose to leave. "A pity," he murmured, looking down at Lauren. "I don't think I have ever regretted winning such a large sum."

Lauren had no reply to that, so she merely smiled and offered her fingers for Felix to kiss. When he had gone, she stole a glance at Jason. He was watching her, with a look in his eye that warned of the reckoning still to come.

Holding her gaze, Jason slowly stood up. "Shall we go, mademoiselle?"

She knew better than to protest as he came around the table to assist her from her chair, but she had a momentary reprieve when Desirée stepped between them. The beautiful brunette touched Jason's sleeve, looking up at him with a pout. "Will you not stay, M'sieur Jason? I have been very lonely without you."

Jason flashed her a regretful smile. "Thank you, my sweet, but I mean to escort Mademoiselle Marguerite home."

As they walked away, Lauren could hear Desirée grumbling to herself about Amazons.

They were required to wait for Jason's carriage to be brought around, and Lauren found herself growing more nervous in the ensuing silence. She considered asking the majordomo, Kendricks, for help, but decided Jason's temper was uncertain enough that he might carry her bodily out of the casino if she refused to accompany him.

Jason's grip on her arm was painful as he escorted her to the phaeton which drew up before the casino. After assisting Lauren up, he tossed a coin to the black youth holding the two horses, then took his own seat and set the pair in motion.

Not until they were well out of town did he speak. "Putting yourself," Jason said, not taking his eyes off the road, "at the mercy of a man like Duval is one of the stupidest things I've ever seen you do."

His voice was quietly grim, like velvet over steel, and his simmering anger made Lauren uneasy, but she resisted the urge to squirm and turned her head away to gaze at the passing shadows of hackberry and sweetgum trees that lined the road. The sultry night was rather dark, with only a thin sliver of moon lighting the way. "How did you know where to find me?" she asked rather lamely.

"Matthew suspected you might do something quixotic and had the good sense to come to me. Which is precisely what you should have done. I'm far better equipped to handle Duval than you will ever be. I have greater skill at cards, and can afford to lose more, besides having the ability to defend myself. You had no business taking on Duval by yourself."

Lauren stiffened at his tone. She had little defense against Jason's logic, yet she objected to being chided as if she were accountable to him. "I don't need you to tell me how to behave," she replied sullenly.

"It's obvious someone needs to."

"You aren't my guardian, Jason."

"That's debatable, but I won't dispute it at the moment." He shot her an angry glance before turning his attention back to the horses. "I can admire your loyalty to Matthew, Lauren, but this damned determination of yours to remain independent has reached the point of obsession."

Sitting rigidly beside him, Lauren didn't deign to reply.

"What were you planning to give Duval if you lost? No, don't answer that. I can guess all too well."

"I didn't plan to lose," she snapped, her own anger rising. "I meant to expose his cheating before that."

"Sweet Christ," Jason breathed. "And just what do you think his response would have been if you had taken away his livelihood? There isn't a chance in hell I could have protected you if he decided to have his revenge later."

"I didn't ask you to protect me."

Jason took a deep breath and counted to ten before he replied. "As a gentleman, I'm obligated to assist a lady in distress, even one who's fool enough to bring trouble on herself."

"That wasn't chivalry! You just wanted to make sure I remained in your debt."

Jason turned a blazing blue glare on her. "I do not under any circumstances expect or want you to feel indebted to me. For any reason whatsoever."

"No? Then why did you suggest our bargain if not to make me feel obligated to you?"

"Damn it, Lauren, I want you to learn the shipping business precisely so you won't feel obligated to me. So we can meet, if not on equal, then at least equivalent ground. And so you'll be prepared for the responsibility when I turn the Carlin Line over to you in a few months."

His hypocrisy, after his declared intention of winning both her and the Carlin Line, galled her. "You want the Carlin ships, don't deny it!"

Jason clenched his teeth. "I won't."

"And you said it was 'all or nothing.' I can't believe you've given up so easily."

"I haven't." Abruptly pulling the horses to a halt, Jason secured the reins as he turned to face her. "I'd like to be indispensable to you, but not because you need me to organize your affairs. I wanted this past month to be an opportunity for us to get to know each other—"

Realizing at last that she had given him an opening for the very subject she wished to avoid, Lauren held up a hand. "No, please! I don't want to discuss it."

"Ignoring an issue won't make it go away, Lauren. You can't run from it forever."

271

As if to prove his point, he reached out to grip her arms. His grasp wasn't painful, but it engendered panic in Lauren. "You promised you wouldn't speak to me of that!" she exclaimed, trying to pull away.

"Just answer one question. What is it you have against marriage anyway? Are you afraid of something? Of me?"

"No . . . yes . . . I don't know!" she cried, pressing her hands to her ears.

Seeing her genuine distress, Jason forbore to capitalize on his advantage. Suddenly releasing her, he gathered the reins and urged the horses on. Neither of them spoke another word to break the tense silence.

When they arrived at Bellefleur, Lauren jumped from the carriage before it had stopped, and ran up to her room where she remained, refusing to talk to anyone, even Lila. She spent a miserable few hours, pacing the floor and regretting the entire evening. Jason was right, she knew; she should have let him handle Duval. She had been infinitely relieved when he had won back Matthew's note, but she hadn't sounded a bit grateful. Instead she had reacted like the petulant child he had accused her of being, arguing and flinging accusations at him. And what was worse, she had given him the opportunity to renew his proposal at a time when she was least prepared to deal with it. The only good thing that had come of the evening was that they had prevented Matthew from going to jail.

Too involved in self-castigation and self-pity, Lauren was unable to sleep when the rest of the household retired for the night. Even Ulysses had deserted her, for the cat had been gone for hours and hadn't returned. It was well past midnight when she heard his plaintive yowl through the open French windows. Lauren called to him, but when Ulysses didn't come, she stepped outside, where only a faint breeze stirred the sultry night air, carrying the heavy scents of Cape jasmine and magnolia blossoms. Searching the darkness, she could see no sign of him, and so she silently made her way along the gallery.

She saw the great feline when she rounded the corner of the house. He was sitting in a soft pool of light that streamed from one of the rooms. Lauren softly called again, but to her dismay, the cat stretched, then bounded inside.

Lauren hesitated for a long moment. There was only one occupied bedroom at the back of the house, and that had been given to Jason. She shrank from the thought of having to face him. But he might be asleep, she reflected. Or he might not be there at all. He might have returned to the gaming house in search of more congenial company. Half hoping he would be gone, Lauren followed the elusive cat.

When she reached the door to Jason's room, she stopped abruptly. Jason was there, Lauren saw at once. He was stretched out on the large four-poster bed, wearing nothing but his breeches, the light from a single candle illuminating his long, muscular body. He had obviously not yet attempted to sleep, for the covers hadn't been turned down and the mosquito net was still open.

He seemed lost in thought, for he lay on his back, one arm supporting his head, his free hand absently stroking the cat's orange fur as Ulysses rubbed against his thigh.

Lauren decided not to disturb him, but before she could turn to go, Jason sensed her presence. Raising his head from the pillow, he regarded her with a frown.

When she felt Jason's gaze rake her scantily clad body, Lauren suddenly became quite conscious of her state of undress. Her nightgown, little more than a thin cotton shift, left her arms and throat bare, while her golden hair was loose and flowing around her shoulders. Yet she knew Jason wouldn't approve of her presence there if she were fully clothed with her hair bound in a tight chignon. "I came for Ulysses," she explained hastily before he could order her out.

He didn't reply. He made no move at all. Lauren's trepidation increased as she stepped into the room. "May I have my cat?" she repeated. "He usually sleeps with me."

Jason exhaled slowly, as if he had been holding his breath. "Lucky cat," he said in a strained voice.

"I offered once," Lauren reminded him. "I seem to recall you were the one to refuse."

Jason sat up then and arranged the pillows behind his back. "Lauren, come here."

She lifted an eyebrow. "Really, Jason, you surprise me. I expected you to remind me that it is highly improper for me to

273

be here in your bedroom."

"It is improper. Particularly when both of us have so few clothes on. But I'll try to restrain myself." He held out an inviting hand, his gaze compelling her to obey.

Lauren found it impossible to resist the arresting power of those blue eyes. She moved closer, yet halted at the foot of the bed, clutching at the poster as if at any moment she would be pulled into the vortex of a storm. "I suppose," she replied, her tone defensively mocking, "that I should be flattered you deigned to notice. You've been so occupied with Desirée lately, I thought you had forgotten me. Indeed, I expected you to return to the casino. What could you be thinking of, to disappoint Madame Gescard's girls so? Desirée must be heartbroken."

Jason's mouth twitched as if he were repressing a smile. "I do wish you would give me a chance to defend myself against your broadsides, Lauren. Come here," he repeated, indicating for her to sit beside him.

"Why?" she countered warily.

"Because, my sweet, the candlelight behind you makes your nightdress nearly transparent. It gives you a decided advantage."

"Oh!" Lauren flushed. Reluctantly she obeyed Jason's command, gingerly sitting beside him on the edge of the bed.

Jason took her hand and held it loosely between his. "Furthermore," he added, "I'm quite receptive to a midnight tête-à-tête, but only if I have some assurance that you will stay to finish the conversation."

When Lauren nervously attempted to extricate her hand, she discovered it to be imprisoned in a painless but immutable grip. "I suppose," she said stiffly, "that now you mean to use brute force?"

Jason met her gaze steadily. "Your accusations are beginning to bore me, Lauren. You don't really think that, any more than you believe I would force you into marriage. Or for that matter, that I only want to marry you for the Carlin ships."

Ulysses jumped off the bed and disappeared into the night shadows, but Lauren never even noticed. "Then why *do* you want to marry me?" she asked in a breathless voice.

"Probably because I love you." When Lauren gave a start, a slight smile played at the corners of Jason's mouth. "I've loved you ever since I first saw you," he said softly. "Why else do you suppose I proposed to you then?" Lauren remained staring at him speechlessly. "What?" he teased. "Are you still here? I had assumed that confession would send you scrambling for cover."

Lauren heartily wished she hadn't allowed him to open the subject again. "You won't release my hand," she said rather lamely.

"Answer my question first." Bringing her fingers to his lips, he kissed the tip of each one, sending warm sparks shooting up Lauren's arm.

"What question?" she murmured vaguely.

"Tell me what you're afraid of." He noted the haunted look in her amber-flecked eyes, but he held her gaze as he continued to press. "You don't fear me," Jason said gently. "You never have. So why do you panic every time I suggest marriage?"

Lauren knew she had to give him some kind of answer. "I . . . I don't want to give any man that kind of control over me."

Jason shook his head. "That isn't your reason. You don't truly believe I would abuse the privilege of caring for you."

"No, but . . . but you want to live in England and I don't. My life is here."

"I can't accept that, either, Lauren." Slowly he reached up to touch her lips, gently tracing them with a lean forefinger. His eyes searched her face as his voice dropped to a mere whisper. "What I would give to penetrate those defenses you show the world. . . ."

Lauren hesitated, her mouth working silently as Jason's long fingers stroked her cheek. She didn't want him to love her. Nothing could come of it. Her origins, if nothing else, prevented her from marrying him.

When she didn't speak, Jason gave a sigh. "Well, I've waited nearly four years for you. I suppose I can wait a while longer."

"No, you mustn't!"

She tried to pull away, but her protest was cut off as Jason drew her into his arms. "Hush, my love," he murmured,

275

stroking her hair. "I didn't mean to distress you."

Resting her cheek on Jason's bare chest, Lauren closed her eyes. She felt a painful tightness in her throat, a throbbing ache deep in her chest, as she regretted more than ever the past which hung like a millstone around her neck. But though she very much felt like crying, her eyes were dry.

She couldn't have said how much time passed before the candleflame sputtered out, leaving the room in semidarkness, but that was when she first realized that Jason's arms were no longer a place of solace. He remained quite still, yet she suddenly became conscious of the musky-clean scent of his skin and the intimate way her breasts were pressed against his sinewy chest. Something strong and vital was flowing between them, something almost tangible. She could actually feel her senses coming alive as longing stirred within her.

She wanted Jason to hold her more tightly, but she was afraid to move. She was well aware that he would send her away if he knew what she was thinking.

But he knew, she realized a moment later. His hand swept slowly down her back, moving possessively over her hip and thigh, then up again. All her nerve endings started to flicker.

After a moment, she felt Jason grasp her shoulders. When he held her away from him, Lauren looked down into azure eyes that glittered with molten desire. "Lauren," he murmured hoarsely. One of his hands twisted in the silken curtain of her hair while the other reached for the buttons of her nightdress.

"Jason . . . please," Lauren whispered, not knowing herself whether she was pleading for him to stop or continue. She was afraid, either way. Afraid that he might again seek relief with another woman if she refused him. Afraid she would surrender totally to him if she consented.

And so she did nothing—neither encouraged nor denied. She only held her breath while her heart hammered against her rib cage.

Slowly, as if he couldn't help himself, Jason released the buttons and inched her nightdress down over her shoulders, baring her breasts to his gaze. Drawing her closer then, he let his mouth close hotly over a taut nipple. Lauren nearly jumped as a shock wave of pure pleasure jolted through her. She let her head fall back, feeling desire curl and twist in her loins.

Jason's tongue swirled over the sensitive peak till it was rigid and aching from his attentions, then moved to the other ample mound of sweet flesh, sucking and licking and nipping gently, grazing softly with his teeth. Lauren's breath came in muted gasps.

In the end, though, it was Jason himself who banked the fires he had started. He pulled away, his rasping breath loud in the dark. "Not like this, Lauren," he said hoarsely. "Not like this. When I make love to you, I want your total commitment."

She was relieved, and yet . . .

He rearranged the bodice of her nightdress, fastening the buttons with unsteady fingers. "Go back to your room, sweetheart," he ordered in a ragged voice, "before we both lose control."

Lauren honestly tried to obey, but Jason's caresses had left her dizzy and weak. Her knees felt like warm honey. When she tried to rise, they wouldn't support her. She sank back down, unintentionally swaying toward him.

Jason was hardly in a mood to be patient. Aching with unfulfilled need, he had nearly reached the limits of his fortitude. "Lauren!" he growled. Gripping her shoulders, he almost shook her. "Lauren, get the hell out of here before I turn you over my knee!" Whipping his head around, he searched the shadows of the room. "Christ, where is that damned cat!"

His eruption, as sudden as a Louisiana tempest, startled Lauren. She stared at him with apprehension, before realizing the cause of his anger.

She did something totally out of character then; she *giggled*. Actually it came out more as a husky chortle, and she immediately clasped a hand over her mouth to stifle the sound. But it was laughter, all the same. She couldn't help it. Jason's fury, following so closely on the heels of passion, struck her as being ludicrously funny.

At the soft sound of her choked laughter, Jason turned the full force of his glare on her. "What the blazes has gotten you in such high spirits?" he snapped.

Giving her laughter free rein, Lauren wagged a finger under his nose. "Those are hardly the words of an ardent lover," she admonished, heady with the knowledge that she had finally shaken his iron composure. "If you want me to become enamored of you, you should be plying me with flattery and kisses. You should be trying to sweep me off my feet, rather than ignoring me and insulting me and threatening me. You're hardly likely to win your suit by such methods."

He drew a long, determined breath. When his temper was once more in check, Jason eyed her suspiciously. Then after a moment, he relaxed against the pillows. "It seems that I'm unlikely to win my suit by *any* method," he said dryly. "But I think I'll stick to the current battle plan, thank you. It hasn't yet proven a total failure. Do you mean to walk or must I carry you?"

Lauren ignored his question. "So you admit it! You *do* have a plan. Is Desirée a particular stratagem then?" she asked in a deceptively silken tone.

It was Jason's turn to smile. He flashed her a grin that dazzled, even in the semidarkness. "What's this? Jealousy, my sweet Lauren?"

Lauren pressed her lips together. "I am merely curious to know what you find so interesting in that . . . that she-cat."

"Isn't it obvious?"

"Of course it's obvious! I just wondered, why *her?*"

Jason's eyes glimmered with amusement. "Desirée's charms are nothing compared to yours, if that's what you're asking. Of course, she generally treats a man with more warmth than you do. . . ."

His baiting words struck a highly sensitive nerve. Lauren leapt to her feet and stood over him, clenching her fists. "You . . . you . . . cad," she sputtered. "Let me tell you something, Jason Stuart. If you *ever* dare compare me to her again, I'll . . . I'll . . ."

"Yes?" Jason drawled provokingly. He rose, also, but in a more leisurely fashion. Slowly, like a giant cat, he began to stalk her.

Lauren took an automatic step backward. "I'll kick you,

that's what. Where it hurts!" Obviously Jason wasn't worried by her threat, for he kept coming. Nervous, she retreated. "And what's more," Lauren added defiantly, "if you don't stay away from Desirée, I'll go back to the casino again. Every night!"

Jason appeared unconcerned as he followed her all the way across the room and onto the gallery. When the small of her back hit the railing, Lauren held up her hands defensively. "And I won't just play the piano," she warned. "I'll dance on it!"

Jason laughed as he reached down and swung her into his arms. "And you accused me of extortion! Very well, I agree."

Lauren started to struggle, but when she realized what he had said, she ceased fighting and peered up into his laughing blue eyes. "You do?" she asked skeptically.

Carrying her easily, Jason strode along the gallery toward her room. "I do. I'll never go near Desirée again if you promise not to dance on the piano. You drive a hard bargain, sweetheart."

Lauren cleared her throat, wondering if she had somehow trapped herself with her own words. "It's for your own sake. Desirée isn't good enough for you. Even Veronique says so."

Jason made a wry face. "And I was hoping you were jealous."

"Well . . ." She dropped her eyes. "Perhaps I was . . . a bit."

His voice softened. "You shouldn't be, Lauren. I never touched Desirée." When Lauren's gaze lifted, holding disbelief, Jason smiled down at her. "Besides," he pointed out, "it's *you* I want to marry."

Lauren pursed her lips thoughtfully, knowing Jason wouldn't be so anxious to marry her if he knew about her birth. "Kyle says now that you are Lord Effing, you have to find a wife."

"Umm hmm," Jason agreed. "The responsibility that comes with the title. Do you have any suggestions? That wasn't a proposal, by the way. I'm sticking to our bargain."

She tilted her head to one side, considering him. "If I refused to provide you with heirs, would you change your mind about wanting to marry me?"

"No, Cat-eyes. I won't ever change my mind."

Entering her room, Jason gently deposited Lauren on her own bed. As he bent over her to tuck a light quilt under her chin, his gaze searched her face. "Don't you want children?" he asked seriously.

"I . . . I don't know. I hadn't thought much about it."

Jason planted a light kiss on her lips. "Let me know if you do. I'll be happy to oblige. Would you like me to stay till you fall asleep?" When she shook her head, Jason gave her a tender smile and then melded into the night shadows.

His loving look kept Lauren warm long after he had gone. And as she lay there in the dim light, staring at the canopy above her bed, Lauren found herself wondering what it would be like to have a child to hold in her arms. Not just any child, but a little boy with laughing blue eyes. One she could hold and cherish and love. . . .

It was quite some time before she drifted to sleep.

Chapter Sixteen

Jason acted quite as if the incident at the casino had never occurred. As agreed, he arranged to buy the *Kite* and hired a captain for the ship's first voyage, and two nights later he escorted Lauren to the theater.

She did enjoy the play. The Orleans Theater on Orleans Street had been destroyed by fire in 1813, but had been rebuilt to house traveling troupes who made their way to the city. The new building was impressive—boasting Doric colonnades, a spacious parquet, multiple galleries, and two tiers of private boxes.

Since their box was fairly close to the stage, Lauren had no trouble hearing, but she sometimes had to ask Jason to translate. The entire play was delivered in French, for even though New Orleans had been under American rule for a dozen years, French was still considered by many of its citizens to be the only civilized language.

Jason derived less pleasure from the entertainment than she did, for he was far too aware of Lauren sitting beside him. She looked stunning in one of the gowns he had selected for her—a high-waisted creation of ivory sarcenette. The décolletage was modest by current standards, but the bodice still left a great expanse of creamy flesh bare to his gaze. The distraction of those lush breasts kept Jason from concentrating, while the fragrant scent of her skin filled his senses and aroused an acute ache in him. He found himself extremely grateful for the semidarkness of the theater, since it hid the embarrassing swell in the front of his breeches.

By the end of the play, however, Jason had once again gained control of himself. When Lauren laughed again over the last lines of the comedy, he decided that the enchantment of her expression was worth any discomfort he might have felt. Smiling down into her shining eyes, he placed her wrap about her shoulders, then ushered her from the box, holding his arm protectively about her waist to prevent her from being jostled by the crowds filling the mezzanine.

They drew the attention of nearly everyone they passed. Lauren's haunting loveliness and Jason's commanding presence made them a striking couple, and more than a few heads turned to watch their progress as he escorted her down the sweeping staircase.

They had reached the first landing when Lauren suddenly stiffened. Jason followed her gaze to see Felix Duval at the foot of the stairs, staring up at Lauren with unconcealed desire. As Lauren's look of rapt joy swiftly faded, to be replaced by her habitual air of remoteness, Jason involuntarily tightened his arm around her, feeling an overwhelming urge to use his fists on Duval's leering face. "No doubt Duval recognized you," Jason murmured tersely as he steered her away.

Peering up at Jason, Lauren bit her lip. "I suppose you will now say it's my fault he looked at me like that."

The corner of Jason's mouth quirked in a smile. "I don't think you can help being desirable, but I would prefer that you didn't tempt him again by appearing at the casino. Even though rescuing you is becoming a habit with me, I shouldn't care to spend a lifetime at it."

Lauren relaxed with Jason's familiar teasing. "I didn't ask you to," she rejoined.

"No," Jason laughed, "but I keep hoping you will."

After that, however, Lauren had little opportunity to visit the casino. Jason kept her evenings full, taking her to dine at a New Orleans restaurant, or escorting her to various social functions hosted by his growing circle of acquaintance, including a ball at a neighboring plantation.

As construction of the warehouses progressed, Lauren also saw more of Jason during the day. He took her shopping again, and to visit Running Deer at the cabin, but more often, he arranged long drives in the country.

Lauren's favorites of these impromptu outings of Jason's were the ones with no particular destination in mind: long, lazy spring days when they would explore some new spot of beauty and then hungrily attack the picnic lunch they had brought.

She was never alone with Jason on these outings. Kyle was often present, having returned from visiting his family in Natchez, and Running Deer frequently served as a guide, particularly when they explored the bayous by pirogue. When they picnicked on a section of the creek that ran through Beauvais property, Lila was on hand to act as chaperone. So was two-year old Charles, since Jason always insisted on bringing the boy along. Even when their chosen site was the Bellefleur gardens, there was always at least one other addition to the party.

It didn't take Lauren long to realize that Jason was purposely avoiding being alone in her company, and his evasion annoyed her, especially whenever she thought of Jason in Desirée's arms. As far as Lauren could tell, Desirée had lost him for a client. Indeed Jason appeared to be staying away from the gaming house altogether. Yet Lauren couldn't dismiss the image of Desirée's voluptuous body writhing beneath his while he murmured words of passion against her lips. The picture was enough to make Lauren's blood boil, for it made her recall how firmly Jason had rejected her.

One day some three weeks after the casino incident, Lauren complained to Veronique about Jason's indifference.

"Do not worry, *m'amie*," the redhead answered with a shrug of her delicate shoulders. "That one is already caught and he knows it, but he will be the one to decide when to allow you to draw him in." Unconcerned, she continued her tour of the bustling shipping office, admiring the new furnishings and decorations.

Lauren interrupted Veronique's compliments. "You don't understand. Not only has Jason been ignoring me, he wouldn't even make love to me when I offered." When Veronique didn't reply, Lauren caught her by the arm. "Veronique, have you not heard a word I have said? I told you that I threw myself at

283

Jason and he refused to have me!"

Veronique at last gave Lauren her full attention. "I heard you, Lauren. But it is you who refuses to listen. *Sacre!* Sometimes you think like a child! So naive! But of course he would not make love to you. Monsieur Stuart is a gentleman, and you are a lady, *chérie*. A young lady, at that. He would not treat you otherwise, as if you were no better than a doxy. You are lucky you have not given him a disgust of you. You will have to change your ways if you plan to have him as a husband."

Astonished as well as hurt, Lauren threw up her hands. "Not you, too! Oh, can no one understand that I don't wish to be married?"

Veronique raised her eyes to the ceiling. "*Merde!* An imbecile, as well as a child! I go now, me." She began to gather up her shawl and reticule, but then the injured look in Lauren's eyes made her pause. Reaching out, she patted Lauren on the cheek. "*Ma pauvre petite.* I think I understand. No woman could resist wanting such a handsome man for her lover. But think first what you give up. With such a man you could have a lover and a husband as well."

"But I don't want a husband," Lauren repeated, trying to convince herself as well as her friend.

Veronique shook her head. "Take my word for it, Lauren. You do not want to lead my kind of life. It is far too lonely. I dare not even agree to Kyle's wish to have me to himself. He will leave someday and then I will have lost my other clients to the younger girls. But I would give anything to have my own man, a family, children to love."

"But that isn't what I want."

Veronique's look was both shrewd and compassionate. "You do not know what you want, *mon chou*. Give it time."

Lauren clenched her fists. "While Jason carries on with any woman who strikes his fancy? I will not!"

"If you are so jealous," Veronique said seriously, "then you must care for him."

The redhead took her leave then, but Lauren hardly noticed. She was staring blindly at the carpet, dazed, even horrified by her revelation. She had been slowly but irrevocably falling in love with Jason!

Lauren twisted her fingers together, wondering how she could have been so dimwitted. How could she have failed to see that trapping her with love had been Jason's intention all along? She had made a grave miscalculation, thinking she could keep him at a distance. She should have been warned from the first by the physical attraction between them, but instead she had allowed Jason every opportunity to wear down her defenses. Now he had managed to shatter the hard shell she had so carefully erected around her heart. Now she was hopelessly trapped. . . .

It was a bitter moment for Lauren. Despair coursed through her, and deep resentment, as well—resentment directed at Jason for the success of his plan. How difficult it would be to part from him when he returned to England! How much more painful to know she could never go with him!

And what of the present? How could she bear to be near Jason while she pretended not to care? How could she hide her love from him when he always seemed to guess just what she was thinking?

Several hours later, Lauren discovered that facing Jason without betraying her inner turmoil was even harder than she had expected. To her dismay, he had chosen that evening to take her out alone, and her distracted air was all the more conspicuous without the presence of others. She couldn't even meet his eyes for fear of giving herself away.

The first part of the evening passed pleasantly enough, however. They attended another play, and if Jason noticed Lauren's strange mood, he forbore to comment on it.

Afterward they dined in a private parlor of an hotel, amid plush surroundings. The meal of braised veal and herb-stuffed quail was excellent, even though Lauren hardly tasted the little she ate. She drank quite a lot, though. Far too much, she realized during the last course. When the waiters at last left, she rose from the table, decidedly flushed and giddy.

She had never been inebriated before, but she discovered to her surprise that although her head was spinning violently, the wine had helped dull the pain she had been feeling. Clutching her temples, she stumbled over to the chaise longue in the corner and sat down heavily.

After a moment, she lifted her head and looked over at Jason. He was seated at the table, watching her over the rim of his glass. How handsome he is, Lauren thought dizzily, seeing his gilded chestnut hair reflect the candlelight. His compelling masculine looks were enhanced by his formal attire, his burgundy coat fitting his broad shoulders to perfection. She felt the strongest urge to remove his clothes and caress his magnificent body. . . .

"How per . . . fect!" Lauren mumbled, attempting to speak. She was amazed at how difficult it was to keep the words from sounding slurred. "The stage is set for a . . . seduction scene . . . Jason."

Jason's mouth twitched. "No, my sweet. I don't seduce young ladies who can't hold their liquor."

"You don't have to. You see, I plan to . . . seduce you," Lauren announced in a husky voice. Then she ruined the effect by moaning, "if you will only stop moving." Lying back against the cushions, she pressed a hand to her aching forehead.

Jason chuckled. "Don't go to sleep, Lauren. It won't help your reputation if I have to carry you from the hotel."

"Devil take my re . . . putation! What difference does it make, anyway? I'm already a fallen woman. You said I was used . . . used goods at a market. Is that why you don't want me?"

Setting down his glass of port, Jason rose and went to her. "You're foxed and feeling sorry for yourself," he observed unsympathetically.

"You don't want me," she repeated.

Jason sat down beside her on the couch. "Of course I want you, but—"

"Then prove it," she challenged. A provocative smile played around the corners of her mouth as she lifted her arms and tried to wrap them about Jason's neck.

He evaded her embrace by capturing her wrists. "You know the terms, Lauren. I don't intend to take advantage of you, particularly when you aren't even thinking straight."

"I am thinking . . . quite well. I want you to make love to me." Wresting her hands away, Lauren reached up to curl her fingers in his tawny hair.

Jason nearly swore out loud. Ever since the incident in his bedroom, it had been supreme torture for him to keep his vow not to touch Lauren again till she was his wife. He had even wondered if he would be compelled to find another woman merely to slake his physical urges. Now, with a befuddled Lauren rashly begging to be seduced, Jason found himself driven to the limits of his endurance.

"Devil take it!" he growled fiercely, gripping Lauren's shoulders as he tried to fight the enticement of her soft, willing lips. But then his resistance crumbled. Lifting Lauren up, he hauled her against him, crushing her breasts against his chest as he captured her mouth in a rough, punishing kiss.

Lauren knew a triumphant moment of pure power. She no longer wondered if Jason still thought her desirable; she could feel leaping hunger surge through him as his hard mouth slanted bruisingly against hers. He seemed lost to all rational thought.

Then Lauren, too, ceased to think, becoming lost in the world of passion Jason created. His embrace was infusing her entire body with sensation, his lips and tongue devouring her, stealing her breath away. When his hand plunged beneath her bodice, curling around a lush breast, the nipple hardened instantly, eliciting a gasp from deep in her throat.

Jason teased the aching bud, making Lauren writhe, before his kisses followed the path of his hand. When his mouth closed over her pulsating nipple, Lauren felt her loins catch fire. She strained against him, wanting him . . . wanting him *fiercely*. Desperately, she slid her hand down his ruffled shirtfront to the heavy bulge covered by his satin breeches. Jason's groan mingled with her own wild moan. . . .

And then, just as suddenly as it had begun, it was over. Jason wrenched away and stood up, leaving Lauren panting for breath.

"Not this way, Lauren," Jason said in a ragged voice, alluding again to his vow. Catching up her cloak, he tossed it to her unceremoniously. "Put it on. I'm taking you home."

Lauren stared at him, her heart pounding painfully against her ribs. "No!" she replied defiantly.

There was a brandy decanter on the table beside the chaise longue and she reached for it. If the wine had dulled her senses, how much more successful would the potent brandy be at erasing the ache in her heart? Determined to eradicate all trace of feeling, Lauren took a gulp of the amber liquid. Fire raced down her throat, making her gasp.

"Lauren," Jason said warningly.

She shook her head fiercely. "No! I'm not going. You can't do this to me. You can't arouse me and then send me away like . . . like a naughty child. You want me, too, Jason. I know you do."

"Damn it, Lauren—"

"I'm not leaving!" She swallowed again. "If you make me, I'll . . . I'll find some other man who wants me."

His blue eyes narrowed. "You do and I'll beat you." Returning to her side, he unsuccessfully attempted to take the decanter from her.

Tauntingly waving it in the air, Lauren smiled. "It shouldn't be too difficult for me to find a man who is will . . . willing to satisfy me." She took another huge swallow before Jason managed to take the brandy away.

He set the decanter on the floor, out of reach, and captured Lauren's hands. "You've had quite enough," he said firmly.

Lauren's head fell back upon the pillows. "Not enough. I want more. I have a . . . a secret, did you know? Prob'ly I shall . . . take a lover."

"You had better not be serious."

"I am sh . . . erious. Why should you have a lover and me not?"

Jason's patience was wearing thin. "Because, sweetheart, I'm not likely to damage my reputation by such an action. I'm even less likely to end up with a swollen belly as a result from my fall from virtue, whereas you—"

"It isn't fair," Lauren complained, her lids sinking down over her eyes.

"No, it isn't fair," Jason agreed. "For men it's painful."

"You have a lover. Is Desirée better than I? Do you want to marry her, too?"

Jason bent to lift Lauren in his arms. "I told you I never

touched Desirée, Lauren. I've been totally faithful to you."

As he carried her across the room, she peered up at him sleepily. "Why did you go see her then?"

"She didn't satisfy my physical needs, if that's what you are asking."

"I have . . . needs, too, Jason." When he didn't respond, Lauren let her head loll against his shoulder, and giving a sigh, closed her eyes. "Do you want to hear my secret?" she murmured. "I . . . love . . . you."

Jason stopped abruptly, his gaze searching her face. "What did you say?" he asked, his voice strained.

"Love you . . ." she mumbled again.

She would have drifted off to sleep except that Jason shook her. "Is that your secret? Does that mean you'll marry me?"

"Can't . . . love you . . . have a secret."

Jason stood there for a long moment, holding Lauren and staring down at her pale beauty. Then slowly, he turned and retraced his steps. Laying her gently on the chaise longue, he filled a glass with brandy and sat down beside her. Then he lifted her head and put the glass to her lips. "Here, drink this, sweetheart," he urged tenderly.

Lauren brushed it away. "What—what are you doing?" she muttered groggily.

"Satisfying your needs, I hope."

He persisted and at last succeeded in getting her to drink. As she sipped hesitantly, his knuckles stroked Lauren's satin cheek. "I truly hope I can," he added softly.

Then, feeling the need to fortify himself for what was to come, Jason, too, took a large swallow of brandy.

Lauren woke to a dull throbbing in her temples and behind her eyes. Odd fleeting images still spun in her mind, remnants of the unusual dream she had been having. She had fantasized that she had actually married Jason in the middle of the night.

It had all seemed so real. There had been a house in her dream—*her* house now, Jason had said as he carried up to the master suite. He had made passionate love to her in a huge, four-poster bed, and in spite of her headache now, Lauren

289

could swear she still felt the languorous aftereffects of his lovemaking.

Wishing the ache in her head would go away, she forced her eyes open and winced at the bright sunlight streaming in the window. When slowly, painfully, her vision focused, she decided she was imagining the chintz curtains that fluttered in the light spring breeze. None of the rooms at Bellefleur were hung in that particular shade of cream. Nor did the wide windows resemble the French doors of the plantation house. Groggy and disoriented, Lauren blinked, wondering if imbibing too much wine always affected people so, making them see things.

When the unfamiliar sight didn't vanish, Lauren realized with a certain foreboding that the room she was in wasn't hers. Just how much had she drunk last night? She couldn't remember what had happened or how she came to be anywhere but her own bed.

Stirring slightly, Lauren made another disturbing discovery. Under the light covers, the sheets felt cool and smooth against her bare skin. The liquor must have greatly affected her reasoning, she reflected. She had never slept naked before in her life. Vowing she would never touch another drop of wine, Lauren raised herself up on her elbows and looked about her.

The room was furnished beautifully, with soft pastels and creams lightening the rich wood tones of mahogany. Lauren couldn't help but be impressed by the huge bed that must have been built on its current site. The other expertly crafted furniture had obviously been imported from Europe. So had the Aubusson carpet covering the floor and the priceless Sèvres vase standing on the inlaid satinwood table in the corner.

There was no sign of the gown she had been wearing the previous evening. Lauren was about to rise from the bed to go in search of it when a door swung open to admit Jason. Her eyes widened. Jason wasn't exactly dressed for paying calls, for his sun-streaked hair was carelessly tousled and he wore a brocade dressing gown, loosely tied at the waist. The robe's deep blue color was nearly the same shade as his eyes, Lauren thought irrelevantly as he stood regarding her from the threshold. The

290

tray he carried was laden with breakfast, if one could judge by the appetizing aroma.

She caught a glimpse of an elegant sitting room beyond him. "Where . . . ?" Lauren started to ask, before finding that it hurt to talk. Wincing again, she brought a hand to her forehead.

A moment later, she was trying to refuse the foul-looking concoction Jason was urging on her. "You'll feel far better if you drink it, Lauren," he insisted with a hint of humor. "Hold your breath and swallow. That's a good girl. Drink it all."

She sputtered and grimaced, but she obeyed. Exhausted by the effort, Lauren lay back on the pillows. "I seem to remember you saying the same thing last night."

"Is that all you remember?"

Lauren could have sworn that Jason sounded wary. Puzzled, she wrinkled her brow. "Where am I? Have I been sick?"

He was watching her intently. "Not sick, no," he replied slowly. "But you drank enough liquor to put a Scot under the table. I suggest you stay in bed and give that tonic a chance to work. You should put something solid in your stomach as well. I've brought your breakfast, as you can see." When Lauren would have questioned him further, he shook his head. "I'll tell you all about last night, after we eat."

Knowing that he meant to have his way, Lauren gave him no further argument. When she sat up, however, she was reminded of her state of undress. And when Jason bent over her to fluff the pillows behind her back, she was suddenly quite conscious of the intimacy of his action. She tucked the covers tightly under her arms to keep them from slipping.

It was quite obvious to her now that Jason had undressed her the night before. And it was all too possible that his lovemaking had not been a dream. Her memory was becoming more vivid by the moment. Perhaps she really had given herself to Jason with such wanton abandonment. The thought was enough to make Lauren blush. She kept her eyes averted when Jason drew a chair close to the bed.

As they shared the meal, a bluebird warbling cheerfully outside the open window provided the only conversation, for neither Jason nor Lauren spoke. Intent on her own thoughts,

Lauren entirely missed Jason's obvious preoccupation.

When they had eaten, Jason carefully cleared away the dishes and carried the tray to the other room before returning to his chair. Frowning down at his clasped hands, he took a preparatory deep breath. Then, reluctantly, he raised his eyes to meet Lauren's quizzical gaze. "You honestly don't remember what happened last night?"

Not caring for the vaguely ominous note in his voice, Lauren nervously shook her head. "You don't recall," Jason prodded, "the event which took place on board the *Siren?*"

"The *Siren?* No, I . . ." Recalling another fragment of her dream, she suddenly blanched. "You don't . . . No, that isn't possible . . . It was a dream!"

Jason's expression was frightfully solemn. "No, sweetheart. It was all quite real, though you may not remember much of it. Kyle married us last night."

Lauren stared at Jason in horror. "No," she breathed. "You're lying."

His lips tightened momentarily, but his tone was gentle. "I'm afraid not. There were witnesses, if you care to ask them. Tim Sutter and your own friend, Veronique. They will confirm that the ceremony did indeed take place and that it was all quite legal. You signed all the proper papers. You even behaved like a willing bride."

"But I couldn't have!" Lauren said frantically. "I would never have agreed to marry you."

Jason shrugged. "Regardless, you are now my wife. Mrs. Jason Stuart, or Lady Effing, if you care to use the title."

Apprehension and dread rose up before her like specters. She couldn't have married Jason! She was a bastard and he a marquess. She was a penniless orphan, possibly even a criminal. Lauren clutched the covers to her defensively. "I don't care to use your title! I don't want anything to do with you! And I don't remember signing any papers."

"I have our marriage lines, if you would care to see it."

"Yes!" She grasped at that suggestion. "Yes, I would. You probably *forged* my signature and—"

Lauren broke off, staring at the piece of paper that Jason was holding up for her perusal. She couldn't deny that the handwriting was hers but . . . she had signed it Andrea Carlin! All the document proved was that Jason had married someone who didn't exist!

Vastly relieved, Lauren didn't even stop to consider her next words. "The marriage isn't valid!" she exclaimed with exultation.

Carefully folding the proof of the ceremony, Jason returned it to the pocket of his dressing gown. "Why should you think that?" he asked curiously.

"Because, I'm not—" Lauren clasped a hand to her mouth, horrifyingly aware of what she had nearly divulged. She took a deep, steadying breath. "Because you tricked me," she prevaricated. "Because you . . . you deliberately made me drunk so that I wouldn't fight you."

"I only finished what you started, my love."

"See, you just admitted that you coerced me! I won't be manipulated, Jason."

Amusement flashed in his sapphire eyes. "I admit that you had a touch too much to drink, but there is no law against a man sharing a glass of wine with his bride. I'm sorry, Lauren, but we are well and truly wed."

"Then I'll have the marriage annulled."

His brows lifted. "On what grounds?" he asked politely.

Lauren flushed, pulling the sheet up to her chin. "Because it wasn't . . . I didn't . . ."

Jason grinned wickedly. "Oh, yes. It was and you did. Don't tell me you've forgotten the consummation, too? I can assure you, I can't so easily forget, sweetheart." He leaned closer, his compelling gaze warm and intimate. "You were far from the iceberg Howard thought you. In fact, I've never known a more passionate—"

"Don't touch me!" Lauren yelped when he would have stroked her cheek. Jason's expression hardened slightly, but his hand dropped away. Hastily Lauren rolled off the far side of the bed, dragging a bedsheet with her. "And don't try to stop me from leaving here, either," she warned in the most chilling tone she could muster as she wrapped the sheet around, sarong fashion.

Jason stretched his long legs out in front of him and cocked

293

his head to one side. "How swiftly you vacillate, my love. You were quite different last night, even going so far as to reveal your deep, dark secret to me."

Lauren froze as a familiar fear raced along her spine. Slowly she turned to face Jason, her gold-flecked eyes wide and wary. "What secret?" she asked, not daring to breathe.

His eyes widened innocently. "You have more than one? What a mysterious woman I married."

"What *secret?*" she demanded again.

"Why," he said, his gaze never wavering, "your admission that you love me, of course. Or did that conveniently escape your memory, as well?"

Lauren let out her breath in relief. Then realizing she was still trembling, she made an effort to calm herself. "That is absurd," she protested. "I never said such a thing."

"But you did, Lauren. Ergo, I arranged a hasty wedding. I didn't want you to have time to change your mind."

Dragging her defenses in place once more, Lauren presented her back to him. "If I did indeed say anything so ridiculous, then it was the wine talking."

Jason watched her as she moved purposefully toward the tall armoire. "It truly is a shame," he said softly, "that we have to depend on spirits in order to have any honesty between us."

She ignored his remark as she flung open the armoire. Seeing at once that it was empty, she whirled. "Where are my clothes, Jason? Have you taken them again?"

"What need have you for clothing on your honeymoon, my sweet?" he asked provokingly.

Lauren flashed him a look calculated to freeze the blood in his veins. Then, with angry determination, she proceeded to search the rest of the room.

Jason made no move to stop her. Recognizing the frigid set of her features, though, he mentally sighed. But then he hadn't expected this to be easy. "Your gown is being laundered, Lauren," he admitted at last. "But I don't intend to return it to you. At least not until I can be assured you won't try to run away."

Lauren slammed shut an empty drawer to the bureau. "I will not run away. I will scream the house down."

"Go right ahead. The servants all work for me."

Lauren tossed her head, sending her golden mane flying. Defiantly, she turned to the door Jason had used earlier, but she had only opened it a mere crack before Jason came up behind her. His arm shot around her waist, and before Lauren could marshal her thoughts for a battle, he had effortlessly lifted her off her feet. "You aren't going anywhere, my love," Jason stipulated, "unless I have your promise to give this marriage of ours a chance."

Ignoring her gasp of outrage, he carried Lauren back across the room. "How dare you put your hands on me!" she cried. "Release me at once!" But Jason seemed totally deaf. Lauren struggled then, but he easily thwarted her attempts to break his iron hold. Depositing her in the center of the big bed, he followed her down, pinning her with his weight, the powerfully muscled length of him covering her completely. When she tried to strike him with her fists, he captured her hands above her head.

Lauren fought him to no avail; Jason wouldn't budge. He even had the audacity to grin in her face. "Oh, you insufferable . . . savage . . . beast," she sputtered, glaring at him furiously.

"Yes, but you love me."

She would have scratched his laughing eyes out, but she couldn't free her hands. "I despise you, you knave!" she hissed. "Now let me go, or I'll have you arrested for kidnapping!"

Jason seemed amused by her threat, for he kissed the tip of her nose. "I regret to inform you, sweetheart, that you won't find any support for your case. The law accords a husband certain rights and privileges—one of which is the authority to see that his wife honors his wishes." Jason lowered his lips to her right ear. "And just now I very much wish to have another glimpse of the wildly sensuous woman you were last night."

Lauren squirmed, trying to escape the touch of his warm mouth. "You would force me?" she cried as Jason's tongue followed the inward swirl of her ear.

His lips moved lower then, searing a path down her neck. "Perhaps," Jason murmured as he nuzzled her throat, "I

295

merely plan to repay you for driving me to distraction these past weeks. Call it settlement of a debt, if you like."

The next moment he had shifted his weight, sitting up to straddle her hips. Before Lauren could divine his purpose, he had shrugged out of his robe and thrown it aside. Her sheet became the only remaining barrier between them.

Momentarily distracted by the broad expanse of chest above his lean, flat belly, Lauren glanced down. She nearly gasped when she saw Jason's magnificent erection, and redoubled her efforts to escape.

But Jason stretched his long body out again, pinning her hands at her sides. Feeling his swelling hardness against her thigh and realizing she was only arousing him further with her thrashing, Lauren stopped struggling. Although she was breathing hard, she forced herself to lie rigid and unresponsive beneath him. His knee pressed between hers then, moving with deliberate slowness. The sheet rasped against her hidden passion, but still Lauren resisted the erotic stimulation, willing her body not to quiver.

Jason appeared undaunted by her lack of response. His eyes glowed with a warm, determined light as his lips renewed their leisurely attack, playing upon Lauren's mouth.

Clenching her teeth against his gentle assault, Lauren tried to turn away, but Jason's hand moved behind her head, holding her still. She couldn't escape the warm pressure of his lips. His teasing tongue probed for entrance, stirring sensations Lauren found increasingly difficult to ignore.

He changed tactics then, in a single deft movement drawing the sheet down, baring the enticing fullness of her breasts and her long, slender limbs. Pressing boldly against her, he made Lauren feel the burning heat of his body. When she opened her mouth to protest, Jason took full advantage, sliding his tongue between her teeth, probing, searching for some chink in her frozen armor. His other hand was slowly stroking a silken thigh, intimately caressing her smooth skin. Tracing a tantalizing path, his hand slid between their bodies. Unerringly, his searching fingers discovered the reflexive wetness that proclaimed her readiness.

When she remained rigidly still, he whispered against her

mouth, "Open to me, Lauren. Let me in. Let me love you." He knew he had won when her lips began to tremble beneath his. Jason raised his head and gazed tenderly into her eyes, trying to tell her without words that he was surrendering as much as she.

For a long moment their eyes held. Then Jason gently nudged her knees apart. When his velvet spear pressed for entry, Lauren once more tried to move away, but Jason stilled her with another languid kiss. He pressed against her slowly, powerfully entering her, his penetration intentionally unhurried. And when he was deep inside her, he remained totally motionless, as if to savor the moment. Then slowly, he drew away and began the hypnotic motion again, his loins sweetly caressing hers, inviting, urging a response.

A moan rose unbidden to Lauren's throat as her body turned traitor. Jason's slow, languid strokes had kindled a fire within her, melting her ice to a fiery heat. She began to answer his thrusting hips, arching against him.

Jason prolonged the exquisite torture for a time, until he lost control. At once his kisses became hungry and demanding, and when Lauren sobbed and strained against him, Jason grasped her buttocks and drove deeply, fiercely, into her, as if he would pierce the very core of her soul.

Their frantic passion mounted, white-hot, till Lauren thought she would scream with the sweet agony of it. When release at last came, the resultant explosion sent her rocketing to the sky, carrying Jason along with her. Shuddering, drenched in perspiration, they held tightly to each other until the final vibrations faded away.

"Ah, my beautiful wife," Jason murmured in her ear. "Can you doubt that we were made for each other?"

Though his words wrenched her heart, Lauren forced herself to answer coldly. "Nothing has changed, Jason. You tricked me. And if this marriage cannot be dissolved, I will seek a divorce. I mean to see a lawyer."

With a sigh, Jason pushed himself off her and rolled to his feet. To Lauren, the separation felt as if a limb had been severed from her body, and she nearly begged him to come back. But she would get over her weakness, she told herself.

She *would* get over it.

Watching Jason shrug his muscular body into his dressing gown, Lauren was reminded that he had taken her clothes. "I would like to get dressed," she said with renewed hauteur.

Jason looked down at her, his gaze sweeping her lovely body, his eyes feasting on Lauren's nakedness before she quickly covered herself with the sheet. Amused by her misplaced modesty, Jason tied the sash to his robe. "As you wish, my sweet," he replied. "I'll return shortly with your clothing. Perhaps you would care for some privacy in order to freshen up. You'll find water on the washstand, and a brush and comb on the dressing table."

He was gone before she had a chance to reply. Lauren wondered suspiciously why he had given in so easily, but she took advantage of his absence to wash hurriedly. She was sitting at the dressing table, brushing the tangles from her hair when he returned and tossed a number of garments onto the table before her.

Examining them, Lauren wasn't at all pleased to discover several filmy muslin nightdresses, trimmed with lace and ribbons. There were also matching peignoirs, but even worn as sets, they would be transparent enough to appear almost sheer. Lauren's lips tightened. "And just what are these?"

Thrusting his hands in the pockets of his robe, Jason grinned at her. "Proper attire for a bride, of course. Ideal for spending the day in bed with a new husband—or so I was told. I had them made for you along with the rest of your wardrobe, only it wouldn't have been proper of me to give them to you then."

Lauren was dumbfounded by his audacity. Jason was boldly admitting he had been confident of his success all along! "I will not wear these!" she ground out between her teeth.

Jason leaned indolently against the bedpost, surveying her. "Suit yourself, Cat-eyes. I think I like you better in the bedsheet myself. It's easier to remove."

"So you mean to keep me your prisoner!"

His jaw tightened momentarily. When he finally spoke, his tone was gentle, but there was a ring of steel beneath the velvet. "Perhaps we should get a few things straight at the outset, sweetheart. You are my wife, not my prisoner. This house is your home now, as much as it is mine. You will have the freedom of it when I have your promise not to disappear."

Lauren's features had completely iced over. "A promise made under duress isn't worth the breath it takes to utter it," she observed scathingly.

"I will trust your word."

"And if I refuse to give it? How long do you plan to keep me here?"

Jason's gaze never faltered. "For as long as it takes. And since I obviously can't go away and leave you to your own devices, I mean to remain here with you. Though honestly, I can't say that I mind. I can't think of a more delightful prospect than being confined to a bedroom with my lovely new bride. I expect you will soon become accustomed to having me around. Perhaps you might even learn to enjoy my company."

When Lauren continued to regard him in frigid silence, Jason pointed to one of the two exits. "That is the door to the hall. You will discover it unlocked, but I warn you, Sutter has taken up a post on the stairs, and I expect he will be more prepared this time if you try to leave. Certainly you won't find it quite so easy to render him senseless. The adjacent room is a sitting room, but it also leads to the hall. And if you look out the window, you will notice that we are rather high up. The jump is too great to make without risking an injury."

With a sinking heart, Lauren realized that he seemed to have every avenue of escape covered. But surely Lila and Jean-Paul and Matthew wouldn't let him keep her here against her will. That hope, however, was dashed by Jason's next words.

"Don't count on your friends coming to visit. They mean to allow us some time together. They think, by the way, that you are happily married and enjoying your honeymoon with your lustful bridegroom."

Recognizing that further protests would gain her nothing, Lauren folded her hands in her lap. She wouldn't demean herself by begging. Instead she would remain coolly detached while she looked for a way to escape. Her chin lifted as she favored Jason with an arctic stare.

In response, he pushed his shoulders from the bedpost. "And now, if we have that understood between us . . ." His

299

words hung suggestively in the air as he untied the sash to his robe.

In spite of her resolve, Lauren's eyes widened when Jason stripped off his dressing gown. She viewed his magnificent body with supreme wariness, determined to fight him to the death this time if he should dare lay a hand on her. But he merely flashed her a knowing grin and stretched his long, corded length out on the bed. Raising his head then, Jason cocked a quizzical brow at her. "Will you join me in a nap?"

She stared at him incredulously. "You're going to sleep?" she exclaimed, allowing the question to slip out unchecked.

"Have you something else in mind, wife?" When Lauren immediately resumed her pose of frosty disdain, Jason lay down again and shut his eyes. "You might not remember it," he murmured wearily, "but you kept me up most of last night."

Lauren bristled at the soft, satisfied smile that curved his lips.

Chapter Seventeen

Lauren had no choice but to spend the remainder of the morning listening to the soft, even sound of Jason's breathing. When at last he woke, her attitude toward him was not only chilly but hostile. Her anger at being tricked was only surpassed by her fury at being held prisoner. As for the question of their marriage, Lauren refused even to consider the ramifications of the ceremony which had been held on board the *Siren* until Jason set her free.

Jason, on the other hand, appeared to be enjoying the situation. The fact that all his conversations with her were completely one-sided didn't seem to faze him. He talked and teased and laughed, just as if Lauren weren't shooting shardlike glances at him from across the room.

Lauren managed to maintain a stony silence throughout the long day, in spite of Jason's occasional efforts to restore peace between them. She had no intention of even speaking to him, much less making him the promise he wanted. Still, she found it difficult not to respond to Jason's attempts to charm her and coax a smile from her.

She also found that her vow of silence had unsuspected disadvantages. She was thoroughly bored, for one thing, since she had refused to respond to his offer of cards or reading material. And no matter how maddening Jason's calm amusement was, or how insufferable his deliberate patience, she couldn't vent her frustration if she hoped to preserve a barrier of chill reserve between them.

Later in the afternoon, Jason afforded her some privacy for a bath. Grateful for the short reprieve from her provoking jailer, Lauren drew out the moment for as long as possible, then conceded a small victory to Jason by donning one of the seductive peignoirs. She was tired of clutching the sheet about her, even if it meant steeling herself to submit to Jason's admiring perusal when he returned. The amused gleam in his blue eyes, however, was almost enough to make her give up her silence in favor of a few choice remarks concerning his parentage.

For supper, she was allowed into the sitting room. The invisible servants had been hard at work, Lauren noted, for an intimate little table was laden with delicacies and spicy Creole dishes. Taking the seat Jason held out for her, Lauren looked about her curiously. The tall French windows leading to the gallery would be locked, of course, but this chamber had more possibilities for escape than the bedroom.

Her new home, Jason had said, was in the new American quarter of town, the Faubourg St. Marie. From what she could tell, the house sat well back from the street in an enormous lot, and if the size of the rooms were any indication, the house, too, was quite large. Lauren never would have admitted it, but she was impressed by the elegance that surrounded her. If circumstances had been different, she knew she would have very much enjoyed living here and being mistress of this beautiful home.

Jason had dressed for dinner—or at least he had donned a pair of tight-fitting breeches and a loose-flowing shirt. Seeing Jason in such casual attire as he sat across from her was genuinely unsettling for Lauren. The front of his shirt was opened to reveal a glimpse of muscular chest, and a lock of his tawny hair had fallen down onto his forehead, filling her with an urge to smooth it back. Lauren was also very much aware of her own nearly indecent state of dress. Her pulse leapt traitorously whenever Jason's warm gaze lingered on her gauze-covered bosom, and she was quite glad when the meal ended.

That night, they shared the big bed. Lauren lay beside Jason in rigid suspense—until she realized he had once more gone easily to sleep. She relaxed somewhat then, but she couldn't help wondering just how much longer she could hold out against his tactics.

Sometime in the night, she woke to the feel of Jason's hard body molded against her back. His hand was lightly caressing her arm, while his warm lips were nuzzling her bare shoulder. Lauren shut her eyes, willing herself not to respond. But then his hand moved tantalizingly downward, over the swell of her breast and the curve of her hip. His gentle stroking chased away her drowsiness, arousing a desire she found impossible to deny. When Jason began the tortuous path again, Lauren was no longer able to feign sleep; her quivering body gave her away.

As he pressed her back into the pillows, Jason's eyes glinted roguishly in the darkness. "I was right," he whispered against her lips, while his hands sought the feminine secrets veiled by her nightdress. "I much prefer the sheet."

The routine the following day was very much the same, as was the next. But on the third, Jason happened to be out of the room when Lauren heard a tinker hawking his wares on the street. She couldn't see him for the large magnolia tree blocking the view, but he must have heard her low-voiced calls since he came to investigate.

When the tinker peered up at the window where Lauren was beckoning to him, she asked if he would deliver a message for her. When he agreed, Lauren slipped into the sitting room to fetch writing materials. She had one friend who wouldn't be under Jason's influence—Martin Kendricks, the majordomo at the casino. Hastily scribbling a plea for Kendricks to rescue her, Lauren raced back to the bedroom and flung the note down to the tinker, promising that he would be well paid for his trouble.

She had barely restored the writing implements to the desk and hidden the telltale signs of her bid for escape when Jason returned. Lauren dared not look at him for fear he would guess her intent; his uncanny ability to read her mind had always been one of his chief advantages over her.

She held her breath as Jason came up behind her, desperately wishing her heart would stop beating so furiously. When he placed his hands on her shoulders, it was all she could do to remain relaxed. But he gave no indication that he suspected her scheme. He merely drew her back against his chest, resting his cheek against her hair.

When he seemed content merely to hold her close like that, Lauren shut her eyes. What in God's name was she doing? she thought wildly. Why was she trying to leave this powerful, compelling man who claimed to love her? She wanted more than anything in the world to stay with him. Jason owned her heart, now and forever.

Lauren could remember now snatches of the vows she had made. She had promised to love and honor him till death's parting . . . Yet she would be sealing her own death if she returned to England. Her impersonation would be discovered and she would go to prison. Regina Carlin would see to that.

For a single insanely foolish moment, Lauren contemplated confessing to Jason and throwing herself on his mercy. But the thought of what she would be subjecting him to stopped her. She would ruin Jason's life if she returned to England as his wife. He had an ancient and respected title to uphold, and his wife would have to be above reproach. The stigma of her birth alone would create a scandal. She was a bastard, a child born out of wedlock. It wouldn't matter to society that her illegitimacy was the result of her father's duplicity. It wouldn't matter that Jonathan Carlin had tricked her mother Elizabeth and pretended to marry her in a sham ceremony. If the British aristocracy ever found out about her birth, Lauren would be shunned, and Jason with her.

As for her own marriage, Lauren wasn't sure it was any more legal than her mother's had been. But what if it really were valid? Jason would be tied to a woman who was completely penniless. And when he discovered that she had no right to the Carlin ships, he would hate her for concealing the truth. Lauren felt her throat tighten in despair. She couldn't bear to see the contempt in his eyes when he learned she had deceived him all along. No, it would be best for both of them if she left, if she went somewhere far, far away.

As if he had guessed her last thought, Jason pressed his lips against her hair. "Give our love a chance, Lauren," he pleaded.

His whispered entreaty tore at Lauren's heart. She shed no

tears, but inside she wept. It was all she could do to keep from turning and throwing her arms around his neck. It was all she could do to keep from surrendering.

After a time, Jason sighed. Releasing her, he stepped away.

That night, dinner was virtually a silent affair. Jason seemed at last to despair of breaking through the arctic barrier Lauren strove to keep in place. Later, when he didn't retire with her, Lauren lay awake in the large, lonely bed, deploring her need for him yet missing his nearness. Her nerves were stretched like taut wires; she was on tenterhooks to know if Kendricks had received her message and if he would attempt a rescue. Jason hadn't joined her when she at last fell into a troubled sleep.

Some time in the night, Lauren sat up with a start. The moonlight pouring in the open window provided enough light to see clearly, but Lauren knew without even a glance at Jason's side of the bed that she was still alone. Apprehensively, she lit a candle. The ormolu clock on the mantel read a quarter past three. After a moment's hesitation, Lauren rose and quickly pulled on one of the hated peignoirs.

The sitting room was deserted, she discovered shortly, and all the lamps had been put out. In fact, the entire house was wrapped in darkness, Lauren realized as she peered out into the hall. Leaving her light behind, she slipped from her bedroom and noiselessly shut the door behind her. It was very quiet. Her slippered feet made no sound as she crept silently toward the stairs, though her erratic heartbeat seemed abnormally loud.

Lauren couldn't have said whether she was searching for Jason or trying to flee her prison, but when she saw that Tim Sutter wasn't at his post, she was filled with foreboding. Had Jason deceived her when he had said she was being guarded? Or was something wrong? Lauren found herself holding her breath as she began her descent.

Reaching the bottom landing, she took a step toward the front door, intending to cross the foyer, and so never even saw the hand that reached out to cover her mouth. Her cry was muffled as she was hauled roughly against a hard chest, and her heart leapt to her throat. . . .

But the arms that imprisoned her felt familiar, as was the

305

particular male scent. When she realized it was Jason who held her, Lauren managed to swallow her fear, but she had no opportunity to protest his rough handling; Jason unceremoniously thrust her behind him as he wheeled to face the moving shadows.

Lauren nearly fell. Grasping at the banister to save herself, she heard an animallike growl and from the corner of her eye, saw the flashing gleam of a knife clutched in a large hand. By the time she had recovered her balance, Jason had already sent his attacker hurtling to the floor.

In the dim light of the foyer, Lauren recognized Kendricks's powerful bulk. There was no time to wonder how he had managed to enter the house, though, for the brawny man jumped to his feet with the nimbleness of a panther, his weapon poised again in readiness.

For a moment the only sound was the muted shuffle of boots on the parquet floor as the two men circled each other warily. Then Kendricks lunged again, his blade slashing wickedly. Jason sidestepped nimbly, but Kendricks whirled, the razor point catching Jason's midriff, slicing at the waistcoat he wore over his lawn shirt. Lauren gave a cry—something between a gasp and a scream.

Jason was ready, however, for his opponent's next lunge. When Kendricks charged, Jason dropped to the ground, his booted foot contacting the man's stomach, sending him somersaulting head over heels into a room off the entrance hall. In an instant, Jason had flung himself after Kendricks, and there was a loud clatter as some unfortunate piece of furniture was toppled.

Lauren followed, biting the knuckles of her hand to keep from crying out again. She watched, horrified, as Jason grappled for the knife. He was using the weight of his body to pin Kendricks down, while struggling to keep the wicked blade from his face.

Lauren clutched desperately at the doorjamb as the point came within inches of Jason's cheek. She could almost feel the muscles in his back and arms straining as he fought for possession of the weapon. She tried to speak, tried to tell Kendricks for God's sake not to hurt Jason, but her breath was

306

trapped in her lungs.

The picture of Matthew fighting off her attackers flashed through her mind as she hovered helplessly near the bodies locked in combat, and a sob was wrenched from her throat. She would die if anything happened to Jason. She had to stop Kendricks somehow. His palm was shoved against Jason's chin, and he seemed not to hear when Lauren at last found her voice and implored him to stop.

"Ah, *chérie*, I have been searching for you."

Felix Duval! Lauren realized he must have come with Kendricks, but she didn't spare him a glance as her attention remained on the fight. Kendricks had gripped Jason's throat with one hand and was trying to strangle him.

"I have come to rescue you, *ma belle*," Duval said dryly when Lauren paid him no attention. "Now would be an expedient time to leave, do you not think? Come away with me, Marguerite . . . or should I say Lauren?"

Lauren ignored him and shrugged off his grasp when he took her elbow, frantically glancing around her for some tool to pry the two men apart. Even if she were willing to leave Jason like this, she would never accept Felix's help, not after his scheming attempts to make her his mistress. She could never trust such a man. And she had to stop Jason from being hurt.

Suddenly, Jason broke free of Kendricks's strangling hold, and with lightning speed, drew back his fist and let it descend on his opponent's jaw. There was a grunt of pain from Kendricks, and while he was momentarily stunned by the blow, Jason abandoned the struggle for the knife. Straddling the man's waist, he gripped Kendricks by the hair to pummel his head against the carpet a time or two. Then he used his fists again, until finally the brawny man ceased his struggles and lay still.

Lauren hugged her stomach to stem the wave of nausea flooding over her. She felt Felix's arm go around her, but didn't have the strength to push him away.

Jason was breathing heavily as he rose to his feet, and his nostrils flared when he saw Duval's arm encircling Lauren's barely clad form. "Devil take it, what are you doing here?" he rasped.

307

Quite calmly, Felix raised the cocked pistol in his hand and aimed it at Jason's chest.

"Oh, God, no!" Lauren cried, but Felix ignored her.

"I am rescuing this lovely lady," he said mildly, "whom you seem to be holding against her will."

"Felix, please, I beg you—"

Jason's reaction took them both by surprise. In a fierce lunge, he flung himself at Duval, striking the pistol from his hand with a single blow.

The resultant explosion was deafening, but the ball implanted itself harmlessly in the wainscotting. Jason's fury wasn't so easily defused. Grasping Felix by the upper arms, he shoved the lighter man against wall, then gripped him by the throat.

"This is *my* house," Jason snarled, his face inches from Duval's, "and that is *my* wife. I want you the hell out of here. You have three seconds to decide, Duval, before I make up your mind for you!"

His threat was punctuated by the rapid approach of footsteps as Tim Sutter appeared, holding a lamp. In the bright circle of light, Lauren could see Jason's fierce expression, and as she watched, a thought struck her that made her dizzy. How close he had been to death—and she was responsible.

When her knees began to buckle beneath her, Tim grasped her elbow, supporting her weight. "Crimes, don't swoon, ma'am . . . I mean, m'lady," his anxious voice entreated. "His lordship won't kill him. Lord Effing dunnet countenance killing . . . much."

Lauren couldn't form the words to explain that it was relief for Jason, not concern for Felix, that was causing her faintness. But she was grateful when Felix nodded and Jason released his stranglehold.

Coughing, Felix raised a hand to his throat. "Your *wife?*" he said, glancing sharply at Lauren. "I am sorry, *chérie*, but I think under the circumstances, I must bow out."

"Duval," Jason said warningly.

Felix threw up his hands. "Very well! I am going."

Jason watched Duval stride unsteadily from the room, yet he didn't wait for the front door to close before turning to bark at

eyes haunted by indecision. She understood quite well Jason was offering to free her, yet she wasn't sure that was what she wanted anymore. Those moments when his life had been threatened had shaken her to the very depths of her being.

Jason had frightened her as well. Not physically, for although his violent rage had scared her witless for a moment, she realized now that she had never been in any actual danger. He would never deliberately hurt her. But still she was afraid of what a future with Jason might bring. Her fear had kept her silent until now—yet she couldn't just let him walk away.

She was struggling for the words to tell him so when her gaze was arrested by the long rip in Jason's gray waistcoat and the dark stain that discolored the material. Whatever else she might have said flew from Lauren's mind. "You are bleeding!" she exclaimed.

Absently Jason glanced down. "I expect so. It seems I wasn't quite nimble enough. But what did you mean, don't go?" His blue eyes returned to hers, searching her face.

Ignoring his question, Lauren came to stand before him. "Kendricks must have cut you with his knife. I want to see it."

Jason waved his hand impatiently. "It isn't important, Lauren. What did—"

"It may be serious," she interrupted, trying to part the ripped material.

Jason was heartened by Lauren's obvious concern. "Shall I undress so you can inspect the damage?" he murmured, lifting her chin with a finger.

Exasperated by his casual attitude, she frowned. "Just the waistcoat and shirt, please," she said sternly. "You may need stitches."

While Lauren fetched soap and water, Jason stripped to his breeches and obediently sat in the chair she indicated. The wound, he knew, wasn't deep, nor did it pain him, but it had bled freely.

He noted Lauren's slight hesitation as she knelt before him and attributed it to squeamishness, but it wasn't the sight of his blood that shook her. It was Jason's bare torso. The broad expanse of gold-furred chest, the sinewy muscles of his shoulders and arms, affected her composure more than she

311

cared to admit. His body was so beautiful that she was almost afraid to touch him.

Her hand trembled as she gently wiped away the dried blood and probed the area. The cut ran across his taut stomach just above the waistband of his breeches, yet when it was cleansed, she could see that it was little more than a red line after all— nothing to worry about.

"See," Jason said to her bent head. "A mere scratch. Leave it for now, Lauren." Placing his hands on either side of her face, he tilted it up, urging her to look at him. For a long, tension-filled moment Jason's eyes searched hers, while Lauren remained very still, fighting the power of his mesmerizing look.

Oh, God, those blue eyes, Lauren thought wildly. Those blue, blue eyes. She wondered if she was at all successful in hiding what she felt for him.

His next words gave her the answer. "You do love me," he breathed, more in awe than triumph.

She tried to pull away. "I don't—" she began, before Jason cut her off by capturing her mouth.

The passion in his kiss took her breath away. And when Jason drew her into his arms, she went willingly.

His lips slanted across hers hungrily, possessive and urgent, and as Lauren clung to him, the memory of the first time Jason had kissed her drifted into her mind. She had been sitting on his lap, like this, when he had taught her about passion, about desire. And just like now, the touch of his lips had seared her, leaving her panting and breathless. His lips had trailed fiery kisses over her bare shoulder, before he had eased down the bodice of her gown, teasing a taut nipple with his tongue. And just like now, she had arched against him, gasping, winding her fingers through his hair. . . .

But then, he hadn't stopped, as he did now.

Holding himself in check with an iron will, Jason reluctantly raised his head from where he was feasting at Lauren's breast. "You're doing a rather poor job of convincing me of your indifference, sweetheart," he said ironically.

When she slowly opened her eyes, Jason blandly returned Lauren's bewildered gaze. "Why do you look at me that way?

One of us has to keep a level head until we resolve this. I suppose it will have to be me since you seem to lose control each time I kiss you." He smiled when Lauren buried her face in his shoulder to hide her flushed cheeks. "There's no reason to blush, Cat-eyes. If you can't behave wantonly with your husband, then who—"

"Don't tease me about this, Jason."

"I'm sorry, sweetheart. But I'm at a loss to know how to proceed from here. Are you willing to talk about it?" When she didn't reply, he sighed. "How much simpler this all would be if I could just ravish your beautiful body all the time. I don't suppose that would be very honorable, though—not if you don't intend to remain my wife. But I expect then I could get you to admit you love me."

"I don't *want* to love you," Lauren said despairingly.

"But you don't want me to go?" he asked gently. "So what am I to do? I can't continue like this, never knowing when you will pay someone to plunge a knife in my ribs."

Lauren shifted uncomfortably. "I didn't mean for Kendricks to hurt you. I only asked him to help me escape. I never expected Felix to come, either."

"Why, Lauren? Why would you want to destroy what we could have together?" When she didn't answer, Jason's fingers closed over her trembling chin, making her lift her gaze. The haunted look was in her eyes again, and he wanted very much to kiss it away. "Won't you trust me, sweetheart," he said softly.

Seeing his tender concern, Lauren felt her heart turn over. But what he was asking was impossible. They were divided by a gulf that could never be bridged.

Jason took a long strand of her hair and drew it softly over his lips, his eyes searching her face. "I always feel like you're holding something back from me, a part of you that you won't let me see."

His observation was too close to the truth, and Lauren looked down to hide her tormented thoughts. When she nervously began plucking at a frill of her peignoir, Jason's hand closed over hers. How beautiful his hands were, Lauren thought irrelevantly. Vital, long-fingered, strong.

313

"Lauren, whatever has happened in the past . . . I love you. Nothing will change that."

How desperately she wanted to believe him. But it was too late now to reveal the truth about her identity. He would never forgive her. And perhaps she didn't deserve forgiveness. She wasn't worthy of Jason, of his love. He was chivalrous and noble and kind. She couldn't let him sacrifice his future for her, any more than she could bear to lose his love when he learned of her deception.

But he was waiting for an explanation. Lauren took a deep breath, deciding to give him at least part of the truth. "It's not that I don't want to be married to you. I just don't want to go to England. I'm *afraid* to go."

"My love, there's nothing for you to worry about in England."

"There is. Regina Carlin. Perhaps you'll think me foolish, but I'm afraid of her. She wanted the Carlin ships, Jason. And she was willing to lie, maybe even kill to get them. She once tried to have An—me locked up in an insane asylum because of my nightmares. I really would go mad if that happened."

Jason frowned into her pleading eyes. "Aren't you forgetting one or two important details? Like me, for instance? Do you think I would let Regina harm you? Besides, she has no incentive. The Carlin ships will never be hers and she knows it. I think she's even become reconciled to the fact by now. She has been quiet for the past year or more, living in some uncivilized region of Northumberland."

As Lauren returned Jason's intent gaze, she remembered her reasons for refusing his first proposal. It seemed absurd now that she had thought to protect him from Regina. He was capable of dealing with physical threats, even from someone as unscrupulous as Regina. But it wasn't just physical danger that threatened their love.

Lauren shook her head. "It doesn't matter. I can't face her."

Jason's arm tightened about her as he drew her closer. "I hope I can persuade you to change your mind."

"No, please! I beg you, don't try."

Very gently he raised his hand to touch her cheek. "Lauren, I'll have to return to England sometime—sometime soon. As it

314

is, I've already neglected all my other affairs far too long."

"I know." Sighing, Lauren rested her head wearily on Jason's shoulder and absently trailed a finger through the tawny hair on his bare chest.

"Well," Jason said thoughtfully as he kissed the top of her head, "I suppose I prefer a separation of four thousand miles to a divorce."

Lauren drew away to stare at him. "You would allow me to stay here in New Orleans? You wouldn't mind?"

"Of course I would mind. But I expect we can work something out."

Doubting, Lauren searched his face. When she saw how steadily Jason was meeting her gaze, though, she felt the ever-present dread lift from her heart. Such a compromise meant that she didn't have to go to England. Her secret would be safe, and so would Jason's exalted position in society.

Lauren flung her arms around his neck in joyous gratitude. "Oh, Jason," she breathed.

"Just a minute, not so fast." He pried her arms away. "I have at least three conditions. The first is that you promise not to run away."

Slowly, Lauren smiled up at him. "I promise. What is the second?"

Jason stared at her, wondering how the slight lift of the corners of her mouth could be so demure and alluring at the same time. "I'd like you visit Duval in the morning and assure him you're happily married to me. I don't want him interfering in our lives, any more than I want him coveting you."

"Very well. And three?"

"Three is that we make the most of the time we have left."

Lauren's smile never wavered as she locked her fingers behind his neck. "Oh?" she said provocatively, her voice husky with happiness. "You mean like this?" Slowly she brought her lips within a hairsbreadth of his, while her muslin-covered breasts pressed against his bare chest.

Jason nearly groaned as a fierce wave of desire gripped him. "I married a clever lady," he rasped, before capturing Lauren's mouth in a possessive, flaming kiss.

Chapter Eighteen

Morning dawned sodden and gray, the magnificent thunderstorm that had shaken the heavens the previous evening having worn itself out, leaving behind a steady drizzle. Shivering as a draft caressed her bare shoulders, Lauren tried to snuggle closer to Jason's warm body, but his muscular arm was draped across her ribs, its pleasant heaviness effectively pinning her down.

As her eyelids fluttered open, a vague thought teased her. During the two weeks of her marriage, she had frequently awakened to find Jason's arms around her, but this morning he was still asleep. Usually by now he was nibbling on her ear or pressing stirring kisses on her lips.

Not wanting to disturb his peaceful slumber, Lauren lay there watching him, letting her gaze roam lovingly over his face. His sun-gilded hair was tousled, the curve of his mouth as relaxed as the tiny laugh lines about his eyes. Drinking in the sight, Lauren again felt a heart-warming sense of wonder that she should be loved by this devastating man. How could she have thought to keep her affections safe by avoiding him? Forswearing Jason Stuart was like ignoring a sunburst after a fierce storm. But now this magnificent male belonged to her—and Desirée Chaudier was probably green with envy. Lauren smiled softly, contentedly, inwardly hugging her happiness to her like a luxurious fur.

It was this smile Jason saw when he awakened. He returned it, measure for measure, his blue eyes full of tenderness.

"Good morning," he murmured, his simple greeting making Lauren's pulse quicken.

She reached up to touch his face with a slim finger, tracing the dimpled crease in his cheek to the corner of his mouth. "I'm cold, Jason," she whispered in her husky voice.

Jason lifted an amused brow. "And you expect me to be sympathetic? When you insist on having the window open?" Yet he drew Lauren into the warm circle of his arms and pulled the covers up over her chilled shoulders. Entwining his iron-thewn legs with her own shapely limbs, he gave an exaggerated sigh. "I'm fortunate to have such a strong constitution. Otherwise, I'd probably freeze to death, sleeping with you."

Lauren's laughter was muffled against his bare chest as she curled against him. "Not true! You're never cold. Besides, *you're* the one who insists on never wearing clothes to bed. Do you even own a nightshirt?"

"Several, in fact. In England my valet ensures that each of my residences is equipped with at least one. Strictly for appearance's sake when I have guests, of course."

"*Each* of your residences? Goodness, how many do you have?"

Jason lifted a thick golden tress from her shoulder and inhaled the fragrant scent of her hair. "Well, there's the principal seat of the Marquess of Effing in Kent, and the London townhouse. Two country manor houses—one in Yorkshire and the other in Devon. A moldering castle in Scotland and a hunting box in the Cotswolds of Oxfordshire. Oh, and a cottage by the sea in Brighton. Call it a half dozen, for I'm not certain the hunting box can boast a nightshirt."

Lauren's eyes widened as Jason enumerated the properties he owned. No wonder he thought so little of buying her a mansion in New Orleans. He must be well off indeed, if not actually rich. When she thought of the hunting box, though, she drew back and arched a delicate brow at her husband. "I suppose in Oxfordshire your female guests didn't consider it necessary to wear anything to sleep in, either. Tell me, do gentlemen actually find time to hunt *game* at such places?"

Jason grinned and stole a kiss from her sweetly pouting lips. "There generally isn't much sleep to be had, in any case. But

317

now that my bachelor days are over, I don't expect to be inviting anyone there but you. We could have a delightful time if you were to reconsider and come to England with me."

"Jason, you promised—"

"So I did. A slip of the tongue. But I haven't given you any reason to regret marrying me, have I, wife?"

"No, husband," Lauren admitted meekly, pressing closer.

"And yet you almost succeeded in getting rid of me last night. I very nearly drowned."

Lauren laughed as she remembered how the driving rain had lashed at Jason as he tried to shut the window against the storm. His shirt had been soaked before he succeeded. He hadn't closed the window entirely, knowing her fear of being shut in, but only enough to keep the deluge out and create an atmosphere of cozy intimacy. And even though the storm had continued to rage through the night, Lauren had slept easily, feeling safe and secure in Jason's embrace.

Now, however, she realized that the rain would spoil the plans they had made. Raising herself up on an elbow, she glanced at the window, her expression registering her disappointment. "And you were going to teach me how to swim today. My lesson will have to be called off."

Jason stretched with lazy unconcern. "There will be other days—and the sun may still make an appearance later."

Lauren could feel the muscles of his hard body rippling against her skin, while his heat bathed her heightened senses. She met Jason's intent gaze as warmth stirred within her. "So," she said demurely, "what shall we do this morning?"

Jason drew an idle finger along her collarbone. "There is always breakfast," he murmured, his smile burning and lazy.

"I'm not hungry," she replied, knowing his look of desire was mirrored in her own eyes.

"In that case, milady, might I suggest a lesson . . . of a different nature?" When Lauren regarded him in puzzlement, Jason threaded a hand in her silken hair and slowly drew her head down until their lips met. "God, that glorious hair," he rasped against her mouth as her flowing golden mane cascaded over him. "I want it wrapped around me. I want *you* wrapped around me. . . ." His mouth moved gently over hers while his

tongue flicked at her lips, parting them, seeking out the swe̶
treasure within.

As always, the fire of his kiss took Lauren's breath away, but
this highly sensitive play of Jason's elicited a warm excitement
that was somehow new. His tongue coaxed sweetly, fondling
and caressing her into a similar play of her own, while his
fingers closed over hers. She was only a bit startled when he
guided her hand to his hard, proud shaft.

It didn't take long for Lauren to learn what pleased him, for
he murmured softly in her ear, urging, cautioning, encouraging, his words stimulating her as he taught her how to
caress and arouse him. And Lauren soon discovered an
unexpected enjoyment being the one to set the pace.

Wanting very much to give Jason the kind of pleasure that
he had always given her, she drew her mouth from his and let
her lips roam down his corded neck to the satin skin of his
shoulder, while her slim fingers continued their erotic
ministrations. Her nibbling kisses were tentative at first, but
they grew bolder as she watched Jason's face contort with
passion. She fondled each of his tight male nipples with her
tongue, then moved down his powerful body with tantalizing
slowness, delighting in the silken heat of his muscled rib cage.

When she reached his hard, flat belly, she paused briefly to
give him a thoughtful glance. Then kneeling above him, her
hair spilling down to caress his skin, she imitated the way he
had made love to her that day by the pool, touching him with
her tongue.

Jason's grip tightened almost painfully in her hair as he
shuddered reflexively, but the next moment he became very
still, as if he were fearful of frightening her away. Lauren bent
to him again, her mouth sweet and warm as she tasted him
fully. Languidly, lovingly, she teased his rigid flesh, exulting in
the soft groans that escaped him, wanting to make Jason need
her as much as she needed him.

Jason could only withstand so much exquisite torture,
though. He reached for Lauren, pulling her full length on top
of him. "Sweet Jesus, where did you learn how to do that?" he
demanded in a voice that was thick with passion.

Her eyes were questioning as they met his. "Veronique said

men enjoyed that," Lauren said uncertainly. "Didn't you like it?"

"Of course I liked it. It's just not a skill one expects to find in a wife."

Lauren's brows drew together worriedly. "Truly, Jason, I've never done anything like that before—"

He touched a finger to her lips. "I believe you, sweetheart. But you do it so very well, not at all like a beginner. You nearly made me lose control."

Reassured that he wasn't angry, Lauren flashed him a provocative siren's smile. "Perhaps I should practice."

"Oh, no." Catching her wrists, Jason prevented her from repeating her ministrations. "Now it's my turn to torment you," he declared huskily. Releasing her then, his hands slid down her back to grasp her hips, and before Lauren could even guess his intent, Jason had lifted her up. When she found herself straddling his stomach, her eyes widened, but she waited expectantly, trustingly.

Jason splayed his fingers over her abdomen, sliding his hands smoothly upward to her breasts. Almost reverently, he cupped the tempting swells, filling his palms with her lush fullness, and as he held her glowing eyes with his gaze, his thumbs massaged the swollen tips. He teased the sensitive peaks till they were rigid and aching, then slowly, he drew Lauren down till he could draw a nipple into his mouth.

The taste of her seemed to trigger some more primitive instinct within Jason, for his lovemaking became half savage in its intensity. His mouth ravaged her breast . . . devouring, suckling, his teeth raking gently. . . . And then the next moment he was soothing, fondling, kissing.

If Lauren had been a cat, she would have purred. As it was, she could only moan at the delicious heat building inside her. And when Jason's questing fingers found the soft curls between her thighs, she whimpered and arched against him. She hardly heard the sensuous words Jason was murmuring to excite her further, for he was alternately pressing his palm hard against her, then teasing her with skillful, knowing fingers.

Sometime later, he lifted her up and slid easily inside her,

320

possessing her in one continuous thrust that filled her. Lauren gasped with pleasure when she was impaled on his heated velvet spear. Letting her head fall back, she arched her spine. The heat was scorching her, setting her on fire. It was like being too close to the sun. This, she thought dizzily, was how Phaethon must have felt driving the flaming chariot across the sky—giddy and dazed and reeling.

Jason began to move inside her then, but he had only to thrust twice before Lauren burst into flames. Jason watched hungrily, his gratification complete, as she surged to a fiery climax. Only an iron-willed control kept him from succumbing to the white heat consuming her.

When Lauren at last regained her senses, she discovered that was she lying limply, almost lifelessly, upon Jason's chest. His rigid shaft was still full and throbbing within her, like a deep, slow pulse of pleasure. When Jason slowly began to move again, Lauren almost protested; she wasn't at all sure she could survive another shattering experience like the last.

"Come with me, sweetheart," Jason urged as he sensed her holding back. "Come with me." His breath was hot against her skin, while his seeking hands moved intimately over her flesh.

When his lips claimed hers urgently, Lauren moaned. She was completely powerless against the incredible heat that again was mounting inside her. When Jason's masterful control at last shattered, racking his body with uncontrollable shudders, Lauren's passion overflowed as well, bursting forth in a glorious profusion of flame. Exhausted, she collapsed upon him and slept, only to be revived a short while later by his warm, arousing kisses.

Apollo the sun god, Lauren thought languorously as desire for Jason stung with fresh insistence. How could he be married to her? Gods didn't marry mere mortals. . . .

It was well after noon by the time they at last rose to dress. Lauren had thought her desire totally sated, but when Jason leaned over to lingeringly brush her lips with his, that same hot sensation stirred inside her once more. Jason grinned at her knowingly, making Lauren flush as she remembered how brazen she had been with him.

They ate a leisurely meal, and afterward, Jason drove her to the Beauvais plantation. Fortunately, the rain had stopped, and by the time they had concluded their visit with Lila and Jean-Paul, the sun was beating down warmly.

When they were settled again in the phaeton, Jason fished under the seat and handed Lauren the parcel he found there. She unwrapped it eagerly, discovering a pair of knee-length breeches and a shirt with no arms. "You remembered!" she exclaimed with a joyful laugh, before throwing her arms about Jason's neck and kissing him soundly.

Her embrace played havoc with Jason's control of the horses, but he was pleased to see the sparkle in her golden emerald eyes. "I'm beginning to suspect that I erred in decking you out as a female," Jason teased as he gently extricated himself from her hold. "I don't remember being rewarded like that for an entire wardrobe of feminine fripperies."

Directing a mischievous glance at him, Lauren folded her hands in her lap. "It would have been highly improper for me to kiss you then," she observed primly. "We weren't married, you will recall. Besides," Lauren added when Jason looked up at the heavens as if praying for patience, "you didn't offer to teach me to swim."

"Is that the way to your heart, then?"

"Perhaps," she replied provocatively.

"*Perhaps,*" Jason mimicked as he turned the gig toward the creek, "I should throw you in and see whether you sink. That's how they determine if someone is innocent of witchcraft, you know."

Lauren's eyes narrowed. "Jason, are you calling me a witch?"

"Oh, no, my love!" Then his innocent expression rapidly dissolved into a grin. "Of course, I wouldn't be at all surprised to discover that you can float," he observed, and laughed at the face she made.

That was the first of such swimming lessons for Lauren. They were repeated almost daily after that, but the initial one stood out markedly in her memory. Not because it was the first, or even because she was finally learning the mechanics of swimming, but because of what Jason said to her that day.

They had both soon changed clothes—Lauren wearing her

new outfit, while Jason stripped down to his breeches. After giving her some rudimentary instruction on dry land, he made her lie on her stomach in a shallow part of the creek as he showed her how to stroke. Then he took her downstream where the water was deeper.

The pool wasn't as large or as lovely as the one they had found that long-ago golden afternoon on the wilderness trail, but it was deep enough to be over Lauren's head. She eyed it with sudden apprehension, a panic that only nonswimmers can know threatening to unnerve her. When Jason took her by the hand to lead her to the water, her limbs suddenly stiffened, rendering her immobile.

Jason's voice sounded as if from a great distance. "Look at me, Lauren. I love you, sweetheart. You have nothing to be frightened of. I would never let anything harm you. I can keep us both afloat if you will only trust me. Now, put your arms around my neck. That's it, sweetheart. Now relax and let me hold you up. Trust me, Lauren. Trust me."

Very soon, she began to enjoy herself. Certainly she never again felt on the edge of panic because she was afraid of *water*. But she had trusted Jason with her life that day, and more importantly, she had realized that gaining her trust was a prime objective of his. He had been, and was still, attempting to win her completely. *Trust me*, he had said. He had used those same words before, Lauren recalled, and more than once. And it was likely that he would never stop trying until he had gained her trust in its entirety.

That conclusion disturbed her. Jason had promised that he wouldn't try to persuade her to return with him to England, and so far he was keeping that promise. But he was to leave in a few weeks. What would happen then? Lauren found it difficult to think of his impending departure without becoming depressed. She already loved him, perhaps *too* well. So what did he hope to gain by having her trust?

Not long after her first swimming session, Lauren received at least a partial answer to that question. They had attended a ball with Lila and Jean-Paul, and when the Beauvaises decided to stay for a while longer, Jason and Lauren returned home alone in the coach.

323

Lauren had enjoyed the evening immensely, but she was pleasantly tired after so much dancing. She rested her head gratefully against the shoulder Jason offered, looking forward to the peace of her beautiful new home and the contentment of falling asleep with her husband's arms around her.

The night itself was lovely—moonless, but with a million brilliant stars to light up the heavens. The coach swayed gently, while a warm breeze drifted through the open window, carrying the fragrances of jasmine and wild azalea and the din of cicadas. Lauren might have been lulled to sleep, except that Jason decided to make use of the romantic setting.

Unfortunately, his desire was thwarted by the ostrich plumes of Lauren's headdress. One caught him in the eye when he attempted to kiss her, and he drew back, muttering a curse on her blasted feathers.

Smiling in the darkness, Lauren wordlessly removed the bandeau and raised her lips to receive Jason's kiss. She wasn't quite prepared for his impatient passion, though, or for her own response. She emerged from his embrace trembling with need.

"God, you're so beautiful," Jason said huskily, the velvet timbre of his voice stroking her senses. His tongue was teasing her earlobe, stirring hot excitement in her body.

Knowing quite well where another such kiss from her lusty husband could lead, Lauren thought it best to divert his attention. Laughing lightly, she tried to push him away. "How can you tell what I look like? It's far too dark to see."

His arms tightened around her. "Ummm, you *taste* beautiful. Do you know what you do to me?"

"Yes, you do it to me as well. But the driver—"

"Devil take the driver. I want you."

Lauren pressed her palms against his chest. "Not here, Jason."

"Yes, here." His hand slipped inside her bodice, covering a ripe breast possessively.

"Jason, the coachman will hear," Lauren protested weakly.

"I'll shut the window."

She reacted immediately to his words. "No! Please, no!" she cried, twisting frantically in his embrace.

324

Jason released her at once, but the intimacy between them had been broken. In the resulting silence, Lauren hung her head, realizing she had made Jason angry. She could feel his eyes on her, but though she tried to think of something to say that would restore his good humor, nothing came to mind.

As the silence between them stretched into an eternity, Lauren was reminded of the night Jason had spirited her away from the casino. She had been frightened out of her wits then, finding herself trapped in a closed carriage with him.

At last Jason said very softly, "Come here, Lauren."

She peered at him uncertainly, but could read nothing of his expression in the darkness. "You *are* angry," Lauren said gloomily.

"Yes. But perhaps 'hurt' is a better description of my strongest feeling at the moment. It hurts me when you pull away from me in fear. Now, come here."

When he reached out to draw Lauren into his arms, she didn't resist. Instead she rested her head on his shoulder as Jason gently stroked her hair. "I'd like to help you, sweetheart," he murmured. "Perhaps I could, if you would allow me." Then in an almost inaudible tone, he vowed, "I would give anything, *anything,* if you would only trust me."

"I do trust you, Jason," Lauren returned quietly.

"Do you?" There was an odd inflection to his voice, a mixture of skepticism and hope. After a time, he drew back, cupping her face in his hands. "Lauren, I wrote to an acquaintance of mine, a doctor who specializes in phobias such as yours. Many of his patients have suffered various degrees of memory loss because of some traumatic event they've experienced, and he thinks your fear may be similar. That may be why you suffer from nightmares. He also says a cure is possible, but that it's important for you to remember the events that caused your condition."

"But I don't—" Lauren broke off as a chill ran up her spine. Jason was referring to Andrea, of course. Her poor half sister had experienced the horror of seeing her parents murdered, and had nearly lost her sanity as a result. Thinking of it, Lauren wanted to shudder. "There is no reason to assume my problem is similar," she said carefully. "What could there be for me to remember?"

Jason's breath was warm and caressing against her cheek. "I'd like to know that, myself," he replied, before bending to kiss her. When he next spoke, his voice was not only husky with suppressed desire, but was also soothing and coaxing, as it had been when he first urged her into the water. "Lauren, I'd like to help you face whatever makes you so afraid. Will you trust me, sweetheart?"

She regarded him warily. "But it isn't something I can control, Jason."

He put a finger to her lips. "I want to try. Will you allow me?" Hesitantly, she nodded. "All right, then. I just want you to relax and remember that I'm here with you. I won't let anything happen to you."

"What do you intend to do?" she asked apprehensively.

"Nothing that will harm you. Now put your arms around my neck, like you did when you were learning to float."

"Jason, please—"

"Trust me, Lauren. That's it. Now, kiss me."

Tentatively, Lauren complied. But as his kiss deepened, she became lost in the private world of sensation that Jason's caressing lips and stroking hands created.

At first she hardly noticed when he leaned forward to slowly close the coach window. She sensed something was different, but his soft murmurings held her attention. "Feel my love for you, Lauren. My sweet Lauren. Let it surround you. My beautiful Lauren. My precious love."

His hypnotic voice, his words of love, kept the specters at bay for some time, but Jason was unable to prevent their intrusion forever. One moment Lauren was soft and warm and willing; the next she had gone rigid with terror, raising her hands to crush them over her ears. Nothing, not words, not kisses, not embraces, could penetrate her mind while it was frozen with fear.

And even though Jason knew what to expect, he was enraged by his own helplessness. She was hearing ghostly voices no one else could hear, being tormented by something invisible, intangible, something he couldn't fight it as he could an ordinary foe.

Seeing Lauren in such distress filled him with anguish, and as he rushed to open the window, Jason knew he would never again intentionally put her through such suffering. He couldn't stand it, even if she could. Even if it meant sacrificing their future together, he wouldn't try again to make her face whatever horrors affected her so.

"Jason!" she cried in a hoarse whisper.

Her plea knifing at his heart, he gave Lauren's shoulders a desperate shake, trying to bring her back from whatever macabre world she was lost in. As he felt her gradual revival, he let out a ragged breath. "God, Lauren, forgive me," he groaned, pulling her quivering body into his arms, feeling her shaking all over. "Sweetheart, I'm sorry, I'm sorry," he murmured over and over, pressing his lips against her forehead. "I never meant to frighten you like that."

Jason held her till her trembling ceased, yet his agonized thoughts wouldn't be still. He wasn't able to help her, he thought despairingly. No matter how great his love for her, he couldn't help her.

He stroked her damp brow, lost in his grim reflections, and hardly realized when Lauren reached up to touch his cheek. "Are you disappointed with me?" she asked worriedly.

Jason stared down at her, clearly shocked by her question. Then his arms tightened fiercely about her and he buried his face in her hair. "No, Cat-eyes, I'm only wondering how I can ever face you again. Perhaps I don't deserve your trust."

For a moment Lauren was speechless. She had never known Jason to be so gloomy, never known him to sound so defeated. This couldn't be her masterful, supremely confident husband. Certainly she never imagined that she would be in a position to reassure him, to offer him comfort.

Tenderly Lauren wrapped her arms around his neck, feeling her heart swell with love for him. "It was different this time, Jason, truly," she said softly. "I was frightened, but this time I could feel you holding me. And I could see you, a shadowy figure so far away. I thought that if I could only reach you, I would be safe. It was never like that before, Jason."

Jason sighed deeply. When he glanced out the window, he realized the coach had stopped moving. "We're home," he commented absently.

Lauren placed a restraining hand on his sleeve. "Jason, did you hear what I said?"

"Yes, sweetheart."

"Don't you believe me? That you were there in my . . . nightmare, or whatever it is I have?"

"I believe you. You cried out my name once."

"I did? Well, that must prove *something*. Always before I've been alone with no one to help me. You were there for me this time, Jason."

"Yet I didn't help you, did I?"

Lauren was amazed at Jason's despondency. "So? I've lived with this 'condition', as you called it, for years. You can't just expect to come storming into my nightmares and sweep me off my feet the very first time, like you did in real life!"

Suddenly coming to his senses, Jason shook his head. A bitter smile tugged at the corner of his mouth as he caught Lauren's hand and pressed a kiss in her palm. "No, I suppose that is too much to expect. See what you've done to me, Lauren Stuart? Here I am demanding prime billing in your nightmares when I should be content with merely a passing appearance."

She ignored his mockery. "But it is a beginning, isn't it?" she pressed.

Jason remembered that one encouraging moment when Lauren had called out to him. "Yes, my love," he conceded gently. "It is a beginning."

Chapter Nineteen

"Do you suppose there is a fire?" Lauren remarked after being jostled rudely by a couple who was hurrying along Chartres Street toward the Place d'Armes.

Lauren's maid, a young black girl named May, had been keeping a respectful distance behind, but she moved closer when her mistress was nearly thrown to the pavement. "Thank you, May, but I'm quite all right," Lauren said, refusing the girl's support. "Perhaps we should see what is causing all the excitement."

As they neared the Place d'Armes, Lauren could see the large crowd gathered there. A man stood on the platform of a small scaffold which had been erected in the square, and Lauren wondered what he could be saying to so thoroughly hold the interest of the crowd. "May, will you see if you can find out what is happening?"

"Yes, ma'am," the girl replied, bobbing a curtsy. "There be ole Gabe yonder. He tell me."

"Here, let me have that, please." Lauren took the carefully wrapped parcel she had just purchased, then urged May to make haste. She didn't intend to linger at the square, for she had come to the Vieux Carré without Jason's knowledge and didn't want to risk his questions.

Her purpose for the visit had to do with Jason's imminent departure from New Orleans. Jason hadn't set a date yet, but June was fast approaching and Lauren knew he would soon sail out of her life. It was the one dark cloud that menaced her current happiness.

A bittersweet ache filled her whenever she thought of the future, and at times Lauren almost wished she had never met Jason. Yet she knew she would rather suffer that pain ten times over, rather than miss the sweet agony of loving him.

She was very much afraid, however, that when Jason returned to England he would forget all about her. Intending to give him something as a remembrance, she had commissioned an artist to paint a miniature of herself.

Until this morning, she had sat only once for a sketch. Jason had been sincere when he demanded they make the most of the time they had left, so Lauren found it difficult to get away from the attentions of her loving husband for any length of time. When Jason had announced that morning his intentions of inspecting the completed warehouse, she declined his invitation to accompany him, and as soon as he had left the house, she slipped away for another sitting, taking May with her for propriety's sake.

An hour later, Lauren left the artist's studio, well pleased with the progress on the small portrait. She was passing the silversmith's shop on her way home when an object in the window caught her eye: a small replica of a schooner, hammered in silver, its tiny sails spread to the wind. The proud little vessel reminded Lauren of the *Siren* and, of course, Jason. In an instant, she was inside the shop, asking to have "Siren" engraved on the sides of the silver ship. She also purchased a half-finished jewel box as a gift for Lila, though she would have to wait several days until the intricate details on the case were completed.

It was as she was leaving the smith's shop that Lauren was nearly run down by the hurrying couple. Curious, she followed them to the Place d'Armes and sent May to find out what was happening.

As May moved away, a man at Lauren's elbow muttered a remark under his breath. Lauren thought he must be an Arcadian, for he wore rough trousers and a homespun shirt under a loose tunic, and spoke in a French patois that was hard to follow. "An auction" was the most Lauren could decipher, but she was puzzled. Most public business was conducted in the

330

rotunda of the St. Louis Hotel where slaves were bought and sold.

"What is being auctioned?" she asked the man.

He seemed surprised to be addressed by a strange beauty, one who was so obviously a lady, but he wasn't at all reluctant to strike up a conversation. He gave Lauren a large, gap-toothed grin, letting his eyes dwell on her bosom with an interest that made her uncomfortable. "Lafitte's property," he explained in English. "The American government thinks to sell the ships they stole from him. Hah, no one will buy! They know better than to risk the wrath of Jean Lafitte."

Even as he spoke, though, a murmur went through the crowd and the auctioneer made a sign. "*Sacre!*" the Arcadian exclaimed. "Someone has made an offer. There is a fool for you. He will not live long enough to enjoy his prize."

The Arcadian's voice seemed loud to Lauren, for an expectant hush had settled over the square. In the silence, Lauren could almost hear the crowd thinking: Would Lafitte somehow stop the purchase? Who was the daring man who had bid on the ship? Would the government be satisfied with such a low price since the bid was outrageously low?

Just then, the crowd parted and a space opened up before her. Lauren drew a sharp breath. She could see Jason clearly now, for he was a head taller than anyone else and he was standing alone. Realizing that the other spectators were giving him a wide berth, Lauren knew then who had offered to buy the ship. It was the kind of game Jason would enjoy, she reflected with dismay, for the element of danger would pique his interest. Lauren couldn't repress the stab of fear that went through her; Jean Lafitte was not a man to be crossed, even by a man as formidable as her husband.

The auctioneer tugged at his neckcloth as if it gave him great discomfort. Then bringing his gavel down, he proclaimed the tall gentleman the new owner of the three-masted bark *Inferno*. Jason nodded to confirm the purchase, seeming oblivious to the excited murmurs breaking out around him.

Instinctively, Lauren took a step toward him, intending to beg him to reconsider, but she froze when a dark-haired woman reached Jason's side and claimed his arm. Desirée! She must

331

have been standing close to him all the while.

When Desirée smiled up at him seductively, Lauren's eyes narrowed with pure unadulterated jealousy. For a moment she was undecided whether to scratch the witch's eyes out or slap her husband's handsome face. Then Jason grinned down at the beautiful brunette and bent his head to whisper in her ear. Desirée said something in reply, before standing on tiptoe to loop her arms around his neck. Lauren watched, stunned, as Jason accepted without a qualm the fervent kiss Desirée gave him.

A taloned claw raked across Lauren's heart as her thoughts staggered from one conclusion to the next. Jason hadn't told her about the auction, but so little escaped his attention that he must have known about it. He hadn't told her he planned to buy one of Lafitte's ships, either, even though he generally made it a point to discuss such business decisions for her edification. Had he not told her about Desirée as well? How long had he been seeing the ebony-haired courtesan? Or had he ever stopped? Desirée was beautiful. She knew all the tricks of her trade, all the ways to lure a man's attention.

Lauren stared at the embracing couple in anguish, a dull roar in her ears shutting out the sounds of the crowd. Even though Jason had denied taking advantage of what had obviously been offered him, she had never quite believed his assurances. She had tried to excuse his indulgences before their marriage, though, knowing she had no claims on him. But had he forsaken his marriage vows already? In favor of that . . . that woman?

The ache rose in Lauren's throat and threatened to choke her. Perhaps, after all, Jason had only married her for the Carlin ships. Perhaps he had never loved her. Perhaps it was all a tremendous lie.

The Arcadian called out something, but Lauren didn't hear; she was gazing blindly at her husband. Through her haze of pain she saw Jason turn and look directly at her, and for an instant, his expression registered surprise. When he took an involuntary step toward her, though, Lauren didn't wait to see what he would do. She couldn't face him. Not now. Not ever. She wanted to run and hide, to crawl up in some dark little corner and die. Turning, she stumbled into someone blocking her path, but she pushed on, not even knowing where she was going.

Jason called out to her, and when Lauren started to run, he swore under his breath. Beckoning to Monsieur Sauvinet, Jason issued some terse instructions to the banker, then set off in pursuit of his fleeing wife.

He had indeed been surprised to see Lauren in the public square; certainly he hadn't wanted her to find out what he was doing. But the discovery shouldn't have made her bolt like a startled doe.

Realizing she had somehow misconstrued his intentions, he cast his mind over the past few moments and recalled the kiss Desirée had pressed on his lips. That had been entirely too intimate a gesture for a wife to easily accept or forgive. But fiend seize it! Lauren was running from him again without even giving him a chance to explain. He shouted after her, but Lauren neither stopped nor paused to look over her shoulder.

Jason's anger grew as he chased her through the streets of the Vieux Carré. He had a decided advantage in speed since his longer legs were unhampered by skirts, but Lauren had a head start of nearly a block. Jason had closed only half the distance between them when she disappeared into Madame Gescard's gaming house, and when he tried to follow, he was forced to slow his stride.

Kendricks stood there blocking the way, his legs spread wide in a belligerent stance. He wasn't at all pleased to see Jason, but neither was he averse to locking horns again. In fact, he had been relishing the thought of avenging his defeat of a few weeks before. One look at the snapping fury in the blue eyes, however, convinced Kendricks this wasn't an auspicious time to challenge the gentleman—or even to stand in his way. He fell back before the force of Jason's relentless advance.

"My wife, where is she?" Jason ground out, gripping the majordomo by the shirtfront.

"She has a room upstairs," Kendricks replied quickly. "Top floor, last door on the right. But I'll not swear that's where she is."

Jason aimed himself at the stairs and took them three at a

time. When he reached Lauren's room, he didn't bother to knock but twisted the doorhandle. To his great amazement, he found the door locked. Knowing her fear of confinement, Jason wondered if he might have the wrong room. But only for an instant. He knew she was inside.

"Open the door, Lauren, before I knock it down!"

There was no reply to his bellowed command. The silence was shortly followed by the sound of splintering wood as Jason applied a sturdy shoulder to the offending portal. When the barrier crashed to the floor, he stumbled over the threshold.

Lauren stood by the open window, not moving, her complexion very pale. Considering the blazing glare her violent husband was directing at her, though, she faced him with remarkable composure. "Go away. I don't wish to see you."

"That is quite obvious!" Jason retorted as he surveyed the wreckage he had made of the door. "You even overcame your aversion to locks, I see, in your effort to avoid me."

Lauren lifted her chin regally. "I thought it the lesser of two evils."

Jason's jaw hardened, but he managed to keep his volume below a roar. "Why the hell are you running this time? Had you intended on saying good-bye first, or did you plan to leave without a word?" When she didn't answer, he swore violently. "Dammit, Lauren! I had your promise!"

She returned his regard coldly. "I don't mean to speak to you. Go away."

Jason spread his hands wide, as if pleading his innocence. "The least you could do is give me a chance to explain. I don't even know what crime I've been convicted of."

"It doesn't matter," Lauren declared in a chill voice. "You will be leaving in a few weeks. What difference does it make if we end this farce of a marriage a bit earlier than we planned?"

Jason drew in a deep breath. "I wasn't aware you considered it a farce." But as his eyes searched her face, he noted with despair Lauren's remoteness. Her silence now was different from the deaf-muteness she had affected when he had tricked her into becoming his wife. This was the same touch-me-never coldness he had once fought to overcome. Only this was far more serious; she had locked him out of her heart. The barrier

334

was up between them again, as frozen and impenetrable as ever, and he couldn't storm it as easily as he could a wooden door.

"Just like that, you end it?" he demanded. "What we had together has ceased to exist?" When Lauren merely stared back at him, Jason's tone shifted to biting sarcasm. "I can see how deeply you are affected, sweetheart. You might be remarking about the weather instead of the dissolution of our marriage. Come to think of it, most people show more feeling when discussing the weather."

Lauren remained silent, forcing herself to steadily return his gaze. She couldn't explain that making herself numb inside was her only means of self-protection. And perhaps, after all, this was the best way to end their relationship. One swift cleaving stroke. Later she would grieve. Later she would feel. But for now she would be thankful for the deadening of her heart.

"Perhaps it is for the best," Jason echoed her thoughts. "I really have no interest in staying married to a child—one who runs at the first sign of trouble. Christ, you even see ghosts!" He missed Lauren's wince of pain as he bent to lift the fallen door. "Being saddled with a neurotic wife does have its disadvantages," Jason observed derisively as he leaned the wooden panel against the wall.

"Get out," Lauren breathed, her voice holding the barest hint of emotion.

Jason eyed her sardonically. "But then I got what I wanted. The Carlin Line."

Lauren shut her eyes against the wave of pain that assailed her. There, he had finally admitted it. But it shouldn't hurt so much to hear what she had known all along. She faced Jason again, although she was unable to keep a quiver from her voice when she spoke. "You have Desirée, as well. Why don't you go to her? I don't doubt she pleases you better than I."

Jason's mouth twisted in a mocking smile. "She certainly isn't as cold as you are."

Lauren clenched her fists as his words struck her. Not only was he not denying his relationship with Desirée, but he was taunting her about it as well! What a stupid fool she had been to listen to his passionate lies, to let him make love to her while

335

he was playing the rutting stag behind her back.

Seething with humiliation and anger, Lauren hardly felt the nails digging into her palms. "Get out!" she hissed. "Go back to her before she misses you!"

Nonchalantly, Jason turned to leave. "Perhaps I will. At least she isn't a frozen excuse for a woman."

He had taken but two steps when a small parcel wrapped in tissue paper came flying past his head. Lauren had picked up the little ship and thrown it with all her might. "Take that with you!" she cried, dangerously close to losing control. "Consider it a farewell present from your loving wife!"

He turned to rake her with his gaze. *"Loving?"* he drawled contemptuously. "You don't know the meaning of the word, my sweet. I could almost pity you, but for the fact your ignorance suited my purpose. How easy it was to play the lovesick swain, to convince you and the rest of the world I married you for love. Now, of course, I am desolated by your repudiation." He swept her a mocking bow. "It should be the work of a moment to persuade all your dear friends that I have been grievously wronged. I doubt if any of them will protest very loudly when I walk away with your inheritance now."

Lauren's wide, pain-filled eyes contrasted starkly to her ashen face. "I hate you!" she whispered.

"Now, sweetheart, that's no way to look at it," Jason admonished. "You may have lost a fortune, but you've had a little pleasure along the way. And you know more about playing the whore now. Your new skills will come in handy, should you decide to remain here. Certainly you can enter the profession with complete confidence. You were quite an excellent pupil! In fact, if you would like, I'll supply you with references."

Lauren attacked him then, with a cry of wounded fury. Flailing blindly, she pounded at his chest and shoulders, wanting to hurt him as he had hurt her. Jason made no move to defend himself until Lauren attempted to rake his face with her nails, but even then he only held her wrists in a gentle grip, not speaking as she fought him wildly.

When the first sob tore through her, it felt like a knife ripping at her lungs. And then more followed; she couldn't

336

stop them. It was like a great dam breaking, letting loose all the violent emotions she always so carefully controlled. Her body shook with racking sobs, while the tears came, in floods, in rivers, erupting from her as a deluge from a stormy heaven.

Jason's hands came up to seize her shoulders, steadying her until she sank to her knees, unable to support her own weight. Wordlessly then, he scooped her up and carried her to the bed where he sat, cradling her trembling body in his arms while her grief poured forth in a wordless, unending stream.

A worried Veronique came to the door, but went away again when Jason silently shook his head. Lauren wasn't aware of it. She was hardly aware that Jason was holding her. Had she been, she would have found it ironic that Jason should be the one to console her; she was crying because she had lost him, because without him she felt incomplete, inadequate, only half a person.

When at last her weeping became less passionate, she realized that she was lying on the bed with him, sprawled on his chest. His arms were wrapped tightly around her shaking shoulders, while his hand gently stroked her hair. When she tried to move away, though, Jason wouldn't let her go. Giving up the struggle, she lay there submissively, her head on his shoulder, his body warm and hard beneath hers.

Finally her shudders ceased and her tears ended. Jason released her then, only to settle her more comfortably in the crook of his arm. Lauren stayed there, not thinking, not feeling anything, yet savoring his protective warmth as she listened to the vibrant rhythm of his heartbeat.

She felt his lips move gently against her hair. "Feel better?" he murmured.

Lauren considered his question. Her body felt drained and limp, as if it had been pounded by the hooves of a hundred wild horses, yet a kind of peace she had never known before had settled over her. She felt cleansed by the tears, purified by the fires of rage and hatred that had swept through her. "Yes," she rasped, though realizing he already knew the answer.

Her voice was husky from crying, her face damp with tears. When she sniffed inelegantly and wiped ineffectually at her eyes, Jason handed her a snowy handkerchief. Lauren used it

337

gratefully, then rolled on her back, staring up at the canopy. "You did that on purpose," she observed, not expecting or receiving a denial. Jason shifted so that he lay on his side. He was watching her, she knew. "I haven't cried since I left England," Lauren added almost absently.

"Thank God you did," he said softly. "I was running out of insults, trying to break through that frozen shell of yours."

Lauren smiled faintly, wondering how Jason had understood her better than she understood herself. When she turned her head on the pillow, she saw the tenderness in his gaze. "I . . . hit you," she said hesitantly. "I didn't hurt you, did I?"

Jason returned her smile. "I'm sure I have a cracked rib or two." When Lauren's green-gold eyes filled with concern, Jason pressed his fingers to her lips. "Believe me, sweetheart, I would rather have you striking me or threatening to shoot me than so stoically denying your hatred or anger or uncertainty. You feel those things—we all do. But most of us find some way of releasing our emotions instead of keeping them bottled up inside or running from them."

When her lips began to tremble, Jason reached up to stroke her tear-stained cheek, and his voice lowered to a pleading whisper. "Don't run from me, Lauren. I can bear anything but that."

The welling tears threatened to spill over again. "Hold me, Jason," she begged. "Please, just hold me."

Almost fiercely, Jason drew her into his embrace once more, but Lauren welcomed the near-pain of being crushed in his arms. She clung to him tightly, as if by doing so, she could merge into one being with him.

It was some time before either of them relaxed their hold. But they didn't move apart, even then. Their lips met in a kiss that was at first questioning, then reassuring.

Jason was the first to draw back. "So you don't hate me after all." His voice held a trace of amusement.

Lauren bit her lip. "I never hated you. But the things you said to me hurt so much—"

"I meant for them to. I was hurt and angry myself. But I trust you realize that everything I said was a pack of lies."

338

"Now I do. But I believed you then."

Jason returned her gaze steadily. "Only because I voiced the suspicions you've harbored against me at one time or another. You never have quite given up the idea that I only married you for your inheritance, have you?"

Lauren buried her face in the curve of his shoulder, giving a slight shake of her head.

"Sweetheart," Jason said lovingly, "if I thought it would make you trust me, I would sink every last one of those blasted ships. Since that night in London four years ago when you were running away from your guardian, you've owned my heart. And you always will."

Her hesitant reply was muffled against his shoulder. "But . . . what of Desirée?"

"Lauren, I've told you before, and I'll only say it once more. I've never *looked* at Desirée, much less touched her. How could I when I have you?"

Lauren drew back to stare at him. "But she kissed you! I saw her."

Jason pillowed his head on his arm as he held her gaze. "So she did. But I had just rejected her more-than-generous offer, and I could hardly insult her further by refusing her kiss. There was nothing to it on my part. Desirée knew that. In fact, I wouldn't be surprised to learn that she gave that little performance for *your* benefit. I had also told her I had a beautiful wife who kept me more than satisfied."

"I suppose that's possible," Lauren conceded. "She always has been a spiteful cat. Still, that couldn't have been the first time you kissed her. Veronique told me you went upstairs with her one night and didn't come down for an hour."

"Veronique! Sometimes I don't know whether to curse that woman or bless her. Yes, I went to Desirée's rooms. But all we did was talk."

"Talk?" Lauren's brows lifted skeptically.

"Yes, talk," Jason repeated firmly. "My reason for seeing her had nothing to do with lovemaking. I simply wanted to ask her some questions. At the time I didn't think you were prepared for an explanation, and I'm still not certain I should tell you."

"Very well, then, tell me why you were bidding for Lafitte's ships."

Jason's blue eyes sparkled. "Surely you aren't jealous of him as well."

"Of course not. I just don't care to become a widow so soon after being wed."

"Would you miss me?"

Lauren shuddered. "Don't jest about such a thing, Jason. Lafitte is a dangerous man. There is already little love between you, or so Kyle says. This might make him wish you real harm."

"I'm in no danger, sweetheart. Jean is aware that I meant to purchase his ships—in fact, he asked me to do so. I had planned to turn them over to him as soon as I had the ownership papers in hand."

"Turn them over? But I don't understand."

"I owed him a favor."

Lauren's brows drew together in a frown as she recalled Jason had bought only one of the ships. "But that means . . . I must have spoiled your plans. Oh, Jason, I'm sorry. I didn't realize."

Shifting his weight, Jason propped his head up on his elbow and grinned down at her. "I suppose I forgive you. Sauvinet was at the auction, and he took my place. I could have gotten a better price, I think, and now everyone will know what we intended, but Jean will get his ships back. What were you doing in the square, anyway? Not that you have to give me an accounting of your whereabouts, but anything could have happened to you in such a crowd."

"May was attending me. May! Good Lord, I forgot all about her! She must be frantic."

"She'll find her way home, I expect," Jason said soothingly. Bending his head, he pressed a light kiss on Lauren's mouth. "Perhaps that will teach you not to run off. Others do worry about you, you know, including your husband. But you changed the subject. You were going to tell me why you were there in the first place."

Lauren's lashes lowered contritely. "I went to buy you a

present. But I think I might have damaged it."

"The package you threw at me?" At her nod, Jason laughed outright. "Well, it doesn't matter. I'm certain to appreciate any gift from you, damaged or not. Should I open it now?"

"No," Lauren answered firmly. "You should explain to me what you were doing in Desirée's rooms, and how you came to be involved with a notorious smuggler."

There was a long pause as Jason's smile slowly faded. His voice was quite grave when he at last said, "Lauren, have you ever heard of man who goes by the name of Rafael?"

Though she tried to prevent it, Lauren stiffened at his introduction of the past. "Why? Should I know him?" she asked warily.

"Rafael was . . . is a pirate. He killed your father."

"My father was killed by smugglers," she said in a low voice, trying to give herself time to think.

"So the world believes. But George Burroughs told me a different story—of how Jonathan Carlin, along with his wife Mary and daughter Andrea, was held captive by Rafael and his fellow buccaneers. The elder Carlins were brutally tortured and died from their wounds, but the daughter managed to escape. Afterward, she didn't remember anything of what had happened. The horror of what she had seen had been stricken from her memory."

Lauren's eyes widened. "And you think that I . . . that I could have forgotten something like that?"

"Such an experience might explain your nightmares."

It would if I were Andrea Carlin, Lauren reflected. But Andrea had been the one to witness Jonathan and Mary's death, not herself. There had to be some other reason for her own nightmares.

Lauren's lips parted in denial, before she realized that if she protested too loudly, Jason would demand to know why she was so certain. Then she would be forced to confess the entire impersonation.

God, she was trapped in an endless circle of lies.

"I suppose it is possible," Lauren said at last. "I don't remember anything like that." She was unable to meet Jason's gaze, but she heard his sigh.

"Well, to answer your question," he said finally, "I promised your guardian I would find Rafael and see that he was punished. I doubt that Burroughs cared much about what happened to your father, but Mary was his only sister, and he wanted her death avenged."

Sitting up, Jason swung his legs over the side of the bed and ran a hand through his tawny hair. "Actually Rafael is the main reason I came to New Orleans—I had heard he was hiding in this part of the world. When I went to see Lafitte a few months ago, I discovered that Rafael had been one of his buccaneer captains but that they had parted ways because Jean hadn't like his methods. Jean suggested Rafael might be somewhere in the Caribbean. I also learned that Desirée's brother Claude had sailed with Rafael. That's why I went to question her. She agreed to put me in touch with her brother when she next heard from him. Yesterday she received a message from Claude saying that he had returned and is willing to see me."

Lauren felt her heart sink. "You are leaving?" she murmured.

Jason turned to gaze down at her lovely face. "For a few days at least. I must talk to Claude and find out what he knows."

A sudden chill made Lauren shiver. Though not knowing the cause, she was quite sure she didn't want Jason to go. She clutched at his hand and held it to her cheek. "Jason, please, don't go down there again," she implored. "I'm afraid for you."

"Sweetheart, I won't be in any danger. Jean has offered me his hospitality again, as well as sending a man to guide me through the swamps."

"Then take me with you!"

Jason's brows lifted half an inch. "Into a den of notorious cutthroats? Not on your life, Cat-eyes. I'd spend the entire time worrying about you, even if I weren't already occupied in challenging all the men who coveted you for themselves. Besides, Lafitte is a handsome man, and he's said to have quite a way with the ladies. I won't risk having him turn your head as well."

"He couldn't! Jason, please, let me come—"

"No, Lauren," he replied gently.

The underlying steel in his voice, however, convinced Lauren that he wouldn't be swayed. Stiffening, she raised her chin mutinously. "Then don't expect me to be here when you return."

Jason's mouth tightened, although he replied patiently. "I made an oath to a dying man, Lauren. I must see it out. Can you not understand that?"

"Yes, I understand! I understand that George Burroughs has once again managed to destroy any happiness in my life, even now that he's dead. Well, so be it! Leave me, but just don't come back!" She sounded adamant, but fresh tears shimmered in her eyes, making them glitter like jewels. Jason stared sorrowfully into the golden-green depths, not replying.

As the silence lengthened and Jason still made no response, Lauren's tears spilled over. Flinging herself into his arms, she retracted her threat between sobs of remorse. She hadn't meant it! She deserved to be flogged for saying that she didn't want him back! She couldn't bear it if anything happened to him.

Again Jason held her and soothed her and comforted her. And when she was calm again, he took the crumpled handkerchief from her and dried her eyes, then kissed her quivering mouth.

Contritely, Lauren rested her head on his shoulder and gave a shaky sigh. "Jason . . . I love you."

"I know, sweetheart."

"Sometimes I say things I don't mean at all."

"I know that, too."

There was a definite smile in his voice, and Lauren lifted her head from its comfortable resting place to glance up at him. "Must you be so disgustingly *understanding?*"

Jason's blue eyes danced with amusement. "Well, what would you have me say? That I mind terribly that you have ruined my favorite coat?"

She drew back to view the now wet garment. "Perhaps the damage isn't irreparable," she said ruefully, wondering how she could feel like laughing when a moment before her heart had been breaking.

Jason chuckled and wrapped his arms about her once more, pulling Lauren tightly against him. "Now we're even, Cat-eyes—you'll have to forgive me now for saying what I did earlier. Though I can't understand how you could have believed that nonsense. How could you have thought that I wanted your money more than your body?"

When he bent to nuzzle the soft skin at her neck, Lauren felt a familiar desire stir within her. She let her head fall back, giving Jason's lips better access to her throat. "Well," she murmured, "you were telling the truth about one thing. I am a good pupil."

"Is that so, madame wife?"

"Yes. And if you hadn't broken down the door, I would prove it to you."

Jason laughed huskily. "I'll repair it at once, by God! See if I don't."

Chapter Twenty

"Of course it is foolish of me, but I shall miss him," Veronique sighed as she languidly waved her fan. "Lauren, you will not allow Kyle to forget me, will you, *chérie?*"

Lauren looked up with a start, then flushed when she realized what the question implied. Both Veronique and Lila assumed she would be going to England with Jason.

She hadn't told them differently, and now as she sat with the two women in the Beauvais garden, sipping cool lemonade in the shade of a giant magnolia, Lauren couldn't bring herself to speak of it. Nor could she control the sudden tears that stung her eyes at the thought of Jason's leaving. Not wanting her friends to see her cry, she rose abruptly. "It's so hot," Lauren murmured. "I must have some air. I beg you to excuse me."

The warm afternoon seemed to close in on her as she sped down the path toward the rear of the garden where spike-leaved oleanders and lemon-scented verbena were in full bloom. She sank to her knees in the soft grass, sobbing.

Sometime later she was startled by Lila's light touch on her shoulder. "Lauren, is something troubling you?" Lila asked in a concerned voice.

Lauren hastily wiped her eyes. "It is nothing. Just a speck of dust in my eye. Truly, Lila, I'm fine. I needed some fresh air. I will just be a moment longer, I promise."

Lila's smile was a trifle forced, although she nodded and left Lauren alone with her troubled thoughts. Dejectedly, Lauren moved to sit on a wooden bench. She made an effort to regain

345

her composure, but she was soon crying again. Half turning to face the back of the seat, she buried her face in her arms.

A few moments later Veronique joined her. "What is it, *mon chou?*" Veronique crooned, wrapping Lauren in a gentle embrace. "I have never seen you cry. Now you have tears enough to water the entire garden."

"I know," Lauren sobbed. "I can't seem to stop. I don't know what is wrong with me. Oh, Veronique, I am so miserable."

"What has happened? Have you lost a fight with M'sieur?"

"I . . . I don't think so. We did have an argument, but we made up before he left for Barataria. I miss him so much that it aches. This is how it will be when—" Lauren broke off, not wanting to open the subject that would lead to lengthy explanations.

"Ah, you are very much in love, *ma pauvre miette.* Your handsome Jason has been gone only three days. But he will return, and then all will be well again."

"You don't understand!" Pulling away, Lauren buried her face in her hands and wailed. Veronique could only pat her shoulder consolingly.

When the storm at last subsided, Veronique drew a handkerchief from up her sleeve and offered it to Lauren. "Perhaps Lila was right. There is a little one on the way, *non?*"

Lauren sniffed as she dried her eyes. "A little one?"

"*Un bébé, le petit enfant.* Lila says that when she was enceinte, she cried all the time. She thinks you mean to keep it a secret. I fear she is a little hurt."

The hand holding the handkerchief suddenly stilled. "A baby," Lauren breathed. Then she shook her head. "No, it couldn't be. I've only been married a little more than a month."

Veronique gave a tinkling laugh. "Since when does that make a difference with babies? Perhaps you were not careful enough before the wedding."

"But I was only with Jason once," Lauren protested, feeling color rise to her cheeks. "And that was . . . at the beginning of March. I would know by now if it had happened then."

"But your monthly courses? Are they on time?"

Frowning, Lauren tried to recall. "Not my last. Oh, Veronique, do you suppose it's true? I am going to have Jason's child?" There was excitement in her voice, and as she searched her friend's face, a soft light began to glow in her eyes. "Yes, of course it is!" she exclaimed before hugging Veronique joyfully. "I just didn't think it would happen so soon. Goodness, Jason was right. What if he hadn't married me? But it wouldn't have made any difference. I would still have loved his child. Oh, God, what if it isn't a boy? He needs a son, Veronique, Kyle told me. Will Jason be angry, do you think, if it's a girl?"

Laughing again, Veronique shook her head. "I am sure he will be delighted either way. Will you tell him now? Or will you wait till you are certain? You know, I am not the one to give you advice. You should speak to Lila about these things since she has— Lauren, what is the matter?"

The color had drained from Lauren's complexion, turning her face pale. "I can't tell him," she whispered, bowing her head as fresh tears scalded her cheeks.

Veronique's brows drew together. "Would you like me to tell M'sieur for you?"

"No, please!" Lauren cried. Then realizing how hysterical she must sound, she took a steadying breath before turning to Veronique. "I don't intend to tell Jason."

Veronique frowned in puzzlement. "You do not want the baby?"

"Of course I do!"

"But then, what is the problem? You are worried that M'sieur Jason will refuse to claim the child as his?"

Lauren smiled bitterly. "No. I'm afraid he will refuse *not* to claim it. You see, I'm not going to England with Jason when he leaves. If he thought I was with child, he . . . I'm not sure what he would do. But he might demand that I go with him."

Veronique shook her head. "I am sorry, *m'amie,* but I do not understand in the least. Now, explain it to me, and slowly, if you please, so my foolish brain can comprehend."

Haltingly Lauren explained about the agreement she had with Jason. When she was done, Veronique still looked perplexed. "But why do you not wish to go with him? There is

347

nothing here for you in New Orleans. And you have been so happy with M'sieur."

"Veronique, it's not that I don't wish to go to England with Jason. It's that I *can't*. The thought of returning there makes my blood run cold. My . . . my aunt still lives there."

"The one who says you are *un'aliene*, a lunatic? The one who would have locked you away?"

Lauren nodded. "Regina Carlin, my father's sister. I am afraid of what she will do."

"But your husband will protect you from such a one as that."

"He might try. But sooner or later . . . Oh, Veronique, you don't know how often I've tried to tell myself that it is safe for me to go back. But I can't make myself believe it."

"And have you told M'sieur this? What does he say?"

"He has agreed, as long as we make the most of the time we have left. And so we did." Lauren's mouth twisted ironically as she thought of the life growing inside her. And then she thought of Jason's love of children and abruptly started to cry again. Did she have the right to deny him knowledge of his own child? She buried her face in her hands. "This child means so much to me," she declared with a choked sob. "If I must lose Jason, at least I will have something of his."

Veronique pursed her lips thoughtfully. "Lauren, although I have never had to live in fear as you have done, I sympathize with you, truly I do. But I cannot agree with your reasoning. I do not think it wise for you to keep this from your husband."

"You . . . you won't tell him?"

"Of course not, *mon chou*. That is your business. But you may not be able to hide it from him."

"It won't be for long. Jason will be leaving in a few weeks."

"*Alors*," Veronique said helplessly. "And to think I was asking you to remember me to Kyle. But you must stop this crying, *m'amie*. It cannot be good for the baby. And you will never convince Lila that nothing is wrong, let alone M'sieur Jason. Your husband is a perceptive man, that one."

"I know," Lauren sniffed, trying to swallow her tears. "But I suppose I should deal with one problem at a time. What do I tell Lila? She has never seen me cry before."

348

"Why, tell her the truth. That you are missing that new husband of yours. It is only natural. You can also say that you have not had the time to make a baby. After all, you do not really know for a fact that you are enceinte."

"I *know*," Lauren insisted in a half-mournful tone.

Veronique paused. "Lauren, are you certain this is what you want?"

She looked away, her face contorting with pain and longing. "No. It isn't what I want at all. But it is what I must do."

"It is strange," Veronique said, shaking her head slowly. "I thought I knew men, but I never would have suspected that Monsieur Jason would agree to leave his wife behind. Certainly not *you*."

"Do you think he loves me, then?"

"What a question! The man is mad about you. The light in his eyes when he looks at you— If Kyle had ever looked at me that way, I would have agreed to become his mistress at once and counted myself fortunate. Such a love only comes once in a great while."

"I know," Lauren said again with despair in her voice. "I know."

Lauren spent two sleepless nights coming to grips with her decision to keep her pregnancy from Jason. The day before he was to return from Barataria, she went for a walk, needing then to isolate herself from reality for a while. The June afternoon was sultry, the warmth a portent of the sweltering summer heat that could steam a leaf from its vine.

Paying no attention to her direction, she strolled aimlessly over the plantation grounds. She had agreed to stay at Bellefleur during Jason's absence because he had requested it, but actually, there was little for her to do in New Orleans. Between them, Kyle and Matthew were effectively running the Carlin offices and the new distribution network. As for her own ship, the *Matthew MacGregor* had already been outfitted and sent off on its first voyage under its new owner.

More than once, though, Lauren found herself wishing she could have remained at her beautiful new home in New

Orleans. And she missed Jason almost desperately. Even so, she was profoundly grateful that he was gone. Had she faced him when she first realized she might be carrying his child, she would have given the game away immediately. Certainly Jason would have been able to guess that something was wrong . . . or different, Lauren amended to herself. She was unable to consider what was happening inside her body as anything short of a miracle.

When she unexpectedly came across the Beauvais family mausoleum, Lauren realized she was quite a distance from the house. Warily, she eyed the small brick building that stood near a cluster of moss-shrouded live oaks. Usually she stayed away from such places, for they sent chills up her spine, but as she surveyed the elaborate facade, a look of thoughtful concentration crept over her face.

There was a cemetery behind Carlin House, she remembered, where Andrea had been buried. George Burroughs had once taken Lauren there to visit the grave, and he had ranted bitterly because the plot had had to remain unmarked and unblessed. The omission had been necessary, though, for the impersonation to continue.

It was the same cemetery where Miss Foster's funeral had been held, and where Jonathan and Mary Carlin had been laid to rest. Remembering Jason's theory about her loss of memory, Lauren shook her head. She couldn't have witnessed the Carlins' deaths, for the tragedy had happened before she had ever come to Carlin House. It was Andrea who had been captured along with Jonathan and Mary by the pirate Rafael. It was Andrea whose mind had been affected by the shocking murders of her parents and her own terrible experiences.

But perhaps she, Lauren, was more like her poor little half sister than she knew. Was Jason right in thinking that there was something in her own past that she had forgotten? Something so terrible that her mind had shut it out?

As long as she could remember, she had been afraid of confinement, but it was only *after* she had come to Carlin House that she had been roused by the first of her recurring nightmares. Was there some connection, then, between her fear and those strange, horrible dreams in which she heard

350

terrifying cries and saw gruesome phantoms?

Her dreams always began in the same manner: She would be standing in a dark room, clad in a nightdress, staring at the light beyond a partially open door. As she moved closer, the indistinct murmurs she heard became anguished cries and harsh laughter. She would push open the door, then, to find shadowed images outlined by firelight, and while she stood paralyzed by terror in the flickering light, a deathly quiet would descend, only to be shattered by a scream and a plea for her to run. In her dream, Lauren would obey; she would turn and run toward the darkness, trying to escape the horror, but the screams followed her and so did the specters, their evil faces and mournful shrieks frightening her to the point that she was incapable of movement. Then, at last, she would be waked by her own screams, with the words: Run! Run! echoing in her ears.

She reacted similarly to close dark spaces: the hideous images and the terrified shrieks petrified her, reducing her to a state of mindless terror.

Lauren felt her skin grow cold as she relived the horror of those evil images. Yet as she stood there, staring at the mausoleum, she felt her memory stir, as if the foundation of a great pile of stones had suddenly shifted. The shadows in her dream took shape. There was a woman in the room, she realized, and a man—a tall man. But then the images faded before she could identify who they might be.

Lauren clenched her fists, frustrated by the flashes of memory that asked more questions than they answered. Yet there had to be an explanation.

What wouldn't she give to be free of the abject fear that had lived within her for so long? Lauren thought wistfully. Perhaps Jason was right. If she could discover what frightened her, then she might be able to fight it. What if she were to step inside the mausoleum? Now, while the sun was shining brightly overhead? Now, while her mind seemed to be sharp and clear?

Lauren took a tentative step toward the door, then another. With her heart slamming in slow, painful strokes, she placed a delicate hand on the great iron ring.

351

"Lauren!"

Jason's velvet-textured voice was so unexpected that Lauren jumped. Whirling, she stared to see her tall, gilt-haired husband striding toward her. She hadn't expected him for another day at least.

Jason's long stride was rapidly closing the distance between them, but Lauren didn't wait. Instead, she caught up her skirts and ran to meet him, easily forgetting about everything else in the joy of seeing him again.

When she launched herself at him, arms outflung, Jason laughed richly and caught her about the waist. Lifting her high above the ground, he whirled her around until she was lightheaded and breathless.

"Jason, put me down!" Lauren protested, laughing. "You're making me dizzy!" He complied, but before her feet touched the ground, he was crushing her to his chest, kissing her hungrily.

The sparks which leapt between them were hot enough to kindle a brushfire. When Jason drew back to search her face, Lauren could see desire smoldering like azure flames in his eyes. She knew then that he would never wait until they had reached home before he had banked the flames to glowing embers.

She was right. Jason huskily whispered her name against her lips, then swung her up in his arms. Lauren didn't even need to ask where he was taking her; he was carrying her to the creek where she had learned to swim, for it was quite close. A smile touched her lips as she wondered if she had subconsciously chosen this direction when she had set out on her walk earlier.

With a contented sigh, Lauren wound her arms more tightly around his neck and rested her head on his shoulder. "I missed you," she murmured.

Jason pressed his lips against her hair. "It was mutual, I assure you, sweetheart. And I appreciate the welcome. This is far better than the one you gave me the last time I returned from Barataria. If I remember, you charged Beauvais with offering me the Carlin Line so I would leave you alone."

"And you said you wanted us both."

Jason grinned down at the lovely countenance filled with

eagerness and desire. "Right now I just want you."

"Was your trip successful?"

"I'll tell you about it later." Then he effectively put an end to further speech by covering her mouth with his.

By the time he reached a copse of willows beside the creek, his kiss was no longer simply hungry; it was fierce and devouring, his tongue sweetly ravaging her mouth, plundering its treasure. Lauren welcomed his impatience, though, meeting Jason's passion with an intensity all her own, as if she needed to become part of him. She wasn't even aware of his rough handling as he found a soft patch of clover-leaved wood sorrel and lowered her to the ground amid a profusion of wild hibiscus and blue iris and deep purple spiderwort. When he lay down beside her and hauled her against his hard length, Lauren moaned and pressed even closer.

His fingers moved at once to unfasten the hooks at the back of her gown, but he was too impatient to have much success. Intending to give them proper attention, he drew away. But then it was Lauren who wouldn't let go. Her fingers curled in Jason's tawny hair, directing his lips back to hers.

Her need for haste seemed to match his own, for her thighs parted instantly when he raised her skirts to her waist. She was ready for him, Jason thought with a groan of pleasure. Oh, so ready.

He unfastened his breeches as Lauren's hands ran feverishly over his powerful shoulders and down his back. His own hands captured her hips then, and with a swift, relentless thrust, Jason drove deeply, burying his throbbing shaft in her incredible warmth. Gasping, Lauren rose against him, her flesh yielding eagerly to his fierce penetration.

Jason lost all control then, his body pummeling hers with a violence that was beautifully savage, arching into her deeply. He was no longer even conscious of the words he spoke as he poured himself into her.

Willingly, Lauren gave herself up to the ravaging heat of his passion, a deep, surging tension swelling inside her with every driving thrust. It grew . . . and grew. . . . And when it exploded in a brutal, grinding release, Lauren felt as if she was being hurtled over a precipice. Dashed to the ground, she lay there, splintered into a million tiny fragments.

Even so, she recovered before Jason did. He had sagged against her, his face buried in her hair, his breath still harsh and ragged.

Lying beneath him, Lauren remembered the hoarse cry Jason had given during his body's final contractions. She smiled tenderly, feeling her heart swell with aching sweetness. Had she ever been this happy? Jason had returned, safe and unharmed. She was in his arms, loved and cherished. And the spirit of their love had been given life, deep within her body. What more could any woman ask?

It was some time before Jason slowly rolled off her. Shifting onto his back, he drew Lauren with him and cradled her head on his shoulder. "Christ, sweetheart," he complained in an exhausted sigh. "If you mean to attack me like that every time I come home, I'll never survive."

Laughing, Lauren snuggled closer to her husband's large body. "I'm the one who won't survive. You're bigger than I, let me remind you."

He pressed a tender kiss to her brow. "I suppose I should apologize for taking you so roughly and swear never to do it again, but I'm afraid that would be a promise I couldn't keep."

"I didn't mind. You were just 'a lion who missed his feeding,' as Veronique would say."

"Did I hurt you?"

"No, of course not."

Lifting his head, Jason scrutinized Lauren's face. "Sure?" he asked with concern.

"Jason, I'm perfectly all right. I hardly even felt you."

As Jason relaxed once more, his mouth curved in a grin. "There's no need to be insulting, Cat-eyes."

"That wasn't insulting. It was *reassuring*." She pushed herself up and presented her back to Jason. "Will you unfasten my dress, please?"

"Why? Is it feeding time again already?"

A soft blush stained Lauren's ivory skin, but she laughed. "Actually I mean to go for a swim. I haven't been in the creek once since you left. No doubt that's the real reason I missed you. Would you care to come?"

"Go ahead, I'll join you in a while. I haven't had my fill of looking at you yet."

As she shed her clothing, Lauren felt Jason's warm gaze caress her. When it wandered to her flat stomach, she caught her breath. Would he guess, she wondered? There was no indication of her condition, but Jason was so astute that sometimes she was certain he could read her mind. Perhaps she should think of something else, just to be safe. Hurriedly she slipped into the cool water and began to practice the strokes he had taught her.

Jason joined her shortly, and for the better part of an hour, they played and cavorted in the water. Lauren was laughing when she collapsed, happily exhausted, on the bank. "Thank you, Jason," she said when he followed her down. Seeing the question in his eyes, Lauren gave him a smile and looped her arms about his neck. "For giving me such pleasure. My childhood never afforded me much enjoyment, but you're giving me that now by letting me be a child again."

Lowering his magnificent head, Jason let his lips graze her neck. "Somehow I don't think of you as a child."

"Yes, but you let me be young and carefree and foolish when I want to be."

"Ummm, I want you to be happy, sweetheart." His breath was warm and caressing as he nibbled at her skin.

"Why are you so good to me? I don't deserve it."

Jason began licking drops of water from her throat. "Yes you do. Now, hush, or I'll set up a gigantic roar."

"Is that what lions do? I've never seen one. I thought they were just big cats. Do they purr like Ulysses? Oh . . . oh!"

Purposefully, Jason had moved lower, letting his tongue swirl over the ripe fullness of her breast. His teeth grazed her nipple, making it throb. At length his lips moved to the other rosy mound, his tongue flicking the sensitive peak, eliciting gasps of pleasure from Lauren. She gripped his bare shoulders, feeling his muscles as they coiled and slid under the satiny skin.

But his kisses didn't stop at her breasts. Instead, Jason went on to taste more of her damp skin, telling her she tasted of sun-warmed honey as he devoured her slowly, inch by glorious inch.

Paying no mind to the way her fingers twisted in his hair, Jason continued his tender worship of her naked body, his lips moving with warm expertise over the curve of her hip, then down a gleaming ivory thigh. And when her shapely legs had been patiently explored, he returned to the pale skin of her stomach. Erotically then, his hand began to stroke the warm moistness between her thighs.

His caresses nearly drove Lauren mad with wanting him. Panting and breathless, she begged him to take her, but Jason seemed deaf to her pleas. At last, though, he pressed her knees wide apart. Lauren tensed in anticipation as Jason positioned himself above her. But he only lowered his head again, finding the tangle of light curls nestled between her thighs.

His sensuous play scalded her. Lauren writhed at the moist, seeking kisses Jason pressed so intimately upon her, and when his hot tongue claimed her, she arched in ecstasy, straining against him with shameless yearning. At last, Jason's pulsing manhood glided smoothly into her, and a brilliant burst of radiance sent her world careening.

When Lauren opened her eyes, she found Jason smiling tenderly down at her. "My beautiful lioness," he said softly, smoothing a damp curl from her face.

Slowly, then, his hard member began to explore the velvet warmth enveloping him. Lauren was almost too drained to respond, but Jason's exquisite movements soon aroused her desire again. He whispered sensuous words of love in her ear, making her blood quicken fiercely, and when he began the spiraling journey to breathless heights, she soared with him, higher and higher and higher. . . .

Dusk was gathering around them when Lauren's gold-tipped lashes fluttered open. She hadn't meant to fall asleep, but the combined effect of the warm afternoon and Jason's passion had consumed her energy. He was lounging on his side next to her, his head propped up by his hand, his blue eyes soft and warm as he gazed down at her. Guessing that he had been watching her sleep, Lauren stretched lazily and smiled up at him, completely sated and content.

Jason's sharp intake of breath was audible. "Stop looking at me like that, Lauren, if you want to get home tonight."

Provocatively, she trailed a finger down the fine hairs on his muscular chest. "Like what, darling?"

"You know perfectly well what I mean!" Grabbing her exploring hand, he kissed her quickly on the lips and gave her bare thigh a gentle slap. "You're a shameless, wanton wench! And shiftless, too. Now, bestir yourself. Lila kindly invited us to dinner and we shouldn't be late."

"Why didn't you tell me!" Lauren leapt to her feet, catching up her clothes. "Lila will be sending a search party out for us any minute now," she muttered under her breath.

Jason grinned as he stood up and stretched. "I don't think so. I specifically warned her not to."

"Oh, God!" Lauren groaned. "That's worse. Now she'll read me a lecture about how a married woman should conduct herself."

Chuckling at her persecuted expression, Jason pulled on his breeches. As he tugged on his gleaming boots, he asked casually, "What were you doing when I found you, by the way? Grave robbing?"

Lauren turned away, pretending to be occupied with getting dressed. "I . . . it was nothing really."

Shrugging into his shirt, Jason came to stand behind her and solicitously began fastening the hooks on her gown. "Lauren—"

Knowing he meant to pursue the subject, Lauren hastened to speak of something else. "You haven't told me about your trip," she said with false brightness.

She couldn't be sure, but she thought she heard Jason give a sigh. "It went well," he replied. "I saw Claude."

There was something in Jason's voice that made Lauren want to shiver. Turning, she saw that he was regarding her intently. "And?" she pressed, directing a questioning glance up at him, though not really wanting to hear the answer.

"Rafael returned some time ago to the Mediterranean. Claude thinks I might find him in Algiers." There was a pause, then Jason said very solemnly, "I have to go, Lauren."

She lowered her gaze. "I . . . I know. When do you leave then?"

"I've ordered that the *Siren* be ready to sail for England in three days."

Her eyes flew back to his face. "Three days?" she breathed. "So soon?"

Jason touched her cheek. "You still have time to change your mind and come with me."

Lauren held up a hand as if to ward him off. "No, please . . ." Something flashed in Jason's eyes, whether pain or anger or something else she couldn't tell. "I . . . I'm sorry," she said quietly, "but I can't."

This time Jason's sigh was audible. "Very well, sweetheart. It's your choice." Stepping back, Jason looped his cravat around his neck and began the difficult job of arranging it into a fashionable fall.

As she watched, Lauren felt tears sting her eyes. Her beautiful world had suddenly crumbled.

When Jason's face blurred in her vision, she turned away to draw on a stocking. Why now, when she needed it most, had she lost the ability to turn off her feelings? she wondered bitterly. The pain wouldn't go away, and she was unable to pretend otherwise.

She tried to hide her misery in inconsequential chatter, though. As she mechanically finished dressing, Lauren forced herself to ask Jason what Barataria was like. And while she pinned her hair into a semblance of order, Lauren listened to her husband recount the details of his trip.

But she couldn't fully meet his gaze. Nor could she even manage a shaky smile as she took his proffered arm. In fact, Lauren had to bite her lip to stop its quivering. She was totally silent and subdued as she walked with Jason back to the house.

Chapter Twenty-One

From her position on the foredeck of the *Siren*, Lauren could see most of the ship's crew. They were hard at work, unfurling sails and preparing to weigh anchor. Lauren paid no attention to the bustling activity around her, though. She had eyes only for one man—and the tears that threatened to fall again tended to obscure her view of Jason.

She had come with him to the ship in order to prolong the moment of parting for as long as possible. Unfortunately, Jason had been needed almost at once, and he had excused himself, ordering her to stay out of the way of the sailors. Now he was speaking to Kyle and another man. No doubt their conversation concerned when to cast off, Lauren thought miserably, turning away. Perhaps she should have said good-bye at home as Jason had suggested. Now, of necessity, their farewell would be rushed and impersonal.

No! Lauren vowed to herself. She would not let him go that way. She would demand a moment of privacy—

"Sweetheart?"

Lauren gave a start, realizing Jason had come to stand beside her and was regarding her calmly. "Would you come below with me? I can hardly kiss you here as I would like."

Lauren smiled tremulously, grateful this time that he had read her thoughts. Placing a hand on his sleeve, she allowed him to lead her to his cabin.

He didn't take her in his arms at once as she expected, but instead went to the infamous desk and opened a drawer.

Withdrawing a small slim box, Jason presented it to her silently.

Lauren glanced at him questioningly before opening it, then gave a soft cry when she saw the jeweled necklace inside. It was a small golden heart, exquisitely surrounded by emeralds, hung on a slender chain. Giving the heart a closer inspection, she saw the engraving on the face—a tiny but proudly soaring hawk, the symbol of the Carlin ships.

The ache in Lauren's throat was so painful that she couldn't speak. The tears spilled over as she looked up at Jason, meeting his brilliant blue gaze.

When she flung herself into his arms, he held her close, letting her cry, but after a moment, he chided her gently. "If I had known you were going to turn into such a watering pot, Cat-eyes, I would never have allowed you to come. I can't bear to see a beautiful woman cry—especially you."

"You made me by giving me such a beautiful gift," Lauren sobbed against his shoulder.

"I'm beginning to regret it. You're wetting my coat again."

Looking up, she saw Jason's tender smile and was ashamed for spoiling their last moments together. Making a great effort to control herself, she drew away, wiping her eyes. Then she took a deep, steadying breath and rummaged through her reticule till she found her gift to Jason. "I have something for you as well."

She watched anxiously as he unwrapped the miniature of herself. Jason looked at the small portrait for a long while, the expression in his blue eyes inscrutable. Lauren couldn't even tell what he was thinking when he at last tore his gaze away to meet hers. The ache in her throat grew. "So you won't forget me," Lauren managed to say huskily before the tears choked her again.

Setting down the miniature, Jason drew Lauren to him. Cupping her face in his hands, he pressed a kiss on her trembling mouth. "I could never forget you, my precious love," he whispered. "How could I when you own my heart? I leave it with you, Lauren. Keep it safe."

Clinging to Jason, Lauren wept again softly, wishing she could be stronger. She didn't know how long she stood there

360

being comforted by him, but the velvet sound of his voice roused her from her morass of self-pity. "It's time for you to go, sweetheart."

Taking another ragged breath, Lauren nodded and searched through her reticule again till she found a handkerchief. As she dried her eyes, she listened to Jason's last-minute instructions.

"If you need anything at all," he was saying, "you're to contact Sauvinet. I've arranged with him to handle your business affairs, and he'll also see that Veronique is given an adequate income in payment for acting as your companion. I cannot like the idea of you two living in town, but I suppose I'll have to be satisfied. At least Lila and Jean-Paul will be nearby to watch over you. I'll remind you once more, though, Lauren, of your promise to stay away from the casino."

"I remember," she said in a low voice.

Jason smiled. "Good. Then I'll try not to worry about you above twenty times a day."

Her eyes bright with unshed tears, Lauren flung her arms around his neck and held him tightly. "But I'll worry about you. You will be careful?"

"Of course, sweetheart. It may take some time for me to settle my business with Rafael, and I have other affairs that need tending, but I'll try to return in six months or so. Perhaps we may even be able to spend Christmas together."

Jason kissed her once more, then pried himself from Lauren's almost desperate hold. Taking her elbow, he steered her above deck.

She said good-bye to Kyle and took one last glance around her before Jason escorted her down the gangway where Veronique waited for her. He helped Lauren into the carriage, then leaned across to plant a swift, hard kiss on her lips. "Farewell, my love. Take care of yourself." Then he turned on his heel and strode away.

With something akin to shock, Lauren watched him go. A myriad of emotions warred inside her, but amazement was the most prevalent. In her heart she had never quite believed Jason would actually leave her. Deep down, she had cherished a secret hope that he would stay. Certainly she had expected him to try and change her mind. In fact, she had half suspected that

361

Jason would force her to go with him, or trick her into it, as he had when he had married her. Yet, incredulously, he had walked away, without once looking back, as if it mattered not at all that her heart was breaking.

She bit her lip to keep herself from calling him back. The decision to stay had been hers, Lauren reminded herself. She couldn't go with him. Nothing had changed—at least nothing but the fact that she loved Jason Stuart to distraction. She was still a bastard. She would still go to prison if her impersonation were ever discovered. She still had no right to subject Jason to such a scandal. And she still couldn't face his hatred when he learned the truth.

The three days had raced by. Although Lauren had tried to accept the idea of his departure bravely, in truth she had been despondent and depressed during their last days together. Their lovemaking had held a hint of desperation, at least on her part. She hadn't put into words her sorrow and despair, though she had known Jason could sense her feelings.

How desolate she felt already, Lauren thought as she watched Jason board the ship. Not even the thought of his child lying deep in her womb could comfort her. She had longed to tell him about that, but she had known it would be a mistake. She had only been able to console herself with the hope that Jason would return in time to be with her for the birth of their child.

She watched as Jason went to stand at the railing where he could observe her. He was still wearing that inscrutable expression, she saw. Behind him the canvas sails were being raised, while in the muddy water below, a half dozen oar-driven skiffs took up slack in their lines as they made ready to tow the schooner into the river's main current.

When Jason lifted a hand to wave good-bye, Lauren found she couldn't watch any longer. Holding back a sob, she ordered her coachman to turn the carriage around and take them home. Then she made the mistake of meeting Veronique's eyes. Eyes that were filled with compassion. Slumping back against the cushions, Lauren began to cry again, silently, hopelessly. "He didn't even try to convince me to go with him," she said brokenly.

Veronique patted her hand. "Did you wish him to, chérie?"

"It is stupid feminine logic, I know. But yes, I did."

"It is not stupid!" Veronique replied with unusual vehemence. "And love is never logical!" She added a graceful curse to the gods above before she, too, found herself weeping.

It wasn't a long drive to the Faubourg St. Marie; a mere ten minutes passed before the carriage pulled to a stop before the house Jason had bought for Lauren. A small black boy jumped down from his tiger's perch to help his mistress descend, but neither of the ladies moved.

Seeing Veronique's tears, Lauren wiped her eyes. "How heartless of me. You, too, are in love. You've lost Kyle, just as I've lost Jason."

"Non, that is not true. I never owned Kyle's love. But you, mon chou, your case is different."

"You think I am making a mistake?" Lauren asked with a sniff.

"Oui, I do. And I think you know it as well. You love Jason very much, non?"

"So much that it hurts. Oh, Veronique, how am I going to live without him?"

"It is not too late. The ship may not have sailed yet."

"It is too late. It has always been too late."

There was another silence. "Well," Veronique said quietly, "what I know is that if I loved a man so much and he loved me, I would never let him get away. I would follow wherever he led."

Lauren looked up. "Even if you knew it could never last?"

"Even so. I do not think anything would be too great a price to pay to know such happiness, however brief."

Lauren gave a mirthless laugh. "However brief," she repeated bitterly. "Do you know it has only been three months since Jason arrived here? And yet I first saw him nearly four years ago. I must have loved him even then."

"Vraiment?"

"Yes," Lauren whispered. For a moment she stared down at her clasped hands. Then she shut her gold-flecked eyes tightly and took a deep breath. "Samuel!" she called to the driver, "I've changed my mind. Please take me back to the levee."

Veronique stared at her, but when the horses began to move once more, the redhead clapped her hands in delight. "You are going to England!"

Lauren nodded slowly. She had amazed even herself with her decision, but she had realized she couldn't let Jason leave without her. She was his wife, no matter whose name was written on their marriage lines. The possibility that their future together might be hopeless no longer mattered. "I must go," she said thoughtfully. "And not just because Jason is my happiness. I could never be *complete* without him. He is the other part of me. I can't live without him. Nothing else matters."

Veronique squeezed her hand. "I do not think you will regret your decision. Oh, I hope the *Siren* has not yet sailed!"

"If it has, then I will hire a ship and follow him." Lauren wasn't surprised by her sudden calm. Indeed, she felt as if a tremendous burden had been lifted from her shoulders. She hadn't conquered her fears, nor could she delude herself that she was solving anything. She was buying a few more weeks, perhaps months of happiness. If the truth did come out, she would still be facing the threat of prison and hanging, but she had to take that risk in order to be with Jason. And perhaps she could find a way to soften the blow for him.

Now that she had made the decision, however, nothing would stand in her way. She urged Samuel to hurry, then reached for Veronique's hands. "This doesn't change the other part of our plan," Lauren said firmly. "You are not to go back to the casino—the house is yours for as long as you want it. Please, don't argue," she added quickly as Veronique started to speak. "I can't leave unless you are settled comfortably. The house is mine, so I can do as I please with it. But Jason would want you to live there, I know. He realizes what a wonderful friend you have been to me. And I doubt that I will ever . . . I probably will not need the use of it again. Jason said he arranged a salary for you with Sauvinet. Accept it as payment for taking care of the house, if for no other reason."

Veronique protested the generous gesture, but Lauren wouldn't allow her to refuse. Shortly they were hugging and laughing and crying as they said good-bye to each other.

"You will write to me and let me know how you like being a titled lady?" Veronique said as the horses threaded their way through the crowded street.

"Yes, my dearest friend. And please explain to Lila and Jean-Paul and Matthew and Running Deer—"

"Of course, but they will understand. Indeed, Lila will be ecstatic that you have chosen to be with your husband rather than to live with me. *Mon Dieu!*" she said suddenly as the carriage ground to a halt. "Is that not them?"

Lauren wasn't looking where Veronique pointed; instead her eyes were trained on the *Siren*. Amazingly, the ship was still docked at the levee. Even the gangway was still in place, although it was moments before Lauren registered this fact. She was busy searching the deck of the schooner for her tall husband.

There he was, standing beside the gunwale. Odd, but he seemed not to have moved since she had left him there twenty minutes before.

From this distance, Lauren couldn't see how tightly Jason was gripping the railing or how white his knuckles were. But she could see the blue gleam of his eyes as he watched her alight from the phaeton.

She had just stepped down when suddenly she came to an abrupt halt. Staring up at him, Lauren put a hand to her mouth. "My God!" she breathed. "He knew! Jason knew all along I would change my mind." Tearing her gaze away then, she looked accusingly at Veronique. "Were you in on this as well?"

"*Mais, non!* I had no idea! But I think you would not be wrong to accuse Lila. She is grinning like the cat who lapped up all the cream."

"She is! And so is Jason . . ." Lauren began angrily. Then she caught herself. What difference did it make if her husband was a warlock who could read her mind, or that her friends had plotted against her? What mattered was that she would be with the man she loved.

Not that she wouldn't have a few words to say to Jason when they were alone, she silently promised as he came forward to catch her up his arms.

365

He lifted her high, in full view of a crowd of interested spectators. "Back so soon, sweetheart?" he teased.

"Put me down, you wretch! I must say good-bye to Lila and the others."

His blue eyes smiled into hers. "You're going somewhere then?"

"You know very well I'm leaving with you. I decided someone must keep an eye on you. I don't trust Kyle to do it properly."

"Well, say your good-byes," he said, lowering Lauren to her feet. "We'll weigh anchor as soon as your trunks are loaded."

Astonished, Lauren stared at him. Then slowly, her mouth curved in a smile. "Do you mean to tell me they aren't already on board?"

Jason laughed. "I wasn't that sure of you." And since he was unable to resist the lips that curved so provocatively up at him, he bent his head to kiss her.

Before Lauren could reply or even respond, though, she was pulled from Jason's embrace by Matthew. "Ye'll have time enough for that, lass, when ye're alone on the ship," Matthew told her as he wrapped Lauren in his brawny arms.

She hugged and kissed him, then the others, saving Lila till last. Lauren clung to the older woman for a long moment. "Thank you, Lila. For *everything*," she whispered.

"You forgive me then?" Lila asked anxiously.

"There is nothing to forgive."

"I always thought you would be happy with Jason. Promise me you will be happy, Lauren."

Lauren laughed. "I promise I will *try*," she said, glancing up at her husband's sparkling eyes.

Lila turned to Jason then, her expression serious. "I expect you to take care of her, Jason. You had better not let any harm come to my girl, or you will answer to me."

Gallantly he raised Lila's fingers to his lips. "I will guard her with my life," he promised quite solemnly.

When it was time to go, he allowed Lauren one last moment with Veronique, then taking her by the hand, led her up the ramp and nodded to a grinning Kyle. Immediately, the *Siren*'s crew sprang to life.

366

With Jason by her side, Lauren stood at the rail, waving good-bye. As the ship slowly drew away from the levee, she sighed, knowing she would probably never see any of her dear friends again.

A strong arm slipped about her waist. Feeling Jason's lips brush her hair, Lauren gratefully rested her head on his shoulder.

"Regrets?" he queried softly.

"No, not really," she replied, not wanting to tell him the true cause of her sadness. "But they are my family. Lila, my mother. Veronique, my sister. Matthew, my father. I shall miss them."

"You haven't seen the last of them. Lila means to visit us next year when Charles is a bit older. I expect she can persuade Veronique to come, too, and if not, then we can return here. There are some advantages to owning a fleet of ships, you know." When Lauren didn't reply, Jason tilted her chin up. "I should like to be your family now, my sweetheart. Not that I'm interested in being your mother or sister. Or even father . . ."

Looking deeply into his eyes, Lauren couldn't help but be warmed by the tender light she saw glowing there. She nodded solemnly, reaching up to touch his cheek. "I've never forgotten what you said to me that night I first met you. 'Partners, lovers, friends.'"

"I would be all that and more to you," Jason replied huskily. "But come now, Cat-eyes. Let's endeavor to be happy. Said another way: Smile for me or I'll toss you overboard for the fishes."

It didn't take much effort on Lauren's part to dismiss her sad thoughts. Not when Jason was looking at her in that particular way. The gleam in his eyes made her pulse quicken.

Looping her arms about his neck, Lauren gave him a brilliant smile. "No, you won't throw me overboard," she disagreed sweetly. "You would never let me become breakfast for a few fishes if it meant missing your own feeding."

"Perhaps not. But I must devise some sort of punishment for you."

"Why? What have I done?"

"Nothing except put me through one of the worst moments

367

of my life."

She arched a delicate brow. "I don't believe it. You knew perfectly well I would change my mind."

"No such thing!" Jason declared fervently. "I was trembling the entire time. All I could do was hope you loved me enough to come with me."

"But you could have prevented me from leaving here in the first place," Lauren pointed out.

Jason shook his head. "No, my love, it had to be your decision. I had already made my choice, you had to make yours. That was a lesson I learned with our marriage. I realized that I'd been trying to control you, the same way my father tried to control me— Lord, you don't mean to cry again, do you?"

Lauren brushed at the tears that had filled her eyes. "No," she said with a shaky laugh.

Jason bent to place a lingering kiss on her lips. He might have gone on for some time, except that a disturbance behind him recalled him to his surroundings. With regret, he lifted his head.

Lauren followed his gaze upward to where the mainsail was being hoisted up its mast. When the canvas spread and caught the wind, she could feel the schooner leap forward.

As a fresh breeze caressed her face, she turned to look out over the majestic Mississippi. Gulls swooped in low circles about the bow of the ship, their raucous cries blending in strange harmony with the snapping sails. When Jason's arms tightened about her waist, Lauren leaned back against his chest, closing her eyes and tilting her face up to the sun. There was nowhere else on earth she would rather be. For the moment she was perfectly content.

After a time, she asked idly, "How long before we reach England?"

"Three weeks, I expect. More if we run into bad weather."

"I suppose you remembered to bring Ulysses?"

"Much to Kyle's chagrin, yes."

Lauren could hear the amusement in his voice. Twisting her head, she peered up at her tall husband. "You thought of everything, didn't you? But what would you have done if I hadn't come back? How long would you have waited?"

Jason kissed the tip of her nose. "I'm not certain. Maybe forever. Then again, I might have said to hell with it after another few minutes and come after you. I don't really believe I could have left you behind."

She laughed suddenly, then seeing Jason's quizzical glance, explained. "I was remembering my disappointment when you didn't try to make me stay. I think I almost hoped you would kidnap me."

Jason grinned. "If you'd like, my love, I'll hold you prisoner in our cabin—without any clothes on, of course—to make up for disappointing you."

Tilting her head, Lauren appeared to give his suggestion serious consideration. "I think I would like that," she said thoughtfully, and smiled when Jason bent to nuzzle her ear.

Chapter Twenty-Two

Except for one or two instances, Lauren considered the ocean crossing magical. Jason intended the voyage to be their wedding trip since they had missed one earlier, and he was determined, Lauren quickly discovered, to make her time on board the *Siren* both delightful and memorable.

It was certainly that. The days were long and marvelously lazy. And the nights—the nights were indescribable.

She never lacked for entertainment when she wished it. During the day, she played cards or chess, took turns with Jason reading aloud, or simply watched the fascinating activities of the crew at work. Jason had granted her full freedom of the ship so long as she got in no one's way, and Lauren took full advantage of it, spending hours asking questions of an aging seaman who patiently explained the intricate details of keeping a ship trim and fit. And each night when she and Jason dined with Kyle and the ship's officers, Lauren was regaled with fantastic stories of the men's experiences at sea—tales which alternatingly had her staring wide-eyed or joining in the uproarious laughter.

One sailor, a young Englishman named Rory, was blessed with a superb voice, and in the evenings he would bring out his Spanish guitar to entertain the crew with folk songs or lead them in roisterous chanteys. Upon hearing the music her second night on board, Lauren had begged Jason to let her watch. When she went above with him, she discovered a dozen men sprawled on the forecastle, singing in loud, booming

370

voices. Jason found a place in the shadows just outside the congenial circle the men had formed, and settled himself on the deck, drawing Lauren down beside him. She relaxed against him, enjoying the performance and the feel of Jason's strong arms holding her.

She had thought her presence went unnoticed, but a short while later, Kyle called to her and suggested she sing for them. Startled and even a little embarrassed, Lauren demurred, but then saw that the circle had politely opened up and that all the men were looking at her expectantly. She gave Jason a questioning glance, and when he grinned and lifted her to her feet, she could no longer refuse.

She sang a love song then, and she sang it directly to Jason. The verses were poignant and bittersweet, but it was Lauren's tone, more than her words, that expressed the depth and breadth of her feeling for him. None of the men who heard her failed to understand that she belonged, heart and soul, to Jason Stuart. Neither was there one who didn't feel a twinge of envy for the tall, tawny-haired man who possessed her love. And there was an eloquent glow in Jason's blue eyes that showed he was well aware of his good fortune.

The men listened with total absorption, and when the last fascinatingly husky notes died away, they gave a great burst of applause. Lauren was astonished by her reception. Having been introduced to the crew, she knew most of their names, yet they had kept such a respectful distance, always meticulously addressing her as m'lady, that she had felt like an intruder in their world. Warmed by their acceptance of her, she smiled shyly, then laughed along with the others when Kyle gave her a resounding kiss on the cheek and Jason gruffly threatened to feed him to the sharks.

After that first occasion, the group never broke up without demanding and receiving at least one song from the "missus," as they called her from then on. Later, because Kyle took the first risk, some of the men even got up enough nerve to ask Lauren to dance under the eagle-eyed regard of her husband.

There was only one of the sailors whom she had difficulty liking—a small-boned, dark-haired man who always seemed to be watching her. His name was Ned Sikes, and while he never precisely bothered her, his constant scrutiny distressed Lauren enough to make her mention it to Jason. She never knew what Jason said to Sikes, but the disturbing looks ceased after that and she was grateful.

The rest of the *Siren*'s crew members were cordially welcoming, though. Indeed, they tried to outdo each other in an effort to please Jason's lady and make her voyage enjoyable. In her entire life, Lauren had never been so pampered. When the ship put in at St. Thomas long enough to bring on fresh food and water, Jason took her to a hidden cove for a picnic. Lauren had never before swum in an ocean, nor had she ever seen such a breathtakingly lovely vista. She was amazed by the sparkling white sand and the aquamarine waves, while the water was so clear she could see the coral reefs far below the surface, as well as flashes of brilliantly colored fish. Afterward, Jason made love to her beneath the shade of a giant palm tree.

When she boarded the *Siren* once more, glowing with contentment, Tim Sutter worshipfully presented her with a floppy, wide-brimmed straw bonnet. It was to protect her complexion from the sun, he mumbled shyly. Lauren wore it often during the remainder of the journey across the Atlantic, even though Jason teasingly called her his gypsy.

Only one incident threatened to destroy her happiness. It occurred the afternoon Jason brought an abrupt halt to one of her sailing lessons.

Before that, Jason had encouraged Lauren's interest in the ship's operation. He had approved when she learned to tie a score of different knots and to repair a ripped canvas. He hadn't objected when she spent time in the galley with the ship's cook showing him how to prepare a bouillabaisse and a delectable sauce for fish. Jason himself taught her how to take the wheel and keep the ship on course, and he hadn't protested when Kyle started giving Lauren instruction on how to use a sextant and the stars to navigate. But when Jason discovered her trying to scale the rigging, he exploded with fury.

After ordering her down from the ropes in a tone that brooked no defiance, he took Lauren's arm in a relentless grip and escorted her below deck. In the privacy of their cabin, Jason gave vent to his rage, and for two full minutes lashed out at Lauren, roaring about the danger and the risk of being hurt, not letting her say a word in her defense.

Baffled by his anger, Lauren eyed him warily. Jason's flashing blue eyes and his clenched fists reminded her of the first night he had taken her on board the *Siren*. He had been implacable then, as well.

"But I was being very careful, Jason," Lauren reasoned when she was finally allowed to speak.

His blazing glare made her want to flinch. "I don't give a damn how much care you use! You aren't to attempt such a foolish stunt *ever again*. Do you hear me?"

"Yes, but I don't know why I mustn't."

"I've told you why, and I don't intend to repeat myself! Your understanding isn't that deficient."

Lauren grew very still; Jason's commanding tone had struck a highly sensitive nerve. "My understanding isn't deficient in the least," she said stiffly. "You are ordering me to obey you. Not requesting, or even telling, but ordering. Very well, I should like to know if you are speaking as my husband or as my guardian."

"Don't play games with me, Lauren—"

"Because if you are being the protective husband, I will remind you, very sweetly, that for years I climbed trees that were far more difficult than those ropes. But if you are presuming to act as my guardian, I will tell you to go to the devil! And not come back!" Seething now, Lauren turned on her heel and marched to the door.

Before she could throw it open, though, Jason's angry words assailed her. "I'm speaking neither as your husband nor your guardian, but as the father of the child you endanger with your recklessness."

Shocked, Lauren whirled to stare at him. "How did you know?" she breathed.

Jason's expression was as grim as she had ever seen it. "It wasn't difficult to guess. Your nausea, for one. You haven't eaten for several mornings in a row, yet you weren't bothered by the rough seas we encountered a few nights ago, so it couldn't simply be seasickness." A muscle in his jaw tightened. "When did you plan to tell me about the child? Or perhaps I

373

should ask, did you ever intend to tell me?"

"I . . . yes, of course I did," Lauren stammered. "I wasn't even sure myself until after we set sail."

"But you suspected," Jason stated flatly. When Lauren opened her mouth, he barked in warning, "Don't dare lie to me, sweetheart! I'm that close to turning you over my knee and applying my hand to your backside."

Lauren's chin came up at his threat, but her reply was cut off by Jason's oath as he savagely ran a hand through his hair. "Christ! I thought we had *some* honesty in our relationship. You planned to let me sail away without my knowing, didn't you?"

Furious now herself, Lauren clenched her fists. "Yes!" she retorted. "I thought that if you knew about the baby, you would force me to go with you."

"Damn it, Lauren! You still don't trust me, do you?"

"Don't swear at me! I wasn't at all sure that I was increasing then. It was only a feeling."

"Your reluctance to tell me makes me wonder if there are other secrets you're hiding from me!"

At his accusation, Lauren sucked in her breath, the original cause of their argument forgotten. "Such as?" she asked guardedly.

Jason's fierce blue gaze bored into her, but he made no answer. When the silence lengthened, Lauren decided he couldn't have meant anything by his mention of secrets. Seeking a cease-fire, she offered an explanation. "I was afraid to tell you, if you want the truth."

Her attempt at conciliation was ignored; if anything, Jason's mouth hardened even more. "The truth would be nice," he replied with biting sarcasm.

Stung by his caustic tone, Lauren drew herself up to her full, regal height. "Perhaps you would care to know who fathered my child, then," she returned icily.

She hadn't meant to say anything so ridiculous, but the taunting words were out before she could bite them back. And the resultant fire that flashed in Jason's eyes frightened her so much that she took a quick step backward. For a moment, the air between them literally crackled with tension while Jason

374

glowered at her menacingly. Lauren could see the effort he was making to control his temper, but she watched him worriedly, waiting.

When he made no move to beat her as he had threatened, she sat down weakly on the bunk, her gaze dropping to her hands. "I wasn't planning to keep it a secret," she said lamely. "I was waiting for a special occasion to tell you."

"What special occasion?"

"I don't know! Just sometime special. It isn't every day that I have a baby."

"Lila said you were crying about it."

Lauren threw Jason an accusing glance. "Lila! I should have known. I suppose you asked her to spy on me and report my actions to you. Well, Lila was wrong! I was crying because I missed you and couldn't face the idea of you leaving me."

There was a long silence before Jason finally spoke. "You want the child, then?"

Hearing the doubt in his tone, Lauren met his gaze squarely. "That question," she said evenly, "is as absurd as the notion that someone else might be the father."

Jason let out his breath slowly. After a moment, he moved to stand before Lauren and reached out to caress her cheek. "I beg your pardon, then, for shouting at you," he said quietly.

Lauren was relieved to see that the gleam in his eyes was no longer anger, yet she wasn't at all sure that she wanted to accept his apology. She raised an eyebrow pointedly. "Is that all you mean to say?"

A smile tugged at the corner of Jason's mouth. "You want me to grovel, do you? Very well, Cat-eyes." He surprised Lauren by dropping to one knee. "Now, I'm kneeling at your feet, begging your forgiveness. But in my own defense, I'll remind you that it isn't every day a man becomes a prospective father. I suppose I haven't gotten the hang of how to act yet." Tilting his head to one side, he smiled at her with such disarming sincerity that Lauren found it hard to resist his compelling charm.

Seeing that she was wavering, Jason wrapped an arm about her waist and drew her against him. "I will now ask you *very sweetly* to please not climb the rigging anymore. Or any trees, or anything thing else which might endanger your health and safety."

"That is much better, Jason," Lauren observed primly as she tried to repress a smile.

"I married a tyrant, I can see. But you didn't answer me. Will you give me your word? See, I'm not ordering you."

His wide-eyed look was so much like a guilty little boy pleading for reprieve from punishment that Lauren had to laugh. "Yes, you have my word. I would have given it to you before if you hadn't been so beastly. But since you apologized so nicely, I'll admit that you were right. It was very foolish of me. I just didn't consider the consequences." Then remembering the cause of their argument, Lauren searched Jason's face, her green-gold eyes growing somewhat anxious. "You haven't told me yet if you're pleased about having a child."

"Could you doubt it?" Jason whispered huskily, before his lips found hers.

He kissed Lauren deeply, lovingly, chasing away her doubts, and when he at last broke off, it was only to gently push her backward till she was lying on the bed. He nestled his cheek against her hair, while his hand splayed possessively over her abdomen, caressing it lightly. Lauren shut her eyes, savoring the tender moment.

After a while, Jason returned to their discussion. "I never asked Lila to spy on you," he said seriously. "She mentioned that you might be in a delicate condition, but even if she hadn't, I would have come to the same conclusion. You haven't pleaded your woman's time since our marriage, and your breasts are fuller now."

"Only the least bit. I'm surprised you noticed."

Jason raised his head to grin at her. "You forget I've made it a point to become intimately familiar with your body." His grin faded a bit as he studied her face. "There's a special glow about you, as well. It's made you even more beautiful. I think motherhood will agree with you."

Lauren smiled back at him. "That's easy for you to say. You don't have to miss breakfast."

"I want you to see a doctor when we arrive in London. Our family physician in Kent is good, but I don't want to take chances."

Lauren's brows drew together. "Jason, you don't mean to treat me as an invalid, do you? Because if you do—"

"No, but one way or another, I mean for you to take care of yourself and my child. Besides, I've always held the belief that a father-to-be ought to have *some* rights. I think I should be allowed to pamper you the tiniest bit."

"So that's why you've been so considerate of me lately! I can see already that you will spoil him dreadfully."

"Him?"

"Our son."

"A boy, is it?" Jason quizzed with laughter in his eyes. "But what if I want a girl, with golden hair and haunting cat-eyes like her mother?"

"I thought you married me so you could get an heir."

"No you didn't. You thought I was after your money. But actually neither reason is the real one. I married you for the pleasure of trying to get an heir."

Lauren flashed him an impudent smile. "Well, since one is now on the way, I suppose you may stop trying."

Jason began to nibble at her lips. "I'm not as certain as you are that it will be a boy," he murmured. "I think perhaps we should keep at it."

"It has to be a boy. Otherwise I couldn't face all those aunts and cousins you told me about."

Jason drew back slightly, letting his gaze caress her. "We'll face them together, sweetheart. My inquisitive relatives and anything else the future holds for us."

"Together," Lauren repeated solemnly, before an inexplicable chill touched her spine, causing her to shiver. But then, as she had been doing for weeks, she forced herself to ignore any reminder of the past, to avoid any consideration of the future.

Looping her arms about Jason's neck, she gave him a slow smile. "There is one thing, though," she murmured, suggestively trailing a finger down the dimpled crease in his cheek to his sensuous mouth. "I've always found it difficult to believe what happened the night you first brought me here. Did you really do something as scandalous as taking me on your desk?"

Jason glanced across the cabin at the desk. The surface was spread with papers, evincing his recent attempts to catch up on his correspondence. A gleam entered his blue eyes as he recalled the incident Lauren spoke of. "Umm hmm," he admitted unrepentantly, "I did, indeed. And I've enjoyed working there ever since."

"Do you suppose you could refresh my memory sometime before we reach England?"

Eyeing Lauren with amusement, Jason chuckled. "I would be delighted," he replied. "But who is being scandalous now?"

Part III

The Unmasking

Chapter Twenty-Three

England, 1816

Four years before, when she had fled in terror from Burroughs's men, London hadn't made much of an impression on Lauren. Then, she had been a trembling, frightened girl desperately seeking a way of escape. Now, sailing up the Thames, Lauren had ample opportunity to take note of her surroundings. She stood by Jason's side, watching silently as the *Siren* threaded a path through the countless ships on the river.

As they neared London, she was afforded a view of the English capital that surprised her, one of dirt and foul smells and poverty. The city seemed begrimed with the smoke of countless chimneys, while clusters of ramshackle cottages and tenements piled on the banks of the river between counting houses and shipwrights' yards, an odd contrast to the imposing buildings and tall spires that could be seen in the distance.

As the schooner neared the bustling London Dock, memories of that long-ago flight disturbed Lauren, making her uncomfortably aware that the same undercurrent of fear was still with her. Her tendency to shiver had nothing to do with the English weather, even though the day was far chillier than what she was accustomed to in New Orleans.

Her sober expression was far too solemn for Jason, though. Giving Lauren a reassuring smile, he slipped his arm around her waist and indicated the bank with a wave of his hand, drawing her attention to the great fortress of the Tower. For the next two hours, until they actually left the ship, he distracted her with tales about London and of the kings and commoners who had lived there.

London wasn't all squalor and poverty, Lauren could see as they were whisked away from the docks by Jason's town carriage; she noted an instant improvement in the neighborhoods when they had left riverside Wapping behind. The streets were crowded with prosperous activity, while the din from vendors hawking their wares vied with the rattle of carriages and the clatter of horses' hooves.

Looking out the window with wide-eyed interest, Lauren commented whenever something caught her eye, causing Jason to chuckle at her excitement. When they reached elegant Mayfair, however, Lauren grew silent. The spacious, relatively quiet streets were flanked on each side with enormous houses belonging to the extremely wealthy.

A short while later, the carriage turned into Grosvenor Square. When they drew up before the Effing townhouse, Lauren stared at the magnificent Georgian mansion with awe. She should have been prepared for such affluence. The luxurious Effing carriage with the impressive crest on the panels, as well as the liveried footmen should have given her some indication of what to expect. Yet seeing the kind of background Jason came from, Lauren was a bit overwhelmed. She suddenly understood quite well how Lila had felt marrying into the prestigious Beauvais family. And the Stuarts went back much further. Jason could even claim an extremely distant and ancient connection to royalty.

But of course Jason wasn't one to stand on ceremony. Ignoring her protests, he swept Lauren up in his arms and carried her up the wide stone steps and over the threshold, proudly displaying her before the servants and anyone else who cared to watch. Lauren felt like a trophy of war as much as a blushing bride. And she was blushing, to be sure. Her cheeks had turned a becoming shade of pink by the time Jason at last lowered her to the gleaming parquet floor. Lauren glanced about her interestedly, catching a glimpse of crystal chandeliers, sweeping staircases, and railed galleries, before Jason began introducing her to the servants.

There seemed to be an army of them lined up for inspection. At the head was the commander-in-chief, the butler Morrow, a formidable-looking, white-haired man with impeccably formal manners. He welcomed the new Lady Effing in stentorian tones, unwittingly making Lauren feel like an impertinent upstart. But she immediately warmed to Mrs. Morrow, the housekeeper. The elderly woman chuckled delightedly when Jason kissed her wrinkled cheek, and she greeted Lauren with kindness that was unfeigned. There was no question that she at least was highly pleased to have a new mistress of the house.

It took some time to complete the entire line. Jason greeted all the servants by name, except for a new gardener who had joined the household in his absence. He spoke to each of them personally, and he never seemed to tire of accepting their good wishes for his marital felicity. Lauren spent the time trying to memorize all the names and faces.

Afterward, as she was being led upstairs by the housekeeper, she learned that the girl named Molly had been appointed her abigail until a satisfactory lady's maid could be found.

"She's a good, biddable girl," Mrs. Morrow said of Molly, "though a bit nervous to be serving in such a capacity. But she has a way with arranging hair. And no one is better with the irons. No fear that Molly will scorch your gowns. Of course, milady, if you would prefer someone else. . . ."

"I'm certain Molly will do quite well," Lauren assured her. "It is I who may make the mistakes. In America I wasn't used to having anyone wait on me until quite recently, and I found it took some getting used to. I expect there will be a number of other customs I will need to familiarize myself with, if I'm not to shame my husband."

Mrs. Morrow beamed. "You'll not do that, milady. But Morrow and I would be honored to be of assistance, should you have any need of us."

"Thank you . . . Goodness! Is this room to be mine?" Lauren asked as a door swung open. She tried not to stare, but the bedroom was almost overpowering in its opulence. Most of the furniture was elegant Louis XVI, but the large bed was practically obscured by elaborate, pink velvet hangings. Along one wall, fabulous crystal sconces flanked two enormous gilt mirrors, while on the ceiling, a painted mural depicted a half dozen golden cherubs. The suite of rooms had belonged to the previous Lady Effing, Lauren was told.

She was relieved to find the adjoining sitting room much more to her taste. The dressing room on the opposite side of the bedroom was also unexceptional, and the water closet, with its hot water plumbing and marble bath was more modern than anything she had ever imagined.

There was a door on the far side, but Lauren hesitated with her hand on the knob. "May I?" she asked uncertainly.

"Of course, milady. That is his lordship's dressing room," Mrs. Morrow commented. "The bedchamber is just beyond."

Jason's dressing room was similar to her own, Lauren discovered, but his bedroom, fortunately, was quite different—furnished in a tasteful masculine style. Stepping into the room, Lauren looked about her with approval. The enormous four-poster bed appeared far more inviting than the pink confection in her suite.

She was just about to test the mattress when her husband entered, followed by his valet, Gordy. Jason had doffed his coat and was in the process of removing his cravat, and when he noted Lauren's embarrassed flush, a wicked gleam of amusement began to dance in his blue eyes. But he refrained from teasing her, merely saying in a bland voice that it was good to be home again, then asking Mrs. Morrow if she approved his choice of a bride.

"That I do," the housekeeper replied at once. "But if I have your permission to say so, milord, I don't see how you ever found her ladyship among the savages in America."

Jason chuckled. "I expect you will say whatever you wish, Mrs. Morrow, with or without my permission. See what an ally you have, Lauren? I can't imagine how I will ever endure the two of you together. Of course, I've always had a fondness for Mrs. Morrow. She used to give me gingerbread when I was a boy."

"Humph! You mean I used to look the other way when you stole it from under Cook's nose." Shaking her head, the elderly woman turned to Lauren. "His lordship was a real terror, milady, make no mistake."

Lauren smiled as she met Jason's gaze. "I can well imagine."

"Mrs. Morrow," Jason said, while his eyes never left Lauren's, "I expect my wife is fatigued from the long journey. She should rest, don't you think?"

"But of course!" the housekeeper replied. "I'll just send Molly up to wait on you, milady."

Jason forestalled her with a brief wave of his hand. "That won't be necessary. I'll perform whatever services my wife requires. We won't be dressing for dinner this evening. Would you see that a supper table is set up in her ladyship's sitting room? And Gordy, I'll manage for myself. I'll ring if I need you."

Mrs. Morrow took her dismissal with good grace, and if Gordy regretted not being able to perform his duties after his master's long absence, the superior valet was too well trained to show it.

When the servants had gone, Jason drew Lauren into his arms. It was only after he had kissed her quite thoroughly that Lauren took him to task. "Really, Jason, how could you tell Mrs. Morrow such a tale? I'm not at all tired."

He grinned. "Neither am I," he replied, and then bent his head again.

Later, when they were sharing the large bed and Jason was drawing lazy patterns on her stomach, Lauren smiled drowsily. "I fear you will never make a proper lady's maid. You don't seem to care what happens to the gowns you bought me in New Orleans."

He didn't even glance at the garments he had tossed so carelessly on the floor. "I don't. I'm only interested in helping you out of your clothes. At any rate, you'll have to order new ones. Not only will you soon outgrow the gowns you have, but your wardrobe is already a year out of date."

"Jason, that's absurd! It will be some time before my condition is noticeable, what with the high waistlines, and I can make over every one of my gowns before then."

Jason shook his tawny head. "Oh, no, sweetheart. That wouldn't be at all fashionable."

"I don't give a fig for fashion. Think of the waste!"

"I know, but I can well afford it. And you have a position in society to uphold now, m'lady. You'll find London far worse than New Orleans on that score. You won't be able to appear twice in the same outfit without causing comment." At Lauren's incredulous look, Jason planted a kiss on her nose. "I expect to be closeted with my man of business tomorrow morning, but you can go shopping with my aunt Agatha. She's an old dragon, but I expect you'll like her."

Lauren sighed with resignation, before peering at Jason through her lashes. "You don't mean to insist on my being totally fashionable, do you?"

"Like cropping your hair? Don't you dare try it. I like it just the way it is."

"No," she said with a provocative smile. "Like sleeping in separate bedrooms. I understand it is quite the custom among married couples to sleep apart."

Jason grinned. "You aren't pleased with your apartments, then? You have my permission to change anything you like—redecorate the whole. I didn't suppose you would care for pink. My mother didn't either, for that matter. She intentionally had her room done that way to annoy my father."

"Goodness! Did she dislike him so very much?"

"Actually my parents were very much in love. But my father had a way of ordering everyone about and then expecting instant obedience. Mama would put up with it just so far, then dig in her heels. The angels were to remind him that people—including his own family—were mere mortals. I like that touch, don't you?"

"Well, it is a little much with the pink. I like this room far better."

"So did she."

Snuggling closer to Jason, Lauren glanced up at him. "Then I may stay here with you?" she asked hopefully.

He laughed. "I'm counting on it."

Lauren did indeed go shopping the next day—with Lady Agatha Trent, a tall, willowy woman who was now a widow with several grown grandchildren. She had been a Stuart before her marriage fifty years earlier, but even though she had changed her name, it was obvious that she now considered herself the matriarch of the Stuart clan.

For the first five minutes of their acquaintance, Lady Agatha treated Lauren with stiff formality. Then she relented somewhat. "You'll do," was her pronouncement. "You may not have the blood, but you have breeding, that's obvious. Your looks are more than passable, your carriage is excellent, and you have countenance. And you seem healthy enough to give my nephew an heir."

Lauren smiled politely. "Thank you, my lady. And since we are discussing my attributes, please allow me to point out my fine teeth, as well."

Lady Agatha's eyes narrowed momentarily, but then she chuckled. "You have a tongue in your head. Good! I can't abide witless females. You'll need to be wide-awake if you mean to stand up to the gossips. I can assure you, all London is talking about you. I'll do my best to tell you how to go on— family is family, you know. But the rest will be up to you. There wasn't anything havey-cavey about your marriage, was there?"

Lauren's eyes widened. Even for an aunt whom Jason held in affection, that question was far too personal. Besides, she couldn't reply with the truth. She wasn't even sure that she *was* married, since she had used a false name. And what would Aunt Agatha say if she were to admit she had been drunk during the ceremony? Or for that matter, that Jason had found her in a high-class bordello and mistaken her for a strumpet?

Somehow Lauren managed a civil—and untruthful—reply, which seemed to satisfy the silver-haired woman, and they went on to speak of other things. After a time, Lauren even became accustomed to Lady Agatha's frankness, and when the older woman unbent enough to lose some of her rigidness, Lauren did like her, just as Jason had predicted she would. In fact, she soon came to appreciate Lady Agatha's guidance.

She learned three things of importance during just that first session with Jason's aunt. The first was that Jason's position in society was even more elevated than she had supposed. The second was that the same society was waiting like a hungry lion to pounce should she make the slightest slip. And the third was that the story about her being the Carlin heiress was already out.

How that news had spread, Lauren never learned. When she taxed Jason about it later, he denied being the source but suggested that someone else had seen her portrait hanging in the Carlin offices. It was also possible, Jason said, that some astute merchant had pieced the puzzle together since he had never made a secret of the fact that he owned the Carlin ships. Then again, Lauren realized, it could merely have started as servants' gossip. That information network was one of the best communication systems in the world, she quickly discovered. Molly, for example, had a fount of knowledge that Lauren found extremely helpful.

But however the story had started, since her connection to the Carlin Line was known—or at least assumed—Lauren couldn't hope to avoid the issue altogether. Before she had been in London three days, she was having to explain to a number of Jason's prying relatives that she preferred to be called Lauren, rather than Andrea. She was thankful that Jason planned to remove to Effing Hall in Kent at the end of the following fortnight.

She wasn't to be allowed an easy escape, though. Most of the beau monde had already left London for their country estates, but Lady Agatha arranged an impromptu gathering of "merely two or three hundred" of those who remained. She was determined to introduce Lauren to society, and even Jason agreed that it was best to "beard the lions" now.

Lauren was extremely nervous about the event. Indeed, as she was dressing for the evening, she thought of the lion at the Exeter Exchange which Jason had taken her to see, and decided that being thrown into the cage with the beast would be preferable to facing the ton. While Molly added the finishing touches to her toilette, Lauren contemplated every alternative short of suicide that would allow her to avoid the evening's ordeal.

She was seated at her dressing table when Jason entered the room. Grateful for the distraction, she examined his reflection in the pier glass. He looked strikingly handsome in his formal blue and buff attire, with a pristine white cravat and diamond stickpin at his throat. His evening clothes seemed only to emphasize his masculinity and accentuate the powerful lines of his tall body, for the coat molded perfectly to his superb shoulders, while the close-fitting satin breeches blatantly hugged his lean hips and muscular thighs.

He approved of her appearance, too, Lauren realized, feeling the caress of his admiring glance as Jason came to stand directly behind her. When their gazes met in the glass, a queer breathlessness assailed Lauren. She was hardly aware when the maid excused herself and left the room.

Jason held Lauren's gaze as his long fingers closed over her bare shoulders. "Magnificent," he said softly.

She managed a tremulous smile. She was wearing a new, extremely fashionable gown, cut low over the bosom to reveal a large expanse of flawlessly smooth skin. The underskirt of cream shot with gold threads shimmered enticingly, while the overskirt of a deep emerald brought out the green in her eyes. She wasn't wearing the fantastic set of Effing diamonds and emeralds that would have complemented her gown, but had chosen instead to wear the jeweled heart Jason had given her, along with a spray of gems for her hair. The effect was simple and elegant, Lauren thought. She defensively touched the beautiful little heart. "This might not be appropriate, but I would like to wear it."

Jason's smile was infinitely tender. "Nothing could please me more, Cat-eyes. I only wish my name were engraved on it so everyone would realize at once that you're mine. As it is, I'm likely to spend the entire evening fighting off the gentlemen. Doubtless they will besiege you. You look like a queen."

Jason wasn't far wrong in his assessment. The masculine half of the crowd at Lady Trent's gathering received Lauren with open arms. The ladies were more reserved, of course, but even they expressed a genuine curiosity to know more about the beauty who had captured the elusive Jason Stuart. And if the words *Cit* and *trade* and *commoner* were uppermost on their minds, they were too aware of the power the Marquess of Effing wielded in society to risk offending his new marchioness.

Lauren stood in the reception line for what seemed like hours, being introduced to a myriad of elegant people, three-quarters of whom she couldn't even remember later. Afterward, she was allowed to proceed to the ballroom—the only room in the Trent mansion that could hold the many guests—and was immediately surrounded.

Dismayed, Lauren looked to Jason for assistance, but he ignored the plea in her eyes, giving her an "I told you so" grin and shrugging his shoulders helplessly. The next moment, his attention was claimed by some of the guests, and Lauren could only watch wistfully as he disappeared into the throng.

It was more than three hours later before she saw him again, moving toward her with another gentleman in tow. Even in a crowd Jason's presence was compelling, and Lauren felt a surge of pride that such a powerful, magnificent male belonged to her.

"Sweetheart," Jason said when he reached her side. "I'd like you to meet one of my closest friends and classmates, Dominic Serrault, the Earl of Stanton. I beg you not to be insulted by his late arrival, though. Dominic has no manners to speak of and is only tolerated for his charming smile. I'll leave you two to become acquainted while I fetch you a glass of wine."

Before Lauren could say a word, Jason was gone again and Lord Stanton was bowing over her hand. When he straightened, she found herself looking up into a pair of penetrating gray eyes. He was a striking man, Lauren reflected, though not anything like her tall, blue-eyed husband. Lord Stanton's dark hair and aristocratic features lent him an air of cynicism, while he carried himself with a natural arrogance that bordered on haughtiness.

He was assessing her quite seriously, Lauren realized, and although he greeted her in a polite, even tone, it was obvious from his severe expression, that he meant to withhold judgment till he knew her better. Indeed, it almost seemed that he was prepared to dislike her. Yet, strangely, Lauren welcomed his reserve. All evening long she had been showered with empty flattery, and though she hadn't found the compliments abhorrent, they had really meant little to her. She wanted approval, of course, but she would far rather it be because of her character than because she had a pleasing face and figure.

She was accorded time for only a brief exchange with Lord Stanton, however, before a woman Lauren recalled vaguely as being the daughter of a duke came up to her then and rather rudely claimed her attention.

Lauren did her best to remain unruffled by Lady Blanche's sly innuendos, truly she did. She responded politely to the prying questions about her background and common antecedents, and even smiled and bit her tongue when Blanche intimated that Jason had married her for her "vulgar" wealth. But when the woman had the temerity to suggest that it was merely a matter of time before Lord Effing resumed "certain activities" that he had enjoyed before his marriage, Lauren's eyes flashed.

"Alas," Lauren said with a sigh, "I could only hope that you would win your wager, my lady. It is so terribly *exhausting*, being required to satisfy a man as . . . active as my husband. And so unfashionable. Imagine," she added with sugary sweetness, "Jason insists that I share his bed! I fear he doesn't care in the least what other people say of us. Indeed, he doesn't mind telling anyone who asks that ours was a love match, though I have *begged* him not to do so. I can barely hold up my head. Oh, but perhaps I should not have said such a thing to you, my lady. How could you know of such things as the habits of virile men? I do hope you will forgive me."

Lauren viewed the result of her little speech with satisfaction; judging from Blanche's queer expression, the lady was unable to decide whether or not she had just been insulted, and if so, whether to take offense.

Blanche was clever enough to realize, however, that the new Lady Effing hadn't been intimidated. Just as she was clever enough to discern that her ploy to attract the handsome Lord Stanton had failed. He was coughing delicately into his fist, quite obviously in an effort to choke back his laughter. Feeling uncomfortably like she was the object of an unspoken jest, Lady Blanche smiled weakly and pretended to see someone to whom she "simply must speak." When she hastily took her leave, Lauren let out a sigh of relief.

391

"'Which if not victory is yet revenge,'" Lord Stanton murmured, causing Lauren to turn and eye him narrowly. She had forgotten his presence since he had been standing a little behind her, but it was obvious that he had been listening to the entire exchange. When she saw the mocking glimmer in his gray eyes, Lauren recalled what she had said about virile men and flushed. But then she lifted her chin. "I cannot abide cats," she said defensively.

He smiled. "Neither can I. And the Lady Blanche is truly representative of the species. I think perhaps she would have tried to bite as well as scratch, had she understood half of what you said."

Lauren didn't answer, for she was contemplating the amazing change that had been wrought in Stanton's arrogant features. Looking up at him, she silently agreed with Jason: the gentleman did have a *very* charming smile.

Just then, Jason returned bearing a glass of champagne. When Lauren accepted it coolly, he studied her face. "What's wrong, sweetheart? I trust Dominic hasn't done anything that will require me to call him out. He's far too good a shot."

Lauren frowned at her husband in disapproval. "Of course not. Lord Stanton has merely been quoting Milton to me." Her reply earned an admiring glance from the earl, but she missed seeing it as she scolded Jason. "It is you, darling, who is in disfavor at the moment. You were about to prove me a liar. I have been telling everyone how much you dote on me."

Jason's blue eyes widened innocently. "But I do!"

"And yet you leave me to fend for myself all evening. Really, Jason, how could you?"

"I told you how it would be," he replied, unrepentant. "I was unable to get near you for all your other admirers."

"Well, if I had known you meant to abandon me to the mercy of these . . . these *kind* people, I would have asked Lady Agatha to require us all to come in costume. I would have worn a suit of armor at the very least."

Amusement sparkled in Jason's eyes. "I ask you, Dominic, has it seemed to you that my wife has needed my protection?"

"Not at all," Lord Stanton answered easily. "Nor mine. She routed the enemy entirely on her own, without help from either of us. Her wit was sword enough. But I do advise you to take better care of your beautiful lady, Jason, before someone else offers to do it for you. She has already confessed how very wearing it is to be married to you, what with your constant demands . . . on her time."

Jason lifted a brow and looked from his friend to Lauren. When she wouldn't meet his eyes, he noted the slight flush that stained her cheeks. "How remiss of me," Jason said finally. "Come, sweetheart. We must find you a chair away from all this crush. Dominic, if you will excuse us?"

"Jason, there is really nothing wrong," Lauren protested as she was led away.

He steered her toward the doors that led to a darkened garden. "I thought not. But I'm interested in hearing this tale of how demanding I am."

Worried that he had misinterpreted Lord Stanton's words, Lauren tried to explain. "I didn't actually say that—"

"No? Then I shall have to give you a reason to complain."

Hearing laughter in his tone, Lauren peered up at him. Jason was grinning down at her, a warm light in his eyes. Lauren accompanied him meekly then, and when darkness closed in around them, she went willingly into his arms.

Jason gathered her enticing body even closer. This was what he had been wanting to do all evening, this and more. . . . "Aunt Agatha will just have to forgive me for stealing you away," he breathed huskily in her ear. "It has been far too long between feedings."

It was in their own garden, two days later, that Jason told Lauren of his plans to accompany the British fleet to Algiers. The summer day was like a rich wine, to be sipped slowly and savored, but Lauren tasted only vinegar as she strolled arm and arm with Jason between beds of roses and columbine.

"The problem with pirates in the Mediterranean is widespread," he explained. "And it concerns more than just the Carlin Line. No ship is safe from attack unless its country pays exorbitant fees for protection. Generally, the vessels are either captured or sunk, while the cargo is seized and the crew and passengers taken captive. Those who are rich enough are ransomed, those not are sold into slavery."

When Lauren remained silent, Jason went on. "The corsairs operate from bases along the African coast. There have been several attempts in recent years to clean up the area and make it safe for commerce, starting with the American efforts at the turn of the century, but they've generally been unsuccessful. So has diplomacy. Currently the largest fraternity, the most damaging one, is located in Algiers. Lord Exmouth, the commander-in-chief of the Mediterranean, plans to lead a fleet of English and Dutch ships against the pirates there. He means to destroy the base, if at all possible."

Pausing, Jason turned to Lauren. She hadn't said a single word since he had begun, nor had she even looked at him.

Cupping her face, he tilted it up. "I plan to be part of it, Lauren," Jason said quietly.

Lauren looked at him searchingly. "You are going to find Rafael," she said in a hoarse voice.

As Jason gazed down into her troubled eyes, he could see the gold flecks in the deep green pools were more pronounced. "Yes," he admitted, "but I have a purpose besides just finding Rafael. The pirates have long been a menace to Carlin shipping. None of our vessels has ever been captured because none sails alone, but some have been severely damaged. Men have been wounded and even killed. The situation cannot be allowed to continue."

"But you don't have to be the one to rectify it!" Lauren protested.

"I'm responsible for the safety of the Carlin Line," Jason said with a finality she could recognize. "And I can't sit back and allow others to fight my battles for me. I've ordered one of our fastest sloops, the *Capricorn*, outfitted with the newest munitions. She's a good ship. And Kyle will be with me. He and I have done this before, and we've always come out of it with nothing more than a few scratches."

"This isn't the same!" Lauren exclaimed despairingly. "You won't come home until you kill Rafael—or he kills you."

Jason sighed. "I made a promise, sweetheart, you know that." Seeing the worry in her eyes, though, he drew her close and rested his cheek against her golden hair. "I want you to stay at Effing Hall while I'm gone," he said quietly. "I believe you will like it there, and Aunt Agatha will provide company for you, if you wish."

Lauren bit back a sob. She wanted to beg Jason to stay in England where it was safe, but she couldn't force the words past the swelling in her throat. Besides, she knew he would never change his mind. "Oh, Jason!" she whispered. "Just come back to me. Just please come back."

Lauren feared for Jason, but a short while later her foreboding was overshadowed by a more immediate fear. That very afternoon she accompanied Lady Agatha to Bond Street, intending to purchase gifts for her friends in America. It had been uniquely heartwarming to see the look of pleasure on Lila's face upon receiving the silver jewel case, but Lauren hadn't had time to show her apprciation to anyone else before setting sail so abruptly.

As she left a silk mercery, Lauren suddenly came to an abrupt standstill. Across the busy street was a man dressed in seaman's blue, a man she recognized; she couldn't mistake the wizened face and bold eyes of Ned Sikes. And there was someone with him—an older woman, tall and strongly built. Lauren couldn't make out her features clearly, but she could feel the malevolence of the woman's gaze. It touched her as if no distance, no throng of vehicles and pedestrians separated them.

Strangely shaken, Lauren forced herself to enter the carriage. Yet she hardly heard a word of Lady Agatha's praise for the fabrics they'd found, and during the ride home, she could only listen mutely while Jason's aunt spoke about an orphanage she patronized.

Lauren didn't recall what excuses she made, but she managed to make her way upstairs to her room. After removing her gown, she stretched out on the bed to rest, but she couldn't close her eyes. Something was about to happen, she knew. She felt an almost overwhelming sense of dread. It was like she was standing at the edge of a precipice, overlooking a deep, dark chasm. She was expected to jump, or would be pushed. . . .

The knock on her door startled her. When a maid entered, bearing a silver salver, Lauren stared at the folded scrap of paper as if it were a coiled snake. This was what she had been anticipating.

Unable to breathe, Lauren dismissed the servant. Her hands trembled as she broke the seal and read the brief, shattering message:

> My darling niece, Andrea,
>
> Meet me at nine o'clock tomorrow morning, Hyde Park. Take the footpath which leads from the north gate. Come alone and do not mention this to your husband. We have much to discuss, you and I.
>
> Your loving aunt, Regina

It was some little while before Lauren became aware of her surroundings again. Only then did she realize that she had moved to sit at her dressing table and was staring at her reflection. Her complexion was stark white, her eyes enormous in her pale face.

Tearing her gaze away, Lauren looked down at the flowered twig in her hand. She must have picked it up while walking through the garden with Jason and then carried it up to her room. Why she had saved it, she didn't know, for it was only the thorny stem of a rosebush. It wasn't even pretty, for the single, tiny bud was now lifeless and brittle.

It had no meaning for her . . . or did it? Somehow it reminded her of how barren her life had been before Jason had found her again. Had she ever truly been alive before then? He had filled her with love, with hope, with their child. For a short moment in time she had been totally, deliriously happy. And now that happiness would be ripped from her like some vital appendage.

With slow deliberation, Lauren closed her hand around the dry stalk, pressing the thorns into the fleshy part of her palm, wanting to feel the stinging pain. Her past had caught up with her, just like she had always known it would, just as she had always dreaded. Her protected haven had crumbled, just as the fragile petals were crumbling now in her hand.

A feeling of desolation swept over her as she watched the pinkish-gray powder rain slowly to the carpet. Not surprisingly, she found she couldn't stop the violent trembling of her body.

Chapter Twenty-Four

Except for several children playing under the close supervision of their respective nurses, the park was deserted at the appointed hour of Lauren's meeting. The lovely summer morning was quiet—so quiet that the scrape of her footsteps on the gravel path seemed abnormally loud.

Lauren would have liked nothing better than to turn and run, but she had to face Regina and find out what the woman knew. If a scandal were about to break over her head, she would have to leave England at once. That might not prevent dishonor to the Stuart name, but at least it would spare Jason the disgrace of having a wife in prison.

The previous night, Lauren had been afraid Jason would guess something was wrong, yet she couldn't prevent herself from clinging to him, not knowing whether she would ever even see him again. There had been a poignant quality to their lovemaking that was almost unbearable.

Evidently, though, Jason hadn't noted anything amiss. He had merely held her tightly, saying nothing, only offering silent comfort. It had been a stroke of good fortune that he had left the house early that morning, intending to finalize plans for his upcoming voyage. Lauren had ordered the carriage, thinking that it was wise not to arouse suspicion by setting out alone on foot. Once in the park, she had bid the coachman to walk the horses while she went for a stroll.

Her footsteps lagged as she approached the north gate. She could only conclude that Regina was late, for there was no sign of anyone.

Then a woman, the same one who had stared at her with such hatred the previous day, stepped out from behind a chestnut tree. Lauren came to an abrupt halt, her immediate impulse to run from the hostile gray eyes that were scrutinizing her so closely. She shivered, feeling cold all over.

"So you are Jonathan's brat," the woman declared.

Lauren had no doubt this was Regina Carlin, for she bore an uncanny resemblance to a portrait of Jonathan Carlin which hung at Carlin House. Her face was lined with age now, but she shared her brother's facial features, as well as the family height and regal carriage. The stark black gown Regina wore made her seem a somber, almost tragic figure, while her silver-gray hair gave an added appearance of fragility. Lauren was well aware, though, that her aunt was a dangerous adversary. The ruthless, fanatical way Regina had pursued the Carlin fortune for so many years was proof enough of that.

The gray eyes relentlessly bored into Lauren. "You're Jonathan's bastard," Regina accused, shattering any lingering hope that she might not know Lauren's identity. "Elizabeth DeVries was your mother." When Lauren gave a start, Regina's lips twisted in a sneer. "Oh, yes, I knew about you! Jonathan bragged more than once about how he had tricked your foolish mother."

Lauren felt her heart slamming against her ribs in painful strokes. The game was up. "Yes," she said faintly. "Jonathan Carlin was my father."

There was a long, tense silence while aunt and niece simply stared at each other. Then Regina spoke again, almost to herself. "I've been as much of a fool. George Burroughs arranged for you to take Andrea's place, didn't he? How clever of him. I never would have guessed he had the nerve. And you—I wondered what had happened to Jonathan's bastard, but I never connected you with little Andrea. Burroughs said he had hidden Andrea away where she would be safe. I couldn't believe it when Sikes told me of a woman named Lauren DeVries who owned the Carlin Line."

As if on cue, Ned Sikes stepped from behind a hawthorn tree. He kept his distance, yet Lauren couldn't suppress a shudder as his insolent gaze touched her. Her throat suddenly felt as dry as dust. "He was spying on me?" she asked hoarsely.

Hooking his thumbs in his belt, Sikes leaned back against the tree and nodded. "She 'ired me to watch that fancy man of yers," he drawled. He ignored the quelling look Regina gave him, although he refrained from speaking again.

"That interfering Stuart!" Regina spat contemptuously, fixing her gaze on Lauren. "I understand you're married to him now. I suppose he thinks he has tied up all the loose ends quite nicely. First he steals the Carlin ships so I can't get my hands on them, then he marries you to make it look legal. Where is dear little Andrea, by the way? Not that I really care."

"She's . . . she's dead," Lauren stammered.

A twisted smile spread across Regina's lips. "How unfortunate. It would have saved me a great deal of trouble if she had died with Jonathan and Mary, when she was supposed to."

Lauren couldn't stifle a gasp. "When she was supposed— Then you *did* kill the Carlins?"

"I'm surprised Burroughs didn't tell you all about it," Regina jeered, avoiding a direct reply.

"He said you were responsible for my father's death."

Regina's mouth tightened. "Jonathan was evil. You should be able to understand that, considering what he did to your mother. I met Elizabeth once. So unsuspecting. So innocent. She found out to her sorrow what my brother was truly like."

"So you *murdered* him?"

A spark of anger flashed in the gray eyes. "Not I. Rafael."

"The pirate," Lauren echoed.

"He was the man I loved," Regina said with quiet vehemence. "The man I would have married but for my brother. I only told Rafael how to find Carlin House, but I would have helped him kill Jonathan, had I been there."

It was said so calmly, without the least hint of remorse, that Lauren felt a fission of fear run along her spine. She watched apprehensively as Regina's gray eyes took on an unfocused look, as if she were remembering something in her past.

"Jonathan condemned Rafael to *slavery*, just for the crime of loving me. My lover, the man who would have been my husband came back half a man." Her fierce gaze focused on Lauren once more. "Do you know what that means, dear niece? Do you? I was *glad* when Rafael had his revenge. I was *glad* to know my brother suffered the same fate! And, yes, I was *glad* when Jonathan died!"

Lauren knew horror must have shown in her face, for Regina raised an accusing finger and pointed. "Who are you to sit in judgment of me? I had reason to hate Jonathan! He ruined my life when he destroyed my Rafael."

"But Mary . . . and Andrea . . . they had done nothing."

"No," Regina said harshly. "But when they died, the Carlin Line would have come to me. I planned to sell the fleet and give the money to Rafael in payment for what Jonathan had done."

"But then Andrea survived," Lauren murmured.

A mask settled over Regina's proud features. She looked cold, ruthless, and to Lauren, deadly. "Yes," Regina drawled, "somehow little Andrea got away. And while your half sister still lived, I couldn't touch a penny of Jonathan's fortune." She gave a bitter laugh. "And to think all this time I believed you were she! You're Jonathan's daughter all right, with an eye out only for yourself. I should have Ned kill you for playing such a trick on me. You would enjoy that, wouldn't you, Ned?"

Seeing the wolfish, black-toothed grin Sikes threw her, Lauren took an involuntary step backward. "You're mad!" she cried at Regina, the words escaping her lips before she could bite them back.

Regina's short laugh made her skin crawl. "Probably. Madness runs in our family, I expect. But unfortunately for you, I'm not so far gone yet. Your sister was, though. She wasn't even aware of her own name after Rafael's men finished with her."

Lauren dug her nails into her palms, trying to remain calm, knowing she would need all her wits about her if she hoped to escape this coil. Perhaps if she kept Regina talking, she could create an opportunity. . . . "So you tried to have Andrea declared insane?" Lauren prompted. "That way you could have the Carlin ships."

"It would have been so simple. But Burroughs wouldn't allow me. From the first, he protected Andrea, kept her hidden at Carlin House."

Lauren's hand crept to her throat as she remembered another death at Carlin House. "Then you *did* push Miss Foster over the cliff?"

"Who is Miss Foster?"

"My . . . governess."

"Oh, yes. Her." Regina's eyes narrowed. "What if I did? Jonathan's money should have been mine. Burroughs had no right to interfere. No right at all."

"But he had so many men. I wonder how you managed to get past them."

A look of contempt twisted Regina's mouth. "I simply sent a letter to the Foster woman by post, asking her to meet me on the cliffs. She wouldn't agree to help me, though. I had to kill her."

This talk of death on such a beautiful summer morning, while sparrows and finches twittered joyously in the branches above them, seemed totally incongruous to Lauren. Stealing a glance at Ned Sikes, she saw that he was gazing up at a point somewhere above his head. Although she couldn't say why, Lauren had the distinct impression that he was listening intently to the conversation. Still, he didn't seem at all concerned by Regina's admission that she had murdered someone in cold blood. Lauren shook her head, feeling dazed.

"Jonathan's money should have been mine," Regina repeated, taking a menacing step toward Lauren.

Alarmed, Lauren held up her hands to ward off an attack. "But you won't get the money by killing me," she said in desperation. "My husband owns all the Carlin ships now. And if something happens to him, they go to his heirs. He has a very large family. You couldn't kill all of his relatives, too."

Regina's face contorted with scorn. "Don't you think I am aware of that? I expect his lordship will be willing enough to pay to have you returned to him safely, though."

Realizing they meant to abduct her in broad daylight, Lauren had difficulty forcing down her rising panic. Another glance told her she would get no help from Sikes. In fact, he probably was contemplating how he was going to kill her if Jason wouldn't agree to pay her ransom. But perhaps Regina could be brought to change her mind. . . .

"I'm not so certain that my husband will want me back," Lauren said breathlessly. "He doesn't know I'm not Andrea Carlin, you see."

She could tell her confession took Regina quite by surprise. Or at least it made Regina consider how her plans would be effected. Lauren pressed her point, feeling her way as she tried to stall for time. "I was afraid Jason might not marry me if I told him the truth. You were right, I wanted to be Lady Effing, a marchioness," she lied boldly. "And Jason wanted no one to question his right to the Carlin ships. I thought it a fair exchange. Me, a bastard, becoming a titled lady, while he avoided any legal problems. The world believes me to be Andrea. You're the only one who knows the truth." Lauren could almost see Regina's thoughts churning as she determined how to use this new information to her advantage.

"Stuart must have realized," Regina said slowly, "that I wouldn't just sit quietly by while he kept the money for himself. That when I discovered you had returned, I would take some kind of action to recover the ships he had stolen from me."

Lauren shook her head. "No, he thinks he frightened you enough to make you give up the idea. With you out of the way and me bound to him by law, he no longer sees a need for caution. Since he doesn't know who I am, he doesn't yet see the threat my background presents."

"What are you saying? That your parentage would make a juicy scandal? Perhaps you're right. There's no evidence to prove you're legitimate."

"Evidence? Why . . . should there be evidence?"

A taunting smile twisted Regina's mouth. "I always suspected Jonathan lied about his marriage to Elizabeth. *She* certainly thought it was valid."

Lauren stared at her in shock. "You mean my parents . . . truly were married?"

"You'll never know for sure. Jonathan destroyed any records of the ceremony. I know. I went to Ormskirk to check for myself."

When Lauren remained speechless, Regina continued, her

tone contemptuous. "It wasn't too difficult to guess what Jonathan had done. He tried to seduce Elizabeth, and when he couldn't, he married her. He must have realized his mistake, though, for he left her behind when he returned to London. It was only after Elizabeth put up a fuss that Jonathan came up with that tale about a sham ceremony. He had already married Mary Burroughs by that time, at Burroughs's insistence. Mary was breeding, you see."

Lauren was too stunned to reply. She simply stood there, shaken, her thoughts reeling.

"But perhaps you're right about your husband," Regina said, returning to their original subject. "The high and mighty Lord Effing might pay to keep the world from knowing he married a bastard. He might pay more if I threaten to tell the courts about your impersonation of Andrea."

Visions of prison flashed before Lauren's eyes, forcing her to collect her rioting thoughts. "No!" she said, too quickly, "you can't involve the courts."

"Why not?" Regina asked, regarding her suspiciously. "Indeed, that might be the very thing. The Carlin Line is sure to come to me when it's learned you're a fraud."

Lauren took a steadying breath. "I only meant that you wouldn't gain anything by being rid of me, since Jason owned the ships before our marriage. And he would put up a fight in the courts. He might even accuse you of murdering the Carlins and Miss Foster."

"He has no proof."

"Still, it will do neither of you any good to bring in the authorities."

"So we are at an impasse. And I am back to my original plan. Jason Stuart must pay to have you returned to him. As you so conveniently pointed out, he doesn't know you're not Andrea. He should still be interested in getting you back unharmed."

"But I have a better plan!" Lauren exclaimed as Regina took another step toward her. "A bargain, if you will."

"You have nothing to bargain with."

"But I do. Rafael's life." When Regina's gaze narrowed, Lauren went on quickly. "Jason promised George Burroughs to hunt Rafael down and kill him. No matter what happens to me, Jason will still honor that promise. If you know anything about my husband, you must know he'll succeed. And I'm the only one who can stop him. Is Rafael's life still dear to you?" Lauren said slowly, letting her words sink in. "Do you still have any love for him? I could persuade Jason to leave him alone, in exchange for your silence."

"Ned?" Regina said, implying that she wanted his corroboration.

"It's true 'e was askin' questions about Rafael. An' I 'eard tell 'e was fittin' the *Capricorn* with enough bloody cannon to sink a fleet o' ships."

"Jason means to sail next week," Lauren interjected. "I could make him change his mind."

"How?"

She could see Regina wavering. "I'm not sure yet, but I would think of a way."

"But how do I know you will even make the attempt?"

Lauren forced herself to return her aunt's gaze. "I enjoy my present life, Aunt Regina. For once I have all the gowns and jewels I want, as well as the respect of people who previously would have turned up their aristocratic noses at me. I want nothing to ruin that. Jason would be angry enough to kill me if he ever discovered how I deceived him. And even if he spared me, he would find some way to make my life miserable, particularly if I brought scandal to his beloved Stuart name. I could avoid all that if you agree to follow my plan. Later, I would find a way to share the money with you. But I should think you would first want to make sure Rafael is safe from my husband. Give me a little time. I think I can safely promise that Jason will never sail on the *Capricorn*."

"Very well," Regina capitulated. "You have two days."

"That might not be enough—"

"Two days! No more! Or I tell Jason Stuart that you're a thief and an impostor. If he were to kill you, it would be no more than you deserve. I warn you, though, that I will attend to it myself if you fail. Ned will be watching you. Ned, see that her ladyship goes straight home."

Lauren felt relief wash over her. She had managed to buy some time . . . for the moment. She was trembling, though, and her knees felt so weak that she wondered if she would collapse. She had to force herself to turn and walk slowly away from the woman who had been her particular nemesis for so long. She could feel Ned Sikes's presence as he followed close behind her.

When she was out of Regina's sight, Lauren found herself breathing hard, as if she had run a great distance. Her legs had regained some of their strength, however, and she didn't feel quite so faint. When she reached a junction in the path, she turned to face Sikes. Trying to hide her fear, she told him that her coachman would be suspicious if he saw a strange man following her. Lauren thought it quite odd when, rather than arguing, Sikes made her a respectful little bow and, without a word, walked away, leaving her quite alone. Lauren stared after him for a moment before giving herself a shake. She was wasting precious time.

When she was seated once more in the luxurious carriage, Lauren leaned wearily against the squabs. She had no intention of trying to persuade Jason to do anything, of course. As soon as Regina had hinted that Jonathan Carlin's marriage to Elizabeth DeVries might actually have been valid, Lauren had realized her only alternative: she had to go to Ormskirk where the ceremony had taken place, to search for proof that the marriage was legal. She couldn't build her hopes too greatly, though, for she might never find such proof. But if there were any possibility that she was the legitimate heir to the Carlin Line, she had to make the attempt.

She knew the general location of Ormskirk; it was close to Liverpool, and to St. Helen's where she had lived the first twelve years of her life with her mother. She would leave at once, and with luck, she could put a half-day's distance between herself and London before Jason even realized she was gone. Though certainly she would have to do a much better job of disguising her trail than the last time she had run from her husband.

Her husband, Lauren said to herself with mingled anguish and supreme bitterness. What would Regina do if her marriage to Jason turned out not to be legal? It seemed ironic that were she truly Jason's wife, she would be accorded a jury by his peers. She would avoid hanging then, for the strongest sentence meted out would be imprisonment. And it was possible she could avoid even that. Jason might hate her when he learned how she had deceived him, but he would probably stand by her, if only because of his child. He might be unable to save her, though. And she couldn't risk being sent to prison, not while she was carrying his child. Even if she escaped hanging, she would never survive being locked up.

Lauren closed her eyes as a combination of nausea and anxiety overwhelmed her. The knowledge that she was grasping at her last chance for happiness only served to increase the strain of the past twenty-four hours—one that left her exhausted.

How she ever found the strength to carry out her hastily devised plan when she arrived home, Lauren never knew. After ordering her coachman to wait, she mounted the stairs to her rooms and penned the note that she would have delivered to Jason. She was relieved that Molly was busy in the laundry, for she didn't want the abigail to see her packing. With dazed automation, Lauren stuffed a change of clothes and a warm mantle into a bandbox. She would tell the coachman it contained a gown that needed alteration, and when he had driven her to the dressmaker's shop, she would send him home and slip out the back way. She should easily be able to take a hackney to a posting house, where she could hire a post-chaise for the journey to Liverpool.

But she needed funds. Jason had given her an extremely generous allowance of pin money, most of which she hadn't spent yet. As Lauren filled her reticule with coins and bank notes, though, she was forcibly reminded of the last time she had left London in a hurry. Jason had financed her escape then, too. Fiercely, she banished the memory, stifling an hysterical urge to cry.

The seconds were ticking away, but there was one more thing Lauren had to do. Going to the bureau, she unlocked the jewel box containing the priceless family gems Jason had given her. She could never take them, of course, and she would leave behind the little emerald heart, as well, for it no longer belonged to her.

Willing her fingers to stop their trembling, Lauren removed the chain from about her neck. As she brought the jeweled heart to her lips, though, her breath caught on a sob, and when she laid the necklace upon its bed of velvet, the tight ache in her throat threatened to choke her.

Although her plan worked well—without any hitches at all, in fact—it was after midday when Lauren found herself on the first leg of her journey. The pace was rapid, however. The driver, anticipating a heavy reward for reaching Liverpool in record time, set the horses to a steady gallop. At one point, they even passed the speeding Mail.

The journey was grueling. Dust swirled so thickly inside the carriage that Lauren was forced to hold a handkerchief over her mouth and nose, and as the vehicle bucked and swayed, she had to grasp the strap to keep from being thrown to the floor. Yet she made no complaints. The need for speed was far more important than any momentary discomfort she might be suffering. Even now, she knew quite well, Jason might be searching for her.

As she drew farther and farther away from the metropolis, Lauren couldn't help wondering what he was thinking. Had he discovered her absence already? Would he be fooled by the note that said she meant to spend the afternoon at the dressmaker's? There was no question in her mind that he would try to find her. And so she urged the greatest possible haste. She fretted each time she was forced to break her journey, chafing even at the necessity of changing the tired horses for fresh ones.

By the time dusk settled, though, Lauren was half convinced she had succeeded in disguising her destination. At least there was no one immediately upon her trail. When the driver halted to light the carriage lamps, Lauren bit back her impatience and nodded when she was told the pace would be slower. It was far too dark to continue at the same clipping rate. Such speed would be reckless and foolhardy, if not actually dangerous. Still, she found it hard to relax.

A few hours later, she was given real cause for worry, for the coach suddenly gave a tremendous jolt, then lurched along the ground for several hundred yards, before coming to rest at a precarious angle.

Lauren had been thrown to one side, shaken but unhurt.

Realizing they had lost a wheel, though, she couldn't prevent a groan of dismay. A broken wheel would take hours to repair, and even if a wheelwright could be located, it was possible that he would refuse to work in the dark. Lauren found herself wearily tramping the nearly three miles to an inn they had passed, praying that Jason hadn't yet deduced where she was headed. Fortunately, the inn was uncrowded and could accommodate her, so she bespoke a private parlor where she could wait for the repairs to be completed.

Remembering her pregnancy, then, Lauren asked if she could be served some supper. When an obliging landlady brought her a bowl of soup and half a roasted fowl, Lauren forced herself to eat a few bites, even though her stomach was tied in knots. She felt somewhat relieved when her coachman delivered the welcome news that the wheel would be ready by first light.

Abjuring him to get some rest while he could, she called for the proprietress once more and requested a bedroom for the remainder of the night. Convinced, then, that she could do nothing to speed events along, Lauren stretched out on the bed and instantly fell into an exhausted sleep.

She was wakened by a servant at dawn. She almost wished she hadn't slept, though, for her head was pounding unmercifully and she felt extremely weak. Her flushed cheeks indicated that she had a touch of fever, as well, and the warm water she used to wash with did nothing to cool her hot brow. Afterward, she felt even worse when her usual nausea welled up.

Trying to ignore her queasiness, Lauren smoothed her crumpled gown and hid her tousled hair beneath a concealing bonnet. Her morning sickness precluded taking anything solid in her stomach, so she was ready to continue her journey in a very short time. Letting herself out of the room, she made her way down the dark hall.

She was descending the steep wooden staircase at the end of the corridor when she heard men's voices speaking in low conversation—one of which sounded elusively familiar. Remembering hearing the rattle of a coach in the yard as she was tying the strings of her bonnet, Lauren continued down the stairs more cautiously.

She halted abruptly as she caught sight of a pair of rough boots and worn canvas trousers. The man was coming toward her, heading straight for the stairs where she stood. When he came into view, Lauren's heart leapt to her throat. It wasn't Jason who had followed her. She was staring down at the wizened face of Ned Sikes!

For a moment Lauren found it impossible to move. Panicking then, she whirled, intent on fleeing up the stairs. She neglected to hold up her skirts, though, and her foot caught the hem of her gown. Before she could even put out a hand to break her fall, the stairs were rushing up to meet her.

Her stomach suffered the major impact of the blow, the force so great that all the air was driven fiercely from her body. She lay there, unable to breathe, feeling as if she were suffocating. The stars in her vision receded, then appeared again. She heard first a shout and then rapid footsteps on the stairs below her, but she couldn't move, not even to save herself.

Her arms were grasped then, none too gently, but she couldn't even fight. It was a struggle just to raise her hand to protect her face from the expected blow.

But it never came. No one hit her. She thought she must be dreaming when she heard Jason's voice angrily telling her to look at him. She opened her eyes . . . and looked directly into his blazing blue ones.

She stared at Jason in shocked confusion, her lips parting to say his name. Yet no sound came out. Then a cry was ripped from her throat as an agonizing pain knifed through her.

Doubling over, she clutched fiercely at her stomach. "No!" Lauren sobbed. The knifing pain in her midsection was unbearable, but even more unbearable was the thought of losing her child.

Jason lifted her in his arms and bellowed for the innkeeper to fetch a doctor.

"No," Lauren cried again. The last thing she remembered was the look of savage fury contorting Jason's handsome features as he carried her up the remaining stairs.

Chapter Twenty-Five

Pain, sharp and cutting, then dull and throbbing, slowly, too slowly, receding. Heat. Sweltering, suffocating heat. Hands, cool and soothing. Hushed voices.

For three days Lauren lay in a pain-dazed stupor, her body so racked by fever that she was aware of almost nothing happening around her. Once she woke to find Jason bending over her, his gaze trained anxiously on her face as he held a cool cloth to her brow. By the light of the bedside candle, she could see his unkempt, unshaven appearance. He looked so utterly ragged and weary that Lauren wanted to reach up and touch him, to warn him to take better care of himself, but her throat was so parched that she could only manage to hoarsely whisper his name. Immediately he was holding a glass to her lips and forcing a bitter liquid between her teeth.

When next she woke, it was daylight. Lauren lay there, trying to remember where she was, before a slight noise made her turn her head. She frowned in confusion, wondering why Lady Agatha should be sitting beside her bed. The elderly woman was bent over a tambour frame, steadily plying a needle.

When Lady Agatha saw that her patient was awake, she put aside her sewing and leaned forward to feel of Lauren's forehead. "So, you decided to join the living," she said briskly. "I knew when your fever broke that it was just a matter of time. It was my own physician's remedy that did it. Country doctors, ha! How little they know. You'll be fine, my girl. Now drink

410

this and see if you can sleep. Sleep is the best cure for the body, I always say. You'll be up and about in no time."

Suddenly an image returned to Lauren, of a kindly-looking man at her bedside. He was saying something to her, but she hadn't heard because of the pain. She remembered gripping Jason's hand, though, as another wave of agony made her cry out.

Yet a pain more savage raked her when she realized why her body still ached. "My . . . my baby," Lauren whispered hoarsely. She tried to sit up, but Agatha's firm hand prevented her from moving.

"You lost the child, my dear," Agatha said sympathetically. "But don't concern yourself unduly. I miscarried twice before my eldest was born and I went on to have half a dozen healthy children."

"No," Lauren rasped, yet she knew her protest was meaningless. She couldn't change what had happened, couldn't bring back the tiny life that had been lost. The tears that flooded her eyes ran down her cheeks to splash unheeded on her pillow.

"That's it, my dear. Shed a few tears. You'll feel better afterward. Now drink this. . . ."

Again it was daylight when Lauren woke, but this time she found Molly bustling quietly about the room, humming to herself. The abigail had cleaned the small bedroom and simple furnishings till everything sparkled. There were also fresh flowers by the bed, and the windows had been thrown open to let in a soft summer breeze along with the afternoon sunlight.

When Molly greeted her with a gaiety that seemed a trifle forced, Lauren suspected that the girl's cheerfulness had been ordered by Lady Agatha as part of her "remedy". Lauren couldn't summon the energy to respond, though. Physically, she felt bruised and battered; emotionally, she felt devastated.

Fleetingly, she wondered if anyone had ever died from depression. She wanted Jason desperately, wanted him to hold her and comfort her, but she was afraid to ask for him. She was afraid to face Jason, afraid he wouldn't want to see her after what she had done. Besides, she didn't *deserve* to be comforted, she reflected miserably, riding a wave of remorse that was nine-tenths self-censure. Feeling wretched, Lauren closed her eyes and let Molly's bright chatter wash over her.

Yet as the abigail attended her, Lauren discovered answers to certain questions without asking. She was still at the same inn, she learned, for the doctor had said she couldn't be moved. Immediately after the accident, Jason had sent for his aunt and Molly, and they had been there for several days. Lauren herself had been in bed for nearly a week, and at one point, her fever had been so high that they had feared for her life.

Lauren felt a little better when she had been given a sponge bath and a fresh nightgown to wear. Molly offered her a frilly peignoir but she refused, for it seemed far too frivolous. Instead she drew on a thick woolen wrapper, while the abigail changed the bed linens and fluffed the pillows.

And as she crawled between the clean silk sheets that Lady Agatha had brought all the way from London, Lauren had to admit that she was grateful for such devoted care. Everyone was being so kind to her, so supportive. If only she could talk to Jason. If only he could forgive her. . . .

Molly left the room shortly afterward, promising to fetch some food from the kitchens. When she returned with it, Lauren made a halfhearted effort to rouse herself from her despondency. "Do you know anything about a man named Ned Sikes?" she asked as she was being spoon-fed a bowl of nourishing broth.

"Oh, m'lady, you would never guess! The Bow Street Runners were here. Such comings and goings. And him one, too, that Mr. Sikes. Who would have believed it to look at him? And a chief magistrate was here, too, asking to see you."

Shock penetrated Lauren's misery. Ned Sikes a member of that elite corps of thief-takers? An arbiter of the law asking to see her? Dear God, what was going on? Were they here to arrest her? Lauren pushed the bowl away, suddenly too faint to swallow.

"Are you finished with your soup, m'lady? His lordship asked to be informed when you were able to have visitors. The magistrate wants to speak to you."

Jason here at the inn? Yet he hadn't come to see her? Weakly Lauren shook her head. "No . . . please, Molly. Tell his lordship that I'm too ill to face anyone."

"Very well, m'lady," the maid replied with a curtsy. "If there's nothing you'll be needing then . . ."

Lauren turned away, feeling fresh tears sting her eyes. "No, nothing," she lied.

After the girl had left, the room was quiet for several minutes. Then Lauren heard a firm tread and a commanding knock on her door. When someone entered the room, Lauren knew without looking that it was Jason. Her heart hammered painfully as she turned her head so that she could see him.

With the sunlight behind him, it was hard to read his expression. There was nothing to indicate by his immaculate attire that he had spent several sleepless nights by her side while she was burning up with fever. Nor were there dark circles under his eyes or growth of beard on his chin any longer.

"Jason," Lauren whispered. "I . . . I'm sorry—"

"Now isn't the time to discuss it, Lauren," he interrupted, shocking her with his coldness. "There is someone below who has some questions to put to you. It is a matter of some importance. Sir John has been waiting several days to see you, so I'm afraid I must ask that you accommodate him. May I bring him up?" The question was asked briskly, as if he expected her agreement.

For a moment Lauren could only stare at Jason, bewildered by his distant, chillingly polite manner. She had expected anger and rage, yes, perhaps even bitterness, but not this coldness from a dispassionate stranger.

But as the silence stretched between them, Lauren's bewilderment turned to despair. She had indeed lost Jason. He couldn't forgive her for what had happened to their child—or for any of her crimes. By now he had to know she wasn't Andrea Carlin, that she had deceived him from the start. Lauren shut her eyes, feeling desolation sweep over her. She couldn't bring herself to speak, to say the words that desperately needed to be said.

But it seemed she was to be spared a confession anyway, for Jason turned abruptly on his heel and left the room. When he returned, he brought with him three men, one of whom was

413

Ned Sikes. He introduced the other two as Sir John Marley, a magistrate from London, and Mr. Rorke of Bow Street.

Jason spoke more kindly to Lauren in their presence, calling her "my dear" and helping her to sit up, but she was certain his considerateness was an act. His ministrations were mechanical, his touch impersonal, and when she searched his face, trying to read his hooded expression, he wouldn't meet her gaze or even look at her.

Still, Jason was a familiar figure, and Lauren felt quite alone when he moved to one corner of the room. He stood among the shadows where he could observe the proceedings.

Mr. Rorke took over at once, apologizing for inconveniencing her, then saying in a brisk, official tone, "Now, milady, if you will kindly tell us what occurred during your meeting with one Regina Carlin. She was your aunt, I believe. Could you repeat the conversation you had with her, word for word?"

Bewildered and somewhat frightened, Lauren looked first to the magistrate, then to Ned Sikes, and finally to Jason. "Are . . . am I to be arrested?" she asked, unable to subdue the quiver in her voice.

The officials seemed surprised by her question, but Jason stiffened, a brilliant flash of anger flaring in his eyes. He answered calmly enough, though. "No, my dear. These gentlemen are here to obtain evidence against your aunt Regina. Sikes was a witness to your meeting with her, but your testimony is needed as well. You must tell them what was said. The *complete* truth, Lauren."

There was a cold edge of irony to his tone, and although Lauren didn't understand why they should want her testimony, she knew she had to comply if she ever hoped to regain Jason's respect. She swallowed then in a shaking voice, repeated her conversation with Regina to the best of her recollection, revealing her aunt's confessions.

Out of her own mouth Regina had admitted to being Rafael's accomplice when he murdered Jonathan and Mary Carlin. She had also confessed to killing Sibyl Foster and trying to do away with Andrea Carlin so she could inherit the Carlin fortune. Mr. Rorke nodded solemnly as he listened, jotting down notes and

414

occasionally interrupting with a question or two for clarification.

Lauren faltered when she came to the part where she had convinced her aunt to let her go rather than hold her for ransom. She stole a glance at Jason, then lowered her eyes once more. The grim set to his jaw, the tight line of his lips, told her more eloquently than words how thoroughly she had destroyed whatever love he had felt for her.

A numbing weariness engulfed Lauren as she completed her tale, and when she was done, she pulled the covers up to her chin and sank back among the pillows. Somehow she no longer cared what they did to her.

"You have our sincerest thanks, Lady Effing," the magistrate assured her, speaking for the first time. "Your story coincides exactly with what Sikes has been telling us. What with the evidence we already have, that should be enough to convinct Regina Carlin for her crimes. You have been very courageous. I know what an ordeal this must have been for you—"

"Sir John," Jason interrupted. "My wife is extremely tired, as you can see, so if you are quite finished with your questions, perhaps you will allow her to rest."

"Of course," he replied at once, and with a deep bow to Lauren, took his leave, as did Rorke.

Ned Sikes, however, approached Lauren hesitantly, hat in hand, his head bowed humbly. His mumbled apology for causing her grief seemed as genuine as it was uncharacteristic, but his next words only confused her. "It were me that asked 'is lordship not to tell you 'oo I was," he confessed. "I thought you would act more natural-like if you didn't know it was a trap for Mistress Carlin. But . . . well, I'm fierce sorry."

Again Jason spoke. "Thank you, Ned. No one blames you."

"We should 'ha told 'er." When Jason said nothing, Sikes quietly left the room, shutting the door behind him.

Lauren was puzzled by Sikes's apology, but more puzzled that Jason had stayed behind. She hadn't thought he would even speak to her. Indeed, he didn't seem to be finding any joy in her company, for he had moved over to the window and was standing with his back to her, his palms facedown on the sill as he stared down at the tiny garden below.

They might have been total strangers, so great was the gulf between them. Lauren felt she had to break the terrible silence. "What . . . what happens . . . now?"

There was a long pause before Jason replied. "Regina has been arrested and charged with murder. Based on your statement, I have no doubt she will be convicted."

"What did Sikes mean? What should you have told me?"

As if the entire subject was wearisome, Jason gave a deep sigh. "It was my idea to force Regina's hand. I devised the entire plan. Regina was sure to be angry when she recognized you and realized that she'd been tricked. I had hoped she would let something slip, though I never expected to get results so quickly or so decisively."

There was another long silence while Lauren registered the significance of his confession. Then her breath caught in a gasp, and she stared at Jason's broad back, stunned. "You knew," she whispered. "All this time you knew I wasn't Andrea."

She hardly saw his slight nod. "Burroughs told me long ago," Jason said quietly. "He also told me of his suspicions concerning Regina—about her involvement with the Carlins' deaths and her murder of the Foster woman. I presented what evidence we had against Regina to Sir John, but he could do nothing without more definite proof. When I found you in New Orleans, I wrote to him, and he sent Ned Sikes over. You didn't realize it, but Ned was keeping an eye on you, just in case Regina had heard of your whereabouts. Alive, you . . . Andrea posed a threat to her, or an opportunity."

When Lauren remained speechless, Jason brought a hand up to rub his forehead in a weary gesture. "As soon as we reached England, Sikes went to Regina with word of your return, hinting that you might not be Andrea. She guessed your identity, then, as I suspected she would, and couldn't resist the temptation to make another bid for the Carlin Line. From there, it was only a matter of baiting the trap and staying on top of the situation."

"Then I was the 'bait'," Lauren observed dazedly. All she could think of was how afraid she had been that Jason would discover the truth, how terrified she had been of losing him because of her deception. She could have been spared that fear, had Jason been more honest with her. But he had manipulated her, made her a pawn in his games, just the way Burroughs had done. Jason had tricked her again, just as he had when he had married her. But perhaps that had been his true motive in wedding her.

Lauren felt her throat constrict. "You needed me to come to England," she concluded in a shaking voice. "Is that why you married me, then?" When Jason didn't answer, Lauren added bitterly, "How clever you are. Now all the loose ends are neatly tied, except for me—"

"It isn't finished yet," Jason said quietly. "Rafael is still free."

Lauren clenched her hands together, her knuckles showing white. "Oh, yes. Your promise. I suppose you also told Burroughs you would see that Regina was punished. Did you promise to take care of me, as well?"

"I pledged to do what I could to protect you, yes."

"How well you succeeded!"

Jason spun around, pinning her with his fierce gaze. "That is quite enough, Lauren! I should have given you some indication of my plans, yes, but I counted on you to have more faith in me. Certainly I never thought you would leave without a word. Though I see now I should have expected it of you. You've let fear rule your life so long that you couldn't hope to stand up to someone like Regina."

Lauren tried not to flinch at the fury in his voice as she returned his gaze. "It wasn't only Regina I feared. I . . . I thought I would be sent to prison for impersonating Andrea."

"You thought *what?*" Jason's face darkened thunderously, but then he seemed to recollect himself, for he relaxed his clenched fists. "That's why you ran? Because you were afraid of going to prison?"

"In part. I also . . . wanted to spare you a scandal. Can't you picture the story in the papers? A marchioness in Newgate. A bastard marchioness, no less."

"Damn it, Lauren, you aren't a bastard! You never were." When Lauren stared at him, Jason ran a hand distractedly through his hair. "Your parents' marriage was entirely legal. Jonathan managed to conceal it, though, by removing a page from the church register. Burroughs found the page hidden among Jonathan's personal effects after his death, along with his marriage lines and a will naming you as his sole beneficiary."

"But that . . . that is why I was going to Ormskirk. To see if I could find proof that my parents' marriage was valid."

Jason took a step towards her, his hands spread in supplication. "You couldn't have come to me, could you? You couldn't have trusted me to help you?"

Lauren had dreaded seeing his contempt and hatred, but this was far worse: a look of bleak despair filled Jason's eyes, a look of raw, primitive grief. He was suffering as much as she. "I couldn't," she said at last, wishing she could erase his pain, "take the risk of going to prison. I had our child to think of."

Jason's voice dropped to such a low pitch that Lauren had to strain to catch his words. "Did it never *once* occur to you that I would have torn Regina apart with my bare hands before I let her harm you . . . or our child?"

The anguish in his eyes was too much for Lauren to bear. Tears scalded her cheeks as she dropped her gaze to her lap.

Jason turned away abruptly, returning to his place at the window. "I wish you would tell me how you ever thought I would let anyone take you to prison. Even if you had done anything to warrant it."

"You couldn't have prevented it," Lauren said in a dull voice. "Not if they chose to arrest me. We aren't truly married. The marriage ceremony wasn't legal. You married Andrea Carlin."

"Our child would have been born a bastard like you," Jason returned harshly. "Is that what you're saying?"

Lauren winced. "That isn't what I meant. But yes, that would have been true if . . ." She couldn't bring herself to add, "if our child had lived." The pain was too fresh to speak of it.

Jason, too, seemed desirous of avoiding the subject, for he shrugged wearily. "It hardly matters now, does it?"

"No, it doesn't matter . . . now."

There was another pause. Tears were streaming silently

418

down Lauren's cheeks, but the only indication that Jason knew was the tenseness of his body.

Finally he took a deep breath and turned to face her. "Well, I'm afraid at the moment I don't have the time to settle the issue of our marriage. The *Capricorn* is sailing in a few days, and I'm needed in London. We can discuss our future when I return." When at length Lauren gave a faint nod, Jason forced himself to let out his breath. "I thought I would leave this afternoon, since you seem to be recovering your health."

She nodded again, her voice too choked even to wish him Godspeed.

Without another word, Jason moved to the door. He had one hand on the latch when Lauren called his name in a hoarse whisper.

"Yes?" he replied, not turning.

Lauren looked at him, seeing him through a blur of tears. She had to know the answer to one question. "Why?" she asked wretchedly. "Why didn't you tell me that you knew I wasn't Andrea?"

"Why did you keep the truth from me?" Jason returned in that cold stranger's voice. Then he bent his head, as if racked by despair. "I suppose I wanted you to tell me of your own volition," he said softly. "It would have meant that you had at last come to trust me."

Lauren could find nothing to say to that. Turning her face away, she bit her lip to keep from sobbing.

A moment later she heard the soft click of the latch as the door closed behind him.

Chapter Twenty-Six

It was several days before Lauren regained enough strength to rise from her bed for more than a few minutes at a time. Then, at the urging of Lady Agatha, she spent the afternoons in the inn's lovely garden. Yet even surrounded by roses and forget-me-nots and flaming lupin, Lauren couldn't seem to shake her listlessness; despondency weighed her down like a sodden cloak.

She didn't cry. The pain cut too deeply for tears. But not even Lady Agatha's assurances could raise her spirits. When Lauren had confessed the entire tale, adding that Jason wouldn't forgive her for losing his child, Agatha had airily waved a hand. "Of course he will," the elderly lady declared firmly. "Men never see children in the same light as women do. To men, children are simply heirs. Jason is bound to get over it, since you can still breed."

Knowing his love of children, Lauren was doubtful. Her fall had been an accident, one not entirely of her own making, but there was no denying it never would have occurred had she trusted Jason as she should have. She had hurt him terribly, possibly enough to destroy any love he had felt for her.

If indeed he had ever felt any. Lauren was half convinced that his reasons for marrying her had little to do with love. He had wanted the Carlin Line, certainly. And if her father truly had left a will naming her his heir, then she was the legitimate owner. There would be no one to challenge her claim to the Carlin fortune now, either. Jason had effectively and legally removed Regina from contention, ensuring that at the very least the woman would go to prison. She might even hang for her crimes.

There were other possible motives for Jason's marrying her, as well, Lauren knew—motives that were nearly as compelling as the Carlin ships. For one, Jason had promised Burroughs to see to her future. For another, he had needed her in England to help expose Regina as a murderer. And he had wanted an heir.

He could only gain those objectives, however, if they actually were married, which was why she was puzzled by the marriage lines he had shown her naming Andrea Carlin as his bride. Jason was too clever to allow any serious oversights in his plans.

But married or not, Lauren despaired of ever being able to regain his love. Jason had been right, she reflected, remembering his manner of leave-taking. She had been letting fear rule her life. And not just her fear of confinement. More damning was her fear of trusting him. She had been afraid to truly love him, to expose herself to hurt and pain, to let herself become vulnerable the way her mother had been.

Thinking back on her past relationship with Jason, she remembered all the times he seemed to be able to read her mind, all the times he seemed to be waiting for a certain response from her. He had been waiting, she realized now. Waiting for her to take the first step.

And during those long, lonely days of recuperation, it dawned on Lauren that if she was ever to be given a chance to win Jason's love back, she would have to overcome her fear—beginning with her phobia. It was this conviction that made Lauren decide to go to Carlin House rather than return to London or remove to Effing Hall in Kent as Jason had suggested.

Her decision distressed Lady Agatha. The elderly lady had just been congratulating herself of the success of her charge's recovery, but upon hearing of Lauren's plan, Agatha vowed that she would *not* be dragged off to heathenish Cornwall and that Lauren *absolutely* could not go alone.

"I shall go, Aunt," Lauren insisted in a tone that Lila would have instantly recognized as unshakable determination. "My sister was never given a proper burial. It is something I must do." *And there is something else I must do,* Lauren added only to herself, not wanting to worry Lady Agatha unduly.

Despite the protests and threats voiced by Lady Agatha, Lauren remained adamant, and when she had sufficiently recovered her health, she set out for Cornwall with Agatha and Molly in tow.

Seeing Carlin House again was like stepping back into a nightmare. Lauren found that time hadn't made her lose her hatred of the place. Nor had time wrought many changes to the estate. Although the furniture was swathed in Holland covers and the grounds showed signs of neglect, the elderly couple who acted as caretakers had kept the house in good repair. They had prepared bedchambers, having been advised of Lady Effing's arrival, but Lauren made a change in the arrangements, requesting her old room instead of the master suite, meaning to take her experiment to the fullest.

Since it was late in the afternoon when they arrived, Lauren was unable to put the rest of her plan in action. She went to bed, intending to visit the graveyard first thing in the morning.

Under the circumstances, it wasn't surprising that she dreamed her usual terrible dream. Yet this time the images seemed clearer than ever: a woman was screaming, while a man was laughing evilly. He was holding something long and dark in his hand, and as he moved toward Lauren, she heard the voice shrieking for her to run.

He was still chasing her when Lauren woke herself up with her own cries, shaking with fright and wishing fervently that she had brought Ulysses with her. The only way she was able to go back to sleep was to leave a candle burning.

In the morning, Lady Agatha offered to accompany her to the cemetery, although admitting an aversion to graveyards. Lauren politely declined. She wanted to go alone, for this was to be a time for burying her past, as well as one for honoring the dead.

The iron gate shrieked in protest as it swung open before her. Clutching the bunch of wildflowers she had gathered along the way, Lauren stepped inside the walled square.

She was surprised to see that this small area of ground

had been better maintained than the rest of the estate. The grass had been regularly scythed and weeded, and although there were no trees or shrubbery to relieve the stark bareness, the atmosphere was unmistakably peaceful. Lauren's slippers made no sound as she made her way along the narrow aisle to the far wall. There, she knew, was where Andrea had been buried.

When she reached the grave, she was puzzled to see a headstone where none had been before. It appeared to have been recently set, for the earth was disturbed at the base, and the stone was clean and unweathered. Kneeling beside the grassy mound, Lauren's eyes widened as she read the simple inscription. The name "Andrea Carlin", along with the dates of her birth and death, had been carved on the headstone.

So her poor little half sister had been properly laid to rest after all, Lauren thought with a tearful smile. It must have been Jason's doing, another of his promises to George Burroughs.

Giving a short prayer, Lauren laid a spray of goldenrod and Queen Anne's lace on her sister's grave, then wandered slowly around the small cemetery. More flowers went for Sibyl Foster, and for the graves of Jonathan and Mary Carlin, and when finally Lauren moved on, she made another revelation: George Burroughs had been buried beside his sister Mary.

Lauren hesitated a long moment before she knelt beside his grave. She no longer felt such intense hatred for Burroughs, but she found it hard to forgive him. All those years he had let her think she was a bastard, a criminal. And more unforgivably, he had allowed her mother to suffer needlessly. Elizabeth DeVries had died in great pain, unable to afford the simple comforts the Carlin wealth could so easily have provided.

It was a long moment before Lauren bowed her head and said the same words of prayer as she had for all the others, and longer still before she placed the remaining wildflowers on George Burroughs's grave. But when she stood once again, she felt as if some inexplicable burden had been lifted from her heart. It was as if a hard knot inside her had suddenly become unraveled after a great many years.

The other task she had set for herself was more difficult,

423

physically if not emotionally. As she stood on the clifftop overlooking the cove, Lauren doubtfully eyed the jagged rocks and white-tipped breakers below. Not only was she out of practice in climbing cliffs, she could well imagine the scolding she would get from Jason were she foolish enough to attempt the dangerous descent wearing slippers and long skirts. And even if Jason agreed with her intent, he wouldn't want her to attempt the cave by this approach. Nor would he want her to go alone.

As she turned away to begin the trek back to the house, Lauren couldn't repress a bitter smile. How ironic that Jason should suddenly become the voice of her conscience, now, when she might have lost him forever.

It was also ironic to be able to command the few servants at Carlin House to do her bidding. Being the titled mistress of the manor, rather than the ward and near prisoner of a man with an obsessive drive for revenge, had its advantages. Lauren was able to secure the services of the caretaker's brawny son with very little persuasion.

Together they gathered up the items she specified, then descended a flagged stairway to the wine cellar. At Lauren's direction, the lad began chipping away at the plaster of one wall, and in a short while, he had carved out a hole big enough to walk through. It was only then that Lauren ran into any opposition, for when Lady Agatha heard the pounding, she came below to investigate its source.

Alarmed to find a half dozen lamps scattered about the dank cellar, Agatha demanded to be told at once what was going on. All the lamps were lit, making it nearly as bright as day, for in spite of Lauren's determination to test her courage in the cave, she hadn't thought herself quite ready to face the darkness.

By the time Lady Agatha demanded that Lauren stop whatever nonsense she was up to, though, Lauren was too determined to quit. Trembling, she picked up one of the lanterns and moved slowly toward the newly made narrow gap in the wall. Then holding the lantern high, Lauren took a deep, deep breath and cautiously stepped over the debris into the tunnel.

She was disappointed with the results of her experiment.

Absolutely nothing happened. The sloping tunnel of roughly hewn rock didn't frighten her in the least.

She wondered if perhaps the amount of light had something to do with it, but when she extinguished the lantern, she didn't feel at all faint. Nor did she freeze with terror or show any of the usual symptoms of her phobia. Not even when she asked the caretaker's son to cover the opening behind her did she feel the slightest unease. Being shut up in a dark tunnel no longer seemed to bother her. It was the same when the seal to the giant cave was broken and the process was repeated.

Frowning, Lauren at last retraced her steps through the tunnel. As she emerged from the cellar, though, she noticed the queer way Lady Agatha was observing her. "I haven't gone mad, I assure you," Lauren said wryly, before explaining about the fear that had haunted her all her life. "Jason suggested that if I could remember whatever originally caused my fear, I might be able to overcome it. But now it seems to be gone, without any effort on my part at all." Lauren sighed. "I had hoped otherwise. I wanted to show Jason that I could face my fear, that I wouldn't permit it to rule my life any longer. Then perhaps he would think more highly of me . . . or at least he might not despise me quite so much."

Lady Agatha wagged her finger under Lauren's nose. "Jason doesn't despise you, girl. He was upset over the babe, yes, but he was far more worried about losing you. When you were ill, he wouldn't leave your side for more than a moment. Just the slightest change in your breathing sent him into a frenzy. A man doesn't act that way toward his wife unless he loves her."

Remembering their bitter parting, Lauren sighed again. "I'm not even certain I am his wife."

"Nonsense!" Agatha said emphatically. "Of course you're his wife. I introduced you as Lady Effing at my rout, didn't I? Jason would never play such a shabby trick on me. And if there is a problem with your marriage lines, I'm certain it can all be rectified with another ceremony. Come to think of it, it might not be such a bad thing after all for you to be married again. No havey-cavey shipboard romance this time, but a proper wedding at St. George's in Hanover Square, with all the ton in attendance. Come now, my dear," Lady Agatha added when

425

Lauren wouldn't be cheered. "A man can't shed a wife like he can a coat. Besides, Jason would have to deal with me first, and I'm still young enough to hold my own in a skirmish with him. He knows I won't stand for that sort of nonsense, even if he wanted to be rid of you—which he doesn't."

"I wish I could believe that," Lauren said faintly. "How I wish I could."

Chapter Twenty-Seven

"A message for you, milady. Delivered by the cabin boy of the *Capricorn.*"

Startled by Morrow's announcement, Lauren lifted her head abruptly. Her sudden, sharp intake of breath echoed in the silence of the elegant parlor. She had been sitting there for hours, ever since she learned that the *Capricorn* had dropped anchor, and her spirits had grown more and more despondent during the interval. With each successive moment that she awaited Jason's arrival, the conviction that he hadn't been able to forgive her became stronger. Now she prayed that he was writing merely to say he had been delayed.

Lauren's hand trembled as she reached for the missive. It was a single sheet of folded vellum, sealed by a plain wafer. When she recognized the handwriting, however, the flicker of hope that had shone so briefly in her eyes died away completely. *He cannot bear to see me,* Lauren thought as numbing weariness engulfed her once more. Absently, she dismissed the butler.

For a long moment she sat perfectly still, staring blindly at the proof of Jason's condemnation. She had hoped he would at least give her a chance to plead her case. But he hadn't come. He hadn't even written. He had left the task to Kyle.

At last she broke the seal and mechanically began to read Kyle's message:

Lady Effing: Jason asked me to write in order to set

your mind at ease. Our mission was an unqualified success, I am pleased to report. The British fleet under Lord Exmouth was victorious, as was your husband. Jason accomplished his self-imposed task with more compassion than I would have shown. His words upon the occasion, as I recall, were "Thank God, it is at last finished."

Allow me, please, to express the hope that he is right. Indeed it is presumptuous of me to say so, but I sincerely trust the troubles of the past can be properly buried. Jason is well, at least in body if not in spirit. He has not made his plans known to me, but I venture to guess he will remain on board the *Capricorn* this evening. I presume again when I urge you to make the first overture. It is my belief that Jason blames himself for what happened—

Letting the letter flutter noiselessly to the carpet, Lauren pressed a trembling hand to her brow. She couldn't accept Kyle's well-meant advice. Jason blamed not himself, but her, for the loss of their child. She had been the one to destroy whatever hope for happiness they might have shared.

Bowing her head, Lauren clasped her hands tightly in her lap. Jason was thinking of her, she could feel it. She closed her eyes, remembering what it had been like to experience his love. . . .

It was only when a maid came in to light the lamps and stir the coals in the grate that Lauren realized how late it had grown. She shivered in spite of the fire, yet it wasn't the September chill which made her feel cold. It was knowing she would never feel the warmth of Jason's arms around her again.

Forcing her numb limbs to move, Lauren rose from her chair and slowly made her way upstairs to pack. She wouldn't wait for Jason to ask her to leave his house.

After her visit to Carlin House, she had come to London to await his return from the Mediterranean. She had persuaded an urchin down at the docks to send word the moment the *Capricorn* was sighted on the Thames, but more than six weeks had passed while she worried about what might have befallen

Jason and his crew. Two events occurred in the meantime.

The first and most shocking was that Regina Carlin had hung herself in her cell. Lauren had visited her aunt once at the prison, but Regina had greeted her with such hostility, cursing Jonathan Carlin and his bastard daughter with such vehemence that Lauren had never ventured there again. She could feel pity for the embittered old woman, though, and sorrow. Regina never had admitted any remorse for killing the innocent people who had gotten in her way. Perhaps her end was only fitting after all, Lauren thought when she learned of her aunt's death. And at least Jason's family had been spared the trauma of an explosive scandal. The case would never be brought to trial now.

The second event of note was that Lauren turned twenty-one. She was astounded when Jason's solicitors called on the very day of her birthday, bringing with them some documents for her to sign. To her dismay, the papers not only dissolved the trust set out in Jonathan Carlin's will for his daughter Lauren Carlin, but gave her full ownership of the Carlin Line, including the share previously owned by George Burroughs.

Although the lawyers called the transaction a mere formality, they were rather unhappy when Lauren refused to sign anything until her husband returned. But the ships had to be turned over to her, they exclaimed. Lord Effing had ordered it so, and no one would dare dream of defying his lordship's wishes. They begged her to reconsider.

The man in charge of the London branch of the Line, a Mr. Pierce, added his pleas also, but Lauren remained adamant. She was determined not to do anything until she had spoken personally with Jason.

Yet now he was denying her the opportunity even to see him, Lauren thought dismally as she searched her wardrobe for the clothes she would take. Her breath caught on a sob. How could she decide what to wear when she didn't even know where she would be going? And how could she consider something so unimportant when her heart was breaking?

It was foolish to cry, though, for tears wouldn't bring Jason's love back. Besides, she had few tears left. Brushing away the telltale moisture from her eyes, Lauren reached for her gray silk mantle.

Then her hand wavered.

She was running away again, she realized with a sense of shock. Again she was leaving without facing her problems. And not only that, she reflected, but even if Jason didn't want her, he would deem it necessary to provide her with funds and make arrangements for her safe travel. She could see him one more time, if only to tell him that she was going away. . . . And perhaps if she could speak to him then, she could persuade him to let her stay with him, if not as his wife, then as his mistress. She might never earn his forgiveness, might never have another chance to be deserving of his love. But at least she could fight for what she wanted, rather than leave before defeat was absolutely certain.

The lethargy that had gripped Lauren fled, and within minutes, the Effing carriage was speeding through the narrow, cobbled streets of London, conveying her to the London Dock where the *Capricorn* was riding anchor.

By the time the coach slowed to a stop before the gate of the great wall, Lauren's heart was hammering. She dismounted, then shivered as a chill mist enveloped her. Except for the chill, she could almost imagine that the clock had been turned back. Once more she was a frightened sixteen-year-old trying to find a ship to take her to America. Her guardian's men had nearly caught her, but then Jason had rescued her. . . .

"Do ye wish me to accompany you, m'lady?"

With a start, Lauren realized that the coachman was asking if she wanted his escort. Shaking her head, she declined and bade him wait. She hadn't yet decided what she would say to Jason, but she wanted their meeting to be private. She spoke to the Thames police constable who was guarding the gate, then slipped inside, and made her way down the stone steps to the quay. Seeing the shadowy form of the *Capricorn* looming through fog, Lauren moved toward it slowly, almost fearfully.

She would never have guessed that the clock had been turned back for Jason, too. On board the sloop, he stood at the railing, delaying his departure, just as he had several years before. But this time it was because he was reluctant to face Lauren. Kyle's supposition had been accurate: Jason did blame himself for the loss of their child.

A hundred times he had gone over in his mind the actions he could have taken to prevent what had happened—and he was doing so again now. It all came back to his lack of judgment, Jason concluded bitterly. He had wanted Lauren to need him, to trust him. He had been determined to test her love. But he had unfairly asked her to overcome by herself a force she couldn't control. He should have been honest with her from the start. He should have shown more support. He should have *helped* her instead of requiring her to face her fears alone.

He was desperately afraid that Lauren wouldn't forgive him. And more than anything, he dreaded that she might not want to remain his wife. She had never wanted to marry him in the first place, he reminded himself. If she wanted to dissolve their marriage now, he had no right to stand in her way. But would he be able to live without her?

The faint sound of footsteps interrupted Jason's despairing thoughts. Alert now, he let his gaze sweep the dim wharf below, but he couldn't see much beyond stacks of tarred crates and barrels. A concealing fog had drifted in from the river, momentarily obscuring whoever was approaching. But then Lauren materialized from the curling mist, and Jason sucked in his breath.

Even from a distance she aroused him. The wharf was illuminated only by the *Capricorn*'s deck lantern, but the glow of her beautiful face lit up the night for him as surely as any flame. Her figure was enveloped in a mantle of dark gray, her hair hidden by a concealing hood, but Jason had no trouble recalling what lay beneath, from the ripe curves of her body to the shimmering golden hair. How easily he could remember the silken feel of those luxurious tresses, the taste of her skin, the joy of having her writhe beneath him. . . .

Closing his eyes, Jason groaned. For weeks now he had been tortured by visions of Lauren, by the thought of losing her. It seemed now that he had wanted her so badly, his mind had conjured up her image. This wasn't really Lauren he was seeing. He was dreaming.

Her steps faltered, and as she stood looking up at him uncertainly, Jason moved toward her in a daze, not even conscious of his action.

It was with a sense of shock that he realized his dream was real, that Lauren truly was standing there on the wharf below. And in spite of the fierce urge to sweep her into his arms, Jason felt his anger rise. She had come down to the docks alone, without protection. Anything could have happened to her.

Bounding down the gangplank and up the quay's stone steps, Jason came to an abrupt halt before her and stood glaring down at Lauren, trying to control the urge to throttle her for her foolishness. His tone was harsh and forbidding, rather than propitiatory as he had intended. "What," he growled ominously, "in the sweet love of heaven are you doing here?"

Lauren was taken aback by his hostile reception. Her brave resolution to beard the lion in his den fled instantly, and when she opened her mouth, she found her throat too dry to allow speech.

"Answer me, Lauren! What do you mean by coming here at night, alone. Are you trying to get yourself killed?"

"I—I wanted to t-talk to you. But I . . . I'm not alone. I came in the carriage."

Jason breathed a sigh of relief as he scanned the darkness beyond her. "Where is it?" he asked more calmly. When Lauren stammered a reply, he took her by the arm. "Come, we can't discuss anything standing here. I'll take you home."

Meekly Lauren obeyed, but she kept her eyes trained on the ground, afraid that a glance at Jason might reveal the grim-faced stranger she so dreaded. The walk was accomplished in strained silence.

Jason handed Lauren into the coach and took the seat across from her. He could see her clearly, for a small lamp illuminated the interior of the carriage and the hood of her mantle had fallen away to reveal her face. He couldn't tell what Lauren was thinking, though, since she wouldn't meet his eyes. She sat with her head bowed, her hands clasped tightly in her lap.

He waited till the horses were moving before he said quietly, "Well? You wished to speak to me?"

Lauren continued to avoid his gaze. "Yes," she said shakily. "About . . . about our marriage." Jason could feel every muscle in his body clench, but he said nothing. Lauren bit her

432

lip. "Lady Agatha suggested . . . that we have another ceremony if the first one wasn't legal. But it . . . it isn't necessary."

Jason found it hard to breathe. A tight band seemed to be squeezing the air from his lungs. "You want me to release you from our marriage, is that it?" he heard himself say.

Lauren hesitated, twisting her hands in her lap. She was finding this even harder than she had expected. But then she reminded herself what was at stake. Digging her nails into her palms, she took a deep breath and spoke in a rush. "No, I don't want you to release me. I'm trying to tell you that you don't have to marry me if you don't want to. I don't want the Carlin ships, either. If there are some papers I can sign so that no one will ever question your right to them, I'll sign. Just please don't send me away, Jason. I'll go down on my knees and beg, if you want me to, but—"

"Stop, it Lauren," Jason said in a strangled voice. "Don't say any more."

She raised pleading eyes to him, choking back a sob with effort. "Please, please, Jason. Just give me another chance. I promise, I'll never—"

"Oh, God," Jason groaned. In a single, swift motion he pulled Lauren into his arms and held her as if he would never let her go. "I thought you wanted to leave me," he whispered hoarsely against her hair.

"No, I—" she began, but her words were cut off as Jason's lips found hers.

Indeed, this wasn't the time for words, Lauren thought vaguely as she clung to him. She needed the physical reassurance of his arms, needed to touch him, to feel the hungry passion in his kisses. The fierce possessiveness of his embrace said everything she wanted to know, and more.

"God, how I missed you," Jason vowed when he at last drew his mouth away. He relaxed his crushing grip, though he didn't release her entirely.

Trembling with desire and relief, Lauren rested her head on his shoulder. "Can you ever forgive me?" she whispered.

Jason pressed his lips against her smooth brow. "For what, sweetheart?"

"For . . . losing our child."

"But it wasn't your fault, my darling. It was mine."

Lauren lifted her head to stare at him. "Yours? How can you say that?"

Holding her away from him, Jason gazed intently into her eyes. "I should have told you from the beginning that I knew who you were. If I had confided my plans, your fall never would have occurred. I won't even ask your forgiveness, for I don't deserve it."

"Jason, that isn't true! Besides, if I hadn't been afraid to trust you, my fall never would have happened, as well. I know now how wrong I was. And I think I've learned to control my fear of confinement. I'm not afraid of being shut up, anymore." Leaning over, Lauren extinguished the lamp, immersing them in total darkness. "See? And I haven't been troubled by nightmares."

With the light out, Jason suddenly realized what he hadn't noted before; both the shades and windows were shut tight. Lauren showed no signs of panic or debilitating fear, though. In fact, she seemed quite content to curl herself against him once more.

When she threaded her arms around his neck and lifted her face to be kissed, Jason quite willingly obliged. His mouth slanted across hers, his tongue delving deeply to drink her sweetness, while his hand unerringly found the curve of her breast beneath the mantle. He stroked her nipple slowly, exciting it to a diamond-hard point, yet when Lauren strained against him, Jason forced himself to break away.

Lauren misunderstood his withdrawal. "I can still bear children, Jason," she murmured, wanting to reassure him that she had completely recovered her health.

Her naturally husky voice sent a stab of desire racing through Jason's loins, making him shift uncomfortably. He very much wanted to continue what he had begun, but her ardent response had taunted him nearly beyond endurance. Already his arousal was so strong that he feared he might lose control of himself and take Lauren right there on the carriage seat.

Trying to divert his mind from what her soft body was doing to him, Jason eased himself from her embrace and busied himself with relighting the carriage lamp. "I know about the children," he replied almost absently.

Lauren's brows drew together. "But how could you?"

"The doctor who attended you told me before I sailed that there was no evidence of permanent damage from your miscarriage. And a letter from Aunt Agatha was waiting for me this morning when I arrived. She said you had seen a London physician who confirmed that opinion."

"Never say you asked your aunt to spy on me!" Lauren regarded Jason indignantly, affronted by the idea that she required watching.

He put a finger to her lips. "Agatha merely felt it her duty to report on your health," he soothed. Feeling the impact of even that small contact, though, Jason let his hand drop back to his side. What he really wanted was to take Lauren in his arms again and kiss the enchanting pout from her mouth, but the lack of privacy was a deterrent to anything further. Too, Jason realized the necessity of giving her some long-delayed explanations. He drew a steadying breath. "I suppose," he began hesitantly, "that our children should have my name."

Lauren instantly forgot her vexation. "Then you will marry me?"

Hearing the anxious note in her voice, Jason gave her a somewhat rueful smile. "We've always been married, sweetheart. As I told you then, the ceremony was perfectly legal. Everything just as it should have been—except that you were drunk. You just don't remember much of what happened that night. I must say, my love, you don't hold your liquor at all well."

Lauren frowned. "But the document you showed me. . . . It was signed Andrea Carlin."

"A forgery, I'm ashamed to admit. You married me as Lauren Carlin, as you would have known had you checked the *Siren*'s log."

She stared at him, her gold-flecked eyes wide with bewilderment. "But *why?*"

"Why the forgery?" Taking Lauren's gloved hand in his, Jason carried it to his lips. "At the time I thought I might need it to deal with Regina. And I also thought by showing it to you,

you might confess who you were." He held her palm against his cheek, holding her gaze as well. "Instead, I drove you further away."

The remorse in his tone made Lauren's heart turn over. She wanted to reassure him, to tell that she had loved him in spite of her fear of trusting in him, but the coach drew to a halt. Knowing their conversation would be overheard by the servants, Lauren withheld her comments and allowed Jason to help her down. When she saw him glance uncertainly at the house, she asked somewhat worriedly, "You will stay, won't you?"

The teasing grin he flashed her was more reflective of the Jason Lauren knew. "Of course—if I'm invited."

"You don't need an invitation to stay in your own house," she returned in an exasperated undertone.

It was some time before she had further opportunity for private conversation with him. Morrow, of course, was stationed in the foyer to receive their outer garments, and Jason was required to acknowledge the butler's polite greeting. Then Lauren had to wait impatiently while her husband spoke pleasantly to the housekeeper and the third footman. She dismissed all the servants then, but when Lady Agatha swept regally down the stairs, demanding an account of what her scapegrace nephew had been up to, Lauren had had enough.

She waited till the elderly lady had proffered her slightly withered cheek for Jason to kiss before interrupting the fond exchange between aunt and nephew. "Aunt Agatha, I'm sure you will excuse Jason until tomorrow. He is so very tired after his long voyage."

Jason raised an amused eyebrow as he met Lauren's gaze. "Oh, yes, *exhausted*," he agreed blandly.

The knowing gleam in his blue eyes made Lauren flush with warmth, but fortunately, Lady Agatha required no more falsehoods to understand their wish to be alone. After extracting a promise from Jason to tell her all about his adventure in the morning, the elderly lady took herself off to bed.

When his aunt mounted the stairs and disappeared around the corner, Jason slipped an arm around Lauren's waist.

"Well, wife?" he murmured, bending to brush her earlobe with his lips. "Am I too tired to make love to you?"

Lauren's blush deepened, but she ignored his teasing. "Kyle said you meant to spend the night on board the ship," she remarked as she led the way upstairs.

"With you so close?" He seemed to be fascinated by the curl at the nape of her neck, for he wouldn't leave off kissing it.

"Then why didn't you come? For the past nine hours, I've been imagining that you hated me, that I might never see you again."

"I was just leaving the ship to come here when you arrived at the docks. And, if you must know, I was trying to get up enough courage to face you, to find the nerve to beg your forgiveness."

"But none of it was your fault," Lauren insisted. "I never blamed you."

Jason shut the door to his bedroom behind them and immediately began to remove the pins from Lauren's hair. "Perhaps not, but I blamed myself. And I was desperately afraid you might want out of our marriage. *I* spent the last nine hours trying to think of logical arguments I could use to convince you to stay with me." Tossing aside the last pin, he loosened her hair from its elegant coil and spread the golden mass about Lauren's shoulders, then gently drew her into his arms. "Now I remember but one," he whispered, holding her gaze. "That I love you, that I've always loved you."

Dazzled by the compelling light in his blue eyes, Lauren looked up at Jason searchingly. His gaze was filled with tenderness and love, leaving no room for doubt. She knew his love was mirrored in her own eyes.

"I think that is a perfect reason," she returned softly, sliding her arms up to encircle his neck.

When he bent her head and brushed her lips, Lauren curled her fingers in his thick chestnut hair, anticipating a passionate kiss, but Jason only allowed himself a brief taste of her mouth. Determined to go slowly this time, he drew away, controlling the pace.

Leisurely, one by one, he removed each of Lauren's garments till she was standing naked before him. Then

437

stepping back, he drank in the sight, his eyes moving slowly over her curving beauty, admiring every facet of it.

His warm perusal set Lauren's pulses throbbing, but she no longer felt impatience. She was suspended with Jason in an exquisite, private time, and like him, she wanted to savor it, to draw out the moment.

She helped him undress, letting her fingers roam over his sleek, muscular torso as he shrugged off his shirt, delighting in the knowledge that he was hers to touch, to find pleasure in. And when his other clothes followed, her heartbeat quickened. The breathtaking impact of his tall, powerful body, his flat, hard belly and lean hips, his proud, swollen erection, made her feel warm and weak all over.

Jason came to her then, and drew her against his magnificent length, the shock of his heated, bare skin making her shiver. His eyes locked with Lauren's for a long moment, before he bent his head again. His mouth was gentle, his kiss as light as gossamer, but his breath was hot against her lips, and she could feel the explosive power he held in check. With exquisite slowness, he traced her lips with his tongue, then parted them, seeking out the secrets hidden to him. The heady invasion aroused a deep pulse of pleasure in Lauren, making her senses spin.

By the time he led her to the bed, she was quivering with desire. But still Jason refused to rush the moment. He pressed her down, then lay beside her, and began to move his roughened palm gently over her body, softly stroking. Her breaths came more quickly under his skilled ministrations, and the ragged sound could be heard in the silence of the room. When he cupped her breast in his hand, bending to kiss the aroused peak and flick it with his tongue, Lauren whimpered. "Jason, please," she pleaded, trying to pull him closer.

"Not yet, my love," he said with a smile. The hoarseness of his whisper told Lauren how very close he was to losing control, but he maintained a tight rein on his desire as his lips nibbled a tortuous path down her body. His hand moved slowly along her slender thigh, then urged her to open for him.

He fondled her intimately, while Lauren's body grew taut with uncontrollable excitement. When his kisses moved lower, and his breath whispered against the golden curls below her abdomen, she gripped Jason's tawny hair and again begged him to take her.

But his caressing tongue had found the center of her passion. Holding Lauren's writhing hips still, Jason lapped at her slowly, like a contented cat licking cream. The sweet torture was unbearable, and when his tongue gently penetrated her, Lauren's passion exploded. She floated high above him, gliding ever so slowly.

Only then did Jason stretch out to slide deep within her, renewing his claim on the moist, inner reaches of her body. Kissing her flushed cheeks, he waited till Lauren opened her magnificent amber-green eyes. "Take me deeper, sweetheart."

"Yes," she gasped, trembling as Jason filled her completely with his rigid fullness. Then her eyes glazed over again with passion as he began to move his hips with a slow, deliberately escalating rhythm.

His tantalizing thrusts unleashed yet another sweeping wave of desire in Lauren, but the limits of Jason's endurance were exceeded, as well. His hands slid under her to pull her up fiercely, while his sweat-slick body clenched and contracted, raking her, his shudders violent enough to make him cry out her name, before he finally collapsed, his passion at last spent.

It was some time later before he could find the energy to lift his weight from her. Lauren's arms were wrapped around his neck, though, and she wouldn't let him go.

Jason managed to roll on his side, facing her. "Now I truly am exhausted," he chuckled, letting his eyes close.

Curling against his damp, sinewy body, Lauren sighed with contentment. She had almost dozed off when her stomach began an insistent clamoring. "Jason?"

"Hmmm?" he responded drowsily.

"I'm afraid I'm hungry."

"Give me another minute and I'll try to satisfy your insatiable appetite."

"That isn't what I meant," she returned wryly. "I really am starving. I haven't had anything to eat today. I was too worried."

Prying open one eyelid, Jason regarded her with a baleful

glare. "I told Aunt Agatha to take better care of you than that."

"It wasn't her fault. She did try, several times."

Lauren got out of bed and retrieved a filmy peignor from the armoire. Watching her, Jason sat up, fully awake now. "Where are you going?"

"To the kitchens to find something to eat. Would you like me to bring you anything?"

"No, I'm coming with you. I haven't been eating too well lately either. Besides"—Jason grinned a mischievous little-boy grin—"I know where Cook keeps the scones."

Hand in hand, unsuccessfully smothering their laughter, they made their way downstairs to the kitchen. Jason found enough food to feed an entire ship's crew, and shortly he and Lauren were seated at the wooden table, enjoying cold pheasant, leftover kidney pie, and a bottle of vintage Burgundy. Eyeing the date on the label, Jason declared the wine must have been aging in the cellar since the last time he had sneaked a midnight snack fifteen years previously.

"You never did tell me what happened to Rafael," Lauren said when her hunger was somewhat assuaged.

"No," Jason agreed in a grim tone. "Suffice it to say that he was punished for his crimes." He avoided Lauren's gaze as he raised the bottle to his lips and drank deeply; he didn't plan to tell her about the challenge he had made to the pirate.

Rafael had been captured during the fall of Algiers and sentenced to hang, but Jason had offered to fight him for his freedom. The offer had been accepted, but evidently Rafael's fellow pirates hadn't favored the idea that their leader might escape their own fate. That same night, Rafael had been butchered in his cell by his own men. It could not have been an easy death, Jason had realized upon seeing the bloody remains of the body. But perhaps, after all, it was a fitting end to a man who had lost any regard for the value of human life. Jason meant to spare his wife the unsavory details, however.

"Is that all you intend to say?"

Jason looked up to find Lauren watching him intently. Instantly his grim expression vanished and a teasing smile curved his lips. "For now, Cat-eyes. Someday I'll tell you what happened, provided you give me no more trouble for the next fifty years."

Lauren realized she was being fobbed off, but decided to let the subject drop. "I knew you would find some means of getting your way!" she remarked, matching his light tone. "Very well, then, I have a bargain for you. I get to hear the entire story when I present you with your first son."

"Make it my first grandson and you have a deal."

Smiling provocatively, Lauren rose and walked around to Jason's side of the table. "That will take too long."

"Not if we work at it," Jason pointed out as he drew Lauren down onto his lap and kissed her. "But this isn't the place," he added huskily when he raised his head. "I don't intend for the servants to walk in and find me fondling my wife."

Lauren sighed. "It was much easier being poor without a great name to uphold."

"Certainly more private," he agreed. "Don't be disappointed, sweetheart. I fully intend to take you upstairs and ravish your body again, but we have a few things to discuss first."

She raised a delicate eyebrow. "Such as?"

"Such as George Burroughs." When Jason felt Lauren's body stiffen, he tightened his hold around her waist and went on doggedly. "Before he died, Burroughs made two last requests of me. One was that he be buried next to his sister Mary. The other was that I explain to you his reasons for using you as he did. He greatly regretted his actions toward you, Lauren. He wanted your forgiveness."

Lauren searched Jason's face, noting how serious his expression had become. When he seemed to be waiting for her permission to speak, she nodded solemnly, knowing that the past had to be dealt with before they could look to the future.

"It began with your parents' marriage," Jason said quietly. "Jonathan Carlin was visiting friends in Lancashire when he met your mother and married her. It wasn't common knowledge, though, since he returned to London without her. Shortly afterward, Jonathan . . . seduced Burroughs's sister Mary.

"Burroughs was livid when Mary came to him in tears,

claiming she was pregnant. He wanted to call Jonathan out, but Mary declared she loved him and wanted him for her husband, so Burroughs gave in. He was a major partner in the Carlin Line by then, and he threatened to withdraw his entire investment unless Jonathan married his sister. As a result a ceremony was held. The marriage was meaningless, though, since Jonathan already had a wife."

Lauren gave Jason a puzzled frown. "But why didn't he simply admit it?"

"Because, my love, an unlawful marriage to Mary gave him the perfect leverage. Burroughs couldn't pull his capital out of the company, not as long as Jonathan held the threat of scandal over Mary's head. Bigamy is illegal, but Mary would have suffered far more than Jonathan if the truth had come out."

"So that's why he destroyed the proof of his first marriage?"

"Not destroyed, confiscated. He had the page of the church registry removed in case Elizabeth decided to go to the courts. The record is back where it belongs, incidentally. Jonathan had kept it hidden along with a will naming you his sole heir. . . . But I'm deviating from the story. Elizabeth was growing desperate since Jonathan hadn't returned any of her letters, so after your birth, she came to London to see him. She was refused admittance to his house, but she managed to find out about Mary and Andrea. Elizabeth went to the Carlin offices then, and confronted Jonathan in a big scene. He lied to her, of course, told her their marriage had been a sham. And Burroughs didn't contradict him."

"Burroughs knew the truth, though, didn't he?"

Jason nodded. "But his overwhelming concern was to protect Mary. She was his only sister and he felt responsible for her, especially since her had insisted on the marriage in the first place. He was determined that Mary should never find out that her marriage was illegal. As far as I can tell, she never did. At any rate, Burroughs never saw Elizabeth again. Jonathan went to see her some years later, after she had written him asking for money, but when he returned, he told Burroughs he had settled the matter."

Lauren looked away, fixing her gaze on a point beyond Jason's shoulder. "All that time . . . my parents really were married," she murmured.

Gently, Jason took her face in his hands. "That's right, sweetheart. You were Lauren Carlin before you became Lauren Stuart. You never were illegitimate."

"But *why?* Why didn't he tell me?"

"Burroughs, you mean? Because he didn't want any shame attached to his sister's name, even after her death."

"But what about my mother? What about her shame? Her family disowned her because of the disgrace!"

Jason's gaze was sympathetic. "I'm not condoning what Burroughs did. I'm just telling you his reasons for keeping silent. Later, he had Andrea to consider. She became his responsibility when Mary and Jonathan were murdered, and he felt it his duty to protect her inheritance. After Andrea died, he decided that you should have the Carlin fortune."

"Not because it was rightfully mine, but because he wanted to keep it from Regina!"

Jason reached up to stroke Lauren's hair. "For both reasons. By then he suspected Regina of being an accomplice in the Carlins' deaths, and was determined that she shouldn't benefit from her crimes. He also wanted to protect you from Regina, which is why he arranged your marriage to me. He meant to explain it all to you when we were safely wed."

Lauren's eyes clouded with pain. "But I would have understood. I would have helped him thwart Regina, had he told me the truth. Instead he threatened to lock me in the cellars to ensure I would do his bidding. And he called me 'Jonathan's bastard'."

"I expect he was still grieving, my love. You were a living reminder of Jonathan's duplicity, and he probably blamed you—wrongly—for even existing. Besides, he didn't know what a loyal friend and ally you could be."

Lauren shook her head slowly. "It isn't just what he did to me, Jason, but what he did to my mother. He let her suffer needlessly. We couldn't even afford to buy laudanum so she could sleep with the pain. I don't know if I can forgive him for that."

Pulling Lauren more closely against him, Jason rested his cheek against her hair. "Well, he did do one thing for which I'll always be grateful. He arranged our marriage. If not for him, I might never have obtained the Carlin Line."

Lauren heard the teasing note in his voice and knew Jason was trying to ease her distress. She sighed, realizing it was foolish to let the past upset her. She had Jason now and that was all that mattered. Drawing back to gaze at him, she let her eyes roam lovingly over the noble features of his face. "Well," Lauren replied, making an effort to smile, "I suppose we made a fair exchange. I ended up with a title."

Jason returned her gaze as he took a strand of her hair and drew it softly over his lips. "I hope, Cat-eyes, that you finally believe that I love you for yourself and not for whatever wealth you have."

"I do, Jason. And I hope you realize how much I regret not having more faith in you. I had a great deal of time to think about it while you were gone, I came to realize why I was so afraid to trust you. I was afraid to expose myself to the kind of hurt and pain my mother knew. But I should have told you the truth."

"Well," he murmured, "we've had too many secrets between us, but that's behind us now. You do, however, have a decision to make concerning what to say about your own past. You could tell the truth, or you could let the world assume your mother passed away before Jonathan remarried."

"You mean not reveal that his marriage to Mary Burroughs was illegal?"

"Yes. You could simply let people think that Mary was your father's second wife and Andrea his legitimate daughter. It isn't a question of inheritance any longer. The Carlin Line is yours by right, since Jonathan's will is valid and Burroughs left you his half. And you would be sparing Mary and Andrea memories. They really were blameless in this whole affair."

Lauren nodded slowly. "I suppose it doesn't make any difference now. But what if someone finds out about my mother?"

"Then we don't deny it. I doubt if anyone will, though. Regina was the only one who could dispute the story, and she's gone."

Remembering her murderous aunt, Lauren shuddered. "I

can't believe it's all over."

"It's just beginning, Cat-eyes," Jason whispered huskily in her ear. "I expect it might be wise, though, for us to hold another wedding ceremony here in England. I don't want you or anyone else having any doubts that we're irrevocably married."

Lauren sighed as she rested her head on his shoulder. "I suppose we have Burroughs to thank for that," she admitted grudgingly.

Smiling, Jason shook his head. "Burroughs might have arranged our original contact, but he had nothing to do with our marriage. That was all my own doing. I got you drunk, remember?"

"I remember that you tricked me—"

"You deserved it."

"I did not!" Lauren protested.

"You did. And I considered it adequate payment for the time you drugged my wine and took my hundred guineas."

"A sum I thought I had earned."

With a finger, Jason tilted her chin up. His blue eyes were alive with warmth and love as he bent to kiss her. "Would you agree to call the score even, sweetheart?" he murmured against her lips.

"I might," Lauren said thoughtfully. She let Jason kiss her again, then added huskily, "I'll give you my answer when we have our first grandson."

"Wake up, sweetheart," Jason urged several hours later. "Lauren, wake up!"

Abruptly Lauren opened her eyes to find Jason shaking her. Above the fading echoes of a scream, she heard his soothing voice directing her to breathe deeply. She reached for him and clung, chilled and shaking.

Eventually the strong beat of his heart beneath her chest reassured her, as did the soft glow from the lamp he lit. Yet an elusive phantom was tormenting her memory. Confused, Lauren held a hand to her throbbing brow.

"You were dreaming again," Jason said as he briskly rubbed

her ice-cold skin. "I thought you said you were over your nightmares."

There was no explosion, no blinding light. The return of her memory was accompanied by nothing more than a soft whirring in her ears. "It really happened," Lauren said in a strangled voice.

Jason pressed his lips to her hair, gently brushing a tangled strand of hair from her face. "What really happened, my love?"

"My dream." Lauren sat up, pulling the covers up to her chin, as if they might offer protection. "I remembered what happened . . . and it wasn't a dream. It was my father, all along."

Jason grasped her chin with his fingers, forcing her to meet his gaze. When Lauren saw his blue eyes regarding her with tender concern, she realized that she was making little sense and began again. "I dreamed the same nightmare as always, but this time it had a conclusion. And I know what, or rather who, I was running from. It was my father."

Jason gathered her in his arms once more, cradling her protectively against his chest. "Tell me about it, sweetheart," he said gently, holding her close.

Gratefully, Lauren rested her head on his comforting shoulder. "I was in bed, asleep, and when I woke up, I heard shouting. I remember now walking through this dark little room. It must have been a dressing closet of some kind, for it led to my mother's bedchamber. I opened the door—" Lauren shivered, then after a moment, continued in a shaking voice.

"My mother and father were having a violent argument. He held something in his hand . . . a stick, with a red tip . . . and he was threatening her with it. I saw Mama back away, but he grabbed her. . . . When he held the stick to her arm, she screamed . . . again and again. My father only laughed. I think it must have been a hot iron from the fireplace," Lauren said in a hoarse whisper. "I could smell her burning flesh."

Shuddering, she buried her face against Jason's bare chest. He stroked her hair wordlessly, offering silent comfort, but it was some time before she could go on. "I must have made a noise, for my father turned and saw me. Mama cried out for me

446

to run, but he reached me before I could move. He . . . he burned my . . . hand." Lauren raised her left hand, palm up, and Jason caught it in his own, kissing it gently. "Mama tried to hit him," Lauren whispered. "When he let me go, I fled back to my room and hid in the trunk which held my clothes. It was so dark, and I couldn't breathe. I . . . I don't . . . remember any more."

"Perhaps," Jason said after a moment, "that was when Jonathan went to Lancashire to see Elizabeth. You could not have been very old at the time. It's possible you witnessed him forcing your mother to give up any claims on him. He must have threatened to hurt you unless she agreed to forget there ever had been a marriage. I wouldn't put it past him. Burroughs said Jonathan Carlin wasn't a very likable man."

There was a hint of fury in Jason's tone, but he managed to repress his anger for Lauren's sake. Tightening his arms around her, he said firmly, "But all that's in the past, Lauren. Come now, you must try to forget. You have only to look to the future, one with me by your side."

His tender assurances lightened the pain in her heart. With tears sparkling in her gold-green eyes, Lauren lifted her face to his. "Love me, Jason," she pleaded in a whisper.

"Always, sweetheart," he said as lips found hers. "Always."